THE BAD LUCK WEDDING CAKE

BAD LUCK WEDDINGS SERIES BOOK TWO

EMILY MARCH

EMILY MARCH
BOOKS

For Caitlin Michelle Williams

I sang it on the day you were born,
And it is still the song in my heart.

You are my sunshine.

CHAPTER 1

IF YOU ROLL OUT A PIE CRUST BEFORE DAWN ON NEW YEAR'S DAY, YOU'LL HAVE A YEAR OF BAD LUCK.

FORT WORTH, Texas, 1880

Tye McBride's nose twitched, then wrinkled. His eyes cracked open and immediately started to water. Grimacing, he muttered into his pillow, "What in the world died?"

The smell was enough to knock a buzzard off his dinner.

The stink interfered with his thinking, too. His thoughts flowed slow as molasses, and he had to work to make sense of his surroundings. Where was he?

Scenes from the previous evening flashed in his mind. Hell's Half Acre. Rachel Warden's whorehouse. Ah, damn. Afraid to look, Tye rolled onto his back and cautiously felt the mattress beside him. Nobody there. Good.

Slowly, he opened his eyes fully. The familiar gaslight fixture hanging from the wall established his position. He lay in his own bed in the apartment above his sister-in-law's dress shop, Fortune's Design. So, if he was home, alone, then what the hell was the stench?

He twisted his neck toward his armpit and sniffed. Wasn't him. Lifting his head, he squinted against the light filtering through the windowpane and attempted to gauge the time. Early

1

morning. Very early morning by the looks of it. When had he come to bed? Had he slept at all? The weariness clinging to him like a hangover suggested otherwise.

Groggily, he sat up. He grabbed his pillow and held it against his face, cloaking the odor permeating the room. He forced himself to focus, and finally, one by one, memories of the previous evening trickled through the muddle in his mind. Tinny saloon music. The scent of stale perfume and hard liquor. Gunshots. Blood.

Just another night in Hell's Half Acre.

Located in the heart of town, the Acre specialized in serving up violence and vice to any and all who wished to partake. Liquor, gambling, and women were the core industry of the Acre; murder and mayhem oftentimes its product.

Because he was a man who indulged in a vice now and again, Tye had visited Fort Worth's tenderloin a time or two during his extended visit to town. His favorite haunt, the Green Parrot Saloon, billed itself as a one-stop entertainment emporium. Services provided on its first floor included dining, drinking, and dancing. Gambling and whoring remained strictly second-story sport. Tye enjoyed the ambiance and convenience the Parrot presented. He had made friends of the owner, who, in deference to the fact that Tye had sworn off liquor, laid in a generous supply of his favorite root beer.

But Tye hadn't been drinking soda water last night. He had not visited the Parrot at all. "I went to Rachel Warden's," he said, remembering. "Why?"

He groaned as the reason came to him in a flash. His nieces. His brother Trace's daughters. The girls known in Fort Worth as the McBride Menaces.

And the puppy.

The dog was the reason for his mush-mindedness. He'd paid for a puppy, not a poke, at the whorehouse last night. After putting his nieces to bed, he'd headed to the Acre and bought the six-week-old mutt from one of Rachel's girls.

The puppy was a cute little boy dog with small dappled paws, a terrier snout, and a beagle body. Tye knew the girls would love him. They adored animals and their menagerie included everything from a pet armadillo to a prized collection of doodlebugs. Tye had decided a friskier—and hardier—pet was needed once he realized the extent of their enthrallment with Spike, their so-called fortune-telling perch. Besides, he'd much rather take a dog for a walk than cart along a fishbowl on neighborhood treks with the girls, like he'd been doing of late.

He had reminded himself of that fact off and on all night when the pup's constant crying kept him awake. It wasn't until he'd let the damn thing sleep in bed with him, curled up against his belly, that the animal finally went to sleep.

But the dog wasn't in his bed now. He glanced around his bedroom. The animal wasn't anywhere to be seen. Then Tye spied the half-opened door. "Aw, hell."

He swung his legs from the bed, and a fresh whiff of the putrid scent hit him like a fist and served to clear away the last of the cobwebs clinging in his mind.

The puppy. The smell.

Even as his gaze searched the floor, he realized the odor smelled different from what he could expect an untrained puppy to leave behind. This was more of a burnt-fur smell.

His eyes widened and his chin slowly dropped. The puppy. The smell.

His troublemaking nieces.

In his mind he heard the echo of little Katrina's voice as she begged him for a pet. *I'll take good care of it, Uncle Tye. I'll feed it and brush it and give it nice warm baths.*

Warm baths. Hot water.

"Holy hell!" he cried, shoving to his feet "They've cooked the dog!"

~

CLAIRE DONOVAN DABBED a handkerchief at her tearing eyes and wondered once again at the creative thinking behind her great-grandmother's recipe for the flavoring extract the Donovan Baking Company used to such success. The family called the brew Magic, and its formula remained a closely held secret.

Unlike her brothers, who had received the recipe upon their eighteenth birthdays, Claire had waited until she turned twenty-three before her parents entrusted her with the knowledge. Even then she'd suspected they'd misled her. Sugar and honey and lemon peel in the recipe, yes. But chopped cabbage, pickled beets, and cauliflower?

Her mother had only smiled and urged her to give it a try. Claire then made her first batch of Magic and sure enough, the strange combination of thirty ingredients did indeed cook down to a syrup so extraordinarily delicious that a single spoonful added to a batter turned an appetizing cake into a Magical Cake.

Magical Cakes, in turn, had propelled a small family bakery into a prosperous business whose three bakeries produced goods of renown all along the Gulf coast.

Of course, it had taken more than extra-special bakery items to make the Donovan Baking Company the success it was today. It had taken Claire's brother Patrick and his idea for an advertisement. Patrick had been the one to parlay a musing from Great-grandmother Gertrude's journal into a legend. She had written that the marriages of those couples who served a Magical Cake at their weddings appeared to be blessed with an extra measure of happiness and prosperity. Patrick had publicized his great-grandmother's observation and, five years ago, the first of many articles about Donovan's Magical Wedding Cakes had appeared in the *Galveston Gazette*.

It proved to be the beginning of the end for Claire.

"Oh, stop thinking about it," she grumbled to herself, her

knife slicing emphatically through a head of cauliflower. She was in the midst of a new beginning—a new business in a new city, far away from family and former fiancés. Besides, she needed to keep her mind on her work. It wouldn't do to make a mistake in the recipe.

The ingredients for Magic were expensive; her money in limited supply. The rent and renovations on her bakery shop space had used up more of her cash than she had anticipated. "That's another mistake I made," she said with a sigh. If she'd better estimated the cost of establishing a new life, she'd have taken more than her jewelry and half her designated dowry funds with her when she fled Galveston on her wedding day.

Claire stirred the final ingredient into her mixture, checked to ensure it remained at a slow boil, and placed the lid on her tall soup pot. Flipping her favorite hourglass timer, she paused as her gaze fixed on the trickling sand. Sixty more minutes of cooking, then another hour or so of bottling, and she'd be through with this chore for a good three months. Thank goodness.

Of course, as much as she disliked making Magic, she'd be happy to repeat the task weekly if it meant the citizens of Fort Worth found The Confectionary's baked goods worthy of their support

The Confectionary. Claire thought it a particularly good title for her shop. The name Donovan wasn't part of it anywhere.

Lining her utensils, pots, and pans in customary washing order on her cutting board, she hummed an upbeat tune as she mentally inventoried her supplies. She needed to order more sugarhouse molasses, cloves, and gelatin from Mr. Hankins at Fort Worth City Mercantile. She likely had enough flour, pulverized sugar, and cinnamon. Better check on the carbonate of ammonia. She hoped to be ready to open for business within two weeks.

She had finished washing and had picked up her dish towel when she heard the first thud coming from the rooms above her. Alarmed, she glanced toward the ceiling.

When she leased the shop space a little over a month ago, she had also asked to rent the lodgings above it. Her landlord, Trace McBride, had been apologetic but firm in his decision to keep the rooms reserved as a haven for his expectant wife on the days she insisted on working at her dress design shop next door. He kindly offered her another property, which she now shared with the local schoolteacher, Miss Blackstone.

But shortly after Claire signed her lease, the McBrides had left town on a belated honeymoon. Jenny McBride certainly wasn't resting upstairs today. The place should be empty.

Don't borrow trouble, Claire told herself. She had no reason for worry. Despite the fact that Fort Worth had become the murder capital of the world west of the Mississippi, the sheriff kept that type of activity primarily confined to the Acre. She had never once felt less than safe here in this building.

Well, except for when the sisters from the Catholic church across the street paid a call. That Sister Gonzaga was downright scary.

Still, when she heard a second noise above her—one that sounded suspiciously like a slamming door—she realized just how alone she was in the building this early in the day. Jenny McBride's employee, Mrs. Moore, wasn't due to open the dress shop next door for hours. Unbidden, the memory of her father's constant caution to keep her doors locked fluttered like a red flag in her mind.

Maybe it wouldn't hurt to heed his warnings now and again.

Setting down her dishcloth, Claire stepped into the public room and gave it a sweeping glance. Her shop was divided into two main sections, with her kitchen in the back portion. The front room contained a display case for her baked goods, counter space, and five sets of small round tables and chairs for patrons who wished to consume their purchases in the shop. The store remained empty, thank goodness.

Her gaze drifted toward the unlocked front door that led to a small vestibule rather than directly onto the street. Upon entering the Rankin Building, customers faced three doors. The center door opened to the staircase leading to the apartment above, the right door to Fortune's Design, the left to the bakery.

Claire took two steps forward until the footsteps pounding down the apartment stairs brought her to a dead stop. She gasped softly when a shadow flickered in the frosted glass that decorated the door. Whirling around, she fled back into her kitchen.

The front door hinges creaked as Claire stepped quietly to her worktable and picked up her paring knife. In her mind, she heard her brother Patrick say, "You're quick, Claire. A man gives you trouble, you go for the throat."

Lord help her, she didn't want to hurt anyone.

She glanced toward the door leading to the alley and quickly debated whether to flee or hide. She chose the latter, thinking it best to stay out of the way of whatever trouble headed her direction. *Besides*, she thought with a sudden burst of courage, *I've done enough fleeing from problems recently*. She was finished with that.

She dropped to her knees and started to duck beneath the broad oak worktable when a near-naked man burst into her kitchen hollering, "Girls, get the dog off the stove!"

Claire froze. He was tall and broad and wore only a pair of white men's drawers, their legs hemmed indecently and unevenly short, halfway down his thighs. Red embroidered hearts adorned the cotton garment. Recognizing her landlord, Claire climbed to her feet "Mr. McBride?"

He paused only long enough to give her a harried, curious look. "Where are the girls?"

He rushed toward the stove where her Magic bubbled. When he reached for the handles on the pot Claire tore her gaze off the expanse of masculine bare chest and lunged forward. "What are you doing? Get away from my Magic!"

"Magic?" He yanked the soup pot off the fire, cursing beneath his breath and waving his hands. He hadn't bothered to grab a towel before grabbing the hot metal. "His name was Ralph."

"What?"

"The Blessings must have thought to give him a bath on the stove."

The Blessings? What was he talking about? And why was he standing half-naked in her kitchen?

Claire couldn't remember ever being this flustered. The last time a man who was not one of her relations huddled with her beside the stove, she'd found herself engaged before sunset. And Reid Jamieson had been wearing clothes at the time.

At least she wouldn't end up betrothed to Trace McBride; he was very much married.

And he was also supposed to be in the Caribbean with his wife, Jenny.

Claire gawked at the stranger's face. "Who are you?"

"Ah, Ralph," he murmured, his stare fastened on the soup pot. "I thought the girls were old enough to care for a dog. They do all right with the armadillo. Of course, it's damn near impossible to kill an armadillo. Dogs aren't nearly so hardy. I should have left the poor pup at the whorehouse."

Green eyes cut in her direction. "They are hiding, aren't they? The stink must have scared them off." He reached for the pot's lid, and his voice sounded grieved as he added, "I'll take care of this, but would you please go find my nieces?"

Still holding the knife, Claire lifted her hand. "Touch that kettle, and I'll take your hand off. It ruins the recipe if you peek."

"Recipe!" The man's eyes rounded in horror. "You've cooked the puppy on purpose?"

"The puppy is under the table."

"You've already removed the corpse?"

Claire pointed toward a basket beneath the table. "He's asleep, you imbecile. I didn't cook your dog. That's my Magic cooking on the stove."

"Magic. Magic?" He strode toward the workbench. "Sounds like a cat's name. You cooked a cat?"

"Cat?" Even in her pique Claire couldn't help but notice the bunch of muscles in his thighs as he crouched down to peer beneath the table. After all, the red hearts embroidered around the hem naturally drew her gaze.

"Well, something died," he stated flatly, reaching a gentle hand toward the sleeping puppy, scratching him behind his floppy ears.

The man's stomach muscles rippled like Great- grandmother Gertrude's washboard.

Face flaming, Claire jerked her attention away from the stranger and slapped the knife down onto the cutting board. She picked up her hot pads and shifted the soup pot back onto the fire before folding her arms and saying, "I killed a cabbage, sir, not a cat. I killed a cauliflower, too."

For a long moment, he didn't reply. Then he twisted his head and grinned up at her, an entirely different person from the harried man who'd barged into her kitchen a few confusing moments earlier. Wicked amusement danced in his eyes, and his smile . . . well, it made Claire's knees go a bit weak.

Lifting the puppy from its makeshift bed, a basket and blanket Claire had provided upon discovering the canine in her kitchen when she arrived at the shop that morning, he cuddled it against his broad, bare chest and slowly stood. "So you're the one the sheriff has been searching for."

"Pardon me?"

"I doubt it. Probably get ten years to life in Huntsville prison. Be a right shame, too, if you ask me. Your eyes are too pretty to be looking out from behind bars. Reminds me of the blue in the Texas sky on a rain-washed morning. Too bad you had to turn out to be the one."

If Claire had been flustered before, now she was downright addled. "What one?"

"The vegetable killer, of course. Tell me, do you limit yourself to "C" plants, or have you branched out, included a squash, or tomato or two?" He eyed the soup pot suspiciously. "I wouldn't be surprised to learn you stalked broccoli, to tell you the truth."

The absurdity of the entire scene struck her then, and she started to laugh. "Well, that takes care of me, I'm the vegetable killer. So who are you?" She gave him a sweeping, pointed gaze. "A refugee from one of the sin parlors in the Acre?"

He glanced down and winced. "I was in a hurry to save the mutt, here. Grabbed the first thing I came across. Emma gave these drawers to me yesterday. She's trying to teach herself to follow in her mama's footsteps."

"I hesitate to even wonder as to Emma's mother's occupation," Claire said dryly.

He muttered something beneath his breath, shoved the dog at her, and strode from the room. Five minutes later he was back, dressed in brown twill pants and buttoning a blue chambray shirt as he entered the kitchen. He rattled off his explanation in crisp, concise sentences. "I'm Tye McBride, your landlord's brother. The puppy is a gift for my nieces, one of whom is Emma. Her mother is my brother's wife, Jenny McBride, who I assume you know is the extremely talented designer who owns the dress shop next door. My nieces have a tendency to tumble into trouble, so when I woke to find the pup missing from my room and a godawful smell coming from downstairs, I naturally assumed they'd gotten into more mischief. But I checked when I went upstairs to dress and they're still in their beds asleep. Now, that explains me. How about you?"

With his rapid recital, the situation fell into place for her. "You're the relative caring for the McBride Menaces while their parents honeymoon."

He frowned. "I know the reputation my nieces have here in town, but I prefer a different term—Blessings. They are the McBride Blessings, Miss . . . ?"

Claire felt a rush of warmth toward Tye McBride that went

beyond her reaction to his handsomeness, and she smiled. The girl who'd grown up to the moniker Calamity Claire appreciated his sentiment more than he could ever know. She wiped her hand on her apron then extended it "Claire Donovan. I rented this shop space the day before your brother left on his trip."

He shook her hand, but his brows arched and his tone held a doubtful note as he asked, "You're the baker?"

"Yes."

He considered that a moment, then asked, "You intend to make food and sell it from this shop?"

Her appreciation faded at the doubt she heard in his voice. She snatched her hand away from him. "You have a problem with that?"

He rubbed his palm across his jaw, then gestured toward the pot of Magic. "I've made the acquaintance of men who drove cattle from here to Wichita, never once washing their clothes. I have to tell you, ma'am, their socks had nothing on your brew here when it comes to perfume. I just hope the stuff tastes better than it smells, that's all."

Claire wasn't offended. The making of Magic was an odorous undertaking. Shrugging, she walked over to the large earthenware jar that sat on her worktable. Lifting the lid with one hand, she gestured with the other. "Molasses cookies. Help yourself."

"Is it safe?"

She challenged him with her smile.

He cocked his head and clicked his tongue. "I purely hate looking like a coward to a woman whose hair is the exact golden color of a West Texas sunset." He approached her and standing close—too close—reached a hand into the jar and drew out a sweet. His gaze never left hers as he took a small bite of the cookie. Immediately, his eyes widened. Then they drifted shut. He chewed slowly, swallowed, and dropped to one knee. "Miss Donovan." He took her hand. "Will you do me the honor of becoming my wife?"

A gasp, a squeal, and a screech sounded from behind her.

"This is wonderful!" a girl's voice exclaimed. "Just what we hoped for."

A different voice. "Yippie! Another family wedding! No animals this time, Uncle Tye. We promise!"

Claire whirled around just as a third girl spoke. "Wait a minute. We've made a mistake. The hair color fooled us!" She pointed dramatically toward Claire. "Look, sisters. That's not her. That's not Loretta Davis!"

CHAPTER 2

IT'S BAD LUCK TO BREAK AN EGG AGAINST THE RIM OF A COFFEE CUP.

TYE CLIMBED TO HIS FEET, tilted his face toward the ceiling, and closed his eyes. Wouldn't they ever leave it alone?

Upon the heels of their matchmaking success the previous year with their father and the former Miss Jenny Fortune, the McBride Blessings had turned their matchmaking attentions in his direction. God help him, they were plumb wearing him out.

He had extended his visit to Texas from his home in South Carolina at his brother's request. When Trace asked Tye to share the childcare burden with the part-time housekeeper, Mrs. Wilson, while he and his bride took a much-delayed honeymoon, he'd swallowed his uncertainty and agreed to help.

Tye had been happy to do his brother a good turn. He owed his twin big, and besides, he truly loved the Blessings. He'd give his life for any one of them. A time or two in the weeks since Trace and Jenny's departure, he'd worried it might come to that. He had never been particularly comfortable with heights, and fetching Katrina off the sharply sloped roof at Willow Hill had reinforced the feeling.

For the first two weeks they'd managed just fine because the girls had behaved like perfect angels. He should have known it wouldn't last. Once the dew dried off the rosebud, so to speak, their gift of good behavior evaporated, too. When Mrs. Wilson's daughter broke her leg in a riding accident and summoned the housekeeper to Dallas, leaving Tye to deal with the Blessings alone, the situation deteriorated. The girls erupted into full-blown mischievousness.

That's where the puppy had come in. Tye was desperate for ways to occupy their time. Ways to distract them from their matchmaking.

His dear, darling nieces had made it their goal to find a bride for their Uncle Tye—whether he wanted one or not. They chose the daughter of a local doctor, Loretta Davis, as their other victim. Tye was still dealing with the storm they'd started the previous week when they'd mailed Loretta love letters signed in his name.

Summoning his patience, he lowered his gaze and pinned his brother's daughters with a stern look. "Girls, I thought we agreed the word 'wedding' belonged on the demerit list."

"But Uncle Tye," seven-year-old Katrina protested. "That's not fair. We talked it over. It's not a naughty word. Not like—"

Maribeth, age nine, slapped a hand over her younger sister's mouth. "Hush, Kat. Not now. We're three marks away from having peas for supper."

"Two marks." Tye had found peas to be an effective threat in dealing with his brother's children. In fact, ordering peas for supper served as the only real discipline he'd managed up to now. Try as he might, he couldn't summon up the mettle to punish the girls, even when he knew they needed it. Then, prodded by the knowledge he should be more firm with them, he folded his arms and added, "You're lucky it's not down to one. I should add a demerit for snooping."

Emma, the eldest at eleven, shook her head. "We didn't intend to eavesdrop, Uncle. Honest. We woke up and went looking for you, but you weren't upstairs. We followed the sound of your voice. I don't believe that counts as snooping because we didn't stop and listen."

"That's right," Maribeth agreed. "We just barged on in."

Tye glanced at Claire and noted the amusement shining in her eyes. Wryly, he said, "Just your average morning at the McBrides'."

"How interesting."

He could tell she was biting the inside of her cheek to keep from laughing. Damned but if that didn't make her all the more appealing. The attraction he'd felt since taking that first bite of her cookie rose a notch, but he did his best to hide it. Heaven help him if the Blessings noticed.

"Line up, girls. I take it you haven't met your father's new tenant?" When they nodded, he moved to stand behind them and said, "Miss Donovan, may I present the most troublesome trio in town, the McBride Blessings." He laid a hand atop each girl's head as he announced her name. "Emma, Maribeth, and Katrina McBride. Girls, this is Miss Donovan. You'll be interested to know she makes cookies that will tickle your tonsils."

"Why, thank you, Mr. McBride," Claire said, smiling. "Girls, it's a pleasure to meet you."

For a long moment, no one said anything. Then Katrina lifted her chin and declared, "I don't want you to marry my uncle. We picked Miss Loretta. She's just as pretty as you and she doesn't stink."

"Katrina." Tye put both hands on her shoulders and gave them a gentle squeeze. He was shocked and more than a little embarrassed. "The smell is coming from the soup pot."

To her credit, Claire Donovan only laughed. "You needn't worry, Miss McBride. I have no designs on your uncle. In fact, it may ease your mind to know I left a fiancé down in Galveston. Your uncle was only teasing me about marriage, you see, because he liked my cookies so very much."

"Oh." Katrina thought about it a moment, then nodded.

"Uncle Tye teases a lot," Emma said with a shy smile.

Maribeth nodded. "He is even a bigger teaser than our papa. He looks just like our papa, too. They're twins. One time he pretended to be Papa and—"

"That's enough, sugar," Tye clapped his hand over the girl's mouth and said, "Let's save the stories for another decade, shall we? In the meantime, I have a surprise for y'all."

"A surprise?" Maribeth asked, twisting her head to beam up at him.

"Yes, a surprise, and you get to guess what it is. Now, what have the three of you been wanting for a long time now?"

"An auntie," Katrina answered.

Tye grimaced. "No, dad blame it. You want a dog."

"A dog?"

"You can't marry a dog, Uncle Tye."

Maribeth folded her arms, and mischief gleamed in her eyes as she said, "I don't know, Kat. That woman Will Tucker married is pretty close to being a dog. Her face is awful furry, and she sure barks a lot when she gets after him."

Tye all but dove for the basket where the puppy lay sleeping and gave silent thanks that a distraction was at hand. As it turned out, he could have shouted his prayer at the top of his lungs and no one could have heard it. Needless to say, his nieces loved Ralph, ear-splitting squeals and screams rising from their throats from the moment of introduction. Ralph's yips and barks added to the noise level, which swelled to near deafening. When Tye finally managed to ease the circus out the back door and into the alley, he halfway expected to hear a cheer of delight from the baker. He told her so, once they could hear themselves talk again.

"I have brothers, Mr. McBride," she informed him, her gaze flicking toward the hourglass timer. "I'm used to a little commotion."

Arms folded, Tye leaned casually against the jamb of the bakery's back door, his gaze shifting often from the happy scene outside to the intriguing one indoors. He jerked his head toward the alley. "Calling that a little commotion is like saying the Acre gets a tad bit rowdy."

She replied with only a smile.

Tye gave his nieces another look and determined they might just stay out of trouble for the next few minutes. Instead of going out to join them, he sauntered over to a table. Pulling out one of two chairs, he straddled it.

"Please, make yourself at home," Claire said.

Tye grinned at the sarcasm in her voice. "Thanks, I will." Actually, he had a bunch of stuff he could be doing—like finding breakfast, for one thing—but he couldn't quite muster up the will to leave. Because his day had started so early, he had a whole hour before he needed to get the girls ready for school. And besides, his nose had grown accustomed to the stink, so it wasn't so hard to hang around. This woman intrigued him.

He cocked his head and studied her. There was more to Claire Donovan than beauty, although her face and figure were enough to stop a stampede. Something about her—some quality he couldn't quite put his finger on— made him suspect her waters ran deep. Most females of his acquaintance would have raised the roof with their ire when invaded like she had been this morning. Not Miss Claire. She'd taken it all in stride.

The woman wore self-confidence like an apron, independence like a feather in her hat. But at the same time, she had the look of an imp—almost like one of the Blessings all grown up.

It was a startling thought, and he contemplated making a beeline toward the door in self-preservation. Then, as she bent over to remove a box of corks from a lower shelf, he eyed the slender curve of her ankles and reconsidered. "So, when you're finished with what you're doing, how about I cook us up a passel of eggs and bacon for breakfast? And maybe some flapjacks to go along with them?"

"A passel?" she asked. "I used that word once, and my father threatened to wash out my mouth with soap."

"Why? It's not a cuss word or anything."

"No, but it isn't refined. My da holds great store in refinement."

Tye grinned and took the opportunity for a little flirtatious teasing. "Then I reckon he didn't chow down on a mess of grits to go along with his passel of bacon and eggs."

Her mouth twitched. "No, but he does enjoy a bowl of porridge for breakfast on cool winter mornings."

"Porridge, huh? Not grits. So the family's not from the South. Are you newcomers to Texas, also?"

"Actually, I've lived here most of my life."

That surprised him. He drummed his fingers on the back slats of his chair. "You don't sound like a Texan. In fact, I'd have sworn I heard an Irish hit to your voice."

She shrugged. "I was an infant when my parents immigrated."

"To Texas?"

"New York, originally. We moved to Galveston when I was ten."

"New York, huh?" The temptation to tease overwhelmed him. "So that's it."

"That's what?"

"It's not Ireland I hear but a Yankee twang."

She arched an offended brow. "Yankee twang!"

"I feel sorry for you, Miss Donovan. If you've lived in Texas awhile, you should have lost it by now. I've been here only a short time myself, and I'm well on my way to speaking with a nice Texas drawl."

Her chin came up. "Well, at least I'm aware that "R" and "E" are letters in the language."

"What do you mean by that?" Tye replied, acting affronted while he secretly wanted to grin. Her blue eyes sparkled like sunshine on dew when she was riled.

"Take your breakfast, for instance, McBride." She shook her spoon at him. "You want aa-yugs, instead of eggs. You stretch that tiny little word into two whole syllables. And when you called your niece sugar, you said, 'shug-ah.' No 'R' at the end."

"So what's your point? You don't want any breakfast?"

"My point is, it's rude to insult a person's pattern of speech."

"That's why I wasn't going to point out that you have a twang, but then you went and dragged it out of me."

She contemplated the cork in her hand, then looked at him. Tye could see she wanted to peg him with it. "Refinement, Miss Donovan," he reminded. "So you'll have breakfast with us?"

For just a moment she appeared speechless. Then her laughter washed over him like warm summer rain. "Thank you, but I've already eaten. You all are welcome to try my apple muffins if you'd like."

"I'd love to try your muffins, Miss Donovan," he drawled, working to maintain an innocent expression as she stabbed a look at him.

"Maribeth told the truth when she called you a tease, didn't she?"

"Yeah. Maribeth is observant. She sees things that fly right past other people."

He went on to share a little more about the girls with the baking beauty. Good points and bad. He figured she should know what she was getting into. After all, he and the girls would be living in the upstairs apartment for the next two weeks, if not longer. The man he'd hired to refurbish the walls and ceilings of Trace's house on the heels of the tomato war couldn't say just how many coats of paint the job would require.

Claire worked while he talked. Tye watched closely as she lined up more than a dozen bottles on her counter, his gaze lingering on the swell of a full bosom beneath her green gingham dress. He wrapped up his summation of his nieces with an apology. "I'm sorry for all the upset this morning. I guess the Blessings can be rather forward."

"Take after their uncle, do they?"

He winced. "Ouch. You do have a sharp tongue, Miss."

She innocently offered him a plate of muffins. He took it as an apology, whether she meant it as such or not.

Tye watched her as he bit into a muffin. Flavor exploded in his mouth, and he couldn't help but give a little groan of pleasure. Except for the cookie he'd tried earlier, he couldn't remember the last time he'd tasted anything near this delicious.

"Good, is it?" Claire asked, her voice confident.

"Mmm . . ." he sighed, his taste buds bursting with pleasure.

His eyes were getting a treat, too. Tendrils of golden hair had escaped the baker's pins to curl against her peaches-and-cream cheeks, and her lips tilted in a secret smile. As he finished his muffin, Tye's simple masculine appreciation for a warm, beautiful woman flared into something infinitely more complex.

He wanted her. The urge hit him quick and hard and had him eyeing the surface of her worktable with an interest that had nothing to do with the bottles waiting to be filled.

What the hell? He froze, not believing his reaction. What was the matter with him? Had his good sense gone south? She said she left a fiancé at home, and besides, she was a lady.

Lady. A four-letter word that made "damn" and "hell" sound downright proper.

Tye made it a practice to keep his relationships with that brand of female on a surface level. He could enjoy their company, even flirt a little. Pretend. No one got hurt. He was safe. Everyone was safe.

When he needed something physical, he looked to the honest women of this world. He limited his liaisons to harlots. A man could trust a soiled dove; he knew exactly what he was getting when he paid for pleasure. It was all black and white with no shades of gray.

Tye couldn't manage gray.

History had proved his instincts toward women weren't worth a Confederate dollar. He couldn't trust his own intuition. He had screwed up royally once and all but destroyed his family and himself. He'd sworn never to take that risk again, especially now that Trace had forgiven him.

If only he could learn to forgive himself.

Not an easy thing to do, considering the magnitude of his sin. Eight years ago, all caught up in a lady's lies, Tye McBride had bedded his twin brother's wife.

With memories of Constance at the forefront of his mind, and cognizant of the strength of his reaction to Claire, Tye set out to put some distance between himself and the baker lady by asking, "So, tell me about this fiancé you mentioned. When's the wedding? It's kind of curious, you being here in Fort Worth and him being in . . . Galveston, is it?"

For a moment, she appeared taken aback, then pink stained her cheeks. "I prefer not to discuss my private life, Mr. McBride. At least, not where Mr. Jamieson is concerned."

"Oh." A beat of silence followed; two beats. "I apologize if I got too personal." Then, in an attempt to lighten the mood, he took the conversation back to his nieces. "I'm not so het up on the idea of talking about nuptials, myself. My ears are worn out from listening to that particular topic. Matrimony is the girls' favorite subject these days."

"I believe many girls enjoy dreaming about their future weddings."

"If only it were *their* weddings they were planning, I'd be happy," Tye said, offering a rueful smile. "But it's not their own lives they are arranging, it's mine. My nieces enjoyed a run of good luck in matching their daddy with their new mother. Now they think they can do it again. To me."

He paused and rubbed his jaw thoughtfully. "You know, when they take to trying to marry me off, I find myself wanting to go along with the rest of Fort Worth and call them the McBride Menaces."

"That's understandable," Claire replied, stirring her witches' brew. After setting down the spoon, she removed a tin funnel from a wall hook and set it beside the bottles.

Tye watched her, intrigued. What was it she'd called her mixture? Magic?

Magic. His gaze trailed slowly down her curvaceous form. He found it easy to imagine her a sorceress.

"You are against marriage?"

"Hmm?" Tye yanked his gaze off the graceful curve of her hips. "Am I against marriage? No, not at all. It's certainly made my brother a happy man. It isn't in the cards for me, though. Not any time soon, anyway." He paused and grimaced. "If only I could get the Blessings to understand that."

She paused in her work and looked at him. "Family can be difficult at times."

He read understanding and something more in her gaze. Sadness. Hurt. Perhaps anger. "Do you have family here in Fort Worth?"

She jerked her gaze away. "No. Are you always this nosy, Mr. McBride?"

"Touché," he said with a grin.

Despite Tye's better intentions, Claire Donovan piqued his interest. She'd left her beau down in Galveston and obviously had some sort of trouble with her family. He wondered what it was. Had love put her heart through a wringer, too?

Boisterous laughter interrupted his contemplation as the Blessings dashed past the door. Ralph bounded along beside them, his excited puppy yelps blending sweetly with the music of the children's joy. Claire smiled at the sound and glanced toward the timer where the last grains of sand slid through the narrow opening. Lifting a pair of padded mittens, she approached the stove.

Tye rose from his seat. "Let me help with that. It looks heavy."

"I can do it."

"I'm sure you can," he replied. "But let me help anyway."

Tye appropriated the pads, then lifted the soup pot from the stove and carried it over to the table, setting it where the lady indicated. She placed a funnel in the neck of the first bottle, then dipped a ladle into the brew and brought it to her nose for a sniff.

Tye was surprised she still had the ability to distinguish scents. His expression must have showed his doubt, because she grinned. The imp was back. "Here, doubting Thomas. Take a whiff."

Wary, Tye leaned forward. He was momentarily distracted by the brush of her arm against his. Then, meeting the challenge shining in her eyes, prepared for a shock to his system, he inhaled. "Good Lord."

It was a shock, all right. The scent blasted through him, a knockout punch of pleasure to his senses. Instinctively, he took a second sniff and groaned with delight. *It's like sex for the nose*, he thought. "All that stink. How in the world did that become this? How did you do it?"

Her brow arched. "I told you. It's Magic."

"Magic," he repeated.

She lifted the ladle to her mouth and sipped. Her eyes slowly closed. She licked her lips and smiled.

Never in his life had Tye witnessed a more erotic act.

The scent of Magic swirled around them, and his nostrils flared to take it in. Her lashes lifted. Their gazes met and held. His breathing quickened; his mouth went dry. Again, arousal hit him, hot and hard and heavy.

Magic.

As though it had a will of its own, his hand rose, his fingers wrapping around hers as they held the ladle. Claire's eyes widened as hot liquid splashed over the sides and spilled to the floor. The effects of the scent roared through him, took hold of him, captured his will.

He wanted to taste the Magic, too, but not from the damned spoon. He wanted to drink the sorceress's Magic straight from

Claire Donovan's mouth. As he lowered his head, he demanded in a raspy voice, "Share."

At her whispered gasp, he paused and his gaze met hers, deep and shadowed blue like the night sky as it gave way to the universe. Magic. Enchantress. Seductress.

What the hell was he doing?

Abruptly, Tye pulled away. The spoon clattered to the floor. Desire remained a driving need within him as he stared at the droplets of amber-colored fluid collected on the tile. What had come over him? Why had he acted so totally out of character?

After a moment's thought, revelation widened his eyes. He glanced from the floor to the soup pot to the muffins on the table.

To the delectable, delicious, and dangerous Claire Donovan.

A breeze from the open door stirred the scent of her elixir around them again, and desire hit him with another wallop. Good God. Miss Donovan's Magic was aptly named. The woman added more than flour and cinnamon and eggs to her baked goods.

Obviously, Claire had cooked up an aphrodisiac.

CHAPTER 3

TO AVOID BAD LUCK, ALWAYS STIR A GOOD ROAST GRAVY WITH A WOODEN SPOON.

I CAN'T BELIEVE he almost kissed me.

Three days after the fact, the memory of the moment continued to shock and befuddle Claire. Even in a place as wild and untamed as Fort Worth, men didn't force themselves on ladies they'd only just met. Not if they were gentlemen. Didn't that give a nice fat clue into Tye McBride's character.

I wonder why he pulled away?

She dabbed her paintbrush at the spot of white she'd missed on an interior wall, obliterating the dry place with an uneven stroke of pale yellow. "You're better off not asking that question, Claire Donovan," she muttered. Pursuing that line of thought any further meant examining why she hadn't pulled away first. Experience had taught Claire it didn't pay to be too curious.

But she was still a woman, with a woman's weaknesses, so when the masculine groan and childish squeal of distress sounded from next door, she put down her paintbrush and hurried to investigate. What she found left her gasping. "Oh, my."

Afternoon sunshine beamed through Fortune's Design's plate glass window, illuminating the interior of Jenny McBride's dress shop. Upon Claire's earlier visits to the store, notions, trims, and bolts of fabric had filled the shelves along one wall. A display table near the front usually held sketchbooks, markdown items, and an ivy plant droopy from lack of water. Normally, the work-table stood flush against the wall.

Today was not a normal day.

Claire stopped right inside the front door and surveyed the surroundings in shock. Directly in front of her lay an overturned chair. Beside it, a thread box rested on its side amidst the broken remnants of a pottery flower vase. "Oh my," she repeated as she stepped around the chair. Her hem collected a web of scarlet thread, and her shoe bumped one of the dozens of wooden spools lying scattered on the floor, sending it rolling across the wood to slam against the baseboard.

"Careful, Miss Donovan," came a man's voice. "I darn near broke a leg on one of those. Never realized a small scrap of wood could be so dangerous."

She followed the sound to the back of the shop. Tye McBride sat on the floor slumped against the wall opposite the dressing room. *Dazed* was the word she thought best described him.

Uncertain how to reply, Claire settled for a dry, "Sewing can be a perilous occupation for some of us. I poked a needle halfway through my thumb one time."

"Do much sewing?" he asked casually.

"Not if I can avoid it. I do have to make curtains for my bakery, though, I'm afraid."

Tye's smile was wry. "Maybe you could barter buns for basting with Mrs. Moore. She manages this shop for Jenny."

"We've met." She glanced from the back of the store to the front and didn't hide her grimace. "She's not working today?"

"She went home sick." Slowly, he pushed to his feet and dusted off his denim pants. "I told her I'd keep an eye on Fortune's Design for her."

"Next time you might try using more than one."

He sighed heavily and nodded his agreement "I put the CLOSED sign up in the front window."

"I guess your vandal couldn't read."

He cut her a dry look, then commented, "A good neighbor might have checked on the situation when she heard a bunch of commotion next door."

Claire nodded. "A good neighbor would have had she not been away doing errands for a time. All has been quiet here for the past hour or two. At least it was quiet until you groaned." Walking back toward the front of the store, she plucked a bright red pincushion out of the center of a potted plant "Reminds one of a tomato."

"Yeah," Tye replied. He stared at the stuffed roundish ball. "I like tomatoes. You use them much in your baking?"

She winced at the thought "No, can't say I do. Why are we talking about this?"

"I'm trying to avoid dealing with reality here."

Claire wanted to laugh at that. How like a man.

"Bet you use a lot of that Magic stuff you make, though, don't you? I figured it out. It's an aphrodisiac."

"A what?"

One of the girls, Maribeth, if Claire remembered correctly, poked her head outside the dressing room curtain. "Hello, Miss Donovan. Uncle Tye, I've picked up all the pins in here. What do I do next? And what's an aphrodisiac?"

McBride wasn't paying attention. Instead, his gaze had focused on a bolt of red gingham now lying on the floor. Claire followed the path of his stare and spied the muddy paw prints adorning the cloth.

Claire wasn't the least bit surprised. She hadn't seen much of the McBrides the past few days, but she'd seen plenty of Ralph. The dog could teach even the three Menaces how to get into mischief.

"Uncle Tye," the child repeated, "what's an aphrodisiac?"

27

He cleared his throat and said, "It's an animal similar to a raccoon, Mari."

Claire gaped at him, then bit the inside of her cheek to hold back an unladylike snort as hope lit the youngster's eyes.

"Like a coon?" Maribeth asked. "They're mischievous animals. Does an aphrodisiac make paw prints like a puppy's?"

Tye jerked his head toward the soiled gingham, and in a boom-lowering tone, stated, "You mean like Ralph's."

Ralph. The obvious culprit. Judging by the wilted expressions on both the McBrides' faces, neither of them was happy with the truth.

The girl asked in a little voice, "What are you going to do, Uncle Tye? This breaks Rule Number Three on Papa's list, the one about animals and trouble. Are you gonna make us give him away?"

"Well..." He rubbed his palm along his jaw. "I can't be breaking any of your pa's rules."

Though Claire wouldn't have thought it possible, Maribeth's face drooped even further.

"But," Tye continued, shooting a sharp look toward Claire. "I'm not a hundred percent certain Ralph is at fault here. We have an unaccounted-for aphrodisiac running around loose."

Emma McBride should have embroidered teddy bears on his drawers along with the hearts, Claire thought. That's all he was, a big teddy bear.

The sudden vision of this particular teddy bear propped up against her bed pillows along with the other mementos of her youth brought a warm flush of embarrassment to Claire's cheeks. *Must be all this silly talk of aphrodisiacs.*

She cleared her throat. "Well, Miss Maribeth, I think your uncle has a point. Another four-footed animal might have made this mess."

Hope lit Maribeth McBride's expression. "So if we're not positive Ralph broke Rule Number Three, we don't have to give him away?"

Tye reached down and ruffled her hair. "Not as long as a trio of two-legged little girls work hard to clean this place up."

"The piano lesson should be almost over. I'll go tell my sisters to hurry up." Maribeth hopped to her feet and darted out the back in a flash.

Claire laughed as the door banged behind the girl. She scooped up the basket lying at Tye's feet and deposited the pincushion inside. After kneeling to retrieve more of the basket's contents, she looked up at him and observed, "You're the Menace, Mr. McBride. Lying to that child. Really now, an aphrodisiac?"

Tye stood frozen in his tracks as he caught a whiff of her perfume. Fresh paint with an overriding scent of Magic.

Damn right an aphrodisiac.

He wanted to reach down and pull her up. Up into his arms. He wanted to taste Claire Donovan's Magic.

A loud *harrumph* shook him from his trance. Glancing up, he spied Trace's housekeeper, Mrs. Wilson, standing in the doorway. He stifled a groan. This day was riding a fast train from bad to worse.

Scandal bristling in her tone, Mrs. Wilson glared at him and said, "Lies and wickedness. You should be ashamed, Tye McBride."

He sighed. Just his luck the old biddy arrived in time to witness his story about animals and aphrodisiacs. Knowing her, she had decided he'd hosted an orgy in Jenny's shop. Wonderful. Just wonderful.

Claire rose to her feet and faced the housekeeper. Disapproval flattened the baker's smile, and for the first time since his brother left town, Tye felt like he had somebody on his side. Despite the tension of the moment, he grinned.

Tye and Mrs. Wilson had been engaged in something of a turf war since the moment Trace and Jenny stepped aboard the outbound train. She didn't trust him with her beloved charges, and he didn't like her bossy attitude. The girls, being the intelligent scamps that they were, had used it to their advantage by playing one against the other until Mrs. Wilson left to care for her daughter. While he admitted to needing help with his nieces, Tye found he didn't look forward to a resumption of hostilities now that the housekeeper had returned.

To that end, he decided to ignore her censure. "Good afternoon, ma'am. Welcome home. How is your daughter's leg coming along? Is it healing all right? Are you back for good?"

She gave an exaggerated sniff. "I'm just here in Fort Worth for the afternoon to check up on the girls and pick up a few necessities from my house. My daughter is doing tolerably well under the circumstances, thank you, which is more than I can say for both Fortune's Design and Willow Hill. Why, I've never seen such a mess in my life!" Turning to Claire, she asked, "And who are you? I won't tolerate him bringing his doxies around my Menaces."

Anger flashed like lightning. "Now wait just one minute," he began.

Claire smiled and extended her hand, deliberately treading on Tye's foot as she took a step toward the housekeeper. "Please excuse my appearance. I've been painting and I do look a fright. I'm Claire Donovan, Mrs. Wilson. I've rented the shop space next door from Mr. Trace. I met Mr. McBride and the girls this morning. Those children are so delightful and they had so many nice things to say about you."

"They are precious girls, aren't they?" Mrs. Wilson beamed.

Tye figured Claire had handled the insult to herself, so he settled for grumbling, "So don't call them Menaces."

Mrs. Wilson wrinkled her nose his way. "I've told you before it's a term of endearment that both their father and I use. You don't know these children well enough to care for them."

She turned to Claire and spoke as though the baker were now her ally. "When I received word my daughter and son-in-law needed me I was so torn. I knew it was a mistake to leave this scoundrel solely in charge of the girls while I help my daughter and grandchildren. If only Mr. Trace had listened to me and arranged for another woman to back me up with the girls while he and Jenny are away instead of this brother of his. I told him it was a mistake to rely on Tye."

"Hold your tongue, lady," he warned.

Claire played referee by stepping between him and the housekeeper, and he couldn't fault her thinking. His temper up, he braced his hands on his hips and kicked another thread spool out of his way. He'd expected holy hell from her should she return before he'd successfully dealt with the tomato chaos at the house, but the woman had no cause to fault his care of his nieces. She'd prodded a sore spot, and he wasn't about to allow her charge to pass. "My brother can depend on me for anything and everything, and he darn well knows it. I'd give my life for the Blessings. I've taken good care of them."

"Too bad you can't say the same about Willow Hill and this poor store," the housekeeper snapped back. "Where is Mrs. Moore, by the way? She probably took one look at this place and had a spell."

"I gave her the day off," Tye replied, biting back the words he truly wanted to say and all but choking on the words he eventually voiced. "You are right, Mrs. Wilson."

Claire tossed a look of surprise over her shoulder. After a moment of shocked silence, the old peahen preened.

Tye wanted to scowl and turn the air blue with a few choice cuss words, but under the circumstances, he reckoned placation was the word of the day. Otherwise Mrs. Wilson was liable to hunt up one of her friends to "assist" him with his nieces.

Despite recent trouble, he still thought he could handle the job alone. He needed to do it, needed to help his brother when that help really counted. He would not sound retreat and call for help from outside sources. At least not from someone of Mrs.

Wilson's choosing.

So he had to appease. "Look, I learn from my mistakes and the girls and I know I have a mess on my hands both here and at the house, but it's nothing a little paint and pickup won't fix. I reckon I should have anticipated trouble when I brought a bushel of South Texas tomatoes into a houseful of warring females. And as far as this place goes, I shouldn't have..."

His voice trailed off as he spied Loretta Davis crossing the street headed for the store, her cheeks about as red as the posy on her bonnet.

Oh, hell. The McBride Blessings must have been at it again.

"Mrs. Wilson, I know you must be anxious to see the girls. Kat had her piano lesson this afternoon and Emma is walking her home. Mari went to meet them, and if you left now, you could catch them near the Emporium." He reached for his wallet and said, "I'll buy y'all a soda." Removing more than enough cash, he shoved the bills into Mrs. Wilson's hands and ushered her toward the back door. "Take the alley. It's quicker."

When the back door banged shut behind the housekeeper, Tye had just enough time before the front door opened to mutter to Claire, "You've been a trooper so far. Don't give up on me now."

As CLAIRE WATCHED Loretta Davis sweep dramatically into the dress shop, she decided she should have a bag of peanuts in her hand. Seeing Tye McBride juggle the women in his life was more entertaining than a circus center ring.

"You need to take those girls in hand, Mr. McBride," the pretty young woman demanded, her eyes flashing behind long, curling lashes. "Immediately. They've stirred up a den of snakes this time."

Claire uprighted the chair and took a seat to watch the show. Tye winced and asked, "What have they done?"

"It's my mother."

"Your mother?"

"Ooh," Claire said softly, dread inching up her spine on the McBrides' behalf. If Tye's Blessings had done mischief to Maybelle Davis, they had serious trouble on their hands. One of the first things Claire learned upon her arrival in Fort Worth was that the doctor's wife was a force to be reckoned with.

She was a tiny woman with an enormous opinion about every issue and occurrence in town. Claire had witnessed her lecture of a pair of rowdy schoolboys in the mercantile just the day before. The woman had gone on for more than half an hour about how children should be seen and not heard. *I bet Maybelle Davis and the McBride Menaces mix about as well as a Baptist choir and bawdy songs.*

Loretta Davis acknowledged Claire and her "ooh" with a distressed nod.

Tye must know about Maybelle Davis, too, because he'd gone a bit green and his voice squeaked as he asked, "The girls have had dealings with your mother?"

"Yes, my mother," Loretta confirmed, her bountiful chest heaving in agitation. "She spoke in my father's place at school for Commerce Day. She talked about being a physician's wife. The teacher invited a number of representatives from local businesses to speak also. Including a blacksmith."

Claire noticed that Tye had to drag his gaze back up to Loretta's face. Men and bosoms. They are never too busy to notice.

"I'm sorry," he said to Loretta. "I'm not making the connection."

"The blacksmith is my beau, Mr. Gus Willard." Loretta blinked furiously as tears pooled in her honey-brown eyes. "It was that Emma. I swear she is eleven going on twenty. She told my mother you . . . you are . . . you are very . . ."

With every stutter, Tye's complexion grew a little greener. He croaked, "I'm very what?"

"Eligible," she wailed.

Tye blinked. "Excuse me?"

"Emma told my mother you are heir to some grand English castle. She said you are rich beyond our wildest dreams. Needless to say, my mother has made an abrupt about-face. She's joined forces with those Menaces to see us wed." Tears spilled down Loretta's cheeks and she cried, "And my Gus heard the whole story. Now he thinks he's not good enough for me."

She clutched at Tye's shirt sleeve and said, "Tell me it isn't true, Mr. McBride. Tell me you don't own a castle."

Claire leaned forward in her chair, dying to hear the answer to this.

Grimacing, Tye scratched the back of his neck. "It's not a castle. It's a manor house. And I'm not the heir.

It's my child who will inherit most of the wealth. My share is only a fraction."

Hope shined like sunbeams in Loretta's eyes. "You're already married? You have a child?"

"No. I have no children."

Claire heard a note of pain in the answer and wondered at it.

"Oh, no. That's it then. My life is ruined." Loretta dabbed at her eyes with a lace-trimmed handkerchief as tears overflowed

Tye cast a what-do-I-do-now gaze toward Claire. She gestured for him to pat the poor, sobbing young woman's back. Awkwardly, he reached out and laid a hand on Loretta's shoulder. His touch gave voice to her tears and she started blubbering aloud.

"Men," Claire said with a sigh. She stood and wrapped a consoling arm around Loretta. "Now, now. Calm down. There's no need to water yourself dry. Matters aren't as bleak as you think. Mr. McBride will have a talk with your Gus and smooth things out."

"It's no use. It's gone too far for that. My *mother* is involved!"

She wrenched away from Claire and threw herself against Tye. She clutched at his shirt with both hands and buried her face against his chest. Though he bore it with a stoic look on his face, Claire noted he didn't resist the proximity of a pillowy bosom.

Her offer of comfort dismissed, but unwilling to walk out on the play altogether, Claire turned her attention to tidying the shop. *First order of business is to get the bolts of fabric off the floor,* she thought.

Moments later, Loretta burst out in a new flurry of tears. "Oh, look. She has that bolt of red cotton. I'm making a shirt for Gus out of that very cloth for his birthday. All I have left is to sew on the buttons, and now he won't want it."

As the waterworks continued, Tye shot Claire a helpless, entreating look. "Miss Donovan?"

Claire rolled her eyes, then set the bolt of gingham she held on the worktable and approached the sobbing woman and uneasy man. Stopping directly behind Loretta, she looked him in the eyes and said, "Yes?"

"I think Loretta could use a little female encouragement about now. Maybe you could take her next door? Maybe feed her one of those cookies of yours? It might be helpful for her to talk with another woman. And as you heard, she seems to think her mother—"

"Is here!" Loretta whispered fiercely, her horrified gaze staring past Tye's shoulder and out the window. She jerked back, hiding behind Tye. "You can't let her find me here. She'll know I've been crying and I'll have to explain and I can't explain. Not until I've talked to Gus. Don't let her see me."

"Lord McBride?" Maybelle Davis called as she entered Fortune's Design. "Lord McBride, is that you? I need to speak with you about the most interesting information I picked up at school-" She broke off abruptly. "Why, Lord McBride, do you have a woman in your arms? Here in your sister-in-law's shop? Have you compromised my daughter? Is that our Loretta?"

Tye's mouth worked but no sound came out.

"The dressing room," Claire whispered to Loretta. Then she whirled around to the rescue. Wearing her most charming smile, she glided toward Maybelle, silently demanding her attention. "It's me, Mrs. Davis. Claire Donovan. Mr. McBride was just helping me get a piece of lint from my eye. All this fabric, you know. I'm so glad you stopped by the Rankin Building. I haven't helped but notice what superior sense of style you have. I need to choose fabric for curtains for The Confectionary and I'm wondering if you would mind assisting me with my decision?" She gestured toward the bolt of yellow gingham on the worktable.

Maybelle raked the scene with a suspicious gaze. "Has your choice been so difficult that you created this mess, Miss Donovan? I do hope you handle foodstuffs with better care than you do dry goods. Otherwise the safety of eating in your shop will come into question."

"Miss Donovan didn't do this. It's all my fault," Tye hastened to say. "I'm afraid my puppy and I got a bit rambunctious while playing earlier."

Maybelle smiled with delight. "You enjoy pets do you, Lord McBride? My Loretta just loves her kitty."

"I'm not a lord. I'm a—"

"Landlord," Claire interjected. "My lease called for the replacement of the curtains in my shop, so Mr. McBride is acting in his brother's stead. He tried to help me choose, but you know how men are. I could certainly use a lady's opinion, Mrs. Davis." She lifted the yellow gingham and hurried toward the front of the shop. "Please, would you mind terribly walking next door with me? I need to know if this will look all right with the color of the paint, and I do so admire your sense of style."

Flattery, along with the idea that Claire's presence in the shop was just business did the trick. Maybelle beamed a smile at Claire. "Why, certainly. I'd be glad to help. I just need a moment with Lord McBride first."

"Tye" he insisted. "Please, just call me Tye. What can I do for you, ma'am?"

The older woman's eyes took on a predatory light as she said, "I'm hoping you can join us for dinner this evening, Tye. Loretta is cooking, and she makes a delicious roast beef. And she has also baked her pecan pie that won the blue ribbon at last year's fair."

"Sounds wonderful, but I'm afraid I can't leave my nieces."

Tye appeared truly regretful. Claire didn't believe it for a minute.

"Oh, pshaw." Maybelle waved a hand. "Please, feel free to bring them along. Loretta loves children."

Tye attempted half a dozen more objections but he might as well have saved his breath. The woman overcame every one. Finally, he bowed to the inevitable and agreed to arrive for supper at seven o'clock that evening.

As Claire escorted the matchmaking mama from the dress shop, she glanced back over her shoulder. Tye McBride sat slumped in the chair, his legs stretched out before him, waving a frilly, white lace fan in front of his face.

The Menaces, Mrs. Wilson, Maybelle, and Loretta Davis. *Yes, Lord McBride, I'd say you're in the hot seat now.*

She stifled a laugh. The man certainly had a way with women.

TYE WAITED a couple of minutes to make sure Maybelle wasn't coming back before he ushered Loretta out the back. "I'm doomed," the distraught daughter said once they'd reached the alley. "The McBride Menaces have ruined my life."

Tye glanced heavenward. "Hush, now. Don't be ridiculous. My Blessings haven't done any more than speak a little out of turn. I'll look up Gus and explain the situation, and before you know it, we'll be dancing at your wedding. Now go on home, girl."

She wore a pleading look as she insisted, "You'll put a halt to this matchmaking your nieces are up to?"

Tye rubbed his palm across his jaw. "Yeah. I'll put my foot down." As he watched Loretta hurry down the alley, he added, "I just hope I don't step in something unpleasant when I do."

Back inside, he started putting Fortune's Design to rights. He figured a good hour's work would be required to make it fit for the store to reopen the following day. As he worked, he kept his ears perked for sounds of Maybelle Davis's departure from next door. He wanted to thank Claire for all her help. Not only had she stood with him against Mrs. Wilson, she'd bailed him out when the Davis women came to call. He figured he owed the baker big time.

"Maybe I'll buy her a hat," he said to the rag doll Katrina had left in the shop. He knew it was Katrina's because of the chocolate kiss stains across the face.

Tye had all the fabric off the floor and half the thread picked up when he saw Maybelle stroll past the window. Trying not to appear too anxious, he told himself to wait a full minute before heading next door.

He held out for thirty seconds.

Claire was wrapping yellow gingham back onto the bolt when he sauntered across the vestibule and into The Confectionary. She hadn't seen him come in. He stopped abruptly just inside the door.

The woman literally sparkled. Sunlight beaming through the front window highlighted strands of fiery red that streaked through her golden hair. Her blue eyes danced, color stained her cheeks, and the grin teasing her lips gleamed. She was the very picture of beauty, and she took Tye's breath away.

Must be the air in here, he thought. All that Magic hanging around. He cleared his throat, trying to break the spell.

She turned her head, then gave him a cutting glance. "I'll have to talk my way out of pumpkin-colored curtains all because of you."

He eyed the freshly painted yellow walls and said, "That's going above and beyond the call of mere acquaintanceship. I guess we'll have to be friends. Can you use a friend, Miss Donovan? I sure can."

She tossed him a droll look. "You probably go through friends pretty fast. All that bailing you out of trouble wears on a person."

Damn, but he liked her spunk. He realized that he meant it when he asked to be her friend. It wasn't simply a throwaway line. He liked Claire Donovan and he would enjoy her friendship. Especially since she couldn't be his lover.

What he didn't like was the way his body responded to her. Damned Magic. Did it affect every man this way? "Do you have many male friends, Claire?"

Arching a brow, she tossed the gingham onto a nearby table. "I don't remember giving you leave to use my given name, Lord McBride."

Tye grimaced. "I swear you could fillet a fish with that tongue of yours. I figured after all we've been through together today, we were already on a first-name basis. Please, call me Tye." After a moment's pause, he added, "*Please* call me Tye."

She laughed and headed back toward the kitchen. "I'm thirsty, Tye. Can I offer you a lemonade?"

"Please."

He remained in the main part of the shop, hesitant to go any closer to the place where she stored her elixir. While he waited he found himself wondering about men and Magic and whether he had cause to be concerned. His innocent, impressionable nieces would be living upstairs for the next couple of weeks. If she planned on parading a passel of fellas high on Magic through here, then he reckoned he had something to say about that.

Another thought struck him, and he momentarily shut his eyes. Good Lord, cattle season started shortly. Imagine the potential trouble when dozens of cowboys— randy by nature anyway— got hold of her cookies. It'd be like mating season on a goat farm. "I'll have to move the Blessings to Dallas."

"Excuse me?"

He gave his head a little shake and accepted the glass she handed him. "The paint fumes are getting to me. Wouldn't you like to go outside?"

She shook her head. "I have work to do, boxes of dishes to unpack. Your problems have already delayed me enough as it is." Her skirt swirled as she turned around and headed for the back room.

Tye remained where he was, drumming his fingers on his knee as he thought. He, too, had work to do, but first he needed to do what he'd come here to do. Pushing to his feet, he braved the lingering Magic fumes and followed her into the kitchen. She was removing a white stoneware plate from a straw-filled crate, and her movements drew her blouse tight across her bosom.

She can give Loretta a run for the money in the breast department, Tye couldn't help but observe. Dragging his stare away from the pleasing sight, he spied a neat row of bottles lining the shelf. Damn Magic. Best get his business done and get out of here. "Thank you, Claire."

Claire set the plate down, then looked at him. "For. . . ?"

Even her neck is pretty, he thought. Slender and graceful. Damn, but she's pretty as a polished pearl.

Tye cleared his throat and tried to drag his attention back to where it belonged. "For helping with Mrs. Wilson and Mrs. Davis and with the shop. And most of all, for backing me up with Maribeth. I didn't know how else to get around Rule Number Three. It would have killed me to have to take the dog away from them."

"I know," she replied. "And you are welcome. And, since I guess I would like to be friends, I probably should warn you about Maybelle. Her daughter was right to be worried. My little tête-à-tête with Maybelle convinced me she definitely has plans for you and her Loretta. She came right out and said she hopes Jenny McBride returns from her honeymoon in time to make Loretta's gown for her wedding to you."

"And I promised to have dinner with her. The woman caught me off guard. I wasn't thinking fast enough."

"I understand that can be a problem for *lords*," Claire replied with a smile that was downright ornery.

"Ouch." Tye reached into the crate and removed a saucer. Brushing away the packing straw, he added, "You picked up on that, did you?"

"It was difficult to miss."

"It also wasn't the truth."

"That's not what Maybelle Davis believes." Claire pulled a cup from the wooden box. "The way she plans it, her daughter is only an 'I do' away from an English castle."

"It's a damned manor house. Not a castle."

Claire fumbled the cup and almost dropped it "You *are* a lord?"

"No. Well, maybe. Yeah, I guess I am. I'm older than Trace by a few minutes, so I guess the title is mine whether I want it or not. Which I don't." He pointed toward the kitchen window. "Is it all right if I open this? The fumes are getting to me."

"You still smell the paint?"

He shook his head. "Magic."

He was debating whether or not to bring up the subject of aphrodisiacs again when a knock sounded at the back door. "Got your evening paper, Miss Donovan," a boy called.

Claire reached into her cookie jar and removed two cookies. She handed them to the paperboy in exchange for the newspaper. "Thanks, Casey."

"You're welcome, Miss Donovan. See you tomorrow."

"I know that boy," Tye said, frowning. "Casey Tate Katrina told me Emma is sweet on him."

"Really?" she murmured, reading the front page. "That's nice."

41

Tye didn't think it was nice. Emma was too young to be looking at boys. And that boy had no business sampling Claire's Magic. "You shouldn't give him food like that. It probably ruins his supper."

She ignored him. Her attention was focused on the paper. "You are not going to like this. Wilhemina Peters simply cannot leave the McBride family alone. You want to read what she has to say about you in today's 'Talk About Town' column?"

"Not particularly."

She glanced up at him. "You need to know this, my friend."

Scowling, Tye tugged the paper right out of her hand and scanned the page for Wilhemina Peters's column.

Royalty Visits Fort Worth

This columnist has learned that the citizens of Fort Worth have been mistaken in their address of Mr. Trace McBride's brother, Tye, during his visit to Fort Worth. The handsome bachelor is no mere mister. He is a cousin to Queen Victoria herself and owns a real, honest-to-goodness castle in England. A great big Texas howdy to Lord Tye McBride.

The newspaper slid from Tye's hands and fluttered to the floor. "Oh, Lord."

"Cousin to the queen, Lord McBride?" Claire asked, scooping up the newspaper.

"God, no," he replied, closing his eyes. That blasted Wilhemina Peters was showing her ignorance again. "I'm not a royal cousin and my title is not my surname."

Claire sounded as if she had her tongue planted firmly in her cheek as she said, "Of course it isn't. As much as I love Texas and her people, I'm afraid we are a bit too far removed to know the ins and outs of British aristocracy. You are not Lord McBride, you're Lord . . . ?"

"Wexford."

"And your title is . . . ?"

He didn't answer.

"Earl?" she guessed. "Duke?"

"Viscount of Wexford," he grumbled grudgingly. He said no more, staring unseeing at the crate that contained Claire's cups and saucers as slowly, one by one, the ramifications of Wilhemina Peters's gossip column made themselves known to him.

He obviously wasn't the only person whose thoughts drifted that direction because after a moment, he heard Claire make a noise that sounded suspiciously like a choked-off chuckle.

"What!" he demanded sharply.

She cleared her throat and looked up from the newspaper, meeting Tye's glare with sparkling blue eyes and luscious pink lips. Twitching pink lips.

"What's so funny?"

Smothered laughter hung in her voice. "I'm sorry. I don't mean to be unkind. It's just that your expression . . . it's so . . . *male*. My brothers would look exactly like you do, under similar circumstances."

"Well I'm not one of your brothers, so don't be laughing at me. This title business is all nonsense, anyway. This is Texas, not England. I don't even know if it counts here. I might not even have one."

"Oh, you have a title." Claire's smile broke like sunshine from behind a storm cloud as she waved the paper in front of him. "As of this afternoon, you sir, are the Most Eligible Bachelor in Texas."

CHAPTER 4

TO END A RUN OF BAD LUCK, THROW THREE SHAKES OF SALT OVER YOUR LEFT SHOULDER DURING A FULL MOON.

THE WOMEN BEGAN ARRIVING SHORTLY after daybreak.

Accustomed to a baker's early hours, Claire was halfway through her day and hard at work washing the storefront window when the first female bearing gifts appeared. Muffins, she decided, her experienced nose detecting the aroma of cinnamon and baked blueberries wafting from the napkin-covered basket that dangled from the woman's arms. Possibly a coffee cake.

"Good morning." Claire beamed a friendly smile. "It looks to be a beautiful day."

"Yes, I have high hopes for it." The woman paused, fiddled with the strings on her bonnet then lifted her chin. Squaring her shoulders, she stepped into the Rankin Building vestibule and rapped on Tye McBride's door.

Claire polished her way closer, making certain to work quietly. She didn't want to miss a word.

Inside the building, a door swished open. Katrina McBride spoke in a sleepy voice. "Hello. May I help you?"

"I'd like to speak with Lord McBride."

After a pause, the littlest Menace replied, "Oh. If you're looking for the Lord, you should try across the street at the church. Ask for Sister Gonzaga. I think she's got an extra good connection to Him."

"Your uncle, child," the visitor replied, her voice tight. "I wish to speak with your uncle."

"Well you should have said so." With every word the girl's voice grew stronger, as though she were shaking off the effects of sleep, preparing herself to launch into the mischief of the day. "Wait here. I'll go get him. Unless he's still asleep, and then you'll have to come back later. Uncle Tye gets really grumpy when we wake him up before he's ready, and after the trouble during supper at Miss Loretta's, my sisters and I need to be extra good today. Part of that is letting him sleep as long as he wants. What do you have in the basket? It smells good. Maybe I should take it upstairs with me now."

The woman protested, but little Kat must have gotten her way because the basket was gone when Claire stepped into the vestibule and then into her shop, pausing to prop her door open with a decorative stop made of cast iron and shaped like a butter churn.

Claire couldn't help but wonder what kind of devilment the girls had contrived the night before at the Davis's supper table. Not that it was any business of Claire's, but she couldn't help being curious. It was in her nature.

The predilection to snoop wasn't the most flattering of traits, but Claire had come by it honestly. She'd learned early on that if she wanted to know any of the juicier secrets her family shared, she'd need to listen at keyholes and spy in windows. Her parents never told her anything, and her brothers were just as bad. After all, they said, Claire was a girl. She need not trouble herself with troubles. So, barred from family meetings of one sort or another, she had learned to adapt. Such ingrained habits were hard to leave behind.

Claire ducked into the back of the shop for her recipe books, then grabbed a pencil and paper for a grocery list. She could pretend she chose that spot because the light was better or the chair more comfortable. But in fact, when she poured herself a cup of coffee and took her seat, Claire Donovan was settling in to eavesdrop. She felt only slightly guilty for doing so.

Within minutes, she heard Tye's scratchy rumble. "Uh, hello."

In a simpering tone the visitor said, "Lord McBride, my name is Eliza Ledbetter. I wanted to welcome you to Fort Worth with a basket of blueberry muffins, but your niece already took them upstairs."

Blueberry. I knew it, Claire thought smugly, marking flour down on her list.

"Well, ah, thank you, Miss Ledbetter. It's nice to meet you. And please, just call me Tye. I appreciate the welcome. Kat showed me the basket, and we surely will enjoy those muffins."

"It's my special recipe."

After a pause, Tye asked in a suspicious tone. "Did Claire Donovan provide any of the ingredients?"

"I don't believe I've met Miss Donovan."

"That's good. Well, then, I'll look forward to sampling your baking."

Claire broke the point on her pencil.

Eliza Ledbetter continued, "Lord McBride—"

"Tye."

"Tye. And you must call me Eliza." She twittered then, and Claire rolled her eyes. "My mother has decided to hold a small soiree on Friday night, and we'd be honored if you would attend."

Again, there was a moment's pause. "Well, I thank you for the invitation, Eliza, but as you probably know, I'm here caring for my nieces. I don't feel good leaving them."

"You'd be welcome to bring the Mena—I mean, your nieces. Perhaps they could assist in the evening's entertainment. I understand young Katrina has a beautiful voice."

"Yeah, Kat can sing, but I'm afraid she's useless when it comes to sitting still. I took the girls with me to supper last night, and

I'm afraid it turned out to be a rather unpleasant experience for all. Please, give your mother my thanks and pass along my regrets. Maybe next time."

"Couldn't you leave them with your brother's housekeeper or Mrs. McBride's mother?"

Tye's voice sharpened. "Mrs. Wilson is in Dallas and Jenny's mother, Monique, is in Europe, so neither is available to baby-sit. Besides, I told my brother *I'd* care for them. That's exactly what I'm going to do."

"Oh."

Claire couldn't tell if Eliza Ledbetter was embarrassed or disappointed. The way she tied up the conversation and hurried off made Claire suspect it was a little of both.

Eliza might have been the first woman Tye disappointed that day, but it soon became obvious she wasn't to be the last. By the time the girls left for school Claire watched women deliver seven more baskets of muffins, four cakes, three loaves of bread, a roasted turkey, and five proposals of marriage. When she spied the woman toting the roasted bird pass her window, Claire had to peek around the shop's door to observe Tye's reaction. His panicked expression when he accepted the turkey had her biting the inside of her cheek to keep from laughing aloud.

Shortly thereafter she heard the children call their good-byes as they hurried off to school. Tye followed quickly on their heels, ducking out the back door wearing a beat-up straw hat and a hunted expression. "I'd bet a dozen bottles of Magic he's going somewhere to hide."

Watching him go, Claire felt torn between sympathy and amusement. Normally she wasn't the type to hold a grudge, but she couldn't forget the snotty comment McBride made to Eliza Ledbetter in reference to Claire's ingredients. What did he have against her cookies, anyway?

She pondered the question for some time without arriving at any answer. Then, shortly before noon, as she prepared to mix up a Snow Cake, a knock sounded at her back door. Tye McBride stood on the stoop, his hands cupped against the glass as he peered inside. The moment she opened the door, he ducked into the kitchen.

"I am so glad you are here. It's getting dangerous out there."

Claire took a good look at him and decided the danger factor in her kitchen just hiked up a notch itself. Dressed in a blue chambray shirt, worn denim britches, and a help-me look, Tye McBride appealed to the caretaker in her. It was all she could do not to set him down at the table and ply him with baked goods.

When he flashed her a grin and sank into a chair with a grateful sigh, it was all she could do not to sit in his lap and ply him with kisses.

Why, Claire Donovan. Where did that come from?

Flustered, she walked to the window and threw it open. "It's getting hot in here," she muttered inanely.

"You think this is hot you should see it upstairs. It's wall-to-wall women up there."

He looked so appalled that she couldn't help but laugh. With that, her tension eased. "What's the matter, Lord McBride? You don't like being popular?"

"Popular, hah," he scoffed. "These gals look at me and see one thing. Some silly bit of inheritance that doesn't mean a dam— darned thing. I'm glad you're not like that, Claire. It's reassuring to know that not all women are feather-heads. I'd hate for the Blessings to grow up that way."

Claire smiled weakly and turned back to her cake. He was right about one thing. When she looked at him she didn't see an English title, she saw a handsome, virile man. Which put her right in there with the feather-heads after all.

Glancing down at her bowl, she saw she'd beat the butter to a cream without awareness of the effort. "So why are you calling on me? Are you hiding?"

"Darned straight, I am. At last count there were ten ladies up there offering to help baby-sit the Blessings. Each one of them had rounded up a kid of some sort— a niece, a nephew, a neighbor's child—to come play at our house. Even Mrs. Wilson showed up since she ended up staying in town overnight and now has time to kill before her train leaves for Dallas. The girls are in heaven, but for me it was pure hell. So I escaped. Told Mrs. W. I'd be back before her train left. What are you making?"

"Snow Cake." She added arrowroot to the mixture, then a half-pound of flour, trying her best to ignore her visitor. She wasn't having much luck.

He rose from his seat and began to pace the small kitchen. He made her feel like a cook in a lion cage. "You're making me nervous, McBride," she said as she stirred in her flour. "Go in the front and pace if you must."

"No, they might peek in the windows and see me."

"Then find something to do." She gradually added a half-pound of sifted white sugar to the mix, sensing the weight of his gaze all the while. At least he'd quit marching.

When she laid down her wooden spoon and reached for an egg, he approached her, saying, "I'll help you with the cake. Except the poison part, that is. I won't contribute to that."

She fumbled the egg. "Poison?"

"That potion of yours. The Magic. Here," he grabbed the egg from her hand, "you're fixing to make a mess. I'll do the eggs." He cracked the shell gently against the rim of her mixing bowl.

Claire stopped him just in time. "No, not in the batter. This recipe uses only egg whites. I'll do it."

She tried to take the egg away from him, but he dodged her reach. "I know how to separate eggs. Get me a bowl."

"No. I—"

"You told me to find something to do. I'm going to help."

That she sincerely doubted. He'd already proved to be a distraction to her. Now that he'd taken up a position at her side, it only grew worse.

He smelled delicious. She tried to put a name to the scent. Spicy, certainly. Hot, zippy spices. Maybe cayenne or red pepper. But savory, too. Like warm sweet cream. And—she leaned a little closer to get another whiff— manly. Musky. Yummy. *Figure out this recipe and you can forget all about Magic.*

"How many?"

His voice jerked her back to the present. "What?"

"How many egg whites?"

"Oh. Um . . ." She couldn't remember. She'd made this cake a thousand times and now she couldn't remember. Disgusted with herself, Claire checked the recipe.

"Six."

He whistled while he worked; a jaunty, bawdy tune. It bothered Claire. Having him around bothered Claire. The fact that she was bothered bothered Claire. "Oh, bother!"

She set her mixing spoon down with a bang and moved away from him, taking a seat in the chair he'd so recently vacated.

"What's the matter?" he asked.

"I'm taking a break. I'm the boss, I can do that."

He nodded and cracked another egg. Despite her best intentions, she couldn't help but watch his hands as they gently juggled the yolk from half-shell to half-shell. "You have good hands."

The quick grin he shot her dripped wickedness. "So I've been told."

Feeling her cheeks burn, she rushed to make conversation. "So where did you learn to separate eggs? Do you do much cooking?"

Those green eyes wore a devilish twinkle as he opened his mouth to reply. Claire realized she'd fed him another line and winced. He chuckled, then, and said simply, "It's about like you and sewing. I cook only if I have to. But since I like to eat, sometimes I'm forced to fend for myself. I love meringue so I got my grandmother to teach me how to make 'em. I'll have you know I can bake a molasses pie with the best of them."

"You put a meringue on a molasses pie?" She shuddered at the thought. "Like sugar, do you?"

"Love it."

"Then you must be in heaven with all the baked goods your harem is providing."

He cut her a chastising look. "C'mon, Claire. Be nice. I told you those women are dangerous. That's why I'm hiding out here."

"And I'm safe?" She sniffed and folded her arms. "Gee, thanks for the compliment. I am a woman, too, you realize."

"Oh, I realize, all right" Appreciation gleamed in his gaze, which raked her from head to foot. "But you're engaged, so that makes you safe."

That's what you think, boyo. She'd like to show him just how "safe" she was, but she knew such action wouldn't be at all prudent. She feared the road to danger ran both ways in this case. Instead, she changed the subject "So tell me about your grandmother and the rest of your family. The McBrides are from where, Atlanta?"

"Charleston." While he beat the egg whites, he told her of Oak Grove, the family plantation now overseen by his sister Ellen and her husband, Scott. She learned his parents died in an accident when he and Trace were but youths, and that the boys and their three sisters had been raised by their grandmother, Mirabelle McBride.

"She's a pistol. I'm afraid we won't have her for much longer, and that haunts me. It made it difficult to leave South Carolina and come here."

"So why did you?"

He took a long time to answer. "Family dirty laundry. I did something really stupid and I couldn't put off dealing with the repercussions." After a moment's pause, he said, "That's enough about me. What about you? Tell me about your family, and especially the part of why you're here and your fiancé is not."

Claire did not want to talk about Reid Jamieson. Nor was she of a mind to discuss her family. *Too much dirty laundry in the kitchen might curdle the milk.* Instead, she walked to her pantry and perused the ingredients. *Anything to distract him*, she thought. Maple syrup. Corn syrup. "Blackstrap molasses."

"What?"

She snagged the bottle and carried it to the worktable where Tye had just finished adding the frothy egg whites to the cake batter. "I'm experimenting with this recipe. In honor of your fondness for molasses pie, I shall add half a cup of the syrup to see what that will do to our cake."

"Molasses to a Snow Cake? Good Lord, gal, you'll end up with mud."

"Better in the cake than attached to my name," she muttered beneath her breath.

"What was that?"

She gestured toward the chair. "Sit back and watch, McBride. A genius is at work."

Forty minutes later, with Tye leading the way, they sneaked out the back door, headed for a place—anyplace—that didn't stink quite so bad. Claire dropped her experiment into the trash can behind Murphy's Hardware. It hit the bottom of the metal receptacle with a clunk.

"Experiments are always trial and failure," Tye said, shaking his head sadly. "Don't let it get to you, Claire."

She smiled at him and said, "Oh, I won't." That's because she didn't see the experiment as a failure. In her eyes the cake had been a huge success. The Donovan family laundry remained wadded up and stuck away, just where she wanted it.

TYE TOOK HER HORNY-TOAD HUNTING. He gave her the choice between that and snagging for crawdads, but the minute she heard the word "mudbugs" she went for the toads. Tye didn't care which they did. All he wanted was to get away from town and the predatory females with their baked-goods bribes.

But he was glad to have the company of a friend. As they stepped across the rangeland south of town, he promised himself he'd continue to consider her just that. *Friend*, and nothing more.

It was a damned difficult assignment.

Even out here in the wide open spaces, with nary a hint of Magic in the air, he felt drawn to her. She was pretty and smart and full of surprises. Most important, she made him laugh. He hadn't laughed with a woman in so damned long.

Look at her now, her bonnet lost and her eyes bright and sparkling as she knelt facing the sun and holding the horned toad in her palms like a pagan offering. She was downright beautiful, even with her tongue flicking in and out like that "What are you doing, Claire? It's not gonna talk back to you."

Wrinkling her nose, she said, "This is the most fascinating animal. I don't know that we have these down in Galveston. I've never seen one before. Look at what he's done, Tye. It's like he's playing dead. See how he's gone all stiff? That must be a defense mechanism, don't you think?"

"That, or he likes what you did with your tongue and he's flirting," Tye replied, pretending seriousness. When she wrinkled her nose at him, she looked so cute he couldn't stop himself from adding, "Well he is a horny toad, after all."

"I can't believe you said that," she murmured, a pink blush stealing across her cheeks.

"I can't believe I did, either," Tye said, laughing. "Ah, Donovan, you are too fun to tease. Now, put your friend in my burlap bag here and let's find us a couple more toads. Even though Maribeth is the only one who'll be interested, one thing I've learned from the Blessings is that if you come home with anything, it'd best be three anythings."

"It was the same way at my house," she told him, slipping the horned frog into his bag. "Whenever my da made us walnut-raisin muffins for breakfast, he had to be sure to make a number divisible by three because heaven forbid one of us kids would get one more or one less muffin than the others. And only one of us even liked walnut-raisin muffins."

Tye smiled along with her as they searched the field for another anthill, ants being the main attraction on a hungry horny toad's menu. While they walked he was pleased to pry a few more details from her about the Donovan family. It had not escaped his notice earlier that she went out of her way to dodge discussion on that subject.

He found he was uncommonly curious about this woman, and as they hunted their pointy prey, he could tell she'd begun to relax her guard. Now was the time to ask about the fiancé. Tye decided to ease into the subject slowly.

"So tell me about your shop. Have you always wanted to be a baker?"

"Always." She stooped to pick up a shiny rock, then moved it back and forth in the sunlight so that it sparkled. "My da is a baker and he passed on the trade to his children. Recently the boys both opened bakeries of their own."

"Both of the boys and you."

She tossed down her rock. "Not exactly."

Claire picked up her pace and Tye had to hurry to keep up with her. They walked right past an anthill, but he chose not to bring it to her attention. He thought he was getting somewhere. Finally, he put his hand out and stopped her. "Slow down, you're paining my sore knee."

"I didn't know you have a sore knee."

"I don't, but I will if we keep running. So what's the deal, Claire? Is The Confectionary not yours after all? Are you getting it set up for one of your brothers?"

"Absolutely not" She whirled around and started walking back the way they'd come. This time she saw the anthill and stopped. "Shh. Don't scare away the frogs."

Tye didn't care about hunting horny toads anymore; he was searching for answers. "The fiancé then? Is he going to run your shop?"

"I'm running The Confectionary. It's not part of the Donovan Baking Company. It's my shop and no one else's. It's my dream and I'm not letting anyone take it away from me. Especially not a pretty-boy banker's son."

Now that threw Tye for a loop. *Pretty-boy banker's son?* Before he could figure out what to say, she'd dived for another toad. "Ooh," she said a moment later, staring down at her hands.

Tye reached for his handkerchief. "They can squirt blood from their eyes when they feel threatened."

"Handy little characteristic, I guess." She deposited the horned lizard in the sack, then accepted Tye's handkerchief to wipe her hands.

"Are you feeling threatened, Claire? Is that why you won't tell me your story?"

Her tone was as dry as West Texas in July. "Look in my eyes and figure it out, McBride."

He laughed. He couldn't help it "Don't squirt me, friend. Talk to me. That's what friends are for, you know, and I'm thinking you can use one. You helped me today. Now let me help you. Who's this pretty-boy banker's son?"

"Reid Jamieson." She spat the name like a curse. "Now leave it alone, Tye. If you're my friend you'll leave it alone. I don't want to talk about this. It won't help anything."

"Sure it will. Believe me, Claire, I have plenty of experience in keeping painful troubles bottled up inside. Let it out. It'll be good for you. Besides, you've got me curious as a calf in a new pasture."

"Well" She drew herself up straight and cracked her words like a whip. "Heaven forbid you don't get your way. You're a man, aren't you, and men's needs and wants and wishes always come first."

"Whoa now, Claire."

She didn't *whoa*. The words poured out. "I didn't love Reid Jamieson and I couldn't go through with it. I'm sorry for the embarrassment I caused the family, but they should have listened to me. I told them and I told Reid. The very day of the wedding I went to him and told him I couldn't marry him. If he showed up at the church and waited at the altar, well, it's his own fault."

If Tye were a horny toad, he'd have squirted blood from his eyes that very minute. Being a man, he settled for backing away.

"You said you left your fiancé in Galveston. Do you mean, left him at a *church* in Galveston? At the *altar* of a church in Galveston?"

She tossed her hair over her shoulder. "With a boutonniere in his buttonhole."

"So you ran away from home?"

"No." She stared at him as though he were stupid.

He couldn't argue with her.

Her eyes burned like a blue gas flame. "I left home. There is a difference. I took my half of my dowry and all my jewelry and set out to build a new life and a new business. This is my life I'm living, not my brothers' lives or my da's life or my mother's life. Mine. My talent is mine, my business is mine. My independence is mine. And no one is going to take it away from me. I don't care if he owns every bank in Texas."

"Jamieson owns every bank?"

"I don't know," she scoffed, disgusted. "I didn't mean it literally."

"But you did mean that you *left* your fiancé. So you're not really engaged. You're not taken."

"That's exactly my point." She threw out her arms. "There shouldn't be any *taking* in marriage. It should be all *giving*. Nobody is ever going to take anything from me. Not ever again."

With that, she turned and flounced back toward the buggy. Tye opened the burlap bag and stared down at the two horned lizards imprisoned inside. "She's not engaged, but she's a lady. Goddamnit, she's *not* safe."

Tye took a step to follow Claire, but then he stopped. He thought about the woman waiting for him in the buggy and the women waiting for him back in town.

He thought of the woman lying in a grave in South Carolina. Constance West McBride, his brother's first wife, his nieces' mother. The lying, deceitful bitch. God curse her soul.

He knelt on one knee and opened the bag on the ground, releasing the sand-colored toads. As they darted off into the brush, he muttered, "If not for the Blessings, I'd run away with you."

CHAPTER 5

PLANT A PENNY WHEN THE DOGWOOD BLOOMS TO AVOID BAD LUCK.

HER TEMPER still high the following day, Claire chose to bake up a batch of Swedish rye bread. Slathered in butter, it was her favorite hot-out-of-the-oven treat. The aroma of the baking bread soothed her, and the subtle blend of anise and fennel delighted the tongue.

This particular day the task served another purpose. The physical effort of kneading the dough was a great way to work off her anger.

She had six loaves baked and muffins in the oven when a fist pounded on The Confectionary's front door. "Catherine Claire, are you in there?" a man shouted.

The flour barrel lid slipped from Claire's hand and clattered to the floor. She closed her eyes. *How in the world did they find me?*

"Catherine Claire Donovan, you open this door this minute!"

Lars. She'd recognize that voice anywhere. Oh, damn. She'd been discovered.

Her hand trembled as she lifted the lid and replaced it. Wiping her suddenly damp palms on her apron, she walked toward the outer door. Sure enough, on the other side of the doorway stood the tall, blond, angelically handsome Lars Sundine. He was her

EMILY MARCH

brother Patrick's best friend. Her friend, too. For years Lars had been like a third brother to Claire. He also had been the only one who listened to her protests about the marriage to Reid.

Claire closed her eyes. How did the family find me so fast? She said a silent prayer, turned the lock, and opened the door.

"Well at least you had it locked," he said, his tone as sharp as her favorite paring knife. Tall and broad, with big, meaty forearms and hands, he seemed to fill the vestibule to overflowing. He wore a mustache and a scowl mean enough to scare a coyote off his kill. "Ah, Clary, do you know what you've done? I have half a mind to put you over my knee and give you the whipping you deserve."

Like a flash fire, her anger ignited. She wasn't going to stand there and be harangued in her own bakery.

"Try it and lose a hand," she replied, slamming the door in his face. She whirled around, ready to march back into her kitchen, knowing he'd follow right behind her. When he didn't, she paused. She waited in the middle of her shop for a full minute, and still didn't hear his footsteps. Pursing her lips, she retraced her steps and slowly opened the door. What she saw brought a lump of emotion to her throat.

The big, burly Swede stood in the vestibule with tears overflowing his sky-blue eyes and rolling down his cheeks.

"Lars?"

He swallowed hard. "Damnation, Clary. We've all been so scared. Come here." He tugged her into his arms and squeezed her tight. "Thank God you're all right. I could kill you for running off like that. How could you do that to the people who love you?"

"Love me?" she replied. "If they loved me how could they force me to marry Reid?"

His expression gentled. "Ah, Clary. I love you. You know that. C'mon, offer me something to eat and drink. It's been a long day and a very long trip."

"How did you find me, Lars?"

60

He reached out and tucked a stray curl behind her ear. "I remembered how you talked about railroad terminal towns and how they'd be a good place to build a business because they were new and fast-growing. I figured Fort Worth was far enough away from the Donovans, but not too far away for a girl leaving home for the first time. It was a hunch that paid off. I got to town late last night and tracked you down real fast. Folks around here are anxious for The Confectionary to open."

"Good." Claire couldn't help but smile at that.

Ten minutes later they were seated around her kitchen work-table drinking strong black coffee and nibbling on molasses cookies. Lars swallowed a bite, studied the cookie in his hand, and observed, "You're a dash short on ginger. Maybe a skosh too much cinnamon, too."

"They are just perfect," Claire shot back.

That started a debate over Claire's baking skills that lasted a good five minutes. After that, the conversation segued into the Donovan family and the state of everyone's health and happiness. For the moment, the subject of Claire's former fiancé and aborted wedding was studiously avoided, a fact she very much appreciated.

While Lars relayed Patrick's latest escapade at a recent horse race, he moved his head and winced in a way that caught Claire's attention. She studied the man. His bloodshot, droopy eyes displayed evidence of more than weariness from travel or worry. He'd obviously had a late night. Wordlessly, she rose and walked over to her cache of Magic. She grabbed a bottle and a spoon and plopped them down onto the table in front of him.

He eyed her offering then rubbed his forehead. "Ah, Clary, you are an angel of mercy."

"I hate to waste a spoonful of Magic curing the hangover you undoubtedly picked up in the Acre, but I can't stand to see any animal suffer."

"The Acre?" His brow furrowed with his scowl. "What do you know about Hell's Half Acre? How do you know about it?"

"How is it you found the Acre before you found me? That's what I want to know."

"Claire," Lars warned.

She rolled her eyes. "How do I know about the Acre? I stage dance at the Green Parrot every Friday and Saturday night. You should see my costume. The stockings are—"

"Catherine Claire!" His eyes narrowed dangerously.

She sighed. "I live in this town. I'm aware the Acre exists. That doesn't mean I have to frequent it."

"You shouldn't know about it at all. You shouldn't be here. You won't be here for long." Lars slapped his hand down on the table. "Go pack your bags, Claire. You are coming home with me. If we hurry, we can catch the afternoon train."

This was it. Time for pistols at twenty paces. "No," she said firmly. "I'm not going anywhere."

"You have to."

"I do not."

"But your mother and father—"

"Tried to make me marry a man I do not love." She shoved to her feet. "It's been wonderful to see you. Please take my love back to Mama and Da along with my apologies for any embarrassment I have caused them, but that is all you are taking back to Galveston. I am an adult I make my own choices and I choose Fort Worth to be my home now. This is where I'm building a new life, the life *I* want. Not the life Da wants for me."

Lars sat back in his chair and frowned. "I knew you'd be stubborn about this. Guess I'll have to give you the letter."

"What letter?" Claire asked, her stomach tensing.

"From your father." Lars reached into his jacket and removed a folded sheet of paper. "Just in case I found you."

Lars tossed the page into the middle of the table, and the brightness seemed to fade from Claire's day. Staring at the paper, her mouth went desert-dry. Emotions she couldn't name and didn't want to face bubbled like hot tar in her gut. "What's in it?"

Lars reached out and squeezed her hands. "Read the letter, Clary. It's a serious situation. Your family needs you."

It was a knife to the heart. If her family truly needed her, how could she deny them help? The paper felt cold beneath her fingertips. She felt cold beneath her skin. "I couldn't marry Reid, Lars."

"I know it seems that way." He tucked a stray curl back behind her ear. "But he's a good man, Clary. He will make you a fine husband."

Will make you. Not *would have made you.* Claire winced.

Lars had listened to her feelings about Reid. He knew how she felt. For him to say what he said now . . . well . . .

Claire's heart dropped to her stomach. For a minute, or maybe an hour, she sat staring at the letter. Finally, she muttered a curse and broke the seal.

Paper crackled as she unfolded it. Quickly her eyes scanned the page. "No. I can't believe this!"

Lars moved to stand behind her. He laid his hands on her shoulders and gave her a supportive squeeze.

"You know what's in here?" she whispered.

"About the rumors."

Scanning the sentences that repeated the newspaper headlines, she read aloud, "The Not-So-Magical Wedding Cake. Donovan's Cursed Cakes. The Death of a Legend." Claire's hands started to tremble and she glanced up at Lars. "All because I didn't marry Reid?"

"You know how your father likes to make every effort serve double duty," Lars replied, shrugging his shoulders. "Before we learned you had left town, he invited the Gazette to the reception hall and made a big production over your cake. So, when the wedding didn't happen, the paper naturally wrote the story."

"About a wedding cake whose magic has turned into a curse

because of a single canceled wedding?" Claire exploded. "That's as ridiculous as the whole legend itself."

"The legend is what made your family's livelihood for the past few years, girl. The legend is what put clothes on your back."

"Well, I'm putting my own clothes on my own back now, thank you very much." Claire took a deep breath and told herself to calm down and be strong. "I'm sorry for the bad publicity, but this is Da's mistake. Patrick's, too, for creating the legend in the first place. It's not my fault."

She nudged the letter. "Papa doesn't say what he wants."

"You know what your father expects," Lars replied. "You know what you have to do."

She shook her head. "No. I won't marry Reid to solve a legend gone awry. Besides, it's too late for that. I stood him up at the altar. He wouldn't marry me now."

"Yes he would. He told your father he would."

"No."

"Yes."

She couldn't believe it. "Why? It makes no sense. He doesn't love me."

"He says he does."

"Well I don't love him."

"Then you shouldn't have pawed him in the kitchen!" Lars snapped.

Claire gasped and tears pressed at the backs of her eyes. In a low, hard voice, she said, "It wasn't like that. Nothing happened. I have tried to tell my family the truth about that night many times. That all of them, and you, Lars, choose to believe him over me offends me more than I can say."

"All right, Clary." He returned to his chair, took his seat, and folded his arms. "Tell me again about that night in the kitchen. Convince me why it's not in your best interests to marry Reid."

"You have more nerve than a toothache, Lars Sundine. I owe you no explanation."

"Sure you do. I may not be a brother by blood, but I am by love. My advantage is I don't have the Donovan hard head. Talk to me, Clary. I'll listen."

She sighed heavily, then acquiesced. She told him how Reid made the innocent doctoring of a cat's scratch appear like an interrupted seduction to her father. She explained how, time and again during their engagement, he had disregarded her wishes and requests. She gave examples of instances when Reid categorically refused to give any consideration to how his actions would affect her.

She finished by saying, "Marrying Reid Jamieson would be like losing myself. I can't live that way. Did you ever hear the story of how my mother wanted to be a teacher? Da didn't want her to do it, so she didn't. Not me. I won't give up my dreams for any man. I won't give up my life here in Fort Worth where I've invested in a business. Invested in myself. I can't lose it all."

Lars nodded. "You make a good case. I'm convinced. But you need to tell these things to your family. You need to face your parents. You know you do. It's not right for a daughter to run off like you did. I'll take you home, and you can talk it over with them."

"I am home. Fort Worth is my home now."

Lars raked his fingers through his shiny blond hair. "You're sure about that? No doubt in your mind?"

"I'm sure."

He drummed his fingers on the table for a moment, then asked, "Do you have anyone helping you here? An employee?"

She shook her head. "I can't afford it."

More drumming of the fingers. Abruptly, he said, "Millicent threw me over."

"No," Claire replied, dismayed.

"Yes. Now she's sweet on Ronald Warfield."

"Ronald Warfield. You're kidding." Claire was shocked. Millicent Ayers and that Ronald Warfield? "The shipping magnate's daughter and a ferryboat hand? Talk about a mismatched set. Don't worry, Lars. It will never last."

"Long enough to get engaged."

"No!"

"Yes. It's making it tough for me to keep working at the shipping company. It was nice to get away to come looking for you." He glanced down at his fingernails and casually added, "I'm thinking a move might do me some good, too."

Claire caught on right away. "I can take care of myself, Lars. I don't need a keeper."

"I wouldn't be such a fool as to think so. No, Clary, I'm thinking we could help each other out. I'm a good accountant. If I could find a position here in Fort Worth—at a bank, perhaps—I could help you in the mornings some with the baking, just like I do for Patrick now. I don't interfere with his business. You know that I wouldn't interfere with yours." He paused a moment and his tone grew serious. "I need away from Galveston, too, Clary. I cared a lot about Millicent."

Claire smiled and reached for his hand, giving it a squeeze. "I love you, Lars. Of course you can help me in The Confectionary —as long as you work for the same wages Patrick pays."

He squeezed her hand in return. "You know, Clary, I always have found your cinnamon buns to be superior to Patrick's."

"Well I should hope so," she replied with a sniff. "You can consider it a raise, then. All the cinnamon buns you can eat in exchange for your help around the bakery."

"So," he said, standing. "I guess we'd best get moving if I'm going to catch that train."

Confusion coursed through her. "The train? You're going back?"

He nodded. "They have to be told, Claire. They're worried sick. I want you to write an answer to your da's letter."

Groaning, she propped her elbows on the table and rested her head in her hands. He was right. She knew it. "Lars Sundine, you might as well change your name to Donovan. You are as big a pain in the behind as any other brother of mine. I have paper and a pen on the counter out front. Bring it to me and I'll write your stupid letter. You know what, I can't wait to go home. This has been a very long day."

ONE FLOOR above the bakery in the parlor of the apartment, Emma McBride lifted her eye from the spy hole and rolled back on her knees. She looked at her sisters. "Have you ever seen a prettier man?"

Maribeth snorted and replaced the woven rug that concealed her own listening post. "I don't like him. Miss Donovan seems kinda nice and he got her all upset."

Katrina sat next to Maribeth and the peephole they had shared, carefully inspecting the old rag doll she'd discovered beneath the horsehair sofa as she lay waiting for her turn to spy. She tugged a hunk of cotton from inside the doll's amputated arm. Rubbing the cotton on the tip of her nose, she observed, "Our Mama had a Bad Luck Wedding Dress, and now Miss Donovan has a Bad Luck Wedding Cake. It's a good thing she's leaving, or she might try to give one to Uncle Tye and Miss Loretta. Just because Mama's dress turned into a good luck dress doesn't mean that lady's cake would change, too. Even if it is magic."

Emma shared a long-suffering look with her middle sister. Recently Kat had developed a fascination with magic and had made it her goal in life to discover how to make objects disappear. Green peas, in particular. "Kat, we have a few problems to solve concerning Uncle and Miss Loretta before we can get to the wedding cake part."

"That's right," Maribeth agreed. "We didn't skip school today to spy on Miss Donovan. We did it to think of a way to make up for what happened at supper with Miss Loretta. Otherwise, she'll never want to marry Uncle Tye."

Kat shook her head. "I can't believe you forgot you had a lizard in your pocket, Mari."

"I can't believe he liked gravy so much." Maribeth glumly propped her chin in the palm of her hand. "But Larry Lizard isn't our only problem. Don't forget the ladies' parades. What are we going to do about that?"

Emma joined her sisters in expelling a heavy sigh. They all were discouraged. Following Larry Lizard's running splash into the gravy boat, Uncle Tye had actually scolded them. He'd been grumpy all day yesterday and today brought no improvement, although Emma blamed the women callers for that.

"Isn't it strange how Uncle Tye is so much like Papa?" she observed. "They not only look the same, they get grumpy the same."

"No, they don't," Kat said, rolling her cotton into a small ball. "I don't think Uncle Tye is the same as Papa at all. He hardly ever gets after us. He never growls, and he doesn't glare. Why, if Papa had been the one to have a bowl of hot gravy dumped in his lap, we'd still be sitting in the corner. Uncle Tye hardly did more than wince and rub his eyes."

"He does that a lot," Maribeth agreed.

Emma stood and walked to the window. "Uncle Tye's being like Papa might help us figure a way to help him past this temper of his. I think we should work on him before fixing things with Miss Loretta, don't you?"

The younger girls nodded. "We are around him a lot more than we're around Miss Loretta," Mari added.

Kat crawled over beside Emma and stuck her cotton ball behind the window hinge. "Stop that, Kat," Emma scolded, grabbing the cotton and tossing it outside. "I'm getting tired of finding cotton stuck in hidey holes all over the house. What's wrong with you?"

Scowling, Katrina stood and stared out the window after her cotton. "Look. Miss Donovan and that man are locking up and leaving. I guess she is going home early."

"What are we gonna do about Uncle Tye, Emma?" Maribeth asked, ignoring her younger sister.

Emma drummed her fingers on the windowsill. "I think we should ask Spike what we should do."

Her sisters nodded, and the three girls traipsed upstairs to their bedroom where Spike the fortune-teller perch swam in his home of clear glass. While Emma used one of Maribeth's socks to wipe dust off a two foot square on the floor, they discussed the options they wished to pose to Spike, settling on three possibilities.

"So," Maribeth said, rolling up her sleeve. "Are we ready?"

"I'm not." Katrina's brow furrowed in a frown. "Tell me again what the rules are?"

Emma groaned while Maribeth said, "Gosh, Kat. Can't you remember anything? How many times have we asked Spike questions since Casey gave him to us? A hundred?"

"Not that many."

Maribeth ticked off on her fingers. "Moving tail only means maybe. Moving head and tail means no. Flip- flopping means yes. Now, Emma you ask the questions." Maribeth plunged her hand into the fishbowl, grabbed hold of Spike, and lifted him out of the water.

While Maribeth held the squirming fish with both hands, Emma chanted, "Spike, Spike, tell us true. Tell us what we ought to do. Do we tell Uncle Tye we're sorry and want to do penance by working in the church garden with Sister Gonzaga?"

All three girls held their breath as Maribeth gently laid Spike on the floor. The fish curled in the middle, lifting both head and tail off the floor. The answer was no.

"Thank you, Lord," Emma prayed as Maribeth lifted the fish and returned him to the water.

They allowed the fish to swim a few moments before Katrina said, "Next question, Em."

"Spike, Spike, tell us true. Tell us what we ought to do. Do we try to sweet-talk Uncle Tye into forgetting about our slipup?"

Droplets of water splattered on the wood as Maribeth again lowered the perch to the floor. For a moment he lay unmoving, but then his tail slowly lifted.

"That's a definite maybe," Maribeth observed.

Emma repeated the rote for the third and final question. "Should we bake Uncle Tye a dessert?"

The second Spike hit the floor, he started flopping.

"That's it!" Katrina clapped her hands. "He said yes. Spike said yes. No tie-breaker this time."

"Thank goodness," said Maribeth, returning Spike to his bowl for a well-earned rest. "It took us seven tries to break the tie last time. I was afraid he would get sick. Perch are hardy fish, but we shouldn't overwork him."

Twirling a pigtail with her finger, Emma smiled with satisfaction. "This is good. I think that's the best choice. We're no different from all those ladies lining up with cakes and stuff. They all wanted to please Uncle Tye, too."

"He didn't complain about the food," Maribeth said, wiping her hands on the bedspread. "Just the women. He liked the food."

"Except the turkey." Katrina kissed the side of the fishbowl. "He doesn't like turkey. And he wished someone had brought a chocolate cake, remember?"

The girls all shared a look and nodded.

"So it's settled, then. We'll get back in Uncle Tye's good graces with a chocolate cake." Emma smiled triumphantly. "And so we won't make a mess that might make him sigh and rub his eyes, we'll bake it in Miss Donovan's kitchen!"

TYE MCBRIDE STOOD on the platform at the railroad station where he'd just said his good-byes to the attorney from Dallas who had overseen Tye's acquisition of a pretty stretch of ranch land southwest of town. "Guess I'm now officially a Texan."

It was something he never would have imagined when he left South Carolina and Oak Grove plantation a few months back. Back then, he and Trace were still the bitterest of enemies, battling over the custody of the daughter each man believed was his own.

Today, everything was different.

He had learned Katrina truly did belong to Trace, and he and his twin had made their peace. Trace had welcomed him back into his life, even going so far as to request that Tye act as guardian for the girls while he was gone.

That's what had made Tye first consider trading his planter's hat for a cowboy chapeau. The years of his estrangement from his twin had twisted his heart near in two. He wanted to spend time with Trace again. To strengthen the bond that had never quite severed, even during the worst of times.

Funny how it was with twins. All their lives they'd shared this strange connection; a deep, subconscious knowledge of each other that was as much a part of them as their hearts or livers or lungs. He'd felt it even when the guilt of betraying Trace had driven him to Europe and into the depths of drunken stupor.

Now that the ugliness was behind them, he looked forward to the good times he could share with Trace, Jenny, and the Blessings. But to do that, he needed to live in Texas, at least part of the time.

Thank goodness he didn't have to worry about Oak Grove. His sisters and his grandmother would oversee planting and harvest. A trip back East two or three times a year should be all that was needed.

Hell, maybe he'd even sign the deed over to his sister Ellen and her husband. Heaven knows, he didn't need the money the plantation produced. "That's the one good thing that came out of this idiotic inheritance," he grumbled, ducking behind a support pole when he spied a familiar feminine face. *I think she brought the fried apple pie.*

Had he not turned away from the fried-apple-pie brunette, he might never have seen the blonde in a bonnet planting a kiss on the lips of a big, brawny stranger.

What was Claire Donovan up to now?

Good Lord, she was handing him a cookie. A kiss and a cookie. That must be like a double dose of Magic. Who the hell was this guy?

Tye eyed the stranger closely. The man was backing away from Claire. Good. He wouldn't have wanted to go break up an intimate encounter atop the baggage cart.

But he would have.

Protecting my fellow man, he told himself. That's all. Hadn't she in effect lied about the fiancé? Hadn't she proved herself to be less than honorable where men were concerned? She'd left this poor Jamieson fellow standing lonely at the altar, for God's sake.

And then there was the Magic business. Intellectually, he questioned whether aphrodisiacs truly existed, but physically, he couldn't deny the symptoms. Claire Donovan's Magic made him randy as a billy goat in spring. He could only hope the brew didn't have a similar effect on everyone. Otherwise, Fort Worth could look forward to a population explosion once she had her bakery up and running.

That was the excuse he gave himself for spying on the cookie queen and her masculine escort. He realized only after the man climbed aboard the departing train and Claire remained behind that he'd been holding his breath. That made him angry. Why did he care what Claire Donovan did? And why the hell had he been awake half the night stewing about the woman? She was nothing more than an appealing, unattached, so-beautiful-she-made-your-teeth-ache *lady*. He'd sworn off the likes of those the day Constance West McBride lied her way into his bed.

Yesterday afternoon everything had changed. She wasn't his friend. She couldn't be his friend. He knew that.

So why was it that now, as the engine slowly crawled away in a strain of gears and a cloud of black smoke, his feet carried him toward her? "Hello, Claire. Whatcha doing down here at the station?"

She looked up in surprise. "Why, hello, Tye."

She had tears in her eyes, dammit. She was crying over that stranger.

"So who was he? Another fiancé?"

"Excuse me?"

"The man you were kissing. Is he someone you've dumped at the altar or just another poor fool you are using?"

The confusion in her expression faded and was replaced by anger as she glanced from Tye, to the departing train, then back to Tye. "You were spying on me? I can't believe you. If you don't have a nerve."

Her fingers tightened around the strings of her pocket-book, and for just a moment he thought she might swing it at him. Instead, she pushed past him, marching toward the street.

Tye stayed where he was; as he watched her leave, fuming. And wondering why it even mattered. Claire Donovan was nothing to him but his brother's tenant. Someone he'd simply passed a few hours with. Why did he care that she proved to be no different from the rest?

Come on, McBride, his conscience scolded. *Who's the liar now? You can't compare dumping a fiancé with the evil that Constance concocted. Be fair.*

Fair. Well, hell.

How could he be fair? Hadn't Constance fooled him? Hadn't she been slick enough and convincing enough and dazzling enough to make him believe vicious, terrible lies about his very own brother? Lies he should have known were false? Trace McBride would never hit a woman, especially not the mother of his children. He hadn't even hit her that night in the cabin when he'd been mad enough to kill. Shooting her had been an accident; he'd been aiming his gun at Tye.

Tye didn't truly think Claire was anything like Constance. Claire Donovan struck him as forthright and honest—for the most part, anyway. But was he fooling himself again?

Could be. She'd admitted to running away from home, stealing her dowry money, and leading him to believe she was still engaged to be married. And then there was the Magic. If that wasn't trickery and deceit in a bottle, he didn't know what was. Could be Claire Donovan had him snowed. Could be she had him thinking with something other than his brain. Just like Constance had done.

Or she could be just the fine, upstanding woman he wanted to think she was.

Tye scowled and kicked at a loose rock, sending it clattering across the platform. This was one of those gray areas he had so much trouble with. This was why he needed to stay away from ladies.

And damn it all, he didn't want to stay away from Claire Donovan.

Muttering beneath his breath, he said, "If you have a brain above your belt, McBride, you'll keep the hell away from her."

Instead he spat a curse, shoved his hands in his pockets, and followed her.

She was halfway up Main Street when he caught up with her and fell in step beside her. She shot him a molten look and the scowl he returned was pure defense. "Look at it from my point of view, Claire. Due to a certain tomato war and the proximity of your shop and my apartment, chances are better than good you'll be spending some time with the Blessings. Those girls are in my charge. It's my duty to ascertain the character of those who make their acquaintance. I saw you puckering up with a strange man, and I felt I should investigate. I'm only doing my job as their guardian."

She rolled her eyes and waved a hand. "Never mind. It doesn't matter. I have bigger things to worry about than being followed around town by an overprotective uncle."

"You do? What things?"

She halted abruptly. Her eyes flashed fire, and she drew a deep breath that lifted her bosom in an enticing manner. "It's none of your business, Mr. McBride. Allow me to say this bluntly. Go. Away."

Seeing her snit and hearing her temper lightened his own mood. Would a wicked woman be so defensive? He wouldn't think so.

"What?" she demanded, peering up at him. "What's put that gleam in your eyes?" Not bothering to wait for an answer, she resumed her march.

"I'm not gleaming," he explained, starting after her. "I'm smiling. I've found it works better than sobbing when problems get you down."

"Sobbing at your problems, McBride?" Her expression turned wry. "What problems do you have? Too many pounds of pound cake perched on your front porch?"

"I do like a woman who alliterates. But you're right. I do have pound cake problems. And you should have seen me carrying that turkey upstairs this morning. I was a blubbering fool."

"A fool, maybe." After a moment's hesitation, she added, "Lord McBride."

He grimaced and gave a long-suffering sigh. "Isn't that the silliest thing? I have enough sweets in my kitchen to keep a dentist flush in the pockets for years. Can you believe the parades of ladies? I'm almost afraid to go back home. No telling what I might find on my doorstep."

"Two more cakes, three more pies, and another dish I couldn't quite identify. I do hope you'll get this situation settled before The Confectionary opens for business. Not that I'm frightened of competition, but I'd just as soon not have ladies lined up at my door giving sweets away when I'm trying to sell them."

They'd reached the corner of Fourth and Main, and Tye took her elbow to escort her across the street. "I understand your concern. I don't know how I'm going to fix the problem yet, but I do understand." He waited until they'd walked a half block down Fourth to add, "What about you? How are you going to take care of your trouble?"

"What makes you think I have trouble?"

He snorted. "You just kissed a fella good-bye with tears in your eyes. Who was he, Claire?"

Claire tilted her head back and lifted her face toward the sky. "You are like a dog with a bone. I can't believe I'm discussing this. I can't believe I'm even talking to you. This is private, personal business, and I barely know you. Besides, only minutes ago you had me cross-eyed furious."

"You're not discussing it, Claire. You're dodging the question."

"Fine. His name is Lars."

Tye waited for her to elaborate, but she didn't. Stubborn, frustrating woman. He opened his mouth to ask more, but before he could get the question out he was hailed by a loud woman in a big hat. Across the narrow dirt street Wilhemina Peters waved a hand in the air. "Lord McBride! Oh, Lord McBri-ide." She picked up her petticoats and dashed out in front of a buckboard. The driver lifted a fist in anger.

"Now *there* is a dedicated newspaper reporter," Claire observed.

"She's a busybody gossip columnist that's what she is. You know, she's the one who named my nieces the Menaces."

"Lord McBride," Wilhemina said, fanning her flushed face with her hand as she drew near. "Here you are. Finally. I've been looking for you all day!"

Tye tipped his hat and tried his best to keep his smile from sliding into a more sickly expression. "Good afternoon, Mrs. Peters. Have you met Miss Donovan? She's opening a bakery in my brother's building."

Wilhemina and Claire exchanged pleasantries. Then, as the reporter launched into her inescapable interview, Claire made her excuses, finger-waving good-bye as she threw an amused grin over her shoulder. Tye eyed the retreating sway of her hips, his blood shooting straight to his loins.

Hell, and I didn't even eat a damned cookie.

Distracted, he answered Mrs. Peters's questions more frankly than he would have wished. By the time Wilhemina pattered off toward the paper and Tye headed back to the apartment, he felt as if he'd gone three rounds with a Spanish Inquisition priest.

All thought of the gossipy columnist disappeared as he stepped into the Rankin Building's vestibule. Foodstuffs lay piled against the wall, a few gaily wrapped packages interspersed among them. But the gifts weren't what made him grimace; the girls managed that.

Emma, Maribeth, and Katrina McBride sat in three chairs lined up just inside Claire Donovan's shop. Covered in flour, smeared in butter—with suspicious red stains dribbling across their bodices and globs of what might have been egg yolk in their hair—the girls each offered him a timid smile.

Behind them, arms folded and eyes narrowed, stood Claire.

Tye cleared his throat and, having drawn a blank on anything intelligent to say, sallied forth with the age-old masculine question, "So, ladies, what's for dinner?"

For her answer, Claire scooped a dish from a nearby table piled high with even more matchmaking offerings. Before he realized her intent she sent it sailing toward his face.

CHAPTER 6

EAT FROG LEGS FOR BREAKFAST FOR A WEEK TO CURE A CASE OF BAD LUCK

TYE TUGGED a handkerchief from his pocket and slowly wiped the pudding off his face, Claire fully expected him to spew a few angry words in her direction. She wished he would. Throwing a single container of pudding hadn't come close to dealing with all the temper she had churning through her at the moment, and she had plenty of ammunition yet to launch. Sally Randolph's custard cake looked like it would fit her hand just right.

But instead of flailing into her like either of her brothers would have done, Tye calmly hung his hat on the tree beside the door, then turned his attention to his nieces. "I want to hear the story in no more than three sentences each. Emma, you start."

The girl's shoulders rose with a deep breath. "You seemed to like the food, if not the ladies, and you said you wished one of them had brought you a chocolate cake, and we felt bad for what happened at Miss Loretta's, and Mrs. Wilson likes to say that a way to a man's heart is through his stomach, and we thought—"

Tye held up his hand, palm out. "I said three sentences."

"But that was only one, Uncle Tye."

"It was long enough for a full paragraph. Mari, your turn."

The middle girl dragged a hand across her mouth and said, "We-ell . . . You see . . . we, uh . . . It's like this, Uncle Tye."

Katrina's thumb popped from her mouth. "That's three, Mari. My turn." She beamed a practiced smile at her uncle and said, "We're apologizing for misbehaving at Miss Loretta's house. We knew we might make a little mess, so we thought we'd be good and use Miss Donovan's kitchen."

"Little mess!" Claire exclaimed. "You call the disaster in my kitchen a little mess?"

"It did get a teeny bit out of hand," Maribeth agreed, wincing. "Everything was fine until we let Ralph inside."

"That danged dog again," Tye muttered. "I'm beginning to think I made a big mistake bringing him home after all. Where is Ralph now?"

Emma answered. "He's upstairs shut in our room. We asked him to watch out for Spike."

"Good," Tye replied, nodding.

Katrina tossed a frown toward Claire. "You said you were going home. Why did you come back?"

"Home? I didn't tell you I was going home."

The youngster whipped a hand up and pointed toward the ceiling. "You told that pretty man. We were watching you through the spy hole."

Claire stood speechless, her mouth bobbing open and closed like a fish. Tye grinned sheepishly and explained, "From what I understand it's an old family tradition."

"That's right," Emma said. "Sometimes Papa says it was love at first sight when he sneaked a peak at Mama."

Her voice lowered confidentially, Katrina added, "That spy hole looked into the dressing room at Fortune's Design."

Trace McBride's own children naming him as a Peeping Tom? Claire threw Tye a scandalized look.

"At least you're not naked when you bake," he said, as if that made spying on her acceptable. A teasing twinkle flashed in his eyes as he added, "Are you?"

She gritted her teeth against the curses waiting on her tongue. One didn't grow up with brothers without learning a few good cuss words. Drawing a deep, calming breath, she said, "I want my kitchen put back to rights."

Tye rolled his tongue around his cheek and glanced toward the doorway leading into the kitchen. "Maybe I'd better take a little look."

"Maybe you'd better not, Uncle Tye," Emma suggested. "We've already told Miss Donovan we'd clean it up. You don't need to waste your time checking it out."

Maribeth shot Claire a narrow-eyed glare before adding, "That's right. We said we'd take care of this ourselves, and we weren't lying. She shouldn't have dragged you into it. We didn't need to sit here like this."

Why, the snotty little thing. It was all Claire could do not to stick her tongue out at the child.

"Button your lips, girls." Tye pivoted and headed for the kitchen. Claire folded her arms and waited for his response. While she didn't expect his reaction to equal hers—she couldn't quite picture him screaming at the sight—she did expect more than a grunt.

A grunt was all she got.

He sauntered back toward them, wincing and rubbing his eyes. "Girls, here's what we're going to do. The three of you are going to march upstairs and get cleaned up. Then I want you to track down your teacher and get the assignments you missed today when you skipped school."

"How do you know about that?" Katrina asked, wonder in her voice.

Maribeth nudged her in the ribs. " 'Cause you told him we spied on Miss Donovan and that man, dummy. That happened during the big middle of the schoolday."

"After that," Tye continued, "I expect you to shut yourselves in your room and read every word, write every sentence, and work every arithmetic problem your teacher gives you. Y'all understand?"

"Yessir, Uncle Tye."

"Then scram."

The McBride Menaces jumped from their seats and darted out the door, Emma pausing long enough to give her uncle a hug, a kiss on the cheek, and a declaration of love. He was grinning when he turned to Claire.

She wanted to kill him. Her fingers itched to let sail a handy custard cake. In a voice that bordered on shrill, she demanded, "What about my kitchen?"

His smile drained from his face like ale from a new tap. "I'll clean it up."

"Sure you will." Claire shot him a scathing look. If he cleaned as well as he disciplined those children, it wouldn't be safe to boil water in her kitchen. She eyed the cake, seriously considering the idea of making him wear it. "Why in the world didn't you have the girls clean up their own mess?"

He rolled up his sleeves. "You've never seen them clean. Since I have to go in behind them anyway, I might as well do it myself the first time."

Claire's attention snagged on his muscular forearms and she absently wondered what physical work he had done to develop those muscles. When he headed for her kitchen, she gave her head a shake and redirected her attention to the matter at hand. "But think of the lesson you are teaching them that way. It's wrong."

He halted abruptly and twisted his head. His deep green eyes bore into hers as he flatly stated, "It's not my job to teach them lessons. My job is to keep them safe until Trace and Jenny get home."

Claire leaned against the doorjamb, her arms folded. Watching him dip a rag into a pan of sudsy water, it was all she could do not to shoo him away and tackle the cleanup herself. But principle glued her shoes to the floor, and she remained standing in the doorway secretly impressed by the attention he paid to scraping every bit of goo from her worktable.

A banging noise out in the alley caught her attention, and when she crossed to the window to investigate she spied a smear of what appeared to be strawberry preserves on her brand new curtain. Slowly, she shook her head. "You aren't doing your brother and his wife any favors by spoiling the girls in the mean-time, McBride."

"I know." His tone was unrepentant "I don't like getting after them. None of their . . . mishaps are malicious. They just seem to have noses for trouble."

"Bloodhound noses," she grumbled. That's what her father had always said to her. That Claire had a bloodhound's nose for trouble. She knew the girls' antics— the mess in her kitchen included—weren't malicious. Watching those girls was like watching herself years ago.

The Menaces' current mess didn't compare to the one she'd made when she'd attempted to bake her first cake unsupervised. But she had managed the cleanup all by herself. Took her an entire day. She'd had to miss the barbecue out at Riverrun Planta-tion. But she'd been better for the lesson, hadn't she? Hadn't she benefitted from the discipline in the long run?

Claire filled a pan with cool water, then removed the curtains from their rod and put them to soak. "They skipped school and destroyed my kitchen, and all you do is make them see to their missed assignments. That's not enough, McBride. Children need to learn that actions have consequences."

"Maybe so, but I don't have to be the one to teach them." Finished with the worktable, he filled a basin with warm water off the stove, added soap flakes, then piled in some of the dirty dishes lying around the room. He lifted Claire's favorite ruffled apron from a peg on the wall and, to her amazement, tied it on. When he plunged his hands into the sudsy water, he added honestly, "I want them to like me."

That stopped her completely. She gawked at him. Tye McBride was big and broad and oozing masculinity. And wearing a frilly apron and washing dishes because he wanted his nieces to like him.

He glanced in her direction and smiled sheepishly.

In that exact moment, Claire fell just a little bit in love.

TYE GAWKED at her and wondered what had put that peculiar expression on her face. "Is it the apron? Is green not my color?"

"What?"

"You look like you just took a bite out of a lemon."

"I . . . um . . . no." She offered him a sickly smile. "Actually the green looks good on you. It matches your eyes."

"Well I'm certainly relieved about that. I hate being poorly dressed in the kitchen."

"At least you're dressed this time."

He remembered how he'd dashed into her kitchen wearing only Emma's drawers. Thank God he had on pants this time around. That damned Magic was getting to him again.

He could smell it in the air. Magic. Like burning cedar chips that have been dipped in peppermint and sunshine—and sex. Despite his best intentions, his head lifted and his nostrils flared. It required a conscious effort not to take a step toward Claire as desire snaked through him.

He dropped a spoon back into the dishwater with a plop, and visually searched the area for a sign of the witches' brew. There, on the floor beside her worktable, a cork. He scooped it off the ground and cautiously lifted it toward his nose. One little sniff.

The scent melted through him. Cedar and sunshine and long, slow, deliriously sweet sex. *Oh, yeah.*

He pegged the cork across the room toward a basket of trash. The aroma didn't fade. Glancing around the room, he finally spotted pieces of glass and a stain puddling out from beneath the worktable. When he hunkered down to retrieve the glass, he heard Claire exclaim, "Oh, no. It was a big bottle, too."

To Tye's discomfort, she joined him, kneeling on the floor just outside the mess. Their hands brushed as they both reached for the same shard of broken glass. Tye's fingertips tingled, and he sucked in a breath through his teeth. Claire Donovan and her damned Magic. "I'll get it," he said gruffly. "Go on, Claire. In fact, why don't you head home. I'll see your kitchen put to rights again. You needn't stay."

When she shook her head a tendril of gold escaped its pins and brushed against her lips. Tye bit back a groan as she said, "No, I can't leave. I have work to do. I lost half a day because of Lars, and if I'm going to open the shop on time, I need to work."

When she stretched her hand toward another shard, the bodice of her gown pulling tight across her bosom, Tye's instincts went to war. Self-preservation finally won out over lust, and he backed away. Slowly, he pulled off the apron and set it aside. "This has been a stressful day. What you really need, Miss Donovan, is a little time to relax. You're strung tight as a two-dollar fiddle."

Of course, Tye was really talking about himself.

She blew a small, disgusted puff of air. "I can't relax. I have too much to do. Too many problems to solve."

Her fingers closed around the ragged edges of the glass. When she flinched, Tye realized she'd cut herself. He mouthed a curse and reached for her hand. "Lemme see."

Blood pearled in a thin line along her palm and smeared the surface of the shard. "Ouch," he said, appropriating the glass. He tossed it into the trash, then took hold of Claire's wrist and helped her to her feet. He reached for his handkerchief, frowned when he found it soiled with chocolate pudding, then discarded it in favor of one of Claire's embroidered tea towels.

His touch was gentle as he dipped a corner in water and dabbed at the cut, frowning as the bright red stain spread across the pristine cloth. "You should have listened to me, Claire. It's not deep, but you'll feel it every time you move your hands the next couple of days."

Out of habit developed from weeks of tending to children, he lifted her hand to his mouth and pressed a kiss to her palm just beside the cut. Then, because he'd lost his mind under the influence of Magic, he placed another pair of kisses at her wrist. Slow, experimenting kisses. Learning her texture and her taste. He licked her skin, and sweetness exploded across his tongue. His eyes drifted shut as he gloried in the flavor.

Claire made a small sound of distress, jerked her hand from his grip, and clasped it to her breast, her eyes wide and clouded with confusion. Sweetness soured in his mouth as the subtle scent of her fear sliced through the Magic like broken glass.

Tye took a vital step back. He shoved his hands in his pockets and tried to calm the pounding in his chest. What the hell was the matter with him? "Claire, I, uh . . ."

Color flushed her cheeks, and her voice sounded breathless. "You were right. I'll go. It's been a long day. Please lock up for me when you're finished cleaning." Turning, she fled from the kitchen and a moment later he heard the outer door bang shut with a rattle of window glass.

Tye muttered an oath and gazed around the small, messy room. He'd scared her with his kisses. Hell, he'd scared himself with those kisses. Another few minutes of that, and he'd have had her on the floor.

What had gotten into him? Had the pudding knocked the brains right out of his head? His gaze drifted to the puddle of Magic at his feet and he scowled. "I've got to get out of here."

As soon as he saw the girls settled in upstairs, he would track down a cleaning lady and pay her double- time—triple-time—to clean the Blessings' mess here at The Confectionary. After that, he'd order supper. The Green Parrot Saloon had a Mexican cook who made chili hot enough to melt diamonds.

Tye tossed down the tea towel he had flung over his shoulder and headed for the door. Pausing beside Claire's produce bins, he snagged a pair of habañero peppers he'd noticed earlier. He'd ask the cook to toss these fiery beauties into the chili pot, too.

Melting diamonds was one thing. Burning away the lingering aroma of Magic was quite another.

IN THE WEEK THAT FOLLOWED, Claire saw little of the Menaces and their uncle. Tye gave her shop a wide berth, and Claire wondered if he always blew so hot and cold with friends.

She wondered about his definition of friendship, considering the way he'd nibbled at her wrist.

Maybe he no longer wished to be her friend. His attitude certainly had changed when she told him about Reid. He'd looked downright horrified. Claire told herself she shouldn't care. If he found her actions so despicable, then she didn't want him for a friend anyway. A true friend offered support, not judgment and condemnation. She had plenty to keep her busy. She didn't have time to be anyone's friend right at the moment. And she certainly wasn't looking for romance. At least, that's what she tried to tell herself.

If only her dreams would cooperate. Almost every night, Tye McBride haunted her sleep. He played the role of knight in English castles and pirate on the Caribbean Sea. Once he'd come to her as Romeo with her his Juliet. It was enough to make a girl blush with embarrassment.

As for the McBride Menaces, following the cake-baking inci-dent they appeared content to confine their mischief to areas outside Claire's domain. Occasionally she observed them playing in the alley with Ralph, and twice she spied them toting a fish in a bowl out onto the back stoop. The first time she saw them lay the poor fish on the boards to flop around she'd been tempted to intervene. But before she could clean the bread dough from her hands and exit the kitchen, they had returned the fish to water. Seeing them coo and kiss the surface of the bowl, Claire decided to mind her own business— at least where the events in the alley were concerned. Those taking place on the street in front of her shop proved much more fun to watch.

The parade of women to "Lord McBride's" front door had slowed somewhat, but by no means ended. Claire found it both educational and an entertaining distraction to watch the different ploys the women utilized in their attempts to gain the man's attention. She considered the early evening serenade especially inspired.

Because she was too much a businesswoman to ignore the increase in foot traffic past her shop, she set up a small display table complete with advertising broadsides and sample cookies in the Rankin Building vestibule. By arriving early and staying late at her shop, she managed to find enough extra hours in the day to keep the sample plate filled, even with the Menaces making numerous trips up and down the stairs. The days were long and wearing, and she looked forward to Lars's return and the help of an extra pair of hands.

Each day while she worked, she tried to think of ways to redeem the Magical Wedding Cake's reputation— short of marrying Reid, of course. To that end, she spent a few minutes every afternoon writing letters to friends and acquaintants along the Gulf coast in which she elaborated on the good fortune and contentment she'd found in Fort Worth. Maybe once people learned of her happiness, they wouldn't view the aborted wedding as such a disaster.

Progress toward The Confectionary's grand opening

proceeded on schedule, but as the day grew near, she suffered a severe attack of nerves. What if no one came? What if her customers didn't like her wares? What if the McBride Menaces decided to pull one of their mischievous pranks?

For her own peace of mind as much as anything, the night before her first day of business Claire rigged a tin can alarm across The Confectionary's back door, then slept on the floor, guarding the front. The night passed without incident.

Before dawn, amazingly well rested under the circumstances, Claire rose and heated up her oven. At precisely six A.M. she raised the shades and turned the front lock. Within minutes her first customer arrived, and soon others trickled in.

A few of her customers came dressed in evening attire and Claire assumed they had yet to find their beds for the night. A dapper young man with beautiful blue eyes confirmed it. "Our poker game broke up less than an hour ago, and when someone in the saloon mentioned you were opening your shop today, I figured I'd come see if you cooked as pretty as you look." He took a large bite of a cherry tart and wiggled his brows suggestively. "A sensual delight, Miss Claire. When I lay my head upon my pillow, I'll be dreaming of your . . . pleasures."

Tye McBride walked in during the man's flirtation, and catching Claire's attention, he shot her a scathing glare. Following on their uncle's heels, his nieces made a dash for the display case. After pondering the offerings, the girls ordered cinnamon rolls and milk, but their uncle intervened. "What do you have that isn't made with that witches' brew?"

"Excuse me?"

"The Magic. I'm not letting my Blessings have it. Can they get something to eat here or not?"

Claire was insulted. "And what do you think is wrong with my Magic, sir?"

He waved a hand. "I just think you have to be extra careful with what you give children. I once knew someone who let their son get ahold of some oriental herbs. The boy started talking and didn't shut up for three days."

It took all of Claire's hostess skills not to roll her eyes. "The most that Magic will do to the children, sir, is make them sigh with pleasure over the taste of what they consume."

"Nevertheless, what can they have that's Magic-less?"

She set her teeth, glared at him, and said, "Raisin muffins."

Tye motioned the girls to take a seat at a vacant table. "Raisin muffins, huh? And why don't you put Magic in the raisin muffins?"

"I don't believe the flavors mix well."

"Interesting."

Maribeth piped up. "I don't care what I eat as long as I eat it soon. I'm starved, Uncle Tye."

When the other two girls joined in with similar complaints, Tye dragged a hand across his face and ordered, "Muffins and milk for my nieces. I'll have two fried eggs and a breakfast steak."

"Steak and eggs are not on the menu, McBride." Claire gestured toward the display case. "You may make your selection from there."

He glanced toward the case, then grimaced. "Sweet stuff. What kind of breakfast is that? What kind of restaurant are you running here?"

"It's a bakery, not a restaurant."

"Well, bake me up some steak and eggs. Toast, too."

At that, he rudely dismissed her by turning to his nieces and inquiring after the status of homework due that day. Claire considered refusing him service entirely, but it would be an inauspicious start to The Confectionary's first morning of business.

She would not, however, serve him steak and eggs.

When she brought the girls their muffins and milk, she set a small loaf of hot Swedish rye bread and a crock of butter in front of Tye. Tye's only remark was to grumble about the noise from the bakery waking them upstairs.

Shortly thereafter, the trickle of customers swelled to a steady stream. Claire stayed too busy to give the McBride table much attention, but when they rose to leave she did notice he'd eaten the entire loaf of bread. She watched him finish off Katrina's milk, too.

Claire grinned about it off and on throughout the morning whenever she had a moment to think, although she didn't have too many of those. By the time she turned the OPEN sign to CLOSED at two P.M., she was exhausted and her baked goods depleted. The grand opening of The Confectionary had been a rousing success.

"The free samples worked better than I thought," she mused, sinking into a chair. Grinning, she glanced up toward the ceiling and gave a silent salute to "Lord McBride."

During the week that followed, The Confectionary's business steadily increased. And every morning, shortly after she opened the doors, the McBrides wandered in. Each day Tye ordered steak and eggs. Each day she gave him whatever she chose from her stock on hand. If she served whatever she felt had turned out best that morning, she saw no reason to make an issue of it. She refused to come right out and admit to herself she was trying to impress him.

They never exchanged more than a few words. He always cleaned his plate and a couple of times ordered seconds—of steak and eggs. He drank more than his fair share of coffee, but made up for it with extra-generous tips. In a few short days, their presence for breakfast became routine, and Claire found herself watching the door for them each morning.

That was why on a Tuesday morning eight days after she opened the bakery, when the McBrides hadn't graced her door by eight A.M., she started to be concerned. By the usual lull in business around nine, she was downright worried.

So she broke one of her father's cardinal rules about running a bakery and closed up shop. When none of the McBrides answered her knock, she tried the door and found it locked.

"There is probably nothing to worry about," she told herself. "Maybe they weren't hungry today."

But she couldn't shake the looming sense of disaster. So, retrieving a spare key from the Menaces' hiding place under a rock in the back alley, she hurried upstairs. What she found when she opened the door at the top of the landing made her heart leap to her throat.

Gas. That distinctive, skunk-oil stink of town gas.

The odor of it stole her breath, and for just a moment Claire stood frozen in shock. *My God, Tye. The children!*

Had the Menaces made the fatal mistake of blowing out the flame of a gas lamp? *Please, Lord. No.*

Instinct had her first rushing upstairs to the attic bedroom where the girls lay sleeping. She couldn't smell it up there. "Emma? Maribeth? Girls, wake up," Claire called, hurrying to throw open a window. She took a gulp of fresh air as it seeped into the room, then turned to the youngest child, the smallest child, and gingerly felt for a pulse. "Thank God."

Moving quickly Claire shook Emma hard, saying, "Darling, wake up." Immediately, she repeated the process with Maribeth. To her enormous relief, the girls began to stir.

"What's wrong?" Emma said, her voice slow and sleepy.

Katrina sat up, rubbing her eyes. "What are you doing here, Miss Donovan? Did you bring us our muffins in bed?"

Maribeth's head emerged from her covers like a turtle from its shell. Beside her, the rapid movement beneath the sheets looked suspiciously like Ralph's tail.

If that little dog was all right, certainly the girls were, too. Claire needed to see to Tye.

"Girls, I want you to grab your robes and hurry downstairs. And take Ralph with you."

Emma, her eyes still heavy with sleep, frowned and asked, "What's wrong?"

"I'm not certain. A gas leak or trouble with a lamp. Hurry,

girls. You need to get out of this building. You can wait in the alley. Where does your Uncle Tye sleep?"

Katrina pointed toward the floor. "Down there. Right below us."

Below them. Where the stink had been strongest.

Urgency gripped Claire. Like a mother hen in a hurry, she rushed the girls downstairs. Awake now and worried, they chattered questions and concerns that Claire couldn't answer. Katrina started to cry as Maribeth turned on the landing as if to lead the way to their uncle.

"No," Claire said, trying to limit herself to only shallow breaths as the smell intensified. "I'll get Tye. You go on outside, away from the building, you hear?"

Emma shook her head. "But Uncle Tye—"

"Will be fine. I'll see to it. Now hurry, girls. And find something to prop open the doors, all right? Both of them."

Claire waited just long enough to make certain they followed her directions, then went in search of Tye, opening every window she spied along the way.

Despite her breaths of fresh air, the gas seemed to pound at her. Her head began to ache. And when she found Tye's bedroom and saw him lying so still—so totally silent—her heart seemed to stop.

First she ran to the window and wrenched it open as wide as it would go. Then she went to the unlit wall lamp and gave the opened valve a vicious twist, turning off the escaping gas. *A draft must have blown out the flame*, she thought. Tye wouldn't have been so foolish as to turn it off without shutting down the gas.

Then she turned to the bed. "Tye? Oh, Tye." She was almost afraid to touch him for fear she'd find the cold, clammy skin of death. Her hand trembled as she laid her fingers against his neck, searching for a pulse. Warmth. A faint, but steady beat. Thank God.

She started slapping his face. "Tye, wake up. You must wake up."

He lay like a corpse, and Claire swore he wouldn't become one as she forced herself to think what to do.

He needed fresh air. But he was too heavy for her to lift. She gazed toward the window. The half-dozen steps between it and the bed may as well have been a thousand. How could she get him over to the window?

Help. She'd call for help.

His bedroom window looked out over the alley. When she gazed outside, no one was there. She glanced back toward the bed. "Tye McBride, you wake up this instant!"

Hating to leave him for even a second, she dashed for the front of the building. She yanked up a window, then slapped at the shutter, shoving it open. Then she leaned out and screamed for assistance. Two men at the comer glanced her way, but only one of them started toward her. Slowly. Too slowly.

As she called for him to hurry, the girls came rushing around the corner of the building from the back. "Emma," Claire said. "Go find more help. Tell them to come fast"

"Uncle Tye. Is he . . . ?"

"He'll be fine. He's just too heavy for me to move. I need help." *Lots of it*, she feared. With a man as big as McBride, it might take more than two people to move him.

Trusting that assistance was on the way, she hurried back to Tye. Either the gas had burned away her sense of smell or the open windows were doing their work. The odor didn't permeate the room like before. Claire gripped Tye's shoulders and shook him hard. "Wake up, McBride."

He groaned.

She'd never before heard such a beautiful sound. She shook him again.

"What the hell?" he murmured into his pillow, his words slow and slurred.

"Wake up, Tye. There's been a gas leak. You must get up and get out of here."

"My head. Hell. I can't . . . the girls." He opened his eyes and lifted his head off the pillow. "My girls?"

"They're fine. They're safe."

His head dropped back. Claire thought he might have passed out again.

Footsteps pounded up the stairs. "Hello? You hollered for help?"

"Here," she called, recognizing the voice as that of one of her customers. "We need to get him outside, Mr. Landry. There's been a gas leak."

Mr. Landry was a good thirty years older than Claire, crotchety and gruff. But the freight hauler had the muscles of a much younger man and, between the two of them, they were able to get Tye to his feet.

"What kind of britches is he wearing?" Landry drawled, scowling down at Tye's hips. "You shouldn't be here, ma'am. Him without a shirt and hearts on his drawers. It's not seemly."

"Well neither is letting a man die," she snapped back.

"You do have a point there. I reckon you saved his life."

A flurry of footsteps coming up the stairs told Claire more help had arrived. As a trio of men assisted Tye downstairs, Claire grabbed clothes for him from a bureau drawer. Soon the men had him dressed and settled in a chair in The Confectionary's kitchen by the opened back door. He didn't complain of any ill effects while the girls reassured themselves of his well-being. When they finally adjourned to the front of the store to partake of their delayed breakfast, Tye confessed to suffering a nauseated stomach and a roaring headache.

Claire poured a dollop of Magic into the warm tea she served him. When he looked at it suspiciously, she said, "This is what my mother always gave me when I had an upset stomach and a headache. It works wonders, Tye."

"More Magic, huh? I guess it can't hurt me, not the shape I'm in at the moment." He sipped at it and sighed.

But as his headache lessened, his frown grew. He asked Claire to explain how she'd found them, and then debated how the lamp may have malfunctioned. "Scares the bejeebers out of me to think about it," he said eventually. "The girls could have . . ."

"Died," Claire said flatly, angry at the thought. "You all could have died. You need to get a man out here to check all the fixtures in this building. Today."

He nodded, then winced at the effort. "I will. But no matter what, I'm moving the girls back to Trace's house. The painting is almost done. Better to live with paint fumes than to . . ." Again, he wouldn't say the word.

Claire didn't hear what else he said. She was too preoccupied with surprise at her reaction to the McBrides' proposed change of address. *I'll miss them,* she realized with a pang in the vicinity of her heart. She recalled some of the Menaces' antics she'd witnessed from her kitchen window. She remembered smiling at the sweet sound of their laughter. The Rankin Building would seem unnaturally quiet in their absence.

"Claire!"

She jumped at the sound of Tye's voice. Judging from his tone and the frustration on his face, he had tried to get her attention for some time. "What?"

"I said I owe you one. A big one. You saved my nieces."

The gratitude shining in his expression was a welcome change from the haunted knowledge of near tragedy that had previously lined his face. Soothingly, Claire replied, "The girls were fine. You were the one who came closest to dying."

"Better me than them anytime. If something bad happened to them it would tear me up. But if it happened on my watch . . . well . . . I couldn't live with it." He drew a deep breath. "Thank you, Claire Donovan. I owe you."

"Tye, I only did what anyone would do. What any *friend* would do. You don't owe me."

"Yes, I do."

He left her no choice but to nod and accept his thanks. When he reached out and took her in his arms for a quick, heartfelt hug, she felt like she'd won a blue-ribbon prize. She was smiling when he turned to leave, humming a happy tune beneath her breath when he stopped at the doorway and glanced back over his shoulder. Her song died beneath the seriousness in his sharp, somber stare.

"And Claire? I'm a man who sooner or later always pays his debts. Anytime, anywhere, you ever need my help, all you need do is ask. All right?"

"All right," she agreed.

Once he left, she pursed her lips in silent contemplation. Well, wasn't that interesting? Whether she deserved it or not, she had a favor from Tye McBride tucked away in her apron pocket.

"Ah, I'll never need it." As soon as she said it, she wanted to bite her tongue. Talk about asking for trouble.

CHAPTER 7

IT'S BAD LUCK TO BAKE WITH INDIFFERENT FLOUR.

TWO DISTINCT CULTURES coexisted in Fort Worth. The refined residents strove to erase the frontier atmosphere of the town, while the ruffians liked to get down and wallow in it. As the days passed, The Confectionary proved to be one of only a handful of businesses in town that catered to both.

Claire now opened the shop a full hour earlier in order to serve those whose sweet tooth attacked at the end of a rowdy night She also stayed open one hour later to accommodate the ladies who wanted The Confectionary's fresh-baked bread to grace their supper tables.

By the end of the first month of business, Claire declared The Confectionary an unqualified success. Her biggest problem was that all the hard work had worn her ragged. Like never before, she appreciated the helping hands her family members gave one another at the Donovan bakeries.

She didn't know how she'd have managed without Lars. He had returned to Fort Worth the day after the McBrides moved back to Willow Hill, bringing with him heartrending news about her family.

Upon learning that Lars had found his daughter safe and

sound in Fort Worth, John Donovan had heaved a huge sigh of relief. When told that Claire refused to return to Galveston and marry Reid, her father's temper erupted. He'd thundered on for hours, eventually declaring he no longer had a daughter. Throughout John Donovan's storm, Claire's mother remained silent and sad.

The boys weren't silent, however. According to Lars, they had maligned her up one side and down the other. It got so bad that at one point, Lars and Patrick actually exchanged a few punches. That was why Lars had chosen not to tell the Donovans he intended to join her in Fort Worth. "They're hardheaded, hard-hearted Irishmen, Clary," he had said, "and if this is the way they're going to be, I want no part of them."

Knowing her father's temper, Claire had anticipated his anger. She wasn't even too surprised he'd gone so far as to wash his hands of her. However, she did expect him to retract his harsh decision once his temper cooled, but as the days passed with no telegram or even a visit by one of her brothers, she was forced to accept that he'd been serious in his proclamation.

The thought that she had lost her family hurt deeply, and at times she second-guessed her choice. But then she'd think about marrying Reid, of retiring to the marriage bed every night with a man she didn't love, and she knew she'd done the right thing.

Family duty went only so far. Had someone's life been at stake or something equally as serious, well, that would have been a different question altogether. She simply wasn't going to sacrifice herself to a legend. The Donovan Magical Wedding Cake fairy tale could find a different fairy godmother. It wasn't going to be her. Still, as the days passed, every other time the welcome bell announced the opening of The Confectionary's door, Claire expected to look up and find a Donovan.

It never happened.

"I can't believe Da really meant it," she muttered to herself at the end of one workday as she closed and locked the shop's door.

"If he did, I can't believe Mama and the boys didn't stick up for me."

Was Lars the only one who truly cared about her? And he wasn't even blood family, but a friend. A good friend. A true friend. *He could teach Tye McBride the real meaning of the word,* Claire thought.

The situation plagued her as she walked to Main Street and splurged by taking the mule-driven trolley to spare her weary body a good ten minutes off the trip home.

Strolling up the dirt lane toward her rented cottage, she spied a figure reclining in the porch swing. Her heartbeat accelerated. Was that Patrick?

Drawing nearer, she saw that no, the visitor was not her brother. Her pulse didn't slow. If anything, it sped up. The man sprawled across the swing on her front porch was none other than Tye McBride.

Suddenly Claire felt a bit . . . fluttery. She hadn't seen much of the McBrides since they'd moved back into Willow Hill. The day after the gaslight incident Tye sent her an extraordinary thank-you gift: free ice for a year from the Fort Worth Ice Company. In his note he said he'd considered sending a diamond bracelet, but thought she'd appreciate this type of ice more. He'd been right.

The Confectionary no longer provided the Menaces their breakfast every day; instead the girls often stopped by for their raisin muffins on the way home from school. According to Emma, Tye was back to eating real steak and eggs for his morning meals. But, Emma allowed, he also ate the sweets Claire sent home for him with the girls.

Claire took it as a victory, considering his scornful reaction to her Magic and especially since the girls also indicated that the parade of pastries and cakes to "Lord McBride's" front door hadn't ended with his change of address. Claire wasn't surprised, having twice spied Tye himself delivering baked goods to the nuns across the street.

"So," she said to herself as she approached her front gate, "what brings Mr. Steak-and-cackle-fruit to my front porch this afternoon?"

Maybe he came looking for some Magic to spice up his eggs.

She forced herself to keep her hands at her sides rather than reach up to smooth her hair like she felt the urge to do.

The sweet perfume of roses drifted on the subtle breeze as Claire arrived at the front gate. Reaching down, she slipped the latch. Hinges squeaked when the picket door swung open, and the man on the swing thumbed his hat back off his brow and sat up. He glanced at her, then tugged a watch from his pocket and checked the time. "Two thirty-eight. You're early, Claire. The Blessings won't be pleased. They didn't want to have to see you."

Affronted, Claire halted halfway up the graveled path and stared at him. For a moment, the only sound that broke the silence was the song of a cardinal from the branches of a nearby Cottonwood. Then, subduing her pique, she asked, "The girls are here?"

"Yeah. Inside with their teacher."

"Why? Did she assign them extra work or something?"

"Not exactly. I've lured Miss Blackstone for extra lessons of a sort. It was all the Blessings' idea. When the teacher wanted the lessons given here, the one thing the girls asked is that it be done at a time when we wouldn't run into you."

"Well, I guess that puts me in my place," Claire replied, surprised to feel the pang of hurt feelings. "What did I do? Substitute blueberry muffins for their usual raisin?"

"Nah. It's nothing like that. Nothing personal." Tye lumbered to his feet and stepped across to the porch rail, where he leaned against a support post and folded his arms. "You have them running scared. I couldn't figure it out myself at first. It took eavesdropping on their latest round of fortune-telling for the pieces to fall into place." He shook his head slowly and added, "I'm starting to worry about that fish."

Claire tugged at her bonnet ties in vexation. "Running scared? What do you mean? They're not afraid of me. They come by my bakery every day. I daresay they like me. A lot. Why, every time I see them they thank me for saving your lives."

Tye nodded. "You put your finger on it Claire. They are grateful you saved us—as I am, I might add—but as far as the Blessings are concerned, gratitude toward you is a fly in their matrimonial buttermilk."

"Excuse me?"

"They posed the question to Spike."

"Spike?"

"Haven't you seen them with their fish? Their fortuneteller fish? I think you know they have their hearts set on marrying me off to Loretta Davis. They worried that they should switch their loyalties to you since you saved our lives. The fish agreed."

"A fortune-telling fish?" Claire pulled off her bonnet and gave her head a shake. "Wait a minute. Did you just say your nieces want me to marry you?"

"No. That's the problem." His lips quirked up in a grin, and a gleam of amusement brightened his agate-green eyes. "They still have dreams of matching me and the fair Loretta. I'm afraid they've even taken their case to Loretta's beau, Gus—after I went to a good bit of trouble to smooth the waters with him after Maybelle stirred them up at the school that day, I might add." He paused and shook his head in exasperation. "Those girls. Now Gus is all in a huff again. I think even Loretta's getting a bit tired of it."

"So where do I fit in to all this?"

"Well, apparently their fish championed you. That's why we are here now. You're not supposed to be home from work yet."

"You've lost me."

"The girls are taking etiquette lessons."

Astonished laughter burst from Claire's mouth. "Etiquette lessons?"

He nodded. "Believe it or not, it was Mari's idea. They intend to learn to be proper young ladies. Last time we had supper with the Davis family, we had an incident. The girls think these lessons will help them avoid similar trouble in the future. Personally I have my doubts, but I didn't see what it could hurt."

"So what does that have to do with me?"

Tye shrugged as he removed his hat and laid it on the railing. Then he resumed his seat on the swing. "I told them I intended to walk them to and from their lessons. I've hired your neighbor Bill Jenkins to be the foreman of the ranch I'm starting up and, since he's home for lunch from his job down in the stockyards at this time of day, it's a handy way for us to meet and discuss business. Today we ordered barbed wire fencing. Have you heard of it? They just started selling it here a year ago or so. Nasty stuff, but according to Bill it's just the thing we need for running cattle."

"And this involves me . . . ?"

"Because they don't want you and me to spend any time together. They planned for us to be gone before you came home from The Confectionary. You see, Spike has spoken in your favor, but, despite that, the Blessings still want Loretta for their aunt."

Claire had no intentions whatsoever of marrying Tye McBride or anyone. She'd just rid herself of one fiancé. The last thing she wanted was to tie herself down to another. Even if he did have the starring role in her fantasies every night.

The fact that the Menaces proved so dead set against the idea stuck in her craw. What made Loretta Davis acceptable and her not?

Those Menaces. Someone needed to show them they didn't rule the world in their parents' absence. Obviously their Uncle Tye wasn't going to be that someone. *I'll have to do it*, she told herself. *Those girls have simply run amok.*

And so, purely for the McBride Menaces' benefit, she told

herself, Claire spread out her skirts and took a seat beside Tye. Close beside Tye. "I took etiquette lessons as a girl."

He eyed the six-inch slat of swing that separated them. "You did?"

She nodded. "Mrs. Avery. She said I walked like a boy. She made me wear shoes three sizes too small so I'd take littler steps. She failed me from the class the day she found my collection of doodlebugs."

A hint of worry coloring his tone, Tye cocked his head toward the window and said, "Miss Blackstone. She's not like your Mrs. Avery, is she?"

"Not at all. Your girls will do well with her. How many lessons do they intend to take?"

"I said we'd start with three. I figured one for each of them. After that, we'll see." After a moment's pause, he asked, "Miss Blackstone won't put 'em in too-tight shoes?"

"Nothing more traumatic than holding a book balanced on their heads, most likely."

Tye pursed his lips and nodded as though reassured.

The movement drew Claire's gaze to his mouth. *How*, she idly wondered, *would Tye McBride taste?*

After a moment's consideration she decided on steamy. And spicy. Like hot gingerbread fresh from the oven. Or maybe cinnamon-sweet, like hot apple pie.

Suddenly Claire felt like Eve eyeing forbidden fruit. But upon reflection, why should it be forbidden? She wasn't in Galveston anymore, surrounded by a pair of overprotective brothers and possessive parents. And it wasn't like she hadn't stolen a few kisses in the past.

Forbidden fruit. Tye McBride. She stifled the urge to lick her lips. Glancing up, she found him watching her, studying her with eyes that slowly caught fire.

All thought of the Menaces and etiquette evaporated from Claire's mind as time stumbled to a halt. The air between them thickened like a hot, July afternoon on the eve of a thunderstorm. Her senses expanded, the world around her becoming magnified. He looked dangerous but smelled of leather and sandalwood and school paste. She wanted to touch him. She craved to test the texture of his late-afternoon whiskers. *Soft or sharp?* she wondered as his nostrils flared beneath her scrutiny. The harsh sound of his breath rasped across the slight distance that separated them.

Claire's insides clenched at the sound.

His gaze dropped to her mouth. She gave in to the urge to wet her lips, and he responded with a low-throated, rumbled groan that sent shivers racing down her skin.

The woman deep within her recognized him. This man could show her. This man could whisk her to that dizzying world of passion and desire. This man, Tye McBride, called to her in a way no other man ever had. She wanted him—no, needed him—to touch her, to hold her.

She needed his kiss.

Her mouth went dry as hunger grabbed her, thrummed inside her, propelled her toward him. "Tye . . ."

"No Magic this time," he said, his breath as soft as a summer breeze. "Just you. This spell is your own, isn't it?"

"Spell?" she breathed.

"Maybe my Blessings are right to be concerned." His hand slowly lifted to cup her cheek. "I don't think straight when I'm around you. You're an Irish-Texan witch, Claire Donovan. A beautiful, beguiling, every-man's fantasy."

She melted on a sigh as his lips touched hers.

This is real magic, Claire thought as he swept her along on a tide of heat and need. She felt the coaxing, entreating brush of his tongue across her lips all the way to the tips of her tingling toes. She opened to him, and at the first warm stroke on the sensitive places inside, her entire body took flame.

She faintly heard a crash like breaking glass and took it to be the sound of her defenses dissolving. Drinking of her passion, he cast his spell around her, through her, into the very heart of her. She ached for him to hold her tight, and somehow he knew it. He pulled her closer, molding her to him. He was hard, so different from her; his chest a granite cliff against the pillow of her breasts, his arms iron shackles holding her captive.

And she gloried in all of it.

Then suddenly he was gone, retreated to the far end of the swing. His mouth, so soft and entreating mere seconds before, now lay set in a thin, angry line. Dazed and confused, Claire lifted her fingers to her kiss-swollen lips.

"Don't try it with me, lady," he growled. "I've been down this road before. I won't play the fool and be tricked again."

The swing swung crookedly as he jerked to his feet.

Swiping his hat off the railing he shoved it on his head and said, "Tell the girls I had to leave. I'll meet them back at Willow Hill."

Before she could muster a response he was gone.

A cricket chirped from the geranium pot beside the front door as Claire sat in stupefied silence. What in the world had just happened here? What did he mean "tricked"?

She sat on the swing for a good five minutes before the shock wore off and she started thinking straight again. She considered getting angry at the way he'd kissed and run, but she recognized the reaction. Tye had acted just like her brothers did when something had them spooked.

A smile tugged at the corners of her mouth. She found the idea of her kiss affecting a man like McBride so strongly downright appealing.

She bent over to unlace her shoes, and kicked them off. With one stockinged foot she gave the swing a push, then tucked her legs beneath her, humming her brother Brian's favorite drinking song in a low, indulgent voice.

She felt wonderful. Warm and tingly and happy. He'd made her fly.

An Irish-Texan witch, he'd called her. Claire leaned her head back against the swing and smiled as she relived his kiss in her mind. He certainly had done his share of enchanting. He'd held her spellbound.

In a voice that all but purred, she closed her eyes and murmured, "Well, if I'm a witch, then Tye McBride most certainly is a wizard."

⁓

IN KATRINA'S bedroom at Willow Hill, Emma practiced flirting smiles in a hand mirror while Kat searched her wardrobe for her hidden hoard of cotton. Maribeth sat on the edge of the bed, her brow puckered with worry as she stared at Spike's bowl. Abruptly, she stood and plunged her hands into the water and yanked out the fish.

Holding him up to her face, she chanted, "Spike, Spike, tell us true. Tell us what we need to do. How do we pay for the vase we broke in Miss Blackstone's front parlor? Should we steal money from Miss Donovan's bakery?" Maribeth gently laid the perch upon her bedroom floor and waited for it to foretell her future.

"Oh, put Spike away," Emma said, lowering the mirror as the fish flopped under the bed. "We're not going to steal money. Even we aren't that bad."

"That's right," Katrina said. "If we did that and Mama ever found out about it she'd cry. I don't ever want to make Mama cry."

Maribeth sighed heavily and, careful of the fish's prickly fins, lifted him and returned him to his bowl. "I guess y'all are right. I wouldn't want to upset Mama. Although I doubt it would bother Uncle Tye. I don't think anything we did would make him too mad."

Emma crossed to the window and looked out over the back-yard. Beneath the big pecan tree, Ralph nipped at their uncle's heels while he hammered nails into boards for the tree house Maribeth had requested. "I think Uncle Tye gets mad. He just doesn't let us know it 'cause then he'd have to get after us, and he doesn't want to do that."

The wardrobe hinge squeaked as Katrina shut it, then joined her sister at the window, rubbing her nose with a hunk of fluffy cotton. "Do you think Papa knew when he left that Uncle Tye would let us run wild?"

"He doesn't let us run wild," Maribeth protested. "For the most part he keeps real close watch on us. If we get in trouble, it's our fault, not Uncle Tye's."

Outside, their uncle glanced up and noticed them watching. Katrina returned his wave and said, "I didn't say it was his fault. It's really all *your* fault, Mari. You're the one who broke the vase when you looked out onto the porch and saw Uncle Tye kissing Miss Donovan." Frowning, she turned away from the window, put her fists on her hips, and added, "I don't know why you're so set in your mind against Miss Donovan anyway. I've decided I like her. She doesn't stink anymore. She makes yummy muffins and she's pretty and she's nice when we're not messing up her kitchen. Uncle Tye likes her. He wouldn't kiss her if he didn't."

"It's not that anything is wrong with Miss Donovan. It's just that she's not as right for Uncle Tye as Miss Loretta," Emma explained, propping her bottom on the windowsill.

"Why not?"

Maribeth pressed a kiss against Spike's bowl, then said, "You know, Kat. Remember what we heard when we snooped on Mama and Papa that day? Remember how Mama said the best way to get Uncle Tye to stay and live in Fort Worth is for him to marry a local girl? Then Papa said Loretta Davis would be perfect for Tye, and Papa ought to know 'cause he and Uncle are twins."

"But Papa didn't know Miss Donovan," Katrina protested, scowling at her sister.

"Did too. He rented her his building and Mama's old house."

"But he never tasted her muffins. He never saw her save our lives. He never watched Uncle Tye kiss her." Katrina folded her arms and stuck out her tongue at Maribeth.

"You two hush," Emma said. "Bickering amongst us doesn't solve anything. The fact is, Katrina, Papa and Mama agreed that Miss Loretta is the one for our uncle so we can feel good that she is the right choice."

"I don't think Uncle Tye feels too good about Miss Loretta, though," Maribeth said glumly. "I don't think he's sweet on her at all. I've never seen him look at Miss Loretta like he wants to kiss her. That's how he looks at Miss Donovan all the time."

"That's what worries me most," Emma said. "Miss Donovan loves that beautiful Mr. Sundine. We heard her say so herself."

"I'm not sure she meant arrow-through-the-heart love," Maribeth said. "She did say something about his being a brother."

"We couldn't hear that part good and, besides, it makes no sense. Look at how gorgeous Mr. Sundine is. I'd love him myself if I were older." Emma slowly shook her head. "No, I don't think we can champion Miss Donovan. If we try to make a match with Uncle Tye and Miss Donovan, and he falls in love with her but she doesn't love him back because she already loves Mr. Sundine, then Uncle Tye's heart will be broken and he'll go home to South Carolina for sure. I don't know about you, but I'm not willing to risk it."

Katrina sniffed. "Miss Donovan would be stupid to love Mr. Sundine instead of Uncle Tye. Uncle Tye's the very best there is. Except for Papa, of course."

"Well, I don't think Uncle Tye is all that sweet on Miss Donovan after all now that he's kissed her," Maribeth observed. "You saw how he marched away from her as soon as it was over. He didn't look happy. Plus, he was so very grumpy last night after supper."

"That's right," Emma agreed. "He only played one game of poker with us."

Katrina obviously wasn't ready to give up. "He was grumpy because he lost the game."

"He always loses, Kat." Emma wrinkled her nose, disgusted with the argument. "He loses to us on purpose, haven't you figured that out yet?"

"He does?"

"Yes, he does. Uncle Tye likes being sneaky. Look at the etiquette lessons. I thought for sure we had worked it so he would hire Miss Loretta to teach us."

"Instead he hires our schoolteacher," Maribeth grumbled. "It's not like we don't get enough of being with Miss Blackstone at school."

All three girls nodded glumly, then Emma continued, "I'll tell Uncle Tye tomorrow we want to quit the etiquette lessons. He won't tell me no about that. But we'll still need to come up with money to pay for the vase. I don't know about y'all, but I don't cotton to Uncle Tye's suggestion we work in the convent laundry for Sister Gonzaga in order to earn the price. Also, we need to come up with another good plan to throw Miss Loretta and Uncle Tye together. Mama and Papa will be back from their trip soon, and unless Uncle Tye is married to Miss Loretta, he'll go back to South Carolina. We're running out of time, sisters."

"I agree," Maribeth said. "But what can we do about it?"

Emma stared at her sisters. "I think we have no option but to use our secret weapon."

Katrina gasped. "You mean, Madam LaRue?"

"I'm afraid so." Chewing on her lower lips, Emma looked at Maribeth. "We could use our spelling bee plan and pay for both the vase and Madam LaRue. What do you think?"

Mari scrunched up her face in thought and scratched her head just behind her left ear. "The spelling bee. I don't know, Em. Like Papa sometimes says, that's heavy artillery. It could backfire on us."

"True. But, like Papa also says, if a person wants something bad enough, sometimes he's simply got to take a chance. Remember, we robbed a train to help Mama before she married Papa. The spelling bee plan isn't any worse than that."

"Yeah it is," Maribeth protested. "Remember how upset with us Papa was after the train incident? Remember what he said about stealing? Why, if we were to get caught doing the spelling bee plan, he'd sure as a Sunday sermon kill us."

"We won't get caught," Emma assured her. "Not this time. And besides, Papa isn't here, and Uncle Tye wouldn't do anything to us even if we deserved it."

Maribeth nodded, then turned to Katrina. "What do you say, Kat? For this to be a success, we have to work together."

"I still say there's nothing wrong with Miss Donovan, but I do like Miss Loretta and I love kitties because I'm Papa's Katie-Cat I reckon dealing with Madam LaRue is worth Uncle Tye's happiness. I'm a little scared of the spelling bee plan, though. How about we talk it over with Spike?"

As one, the three girls turned to stare at Spike, the fortuneteller fish, swimming placidly in his bowl.

THE KISS HAUNTED HIM.

The Kiss replayed itself nightly in his dreams, stealing the rest from his slumber, causing him to awaken tired and grouchy more mornings than not. Tired and grouchy and horny as hell.

He needed a woman. If he had any sense at all, he'd visit Hell's Half Acre and partake of one of the physical pleasures for sale within its confines. But he didn't. When it came right down to it, he didn't want a whore. He didn't want black and white. He wanted gray this time. Gray, all wrapped up in a package of sunshine and laughter and Magic.

He wanted Claire. Damn him for a fool.

After the Kiss he stayed away from her for a week. Then one day, unaccountably, his feet carried him right into her shop.

And now here he was sitting at a table in The Confectionary sipping on a root beer as he debated an editorial in today's *Daily Democrat* with the sorceress herself.

I don't have the sense God gave a horned lizard.

He couldn't say why he'd stopped by the bakery after helping Mrs. Moore rearrange furniture in Fortune's Design. He couldn't say why he was enjoying the debate so much, either. But he was. Claire Donovan was sure something else. Despite being a newcomer to Fort Worth, she was obviously quite civic-minded. She certainly demonstrated an interest in local affairs and a good grasp on the politics of the town. Plus, the woman loved to argue.

Tye enjoyed the intellectual stimulation himself. He found it helped keep his mind sharp, a critical component to a man whose primary job at the moment was riding herd over the McBride Blessings. He'd be glad when the ranch was up in operation. As things stood, he didn't feel like a rancher, but he couldn't honestly call himself a planter anymore. Be damned if he'd list babysitter as his current occupation. Still, that was better than the title some folks around here wanted to pin on him— British Lord with Money to Burn.

Claire thumped the glass top of the display case with her little fist. "The system is essential if this town ever wants to be more than just a frontier outpost. Just yesterday one of my customers told me a survey taken a couple of years ago found that a full third of Fort Worth's youngsters can't read or write. Private schools simply aren't doing the job."

Tye wanted to lick his lips at the picture she made. Instead he arched a brow and drawled, "Careful you don't break your case, there, gal. Can't sell crullers filled with glass. And listen closer to me next time. You misunderstood what I said. I'm not against public schools. I think the city should offer its children a public education. All I said was that Trace's girls have done well in private school."

Warming to his subject, he leaned forward. "Why, you should see Emma do arithmetic. She's so fast she all but burns up the chalk. And Maribeth, she can spell like no other nine-year-old I've ever seen. She's even entered in the next monthly spelling bee the Fort Worth Literary Society holds."

"I've just joined that society," Claire replied, rearing back in surprise. "I understood they implemented the spelling bee a few months ago in order to raise funds. I have to say I'm surprised to hear that Maribeth is entered. I was under the impression that the contest was just for adults."

"No." Tye shook his head and took a sip of his drink. "Emma asked the group's president. He checked the bylaws and found no rule saying a child couldn't enter, so he told her to go ahead."

Claire pursed her lips. He wanted to run his thumb across them. She said, "I'm told Miss Loretta Davis wins the contest every month. How does Maribeth feel about losing? Is she competitive?"

"That might not be a problem," he replied, shrugging. "Mari's been studying like she means it. I won't be a bit surprised to see her do well."

Claire poured herself a cup of coffee, then brought it to Tye's table. Sitting down, she said, "I guess she has plenty of time for it now that etiquette lessons have been canceled."

She smelled of marshmallow and Magic. Grimacing, he took a sip of root beer. "I hope Miss Blackstone's feelings weren't hurt. But once Emma told me they would be too nervous to continue, I didn't see any sense in taking more lessons."

Claire laughed softly. "Believe me, Letty's feelings were far from hurt. Unlike her vase."

"Hey, now." Tye was affronted. "I paid for that vase. And I'm even gonna make the girls work to earn off the price."

Feigning surprise, she reared back in her seat. "Careful there,

McBride, you're sounding like a proper papa. Just think, perhaps by the time your brother comes home, you'll actually have administered a disciplinary act."

"Oh, hush," he grumbled, his mood somewhat dampened. Funny, but the thought of Trace's return left him feeling a little strange. He truly enjoyed playing father to the girls. But, of course, playing was all it was. Katrina wasn't his. For years he'd believed a lie, believed that his twin had stolen Tye's own daughter when he ran away from Oak Grove and disappeared in the wilderness of the West. Only recently had Tye found out otherwise. The knowledge that he wasn't a father after all was, at times, a bitter pill to swallow.

Claire eyed him thoughtfully, then nodded and changed the subject by reaching for the newspaper. "Other than the battle over private versus public schools, let's see what else is in the *Daily Democrat* today. Hmm . . . here's a pleasant headline:

FIEND ATTACKS AN INVALID LADY IN HER BED, CHOKES HER UNTIL THE BLOOD OOZES FROM HER MOUTH AND NOSE, ACCOMPLISHES HIS DESIGN!!"

"The newspaper's journalistic style does lean toward the sensational, doesn't it?" Tye wryly observed.

Nodding, Claire licked her thumb and started turning through the pages.

So much for dampened moods. Now he wanted to mimic her actions with his tongue.

"Well, look at this," she said, her voice lifting with delight. "It's an article about my shop. He never even told me he'd been interviewed."

He. The word jerked Tye from his sensual haze. She must mean this fella Sundine she'd hired. Scowling, he reached over and grabbed the newspaper away from the baker. He'd heard that Claire had a helper working for her now, another newcomer to town. And to be honest, that was one of the reasons he'd decided to stop by for a soda. Mrs. Moore had mentioned that the Swede usually worked this time of day. And Claire didn't. He'd wanted to see what this fella Sundine was all about without running into Claire.

So why, when he'd walked in the door and found her instead of him, hadn't he turned around and left? Why had he ordered a root beer and made himself at home?

She's a dangerous woman, McBride. A dangerous woman.

He turned his attention to the story, quickly scanning the text. It was a typical welcome-a-new-business-to- town type piece. Lars Sundine. Lars. Why did that name seem familiar? "This is all about The Confectionary. Why did they interview him instead of you?"

"Because Wilhemina Peters is a woman, that's why. And Lars is very much a man."

Tye snorted and continued reading. As he reached the end, his frown slid into a scowl. "He shouldn't have quoted a sales figure. It's an invitation to robbery."

She waved off his concern. "I don't worry about robbers. Lars is huge. Hands as big as a bear." With a chuckle she added, "I wouldn't want to find myself on the wrong end of a rolling pin around him."

Good Lord, she actually giggled. The sound grated like chalk on a schoolboy's slate. What was wrong with Claire, acting like a simpering female? She was smarter than that, wasn't she?

Maybe she'd gotten stupid over the past few weeks. Women had been known to do that for various reasons, and he hadn't seen much of her since he moved the Blessings back to Trace's house. Except for the other afternoon, he'd kept far away from Claire Donovan and her damned Magic shop. Except for the Kiss. He'd been up close and personal with her then, by God. The ache in his loins had reminded him of that fact off and on ever since.

Tye yanked his attention away from the memory. "I was under the impression you hired an old man."

This time she chortled. "Well, you assumed wrong. You've seen Lars before, Tye. You spied on us at the railway station, remember?"

His hand jerked, almost knocking over his glass. "The blond fella?" *The one you kissed? On the mouth?*

She nodded. "He's just about your age, and having him around has only increased The Confectionary's business. Listen to this, Tye." She leaned forward, her eyes sparkling.

She looked good enough to eat. Tye shut his eyes.

"I had a visit from a gentleman earlier today. He wanted to lodge a complaint. It seems his wife has quit baking her own bread just so she can come down to the shop and drool over the 'Viking god.'"

"Viking god!"

"It was his wife's term."

Tye didn't like the sound of that. He heard that Claire had hired a man named Sundine, but he'd never made the connection with the railroad station fella named Lars. Stupid of him. He should have put the two Scandinavian names together right away.

Viking god. Damn. "You'd better beware or you'll shoot your good reputation to hell without even realizing it." Fort Worth was a lot looser about such things than other parts of the world, but even Texans had their limits. A Viking god working with a beautiful woman was asking for trouble. Especially with all that Magic around.

His gaze flicked over the newspaper article a second time. "They didn't mention Magic in the article," he grumbled. "Instead of announcing how much money you made, Wilhemina should have included a warning for unsuspecting sweettooths."

"What?"

Tye shrugged. "Nothing. Never mind."

He didn't want to go into his theory about Magic and aphrodisiacs again. To be honest, he wasn't sure he really believed it himself. After his up close and personal taste of Miss Claire Donovan, he'd come to suspect the magic wasn't all in the Magic.

He'd dreamed of the woman every night since their tête-à-tête on her front porch. Hot dreams, steamy dreams, erotic dreams. He'd wake up in the dark, hot and hard and hungry. On two separate occasions he'd actually risen from his bed and dressed, intending to go to her and deal with the ache that plagued him constantly.

Thank God he'd recovered his good sense before he ever left Willow Hill. Now if only he could do something to stop the damned dreams. Tye couldn't remember the last time a woman's kiss had affected him this strongly.

Well, he could too remember the last time it had happened. Constance. That's what had him scared half to death. The biggest mistake he'd ever made involved a woman who had stirred his blood then like the baker did now.

He had to stay away from Claire. Completely away. Maybe he'd get lucky and those brothers of hers would fetch her back to Galveston. With that cheery thought in mind Tye lifted his drink to his mouth and drained what was left in one sip.

"So," Claire said, rising to refill his glass. "What else is new up at the castle?"

"Castle?"

"That's where lords and ladies live, right?

Tye eyed the glass and pictured the pleasure of throwing the soda in her face. "You're a real comedian, you know it, Claire?"

She laughed. "I'll tell you something funny. I heard that Wilhemina Peters plans to research your family tree and publish it in the *Daily Democrat*."

"What? For God's sake, why?"

"Community service, I imagine."

Tye snorted and doused his groan with a shot of root beer.

Anxious to change the subject, anxious to leave, he pushed to his feet.

"You want to hear something even funnier than that?"

"Not really, no." He figured from the impish gleam in her eyes she intended to tell him anyway. She did.

"Loretta's not the only one Maribeth will need to beat. I've signed up for the spelling competition, too."

CHAPTER 8

IT'S BAD LUCK TO PICKLE PEACHES ON A WEDNESDAY.

STALE and too many people filled the ballroom inside the Cosmopolitan Hotel as the minutes ticked toward seven o'clock and the beginning of the monthly meeting of the Fort Worth Literary Society. Standing beside the refreshment table, Claire eyed the cookie tray she'd provided and mentally juggled her baking schedule for the following morning. The caraway cookies had disappeared fast. She should slot a batch of them between the hickorynut cake and the Nun's Puffs.

A stream of fresh air caressed her cheek, and she glanced up to see Tye McBride in the process of opening a window. Her eyes widened with appreciation as she got her first look at the Menaces' guardian dressed up in a coat and tie. The cut of his dark gray jacket emphasized the breadth of his shoulders while the jade-green glimmer of his vest complimented the color of his eyes. He was, she thought, a breathtaking man.

And he kept her off balance. The man ran hot and cold and she never knew which to expect. Friend one day, not the next. Kissing her one day, ignoring her the next. It made her dizzy. He made her dizzy.

And for a woman who claimed no interest in attracting the attentions of a man at this particular time in her life, her thoughts drifted in his direction an inordinate amount of time.

Claire lost patience with herself because of it. How foolish could she get? Other than his hesitancy to discipline the Menaces, he reminded her to a great extent of her very own father. Charming, handsome. A steam locomotive when it came to getting his own way.

Just what I need. Might as well have stayed in Galveston and married Reid as get tangled with the likes of Tye McBride.

As if he had felt her scrutiny, his head twisted and their gazes met and held. Nerves danced along her spine. All her self-cautions melted like butter in sunshine when they communicated silently across the crowded room.

Claire.

Hello, Tye.

He gave her a sweeping look of appreciation. *You look beautiful tonight.*

She smiled at him, feeling flattered and shy and a little flirtatious as, once again, she recalled their kiss. She wondered if he somehow read her mind because he slowly crossed the room toward her, his gaze never leaving hers. Though laughter and conversation swirled around them, they might as well have been the only two persons in the ballroom when he stopped before her and said, "Ready for the big contest, Miss Donovan?"

She cleared her throat. "Actually I'm more interested in the literary discussion that comes before it."

He nodded and casually reached for a sweet from the refreshment table. Claire caught her breath as his hand hovered over Loretta Davis's macaroons, then bypassed her own tray in favor of Wilhemina Peters's chocolate cake. But as he lifted the plate from the table, he apparently changed his mind and chose a ginger cookie. One of Claire's ginger cookies.

Satisfaction washed through her even as she wondered why

such a little thing as his choosing one of her goodies from a table full of anonymous desserts pleased her so much. Then, because she'd become so confused, she did something totally out of character. She started to babble. "I met Reverend Leach's wife tonight. She's a very kind woman. She's made me feel quite welcome. She's invited me to attend the Ladies Sewing Circle. I think I'll go."

"You will?" Tye's lips twitched with amusement. He tossed a quick look across the room to where his nieces stood conversing with their housekeeper and two other women. One of the ladies raised a hand and wiggled her fingers flirtatiously as she mouthed, *Hello, Lord McBride.* He smiled sickly, then turned back to Claire. "I swear these people would bow to a donkey if he had a title."

They shared an honest grin. Then he brought the cookie to his mouth for a bite and as he chewed, all sign of good humor bled from his face. His eyes narrowed to slits. "This tastes like heaven. It's yours, isn't it?"

"Yes." Claire preened.

A look of dismay flashed across his face, and he gave a soft groan. "I didn't think. I'll be paying for this all night."

She halted mid-preen. *Of all the nerve.* "Ginger gives you indigestion, Lord McBride?" she challenged.

"No, Miss Donovan. Your Magic gives me a . . ." He paused and raked his fingers through his hair. "Never mind. Excuse me, I need to check on my girls." He turned away from her, then hesitated. Glancing down at the cookie in his hands, he softly muttered, "What the hell."

He popped what was left of the sweet into his mouth, then snagged a second cookie from the tray. "You know what, Claire? Sometimes a fella simply lacks willpower. You sure look pretty in that dress."

Claire sensed that something more than the tasting of a treat had just transpired but before she could make sense of it, the meeting was called to order. Claire took a seat. After a brief welcome, the president asked the secretary to read last month's minutes. Roll call followed, as did committee reports and dispensation of both old and new business.

Finally the evening's exercises began. Readings, songs, and dialogues were followed by a short debate and announcements of this month's spelling bee participants. A hum of interest followed Claire's name. An outburst of clapping from the McBrides trailed Maribeth's.

During the short break that ensued, the membership scrambled to the treasurer's table to place their bets on the outcome of the contest. Unaccustomed to the gamblers' atmosphere so prevalent in Fort Worth, Claire observed the proceedings with wonder and mentioned her surprise to the woman seated beside her, Loretta Davis.

"The people of this town would bet on the sun coming up if the odds were right," the young woman replied. "We've raised good money for needy charities by bringing the betting out of Hell's Half Acre and into our meetings. If someone must profit from vice, better the orphanage or another charity than the sin dealers down in the Acre."

As Claire nodded her agreement, she again felt the prickle of awareness she'd noted off and on throughout evening. Tye McBride was staring at her again.

It was almost a relief when the president called the spelling contestants to take their places at the front of the ballroom. Claire found herself sitting at such an angle as to observe both Maribeth McBride, seated four places to her right in the competitors' line, and the other Menaces, who sat beside their uncle in the second row from the front.

Within minutes Claire realized the girls were up to some sort of shenanigans. The squirming. . . the pointed looks. The winks. Claire recognized the signs because she'd walked in those Menaces' shoes not too terribly many years ago, herself. "Calamity Claire," she mumbled, biting the inside of her lip to keep the smile off her face. She'd agreed to participate in this spelling bee for the sake of business. Now she wondered if it might prove to be the entertainment highlight of her week.

Especially since it was obvious Tye hadn't a clue that the letters rumbling through his nieces minds spelled t-r-o-u-b-l-e.

SOMETHING WAS UP.

The early rounds had whittled the contestants from twelve down to only four. All around Tye spectators shifted to the edges of their seats as tension built. But despite the fact that their sister stood a good chance of winning, Emma and Katrina looked bored.

Something was definitely up.

Tye sat with his arms folded, his head cocked to one side as he focused his gaze on Maribeth, who waited for the secretary to call out her word. For the most part, he could understand her success through the first five rounds. She was a smart girl, true, and the Society's practice of taking its word list from works of Shakespeare had given her a focus for her preparatory study. That could explain Mari's knowledge of the proper spelling of such unfamiliar words as "burdocks" and "samphire." But nothing would explain the almost apologetic smile she'd given Loretta Davis when she'd rattled off "servile." Maribeth was the only child up there. She should look at least a little nervous. Instead, she beamed total confidence.

"Something is rotten in Denmark."

"What's that, Uncle Tye?" Emma asked. "What do you mean something is rotten in Denmark?"

A man seated behind them tapped Tye on the shoulder. "You muddled the quote, son, and besides, that's *Hamlet*. This month is *King Lear*."

Tye flashed him a brief, impatient smile, then leaned toward

125

Emma and lowered his voice. "Did y'all somehow fix it so your sister would win?"

Emma's eyes went wide with innocence. "How would we do that?"

That's what he wanted to know.

Katrina added, "*Why* would we do that?"

That particular question had him shivering in his boots. "I don't know. I have to admit, however, I'm surprised at how well Mari is doing. She's staying right with them, and I'm beginning to think she might win. She's got that air about her."

The two girls shared a look, then Emma offered an angelic smile. "She badly wants to win. In a weak moment Maribeth promised Sister Gonzaga she'd donate half of tonight's pot to the church. I don't know about you, Uncle Tye, but I don't fancy telling Sister the money isn't coming."

Tye dragged a hand along his jaw and studied his niece. Was Emma telling the truth? Perhaps. Sister Gonzaga could put a squeeze on a person like a lasso. Still, those cherubic expressions made him suspicious.

"Maribeth might not win, you know," he said, stretching out his legs and crossing them at the ankles. "It'll be hard to beat Miss Davis. Too, the Reverend Littleton looks like a speller to me, and Miss Donovan appears plenty confident. This could be a real horse race."

"Horse race! Silly Uncle Tye." Katrina stuck her hands beneath her legs and started rocking. "This is the most exciting spelling bee I've ever been to. I'm so nervous."

Nervous, hah. Like a fox slipping into a henhouse was nervous, maybe.

The sergeant-at-arms rang a bell signaling for quiet, and round six of the Fort Worth Literary Society monthly spelling bee commenced. Twenty minutes later, Reverend Littleton, so distracted by Loretta's previous word, "codpiece," fouled out by forgetting the K at the beginning of "knave." Now only Maribeth,

Loretta Davis, and Claire Donovan remained. Tye couldn't keep his gaze off the baker.

The woman glowed—glittered like a fire on a moonless night—her eyes alight with a hint of impishness that appealed to the devil in him.

He didn't want to be attracted to Claire. She was Magic and mischief all wrapped in a package pretty enough to raise steam on an icy heart. On his heart. She made him yearn for something he had not the right to want.

The voice whispered through his mind like the devil's own temptation. *Why don't you have the right? She's not engaged. She doesn't belong to another man. Not any longer. Nothing is stopping you.*

Bitterness washed through him. Yeah, something was too stopping him. Claire herself. That was the tangle in all of this. That's why he didn't have the right.

If Claire Donovan was an honest lady, a truly good woman, a special woman like the one Trace married, then she deserved a better man than him. If she was as good as his senses were telling him, then she deserved a man without the ugly baggage he toted around. She should have someone whole, someone whose heart wasn't dead. Someone who could love her like she deserved to be loved.

That man wasn't him.

Tye watched her, wanted her, and regretted it as she hesitated over a word. When her teeth nibbled at her bottom lip, his own teeth ached to do the same. The entire ballroom held its collective breath until she properly ended the word "ratsbane" with an NE rather than an A-I-N. Tye rubbed his eyes, determined to focus in on his niece and no one else.

Two words later, and to the spectators' surprise, Maribeth vanquished Loretta Davis, leaving victory in the grasp of either the child or the baker. With such a unique development in the offing, the president of the Society called for an intermission in order to allow the membership an opportunity to place additional wagers.

With the pause in action, Emma and Katrina rushed toward their sister. Tye leaned against the wall and folded his arms, studiously looking anywhere but at Claire.

And so she caught him by surprise when she appeared in front of him. Her eyes shimmered and her grin lit up the room. She had that impish, mischievous look about her that had him bracing himself as she leaned over and whispered, "Don't look now, McBride, but your niece is cheating."

Dammit, he'd guessed right. While he would have liked to have asked Claire how she figured it out—Tye himself was still in the dark—he felt obliged to take Maribeth's side. "That's a fine thing to say, Miss Donovan. Sounds like sour grapes to me."

"Not at all. I have no intention of spreading the fact around. However, since you are currently acting as her guardian, I thought you should know what is happening."

Damn right he needed to know what was going on, and he itched to ask Claire for the details. His problem was he couldn't come out and ask without admitting he doubted Maribeth's honesty, and he wasn't about to do that. He settled for silently encouraging Claire to continue when she observed, "The girls are clever, I'll give them that. I'd like to know how they got a list of the words being used tonight."

The word list. Tye's gaze drifted toward his nieces. Yep, it made sense. Mari couldn't have memorized an entire play, but she could file away a list of words with relative ease.

Claire continued. "What are their plans for the prize money? Have they mentioned it to you?"

It was a question Tye wanted answered himself. He simply didn't buy the Sister Gonzaga explanation. Rather than trying to defend his charges, he went on the attack. "You act like Maribeth has already won. Do you plan on throwing the contest? Now that *is* cheating, Miss Donovan."

The grin she flashed was downright naughty, and Tye froze like a birddog on point when what felt like every drop of blood in his body rushed to his loins.

Her eyes twinkled wickedly as she said, "Oh, I have a spelling word or two up my sleeve, Mr. McBride. You can count on that."

Tye's blood ran so hot he halfway expected to see steam rising from his skin. Damn all his good intentions. A mischievous Claire Donovan was alluring; a saucy Claire Donovan irresistible.

The spelling match resumed, but now he observed it through a sensual haze. He imagined the people seated around him took his fidgeting for nervousness on Maribeth's behalf. The fact was, he couldn't get comfortable sitting down.

Tension crackled in the air like summer lightning as Maribeth and Claire both rattled off their next four words. From out of the corners of his eyes, Tye spied Emma reaching out to clasp her sister's hand. All signs of boredom had vanished as the two girls shared a nervous look. A very nervous look. Up on the contestants' platform Maribeth had begun to bear a distinct resemblance to good old Spike; she'd gone a bit green around the gills.

The president faced Claire for her next word. "Miss Donovan, from Act Four, scene one, please spell for us the word 'esperance.'"

"Esperance?" Claire repeated, as many in the audience flipped through their copies of *King Lear* to locate the word.

"Esperance."

"*Hmm*. Esperance." For the first time all evening, a frown of consternation settled on the beautiful baker's face. She folded her arms and tapped her pursed lips with a finger. "Well, my brain seems to have reached its limits. How many words have we used so far in this contest, Mr. President? Forty-three? Forty-five?"

"This is our fiftieth word, Miss Donovan."

"Fifty!" She laid a hand against her breast and turned her head, flashing Maribeth a gaze of amazement that Tye didn't believe for one second. "Fifty. Imagine that. And how many choices are left on your list?"

The president cleared his throat. "Actually, yours is the last word. After this I guess we'll resort to pulling words from the play itself. I'm afraid we never expected this to go on so long. Never has before."

Maribeth shuffled her feet as Claire said sweetly, "Obviously Miss McBride and I are exceptional spellers. Perhaps we should call this a draw?"

Suddenly Emma surged to her feet. "No! The word is yours, Miss Donovan. You have to spell 'esperance' correctly first. You might miss. Even if you get it right, it's not over." Though she continued to speak to Claire, she shot her sister an encouraging look. "Mari is a very, very good speller. She always has been. She can do this. She can still win!"

"I'm sure she can." Claire smiled tenderly at Maribeth. "You are a worthy opponent, Maribeth. No matter what the outcome, I've been honored to share this competition with you."

Tye wondered if anyone other than he and Maribeth was watching Claire closely enough to see the wink she gave his niece.

"Now," she continued, "please forgive me for the delay. I believe my word is 'esperance'? Very well. Esperance. E-S-P-E-R-E-N-C-E. Esperance."

"She missed it!" Katrina shouted with glee. "Miss Donovan missed it! Maribeth is the winner!"

The room erupted as the membership of the Fort Worth Literary Society surrounded their spelling bee champion and runner-up, offering effusive and heartfelt congratulations. Tye observed the goings-on from the sidelines, slowly shaking his head. Was he the only person in the room who realized a seven-year-old just now learning to read recognized the misspelling first?

"Little criminals," he murmured, indulging in a reluctant grin at his nieces' joyous reaction when the treasurer announced the record-breaking kitty. Accepting the leather bank bag heavy with winnings, Maribeth named the sisters of St Stanislaus Kostka Church and the homeless animals shelter as this month's charity recipients.

And Tye didn't believe it for a minute. The Blessings had mischief on their minds. Fiduciary mischief, he suspected. Of course, he'd put a halt to whatever impish goal they had in mind, but after watching their happiness, he'd decided it could wait until tomorrow. Tonight he'd let them enjoy the sweet taste of victory. Tomorrow was soon enough to throw a fly in their buttermilk.

Claire Donovan's laughter rang out over the buzz of the crowd, and his body reacted to the sound. *Magic*. He had a taste for it tonight. A taste for her. It was a damn good thing he and the girls were heading straight home.

He ambled toward the row of hooks along the back wall of the ballroom and retrieved his hat. Casually he held it in front of his fly.

He'd heard of a sweettooth before, but this was ridiculous.

CHAINS SQUEAKED and wood creaked as Claire gave a push with her feet sending the porch swing into a gentle rock. She gazed out over the lawn toward the flickering lights of town that were clearly visible from here, at Trace McBride's home, built at the crest of Willow Hill. Two and a half hours after the spelling bee ended, she shouldn't be here, alone, surrounded by night and a magnolia's perfume, waiting for a man.

What passed for proper in daytime changed with the setting of the sun. She risked her reputation by coming here unchaperoned at this time of the evening. She knew it, but at the moment she truly didn't care. Never before in her entire life had she felt this excited and bold; daring and alive.

Tye McBride stirred her juices.

High spirits and a good dose of curiosity had prompted her to approach the McBrides following Maribeth's "victory" and offer a congratulatory treat at The Confectionary. When Gus Willard stormed out of the hall following a public spat with Loretta Davis, Lars had suggested including the former champion in the party.

Lighthearted best described Claire's mood during the time that followed. Lars devoted himself to soothing Loretta's romantically ruffled feathers, and Claire watched the pair with amused interest. Over the years she'd seen her friend charm many a woman, but never with quite this same degree of intensity. Could it be the mighty Lars was finally falling?

If so, the blacksmith had missed his chance with the fair Loretta. No man would defeat Lars Sundine in the battle for a lady's affections. Except, maybe, Tye McBride.

Claire wondered if the Menaces had noticed the spark arcing between their Miss Loretta and Claire's right-hand man. If so, she tried to guess what mischief they'd next commit. Once they finished with the current bit, of course.

At The Confectionary she had taken pleasure in watching Tye down not one but two pieces of her devil's food dessert, and his praise of her baking, though grudgingly offered, had been music to her ears. Once the girls had licked their plates clean—literally, in Katrina's case—the McBrides had done the dishes while Claire sat and giggled along with the girls to silly stories about Trace and Tye as boys. Lars had kissed Claire's cheek and offered a good-night and the information that he intended to escort Loretta home. Tye, rather reluctantly, she thought, had volunteered to see Claire to her front door.

Ordinarily such an attitude would have offended her, but tonight two things prevented that reaction. First, in between his grumpy remarks Tye sent her hot, heated looks that stirred a fire inside her. And second, tonight simply felt different. She felt different. She sensed a magic in the air, an excitement. Inside herself she felt a daring, vibrant sense of independence; a tension that zinged through her blood like the finest of wines.

Claire reveled in it. She was a true, independent woman in charge of her own fate. And tonight that fate declared she pass the time with Tye McBride.

During the walk home she'd gotten so involved in a debate with Emma about the superiority of chocolate pudding over butterscotch that she hadn't noticed they'd traveled the wrong direction until they started up Willow Hill.

"I thought I'd get the girls to bed first," he'd explained, moonlight illuminating his face. "It's been a long day. Too, I hate to carry this much money around. It's asking for trouble."

Boldly she replied, "And sometimes trouble does follow us home, doesn't it?"

He stared hard at her, then looked away. But his gaze returned, and with it, a long sigh. "So, Claire," he'd said softly. "Come up the hill with me?"

She sensed he asked for more than a walk, but the web of enchantment that held her in its grasp provided no defense. Now, as he read a bedtime story to his nieces and the sensuous rumble of his voice drifted from the open window above, shivers of anticipation danced across her skin.

She knew she shouldn't be there. *Calamity Claire*. Some things never changed. This mischief simply took another path. A grown-up path. Papa would kill her if he knew what she was up to. "The boys would break his face."

"What's that?" Tye stood in the doorway.

"I was thinking about my brothers."

He ambled out onto the porch. At some point between the time he went inside with the girls and now, he'd removed his jacket and unbuttoned his vest. His necktie hung loose and he'd rolled the cuffs of his shirtsleeves back, halfway up his forearm. He looked disheveled and dangerous, and as he took a seat beside her on the swing, Claire's mouth turned to cotton.

"I've thought about your brothers a time or two myself. I'm surprised they haven't been up here checking on you half a dozen times already. That's what I'd have done if one of my sisters had run off all alone."

"You're a good brother, Tye McBride."

"No, Claire," he said softly, sadly. He reached out to tuck a stray curl back behind her ear. His fingers brushed her skin, traced the curve of her ear as he added, "Believe me, I'm not. I'm a bastard. A real son of a bitch."

"No." Claire protested, resisting the urge to lean into his hand. "You are wonderful, Tye McBride. Wonderful."

Their shadowed gazes met. The air thickened, and she blinked twice. Ever so slowly his hand cupped her face, pulling her toward him as he lowered his head.

Tenderly he kissed her, and she responded without hesitation. Recklessness had hold of her, and tonight, being here felt right. This man felt right, in a way she'd never known before. It was as if his mouth belonged to her, had been made just for her. And hers, for only Tye McBride.

He deepened the kiss, and she surrendered completely, her head falling back against his supporting arm. His kiss was pure magic, transporting her to another time and place. He wove a fantasy of rainbows and medieval knights and of pledges sworn before a cheering crowd. Claire heard music in her head as his tongue pillaged the warm, sweet interior of her mouth.

"Claire." Her name was a groan, and the fantasy disappeared in a fireburst of need. She moaned softly against his lips, her body trembling with an ache so fierce it threatened to consume her. It frightened her so much that she abruptly pulled away from him. She pushed roughly to her feet sending the porch swing into a crooked twist. *Like my emotions*, she thought. "Tye, I don't know . . . I've never . . . I need . . ."

"Me too, honey. Me, too." Standing, he grasped her hand and gathered her close. He murmured in her ear, "I've tried my best to ignore this, but you get to me. Tonight I simply don't have the energy to fight. You make me remember, Claire, and you make me forget. You make me want what I know better than to want. For that alone I should run hard and fast away from you. You make me remember what it's like to feel, damn you. You make me want to feel again."

His mouth took hers, no longer tender or gentle but fierce and needy. Angry. Desperate.

And Claire gloried in his desperation.

His tongue stroked hers; a rough, rhythmic pulse that called to something primitive inside her. His kiss was so intimate, demanding and needful and . . . hungry. But Claire was hungry, too, and so she met his tongue thrust for thrust. She whimpered when he released her mouth. She moaned when he nibbled his way to her neck, nipped at her, then licked the spot with his tongue. His hands swept freely up and down her back, then lower, touching her in ways no man ever had before. He drew her tight against him, holding her, molding her, and through the layers of lawn and petticoat Claire felt the unmistakable evidence of his desire.

Her blood raced hot. Her lungs strained for air. At the first brush of his hand against her bosom she startled, and for the briefest of seconds considered saying no. But she didn't want him to stop, so when he kneaded her breast and walked her backward, around the corner of the porch and into the darkest, most private corner, she allowed it without protest.

Nimble fingers worked her buttons and before she realized what was happening, her dress fell to her waist. "My beautiful, magical Claire."

She quit thinking at all when he made quick work of her corset. All she did was feel. And moments later when the mild night air caressed her bare breasts, she felt wicked and wanton and more free than she'd ever felt before. *Free.* Delicious freedom. Delectable independence.

And yet so dependent on this man, this moment.

As Tye bent his head, Claire's eyes drifted shut. She gave herself up to the scratch of shadowed whiskers, the brush of soft lips, the wet stroke of his tongue. His every touch stoked the fire inside her, driving her onward, upward, toward an invisible summit. Then his mouth—*oh God, his mouth*—sealed itself around her. And Tye McBride suckled.

A lightning bolt streaked from her breast straight to her womanhood, and Claire went taut with pleasure. But it wasn't enough. Instinctively she arched her back—offering, wordlessly asking . . . begging for more. Growling at her response, Tye tended each breast in turn until her knees turned to water and she sagged against him, overwhelmed by the magnitude of her need. "Oh, Tye, what are you doing to me?"

His mouth released her, and he slowly straightened. His breaths sounded harsh in the shadowed darkness of the porch. "It's you. You've bewitched me."

"No. I'm no witch."

"No?" He trailed a finger down the bare expanse of her bosom, caught her swollen nipple between thumb and forefinger and gently tugged. He answered Claire's soft gasp in a husky tone. "I think you are. I think you've dosed me up with Magic to make me forget I can't have a woman like you."

It took a moment for his words to sink in, to douse the heat burning inside her. She wrenched from his arms. "What do you mean 'a woman like me'?"

His laugh was strangled, harsh and self-directed. "A lady. A beautiful, tempting, magical lady."

"I don't understand." Now Claire had grown cold.

Tye shoved his hands in his pockets and took a step away from her. "A man must be careful when dealing with a lady. Your kind can fool a fella, Claire. If y'all deploy all your weapons, your kind can tell a man blue-bonnets are red and he'll believe it. That's why

I try to stick with whores. Whoring is up front and honest. Basic commerce."

His biting words brought a shiver to her skin, and Claire yanked her chemise back over her bosom. Tye made no attempt to stop her, although his gaze remained fixed on her chest. Belatedly her cheeks began to burn with embarrassment. She tugged and hooked and fastened, righting herself as best she could when dressing in the dark beneath the hot, hooded gaze of an infuriating man. As she attempted to finger-comb her hair back into some semblance of order, she snapped, "Is it your intention to be so insulting or are you just stupid?"

He snorted. "Oh, I'm stupid, Claire. Definitely stupid. History has proved that. You see, I'm a poor judge when it comes to picking honest ladies from the crowd, and my mistakes have burned me bad. That's why I've made it a point not to trust any of you. I can't afford another folly."

It made absolutely no sense for Claire to continue to argue, but she did so anyway. "So you'd rather live your life consorting with whores than honorably passing time with ladies?"

This time his laugh was amused. "Is that what this little interlude between us was called? Honorably passing time? If so, then, honey, I damn sure want to see you when you're up to no good."

"You bastard." Mortification fueled her itch to slap him. That, and anger and humiliation and embarrassment and shame. Her feelings were as tangled as a box of fish hooks, and just as sharp.

"I believe I've already owned up to that."

Resisting the urge to strike out, she pushed past him in an effort to flee the scene. She had to go home, to sort this whole thing out in the privacy of her bedroom. Tears pressed at the backs of her eyes and she feared she might cry. She refused to do that in public, in front of him.

But Tye didn't let her go. He reached out, grabbed her arm, and said, "Wait. Sugar, wait."

Don't you "sugar" me. She didn't say it out loud because she decided she wasn't speaking to him.

"Ah, hell." He gentled his voice and continued, "I'm sorry, Claire. I shouldn't have said what I did. I shouldn't have done what I did. I just . . ." His hand released her and his arm dropped back to his side.

Claire waited for him to finish his thought, her mouth dry as yeast powder.

"I just couldn't resist you any longer. I think about you all the time. I dream about you every night. You're my fantasy. And tonight, well, my dreams finally got the better of my reality."

"I don't understand."

This time he was the one who walked past her. He stood at the porch railing and gazed up toward the stars. Moonlight reflected anguish on his face; a wrenching pain she'd never before glimpsed or even suspected. "I've done some wicked, contemptible things in my life. And even if the person I hurt the most can get past it, I . . . well . . . I can't."

He looked at her then, her eyes gleaming like a cat's eyes in the night. "The truth of the matter is, it's not you I don't trust. It's me. And because of who I am . . . what I am . . . I don't dare reach for the dream. I have nothing to give you, Claire. I'm empty inside. And you deserve so much more."

"Tye, what is it—"

"I'm sorry. This won't happen again." He drew a deep breath and blew it out on a sigh. Then, straightening his spine, he gestured toward the front porch steps. "Let me walk you home. I'm not the only bastard in Fort Worth. I'll feel better knowing you got there safe and sound."

She needed to think, to reason out what he had told her. At the moment she was certain of only one thing, and she felt compelled to confess it. "Tye, what happened here tonight wasn't all your doing. I'm to blame too. I don't think—"

"Hush, now. Leave it alone. Like I said, it won't happen again."

"But—"

"It's getting late. You start your mornings early. Let's get you home so you can get at least a few hours' sleep."

Having been raised with brothers, Claire knew well enough when a man had made up his mind. "All right, I'll leave. But you stay here. The girls are upstairs alone. You can't leave them."

"The Blessings will be fine. It won't take me ten minutes to walk you home and come back. They tell me there were times back before he married Jenny that their father left them alone at night for a lot longer than twenty minutes, so they're not afraid or anything. Besides, when I put them to bed I told them what I intended. They'll know where to find me if one of them should need me."

Claire made him go upstairs and check on the girls before she agreed to leave. Once they started down Willow Hill they walked briskly. Neither of them spoke. Claire wouldn't have known what to say to him, and besides, her thoughts were all turned inward. The promise of the night had died, leaving her sad and confused and feeling lonely.

They paced side by side, Tye with his hands in his pockets, Claire with her arms folded, warming herself against a chill that didn't exist.

At least, no chill in the air existed until they turned the corner of her street. Spying the lights blazing in each and every window of her house caused her soul to grow cold. "Oh, dear Lord. What's happened?"

She picked up her skirts and dashed toward her house, her heart pounding from fear rather than exertion, Tye running alongside her. "Claire, wait," he said. "Let me see what might be wrong."

"No. I've got to see . . . look!" Her front door opened and figures began to file out. *Brian and Patrick*. Claire's pace began to slow. *Then others*. Claire came to a complete halt. "Oh, my God."

John Patrick Donovan shook off his wife's cautioning touch

and stepped forward, hands braced on his hips. His roar woke every dog in the neighborhood. "Catherine Claire Donovan! What in God's holy name are ye doing comin' home at this time of the night?"

His gaze raked her, and he suddenly clutched at his chest. "Look at ye now. Mussed and fussed and tousled like a strumpet." He turned his glare on Tye and in a voice dripping with menace, added, "With the devil himself at your side."

CHAPTER 9

AN EGG WITH TWO YOLKS IS A SIGN OF BAD LUCK.

"Run!" Claire whispered to Tye.

He shot her an incredulous look. "Run?"

"Yes. They'll kill you."

Well, that was certainly a flattering assumption. "I'm not going to run anywhere. What kind of man would that make me?"

"A living one!"

Tye eyed the veritable wall of Irish manhood coming toward him and figured she might have a point. The Donovan family had that sort of rabid coyote air about them. Although he would admit to many faults, cowardice had never been one of them. He stood his ground, curling his hands into fists as he prepared to defend himself.

Claire gave a snort of frustration, then stepped in front of him. "You have it all wrong, Da. I was attacked by a drunken ruffian, and Mr. McBride stepped in to save me. He deserves your praise, not your persecution."

Why, the little liar, thought Tye, torn between amusement at her audacity and chagrin at her dishonesty.

The Donovans slowed their approach, the sons glancing

toward their father for guidance as Claire continued, "But never mind that. What are you all doing here? Is something wrong?"

"Is something wrong?" One of the brothers threw his arms out wide. "Is something wrong! I should say so. Reid Jamieson has us by the short hairs, and it's all because of your hardheadedness."

Her father's gaze locked onto Tye's, capturing and measuring. "Don't use vulgarity in front of your sister, Brian."

The other brother shoved the first. "Besides, it's not true. It's not all Claire's fault."

"Keep your hands to yourself, Patrick," Brian shot back. "And it darn sure is too true. The weight of this entire debacle rests on Claire's shoulders."

"Look, this can wait" insisted Patrick. "First we need to find out what bastard bothered Claire so we can kill him."

"Son, your language," the father cautioned.

Brian braced his hands on his hips. "Patrick is right. It's plain as day that someone's been sniffing after Claire. If it's not this fella, then we need to find out who it is."

Tye decided the time had come for him to do a bit of talking. He stepped forward and extended his hand toward Claire's father. "I'm Tye McBride, Mr. Donovan. Welcome to Fort Worth."

John Donovan drilled Claire with a questioning look that she answered with batted-eyelash innocence. Sighing, he clasped Tye's hand in a vicelike grip and gave it one brisk shake. "If my daughter says you deserve my gratitude, then you have it. Come inside, Mr. McBride. Let me offer you a drink."

Claire piped up. "Mr. McBride needs to get home, Da. The children—"

"Are fine," Tye said. "I have a few minutes to spare. Lead the way, Mr. Donovan." The curiosity burning in him came close to matching the intensity of the lust he'd felt earlier.

Ignoring Claire's unspoken suggestion that he reconsider—a sharp elbow to the gut—Tye allowed himself to be escorted into the house by the Donovan clan. There he got his first good look at Claire's mother, which confirmed the source of the daughter's beauty.

Heartache echoed in Mrs. Donovan's voice as she cupped her daughter's face in her hands and said, "Oh, Claire." A pair of tears slipped silently from her eyes and trailed slowly down her cheeks.

"Hello, Mama."

Claire appeared shaken, and Tye felt compelled to wrap his arms around her in comfort. He wasn't stupid, however, so instead he looked around hoping to greet the schoolteacher. He'd been well pleased with the results of Katrina's most recent arithmetic test, and he thought he should tell Miss Blackstone as much. But Claire's roommate had apparently made herself scarce. Smart gal.

John Donovan placed a hand on his wife's shoulder and gave it a squeeze. Emotion cracked his voice. "Dry your tears, Peg. She's here, now, safe and sound. We have much to discuss."

Nodding, the older woman fished in her pocket and brought out a lacy white handkerchief to dab at her eyes. She took a seat in the rocking chair that sat in front of the fireplace as her husband glanced at his sons and said, "Boys, now that we know we won't need to head out searching for your sister, why don't you two find your beds. We've another busy day ahead of us tomorrow."

The term "boys" sounded silly when directed toward the brawny pair, but the Donovan sons complied without complaint. First Brian, then Patrick, kissed their mother's cheek then said their good-nights.

Once the brothers had departed, Tye refused the whiskey Claire offered at her father's insistence, and requested water instead. While she fetched his drink, he took a seat on the horsehair sofa. Donovan pulled a chair away from the small dining table and sat down. He waited, the silence dragging out, until finally he turned to Tye and demanded, "Tell me of this villain who dared to touch my little girl."

Claire returned to the room before Tye could reply. She

shoved the glass of water toward him, saying, "Da, can't we just forget this? I really don't want to talk about it."

Donovan harrumphed. "You'd like to forget it, wouldn't you? Just as, I suppose, you'd like to forget a few other uncomfortable subjects? Subjects like how you ran away with nary a word to us on your wedding day? How you caused your mother to all but worry herself into a decline?"

"Da, please," Claire cut an embarrassed look toward Tye.

"Please what? Please don't shame you in front of a stranger? Please don't call you to task for the embarrassment you caused your family? Please don't make you face the fact your selfish actions brought destruction down upon the Donovan clan?"

"Destruction!"

"Yes, destruction. I borrowed money to expand the business so your brothers could have their own bakeries, to stand on their own two feet and marry and raise families while making their own way in the world."

What about Claire? Tye wanted to ask.

"I knew about the loans, Da," she said. "We discussed them, in fact. Don't you remember? I asked you why my brothers got bakeries, while I was given a token dowry to marry a man I didn't want."

Her father arrowed a glare her way, then continued as if she had not spoken. "After the debacle of your wedding, business fell off dramatically. The newspaper took special delight in reporting all our troubles. My creditors called the notes, Daughter. I couldn't pay them. The Donovan Baking Company was forced to declare bankruptcy."

"Bankruptcy! Oh, Da, no."

Tye watched as Claire took it like a bullet, reeling. He didn't like the way her pa placed the blame on her, and he wanted to call the man on it. But the devastation in her eyes made him hold his tongue. He didn't think she could handle more upset at the moment Obviously John Donovan didn't agree, because he handed her another blow.

"Oh, Da, yes. We lost the bakeries."

Claire grabbed the chair beside her for support. "All three of them?"

"All but this one. That's why we've come, Claire." He squared his shoulders and announced, "The family has moved to Fort Worth to start over. We'll change the name of the shop to Donovan's Confectionary first thing in the morning."

The knife slid into Claire's heart as smooth as a song. "Change the name?"

"Of course. It may take time, but I'm determined to rebuild the reputation of the Donovan name."

Her knees had turned to water, so she found a chair and sat down before she fell down.

Her father continued. "Patrick and I visited the bakery earlier this evening. I'd have preferred a location on Main Street, but this will do."

They must have toured The Confectionary while she and Lars were at the Literary Society meeting. Funny how she'd seen no sign of intruders. Of course, she'd been so wrapped up in her strange mood and Tye McBride that a steer could have sat at one of her tables and ordered chocolate cake and she wouldn't have noticed. Still, she remembered locking the door before she'd left. "How did you get in?"

"Miss Blackstone told us you had an extra key in your bedroom."

Claire made a conscious effort not to grit her teeth. The key had been in her underwear drawer.

"I studied your books," her father said. "You've done surprisingly well for the short time you've been in business. You've made a nice little profit. Of course, I see areas where changes must be made. You're paying too much for some of your staples, and your inventory is underpriced."

She couldn't stand to listen to this. She'd bartered hard to get the best possible prices for her supplies from Fort Worth Mercantile. She knew the prices were fair. True, items were higher here than in Galveston, but Fort Worth wasn't a port city. And as far as what she charged for her wares . . . well . . . this market wouldn't bear higher prices for tarts—of the edible variety, anyway. She was right and her father was wrong. Again. But she held her tongue. She knew he would not listen to her. He never had.

John Donovan rolled his shoulders and stretched, then glanced toward Claire's mother. "Today has been a long day and tomorrow starts early. We'd best be getting over to our rental. Pack up just what you need for tonight, Daughter. We'll fetch the rest of it tomorrow."

Claire's head jerked up. "Pack?"

Her mother spoke in a soothing tone. "Brian found us a nice little house. You needn't be concerned about leaving that Miss Blackstone without someone to share expenses. We worked it out earlier before she left to go to supper with her beau. Apparently her school has hired an additional teacher, who is expected to arrive within the next few weeks. She can move in here with Letty. Doesn't that work out nicely?"

Her head spinning, Claire didn't dare say how she thought it "worked out." Instead, she asked, "Where did you find a house to rent? And when did you find time?"

Her father launched into a description of how they'd stepped off the evening train and gone immediately to work. It had been easy to find out where she worked and lived.

"I must say I'm surprised at Lars. He should have told us he intended to return to Fort Worth. We were all quite put out with him for leaving Galveston so abruptly, especially Patrick. I daresay our boy will have a few words to say to him tomorrow. There's no excuse for his silence. Why, if we'd known he was up here taking care of you, I wouldn't have been nearly so worried."

Claire literally bit her tongue to keep from speaking out at that. *Taking care of me. Does he think I am helpless? And just what was he worried about? The success of my bakery most likely. Certainly not me.*

"So Brian found us a home and all went smoothly, except when it came to you. Where have you been, girl? Why are you quite late getting home? What foolish thing had you done to put yourself in the position to be attacked?"

"Now wait just a minute." Tye shoved to his feet. "This is ridiculous. What do you think you're doing barging in here like this and trying to take over her life?" Glancing at Claire, he added, "And why are you just sitting there swallowing it?"

John Donovan ruffled up like a bantam rooster, and Claire felt the bitter laugh bubbling up inside her. Firmly she forced it down and spoke up before her father found his tongue. "Mr. McBride, you'd best be getting back to the girls." Standing, she walked toward him, her arm extended for a handshake. "I can't thank you enough for saving me from that ruffian. I'm in your debt. Now that you've delivered me to the bosom of my family, it's best you get home to yours."

She watched the protest forming in his eyes and squeezed his hand hard. "Please, Mr. McBride. Go home."

His gaze shouted his unhappiness with the idea, but Tye did as she asked. As he took his leave, her father again expressed his appreciation to Tye for helping Claire, although this time it was offered rather grudgingly.

The door shut behind Tye, and Claire sank back into her chair, her shoulders sagging beneath the weight of her family's presence. When her father again started rambling about his plans for her bakery, she couldn't work up the energy to say a word.

". . . won't need such a big place for long," John Donovan was saying. "Once we're back on our feet, Patrick and Brian want to return to Galveston and their sweethearts. With luck, their weddings won't be delayed more than a year."

A year. Claire licked her dry lips. "How are Cynthia and Eloise?"

Peggy Donovan smiled. "The McClendon twins are well, although I daresay they are pining for your brothers. They want to—"

"Enough of that," John interrupted. "You girls can gossip later. Claire, get your things. On the way home I need you to tell me of any peculiarities I need to know concerning The Confectionary. Any customers we should refuse to sell to? Any idiosyncrasies about your equipment? How much Magic do you have in stock? I didn't see too many bottles in the shop. Do you have a supply laid in somewhere else?"

Claire's head was beginning to hurt. She'd had about all she could stand for one night. "Da, I'm tired. Can we discuss all that in the morning, please?"

"No. I don't want to have to wake you up before I leave for work."

Before *he* left for work? What about her? Slowly, Claire said, "Da, we'll have plenty of time to talk down at the bakery before it opens."

"You won't be there. Your mother will need help setting up the house. Your brothers and I will run the Donovan Confectionary from now on. You won't have to worry your head about it one little bit."

His words gave the knife in her heart a vicious twist. *Dear Lord, my father has repossessed my dream.*

BACK AT WILLOW HILL TYE checked on the Blessings, then brooded. The night felt strange and all out of kilter. Sitting here in his brother's study a nagging sense of being needed tugged at his heart. It reminded him of the intuitive link that connected him and Trace, but he finally pegged the sensation as feeling almost . . . well . . . feminine.

148

Less than five minutes later he was headed back toward Claire's.

He hoped he'd make it before her parents dragged her off to the house they'd rented. He wouldn't know where to look for her otherwise. And the one thing he knew for certain was that he wanted . . . no, he needed . . . to see Claire Donovan once more before he slept.

Striding down her street, he spied her parents coming toward him just in time to duck into the shadows. Out of sight, he followed them a short way, eavesdropping on their conversation.

"Cheeky girl," her father raged. "She's lucky I didn't lay her across my knees and beat the defiance out of her. I would have, had Miss Blackstone not returned. Don't want to air any more of our linen in public, I don't."

"Now, John," her mother said. "At least Claire is not alone. Letty Blackstone appears to be an upstanding young woman, and it's only for tonight. One more night apart from us won't hurt anything."

"Well I've a mind to hurt something. The nerve of the girl. The disrespect. Did you hear that tone in her voice? 'Why, I thought you'd disowned me,' " he mimicked. "What has come over her? Why has she changed so drastically?"

Peggy Donovan's heavy sigh winged on the wind toward Tye. "I don't know, John. I simply don't know."

"Then you're a fool," Tye muttered beneath his breath. "She grew a backbone, that's what." He quit following the parents and switched direction, going to check on Claire.

Approaching the cottage, he saw that all was dark. She must have gone to bed. Apparently Tye's hunch had been wrong. Claire wasn't in need of help. Claire was . . .

Sitting on the porch swing. Crying. And dammit, he hated it when women cried.

It felt natural—too natural—to sit down beside her and take her into his arms. She melted against him, emitting soft, sad whimpers rather than sobs. "Ah, sugar, don't. Everything will be all right."

"All right?" She pulled away from him. "My da barrels in and steals away my dream and you say everything will be all right? What world are you living in, Tye McBride. Obviously not the real one. And what are you doing here? You were supposed to go home and check on the Menaces."

"The *Blessings*, and I did," he replied without the usual steel that crept into his voice when that objectionable nickname was used. He was glad to see the starch return to her spine, so hearing the word "Menaces" didn't bother him as much as usual. "I came back to see what happened to the Claire Donovan I know. She disappeared and left a milksop in her place."

"Oh, Tye. I don't know if I can stand up to them again. I tried a little tonight, but it is so hard."

She rose from the swing and walked away from him, down the front porch steps and out into the yard. Moonlight illuminated her expression, revealing the tracks of her tears. She looked so damned sad that had her father or brothers been standing by, Tye would have decked them.

"I can't believe he's taking my bakery."

He followed her off the porch. "I can't believe you are going to let them."

"You don't understand."

"Then explain."

"I'm not certain I understand everything myself."

"Maybe telling me will help you get it straight in your head."

Wrapping her arms around herself, she nodded. "I guess it's simple enough, really. They are my family and I love them. My refusal to marry Reid led them into bankruptcy. I used Da's money to open The Confectionary. I see why he thinks he has the right to come in and take over."

"And you, Claire? What do you think? Do you think he has that right?"

She paused a long moment before saying, "No. No, I don't. Not if he intends to shove me aside. I'll admit to sharing some of the responsibility for the failure of the family business, but I'm no more to blame than the rest of them. If Brian and Patrick hadn't lobbied so hard to have their own bakeries, Da wouldn't have taken out those loans. But it was his decision to borrow the money. No one else's. Maybe fathers throughout history have sacrificed their daughters on the altar of matrimony in the interests of the clan, but darn it, this isn't the Old Country. It was wrong of them to expect me to marry a man I didn't love, for money. I'm no whore, by God."

Backbone and starch. Good girl. "Now you're talking."

She was also marching back and forth, her voice rising with every word. The woman had passion in her. No denying it.

"Why is it that just because I'm a girl, I don't count as much as the boys? I have hopes and dreams, too. Why are theirs more important than mine?"

"They're not."

She whirled on Tye. "Tell that to my father, would you? And to my mother and brothers, too. They certainly aren't in on that little secret." She stepped closer, staring up at him. "You have sisters. Are they ignored in favor of the boys?"

Tye laughed at the idea. "No, that's not the case at all. My sisters have always run the roost at Oak Grove. Drove me and Trace nuts when we were growing up."

"Well, it's not that way in my family. You should have heard my father after you left, Tye. I built The Confectionary from nothing, and does he acknowledge my accomplishment? No. He criticizes how much Magic I have in stock. How dare he do this? How dare he ignore me and my accomplishments just because my plumbing is different from Brian's and Patrick's? How dare he steal my shop from me in one breath, then tell me he loves me in another?"

Tye cleared his throat "He'll dare as long as you let him, girl.

151

You stood up to him before by running away from your wedding. You gonna stand up to him this time?"

The question doused her fire like a pail of cold water. He again saw the sparkle of tears in her eyes as she looked at him and said, "How can I? Did you see my father's pain when he admitted to losing the business? They are bankrupt, Tye. They have no place to go. What else can I do?"

"I'm not saying throw them out. I'm saying stand and fight for what you want. You want to share The Confectionary with them, then fine. The key word there is share. Don't let them shove you aside. You are a strong woman, Claire. Be strong around them. Show up at the bakery same time as always. Your hard work has earned you that right. Don't give it away for lack of mettle to stand up to your pa. You can do it. You've done it before."

"Once," she said sullenly.

"Twice. You're still here tonight, aren't you, and not at their rental. Make a run at three. Show up at work in the morning and don't let them send you home."

He watched her think about it, watched the idea take hold and grow. "It's hard, Tye."

He nodded. "Most things worthwhile are hard."

"But I can fight for what I want."

"Darn straight, you can. I'll give you one more hint, and then I'd best be getting home. Work on your mother, Claire. I watched her while your pa was going at it. I think the right kind of convincing might bring her over to your side. If you get her standing with you, that might be all you'll need."

Claire spat a laugh. "My mother take a stand against my father? You'd best get to bed, Tye, you're sounding delirious. That will never happen."

"You never know, girl. Folks said Maribeth wouldn't win the spelling bee, either."

"Why, Tye McBride, are you telling me to cheat?"

He shrugged and tipped his nonexistent hat. "Like the saying goes, All is fair in love and war. Seems to me like this business with your family is a little bit of both."

EMMA VIVIDLY RECALLED the last time she'd visited Hell's Half Acre. That was the day that marked the beginning of their papa's courtship of Jenny Fortune, who was now their new mama. The Acre hadn't been half so scary then as it was tonight. Of course, that last trip had been taken in the daylight, not during these shadowed hues of night.

Tinny piano music and laughter spilled out onto the streets, surrounding the sisters as they made their way deeper into the Acre. The girls walked single file with Emma leading the way, Maribeth behind, and Katrina in the middle. Kat had a death grip on the back of Emma's shirt, and Maribeth's hold on the pouch containing the money they'd taken from Papa's safe looked just as fierce. "Papa would blister our behinds if he knew what we were up to," she grumbled. "I can't believe we're doing this."

"Shush!" Emma held up a hand for them to halt. Then, with her heart sitting like a lump in her throat, she yanked her youngest sister toward a nearby horse trough, gesturing that they should hide.

A few seconds later a man came stumbling toward them out of the darkness. He smelled of cigar and sweet perfume, and Emma held her breath until the stink of him dispersed on the warm nighttime air. She made them wait for another seemingly interminable minute before they resumed their trek through the Acre. Their destination was one of the tiny single-room houses called cribs on Rusk Street. According to their friend Casey Tate, that was where Madame LaRue sold her wares.

They had never actually met Madam LaRue, but Casey had told them all about her. She was the one who had sold him Spike, the fortune-teller fish. Emma had been intrigued by the idea of visiting her shop ever since they first learned about it, but up until now, nothing had been worth defying their father to such an extent as to risk a trip into the Acre. Now, though, they were dealing with Uncle Tye's future happiness.

They turned the corner onto Rusk Street, and Emma almost immediately spied the red-and-purple glass lanterns Casey had told them to watch for halfway down the block. "What time is it?" Maribeth whispered.

Katrina pulled a watch from her pocket. "Twelve-fifteen."

Maribeth met Emma's gaze, and the girls nodded at one another. Madam LaRue opened for business only between the hours of midnight and three A.M. Casey hadn't been able to tell them why, but Emma suspected the woman might have another job during the day. After all, how much work could a black-magic priestess find in Fort Worth, Texas?

After hiding from two more pedestrians, the girls finally made their way to Madam LaRue's doorway. Sucking in a breath, Emma linked hands first with Katrina, then Maribeth, and stepped inside.

A cloying scent of incense in the air made Emma want to sneeze. Katrina spoke softly out the side of her mouth. "Ooh, it stinks in here. Reminds me of the time when Papa punished us by making us launder the tablecloths from the End-of-the-Line Saloon."

Emma only nodded in reply as she gazed in wonder and amazement at the boxes and jars occupying the shelves that lined the walls. The items hanging from the ceiling gave her a start: dead animals. Stuffed dead animals, she realized with some relief. Two chickens, a rooster. Oh, yuck, a hog's head. She shivered a grimace.

Dragging her gaze from the ceiling, Emma focused on the imposing figure seated behind a black lacquered desk. Uneasiness sputtered through her. The woman wore a white silk turban and a flowing emerald-green robe. Bright red paint stained her fleshy cheeks and lips. Vivid blue colored the skin above brown eyes framed by the thickest, blackest lashes Emma had ever seen. Big gold hoops decorated her ears, and when she lifted her hand to tap a finger against her lips, Emma spied rings adorning each of her fingers and even her thumb.

"She is more colors than a wildflower field," Katrina said with awe, stepping forward for a better look.

"I shall consider that a compliment," Madam LaRue replied, her voice a soft, whispery hiss. "Now tell me, what quest brings three foolish children to my emporium during the talons of the night?"

Talons of the night? A shiver raced up Emma's spine, but she swallowed hard and loudly cleared her throat. "Hello, Madam LaRue. My name is Emma McBride and these are my sisters, Maribeth and Katrina."

Bells sewn to the trim on the woman's sleeves tinkled as she clasped her hands atop the table. "The McBride Menaces, of course. I have long anticipated your arrival."

Emma glanced at Mari, then asked, "Why?"

Again the bells sounded as Madam LaRue waved, her long, scarlet-painted fingernails flashing in the lamplight. "Your visit was foretold."

"Did you see us in your crystal ball?" Kat asked, her eyes wide with excitement. "Or maybe you have another fortune-teller fish other than Spike?"

"No." She cackled a laugh. "Your friend Casey suspected you might come."

"Oh." Katrina's face fell with disappointment. Emma knew she had long found the idea of a crystal ball intriguing.

Madam LaRue smiled. "He didn't tell me why you would visit me, however. Should I cast the Celtic stones and learn for myself, or do you wish to tell me?"

As the black-magic priestess removed a tiny box containing

three small, highly polished stones, Emma shook her head. "We shouldn't waste time. We should get it and go."

"No," Katrina protested. "Let's see if she can guess what we're here to buy. It'll be fun."

Maribeth agreed with Kat and they stepped toward the table. Keeping a wary eye on the ceiling, Emma followed, positioning herself so that she didn't stand beneath the hog's head. If it slobbered on her she'd have heart palpitations.

Madame LaRue lifted the stones from the box and brought them toward her face. Pursing her painted lips, she blew on them, then recited what sounded like an incantation. At least, Emma thought it was an incantation. The rhythms in her voice sounded similar to her own when she asked Spike for answers.

She shook the rocks, then flung them like dice across the table. When they rolled to rest, she leaned over them, studying the surfaces.

"What do you see?"

"I see you brought cash with you to pay for my services."

Kat nodded. "That's right. Mari won it in the spelling bee, and we're borrowing it from the homeless dogs until we can earn enough to replace it. We have thirty dollars. We need to save some of it for Miss Blackstone's vase, but it should be enough because Casey told us you charged twenty dollars for—"

"Don't tell her," Emma said. "We're trying to get her to guess, remember?"

Madam LaRue flicked Emma a sharp-eyed glance. "The stones tell me you've come here to purchase a love potion; your sister didn't need to say it."

"Wow." Katrina leaned over the table. "Where does it say it? I can't see."

"You should be happy you are blind to the Celtic stones," Madam LaRue said, rising from her seat "You are not versed in the black arts. Such sight could blind you."

Mari yanked her little sister away from the table. "Get back here, Kat."

With a wicked laugh, the black-magic priestess turned to the shelves behind her. "You do prefer a potion to a spell, am I right?"

"Yes," Emma said. "We plan to pour it into sweet iced tea we'll give to our uncle and the woman we want him to love."

Maribeth piped up. "That won't hurt it, will it? Sweet tea won't interfere with its magic?"

Madam LaRue smiled as she picked a small bottle from the shelf and turned around. She set it on the table with a flourish and said, "No, iced tea won't damage the love potion at all. In fact, I suspect the flavors will complement. Your money, child?"

Maribeth frowned. "Twenty dollars is a whole lot of money. That looks like an awful tiny bottle to be worth twenty dollars."

"And how much is your uncle's happiness worth to you?"

Man opened the bag, removed the bills, and counted them out carefully as Emma reached for the love potion. She tilted the clear glass bottle to one side, studying the dark, toffee-colored liquid. "How many doses is this? How much do we use?"

"One spoonful per glass is enough," Madam answered, scooping up the money and sticking it down into her bodice.

Emma contemplated the bottle, and her gaze must have given her thoughts away because Maribeth snapped, "Don't. You're not going to use it on Casey Tate, Emma McBride. You're too young for love potions."

A quick-thinking businesswoman, the priestess turned back to her inventory, this time removing a pink crystal from a jar. "This is a love charm, a more appropriate tool for a young woman your age. It's two dollars."

"Mari?" Emma asked.

Mari snorted and dug into the money pouch for the coins. "Don't forget we have to save four dollars for Miss Blackstone's vase."

After that, nothing would do but to buy something for Kat,

too, so they waited another five minutes while Madam LaRue cast an arithmetic spell over the youngest sister. Emma had almost fainted when the priestess glanced up at the animals hanging above their heads.

Thankfully, Madam LaRue chose a stuffed owl to use in her spell, not the hog, like Emma had feared. Finally, to her relief, they finished their business and departed the shop.

"I feel smarter already," Kat said, her chin lifted smugly in the air. "Wasn't Madam LaRue wonderful?"

Maribeth yanked her sister into the shadows and out of the streetlamp's glare. "I sure hope she's not a fake, and the whole spelling bee plan wasn't a waste of time."

"A fake!" Kat protested. "Why would you say that? You saw her read the stones and learn what we came for. You're not very nice to call her a fake, Maribeth McBride."

"I didn't call her a fake. I said I hoped she wasn't one. She could have figured out why we were there if this love potion is the only thing she sells for twenty dollars."

"I believe in her," Emma said. "Casey says she has the power and that's good enough for me."

"Someone's coming," Kat said, and they flattened themselves against a wall of a small house similar to Madam LaRue's. From inside, Emma heard a woman moan and a man groan, and something about the sounds made her put protective hands over Katrina's ears. A group of laughing cowboys passed their hiding place, followed by a man weaving his way up the street. Emma recognized the banker, Mr. Reece, and slowly shook her head. When Papa got home she'd have to tell him to count his money closely next time he dealt with Fort Worth National.

Emma jumped at the pop of a cork being released beside her. "Mari, what are you doing?" she whispered fiercely.

"I want to see what it smells like."

"Well, don't taste it, whatever you do." Good heavens, Emma

thought. All she needed was a sister in love with Mr. Reece. "I'm not stupid. I just want to . . . oh my."

"Oh my, what?"

"The smell."

"Is it awful?"

"No, it's wonderful. Really wonderful. Smell it, Em."

Maribeth shoved the bottle beneath her nose, and Emma took a whiff. So surprised was she that she forgot to keep her voice down. "My stars. This love potion smells exactly like Miss Donovan's Magic."

Then Emma forgot all about the love potion when a man's voice came out of the shadows.

"Well, well, well. What have we here?"

Emma knew the voice. She knew the voice and the stink of whiskey that swirled around them. Big Jack Bailey. Their mother's gravest enemy. The man who shot Uncle Tye and almost killed Mama and the baby growing in her tummy. "Run, sisters!"

Maribeth jerked the love potion away from Emma's nose and slammed the cork back into it even as her feet took off running. Emma pushed Katrina forward, following right on her heels. For the space of a heartbeat she thought they had safely escaped, but the painful yank at her scalp told her he'd caught her pigtail. He tugged her backward, and she fell at his feet. Gazing upward, all she could see of his face was the eerie gleam of his eyes. Her heart leapt to her throat.

"The M-M-McBride M-Menaces. This must be my l- l-lucky day."

The way Big Jack slurred out his words cued Emma to the fact he was drunk. That and the eye-watering stink of whiskey. When he reached for the gun at his side and placed its barrel against her temple, she almost wet her pants.

The sounds coming from the house escalated, and Emma knew the people inside didn't hear the drama taking place on the other side of the wall. Her gaze darted up the street, then down, as she prayed to see another pedestrian.

Big Jack growled. "The two of you over there behind the water barrel. I see you hiding. Don't you know it's bad luck to use a rain barrel for anything but catching water? Dries up rain for six weeks, it does. Now, you two get over here so I don't have to hurt your sister. It's an omen you fell into my hands tonight of all nights. An omen. I owe your new mama, you know. She brought grief to my family. Y'all bein' here now is a sign I can finally pay her back."

He gave Emma's hair a vicious yank, and she yelped.

"Don't hurt our sister!" Maribeth cried from behind the water barrel.

"Then get your butts over here."

Slowly Maribeth and Katrina did as he asked. Emma heard Kat crying softly, and she wanted to yell at them to run. But to her shame, she couldn't force her lips to form the words.

Big Jack Bailey's gun hand remained steady, pointed to kill, as he said, "Come along. My wagon is back in the alley. Menaces, we're going for a ride."

EARLY-MORNING SUNLIGHT PAINTED the eastern sky a candy-colored pink-and-gold when the welcome bell at The Confectionary rang with a jarring clang. "Claire!"

Her hands sticky with bread dough, she jerked her head toward the front of the shop. *Tye?* He sounded panicked.

She heard Brian say, "Hey, you can't go back there."

As she reached for a towel to wipe her hands, he rushed through the door. Fear knifed through her as she stared up into his anxious face. "What is it, Tye?"

"The girls," he panted, his expression tight. "Please tell me they're here, that you've seen them."

She shook her head. "I'm sorry, no."

His hands curled into fists. "Not at all this morning? Or last night?"

Claire's father broke the silence he'd maintained since she had showed up at The Confectionary three hours earlier and refused to leave. "What is the reason for this disturbance? We have business here to run."

She ignored her father and her brothers and asked, "Last night? Goodness, Tye, what's happened? I haven't seen the girls since they told me good night and went up to bed."

He mouthed a curse, then heaved a heavy sigh, dragging a hand down his face. She could barely make out the words he muttered. "I don't know what made me think I could take care of those children."

She grabbed him by the shoulder and pulled him out the back door, away from the Donovan males. "What happened? Tell me."

A mockingbird sang from its rooftop perch as Tye clenched his fists, then flexed his fingers, then clenched his fists again. "I checked on them both times I came home last night. I saw three lumps under the covers and thought everything was fine. I should have known better. I had that feeling, but I thought it was you. And Ralph slept on the back porch last night instead of in Maribeth's bed like usual. It slipped right on by me at the time. When I went to get them up for school this morning, I found pillows instead of people beneath the blankets. I searched the house. I searched the yard. I went to their school and the apartment and your shop. Where else should I look?"

Oh, no. Poor man. "Have they ever gone missing before?"

"Not from me, but I hear they did it to Trace a number of times." He caught Claire's arm and squeezed it. "The train station. Oh God, Claire, they've run away. That's what they needed the money for."

As he dropped her arm and pivoted toward the end of the alley, Claire said, "Wait. You're jumping to conclusions. This is probably just one of their pranks and they'll turn up safe and sound back at Willow Hill any time. As for the money, did you check the safe? Was it missing?"

"I didn't think of it." He grimaced and added, "I should have checked their room for clues, too. Trace said whenever they run off, they almost always leave something lying around that tells him where to look." His manner distracted, he leaned over and kissed her cheek. "Thanks, Claire."

As Tye took off down the alley in a loping run, she rushed back inside to wash her hands and strip off her apron. Those Menaces, God bless them, had offered her the perfect distraction from her own problems. She could use a break from the wall of silence the Donovans deployed as their weapon of choice this morning. She seriously doubted the girls were in danger. In fact, they probably had guessed their Uncle Tye was onto their little spelling bee caper and had chosen to go into hiding.

Claire knew Tye would worry until they were home safe and sound. He had helped her last night. As friend, neighbor, and woman he'd kissed senseless on his front porch, she could do nothing less than return the favor today.

She made quick time to Willow Hill. Under the circumstances, she didn't bother to knock, but went straight inside and trailed the sounds of a search to Trace McBride's office. Tye stood inside in front of an opened wall safe. The money bag Claire recognized from the night before lay open, its contents spilled across the desk-top. Tye's head was bent as he counted the money. When he finished, he sighed and lifted his head.

Claire asked, "Is it all there?"

"I think some of it's missing, but I can't remember the exact amount."

She did. She always remembered money. "Three hundred twenty-seven dollars and sixty-four cents."

Tye dragged his fingers through his hair. "Then thirty dollars is missing. What would they want with thirty dollars?"

Claire shook her head, baffled.

For a long moment Tye's harsh breathing and the tick of the mantel clock were the only sounds heard in the study. Then he swiped a hand across the desktop, sending bills flying and coins pinging to the floor. "Why did I think I was good enough to care for those precious little girls?"

Ralph bounded into the room and headed directly for Tye. He scooped the whining pup off the floor and absently scratched him behind the ears.

A thought occurred to Claire and she asked, "Did you check the mercantile? A music box in the window had Emma fascinated and that's all she talked about one day last week in The Confectionary."

"No," Tye replied. "I didn't go that far downtown. That's a good idea. I'll check the mercantile and every store on Main Street after I search their rooms. Maybe we could write out handbills to put up, too. Surely someone in this town has seen them."

"I'm sure they're fine. They're just up to some mischief and you'll discover what that is any time now." Claire's lips twisted in a sad smile as she watched Ralph crawl up Tye's chest and lick him on the cheek. She wondered just who was comforting whom.

"You're probably right," Tye said, his gaze turning hopeful. "Tell you what, though. Would you come upstairs with me first? Perhaps a pair of feminine eyes would spy something important I might overlook."

She followed him out of the office and up the stairs. Tye paused outside a bedroom door, explaining, "This is Emma's room. They spend most of their time here. This month, anyway. Last month it was Maribeth's. Trace says they all wanted their own rooms until they got them. It's musical beds around here most nights, and I thought it peculiar when I came to wake them. It was my first clue something was wrong; they never stay in the same bed all night long."

Emma's room was a feminine fantasy. Pink organdy decorated

the windows and draped the bed. Pink rosebuds adorned the wallpaper. Beautifully dressed china dolls stood on shelves that lined one wall. Claire wondered if Jenny McBride had sewn them for her stepdaughter.

Tye disturbed her musings by saying, "Emma is the planner of the three. If any clue as to what they're up to does exist I expect we'll find it here."

Claire took a seat at the vanity, pulled open a drawer, and considered the items inside. A hairbrush, a comb. Three pennies, a doll's dress, and a bead necklace. Nothing out of the ordinary there.

Tye crossed to a rosewood wardrobe and pulled open the door. As he poked and prodded among the clothes, Claire heard him mutter, "I should have paid closer attention to the clothes they wear. I can't tell if anything is missing. I should know what they're wearing. The girls are my responsibility."

Claire prayed they'd find a clue as to the Menaces' whereabouts soon. She expected they'd turn up somewhere with a thirty-dollar prize of one sort or another hidden among their petticoats. In the meantime, however, Tye needed some reassurance. He looked as if he'd aged ten years overnight.

He finished his search of the wardrobe and moved to the window seat where a stack of pillows and books made a cozy little reading area. Claire continued her exploration of the vanity, pausing over the train schedule cut from the newspaper. Her pulse sped up. Surely this couldn't be the clue they were looking for. Surely the Menaces hadn't truly run off. What reason would they have for doing so? They certainly hadn't appeared upset or in distress the previous night when they said good night.

Tye whispered an ugly epithet, catching Claire's attention. He'd been searching a bookcase and now half a dozen books sat stacked beside him on a round table. In his hands he held a small cedar box, and even as she watched, it slid from his hands and fell to the floor with a bang, followed by a rain of white paper. But not all the paper fell. Tye held on to one sheet. Held on to it and crushed it, his knuckles gone white from the force of his grip.

"What is it?" she asked.

"Trouble," he replied, his voice hoarse.

Crinkling the sheet into a ball, he drew back his arm and flung the paper at the trash can sitting in one corner. Then he slumped down onto the window seat and buried his face in his hands. "Serious trouble this time, I'm afraid. Thirty dollars, these letters, and three girls with more guts than good sense. I wonder how long this has been going on?"

"What have they done?" When Tye finally met her gaze, Claire swallowed a gasp. She'd never seen such fear on a man's face.

"I think I just found Pandora's box, Claire." He nodded toward the trash can. "By the looks of it, the girls have taken the lid off. That was a letter to Trace, one of a pile from a Pandora that goes by the name of West. Beatrice West. She's wicked and evil." In a hollow voice he added, "And I'm afraid she has my Blessings.

CHAPTER 10

BAD LUCK ALWAYS COMES IN THREES.

TYE'S HEART pounded like a locomotive's pistons. He propped his elbows on his knees and let his head hang low. The letter had been an explosive charge that blew his past right into his present.

"Who is Beatrice West?"

Old pain and new fear combined to loosen his tongue and allow one of the skeletons to tumble from the McBride family closet. "The Blessings' grandmother. Their blood grandmother."

"Your mother?"

"No. Constance's mother. It looks like she wrote to my brother and an attorney forwarded the letters. Constance left them property. I guess Trace was forced to deal in some way."

"And Constance is . . . ?"

Tye shuddered as the scene flashed before his eyes. *Trace and Constance struggling. The sound of the shot. The dazed look on Trace's face as he stared at the blood soaking his hands. The hatred blazing in his eyes when he turned and looked at Tye.*

"Was," he croaked. "Constance was the girls' mother. She's dead."

Claire nodded. "I knew your brother had been a widower before he remarried. But the only grandmother I've ever heard the girls refer to was Jenny's mother. Isn't she traveling in Europe at the moment?"

"Yeah. That's Monique. The girls have never met Beatrice."

"So the letters are from the girls' grandmother? She lives far away?"

He shook his head. "New Orleans. The girls must have stumbled across them somehow. I'll bet Trace had them locked in his safe and they found them there. We know they have the combination, and Trace would never have mentioned Beatrice to the Blessings himself."

"Why not?"

He didn't have the time or the inclination to explain the entire story. One couldn't summarize extortion, adultery, kidnapping, and betrayal in a few sentences. "I guess bad blood between the families is the simplest way to explain."

She gestured toward the letter. "So why is that trouble? Does she threaten the children somehow?"

Almost against his will, Tye smoothed out the paper and scanned the page. His anxiety rose another notch when he reread one particular sentence. "She wants to see them." Looking up, he shot a worried look toward Claire and voiced the fear ricocheting around his head like a bullet. "God, Claire. You don't think they've run off to New Orleans to visit her."

Claire's reaction wasn't at all what he had hoped to see. She winced as she reached into one of the vanity's drawers and removed a scrap of newspaper. "I found this. It's a train schedule, Tye. But there are many reasons Emma might have a train schedule."

"And I don't like any of them." His heart sank to somewhere around his knees as he stood and headed for the door. "I'll check with the ticket agent and see if they bought fares. Of course, it's more likely they hopped a boxcar. They've done that before."

"But thirty dollars . . ." Claire said, following behind him.

"Could be spending money. It's a nice round amount. Not

much, but to those three, ten dollars apiece probably sounds like a fortune."

They didn't speak as they made their way into town, then caught the trolley for the ride down Main to the railroad depot. Once they took their seats, Claire reached over and clasped his hand in silent comfort. He accepted it gratefully.

Tye was no stranger to fear. Over the course of more than three decades of life he'd learned its different flavors, had thought he'd tasted them all. But the black metallic taste coating his mouth right then was nauseatingly new to him. Fear for the children. Fear of failing the children. Fear of hurting his brother again.

Please, God, let them be all right.

Claire said, "I traveled by myself on the train from Galveston here to Fort Worth, of course. I was pleasantly surprised how polite my fellow passengers were. I visited with a pair of the nicest elderly women between Houston and Dallas. When they saw I was alone they basically took me under their wings."

He squeezed her hand to let her know he recognized her effort, but at the moment he couldn't push any words past the lump blocking his throat.

At the depot he tracked down the ticket agent, who told them he had not seen the McBride Menaces around the station in ages, and especially not this morning before the departure of the day's first train. Tye checked with the porters, the drivers of carriages for hire, and even the laundress who kept a heated kettle opposite the train yard for travelers' convenience.

No one had seen his nieces.

"As much as I hate to, I guess I should telegraph the Wests," Tye told Claire. "Just in case the Blessings stowed away."

"Yes," she agreed. "While you're doing that, I'll stop by The Confectionary and ask my menfolk to help search. If the McBride girls are still in Fort Worth, the Donovan boys will find them."

"You sound so confident."

"I am confident. After all, my family found me, didn't they?"

～

A WARM PRAIRIE wind swept over and around the wagon as Katrina said to Emma, "Do you think he's dead?"

Emma eyed the man slumped across the buckboard's seat and shook her head. "I don't think so. Every once in a while I think I see his chest move."

"He sure stinks enough to be dead," Maribeth observed, inching her way toward the back of the wagon— not an easy feat considering she was bound hands and ankles by a sturdy rope.

Katrina lifted her hands, tied at the wrists, to scratch her nose. "It's the whiskey. Papa used to smell like that sometimes when he came home from the End of the Line."

Maribeth replied, "Except when Papa smelled that way it was because someone had poured whiskey on his clothes, not down his throat."

The three of them shared a knowing look. Emma and her sisters had all been happy that fall when their father had sold his lucrative saloon and returned to the more respectable profession of architecture. Not that they cared about respectability, they simply liked having him home at night.

Emma dropped her head back to rest it against the rough wagon slats and noted a movement in the sky. A big black buzzard circled lazily above them.

"I'm scared, Emmie," Katrina said in a little voice.

"I know. But we'll be all right, you'll see. Uncle Tye will come save us."

"Yeah," Maribeth glumly interjected. "He'll come save us, and then he'll kill us for doing what we did. Of course, we might starve to death before he finds us. Em, your stomach is growling louder than mine."

Katrina swelled up in a pout. "I'm hungry, too. And tired. We didn't sleep very long, did we sisters? And you know what? Even if Uncle Tye is really mad when he finds us I hope he hurries. I need to pee bad."

As Emma reached over and gave Katrina's knee a comforting pat, she spied a second and then a third bird joining the first. She wished her sisters wouldn't talk about hunger when buzzards circled above.

She wasn't as confident in their situation as she had let on. Big Jack Bailey had made all kinds of ugly threats as he'd driven the buckboard out onto the night-black prairie before passing out in a drunken stupor. Emma prayed it had been the whiskey talking, that he wouldn't try to carry out his wicked promises upon awakening. But the bad blood that existed between Big Jack and the McBride family made her worry it might be more than just talk.

The trouble had started the year before, back before Mama married Papa. Big Jack had hired Mama to design the most beautiful wedding dress ever created for his daughters to wear at their upcoming weddings. He was a superstitious fool, and when his daughters all suffered accidents after having worn the gown Mama had sewn, he blamed the dress. Then, when his son died while seeking revenge against Mama, Big Jack went crazy. He'd kidnapped Mama and Uncle Tye—thinking he was Papa because the twins look so much alike—and when Uncle Tye was protecting Mama, Big Jack shot him in the shoulder. But everything turned out all right when Mama outsmarted Big Jack by threatening to put a curse on his family. Because of The Bad Luck Wedding Dress, Big Jack had believed her.

Now it looked as if he'd changed his mind.

"Emmie, I need out of this wagon." A tear rolled down Katrina's cheek. "I'm about to wet my bloomers. And the sun's gonna burn us to crispy critters if we stay here like this all day. We should have worn our bonnets."

Sarcasm riddled Maribeth's voice as she said, "Well, we were fools not to guess we'd be kidnapped and stranded Lord-only-knows-where on the prairie. We should have known to bring our bonnets with us when we snuck out of Willow Hill at midnight."

Emma eyed Big Jack, then the buzzards, then the sun, and finally her sisters. "Set your legs over here, Kat.

Now that the sun is up enough for me to see what I'm doing, I'll try to pick apart the knot. Mari, why don't you work on yours, too."

"I already have been trying," Maribeth protested. "I'm tied up tighter than a fat lady's corset."

So was Emma. In fact, the rope around her wrists was so tight her hands had gone numb, and that made the work on her sister's ropes all the more difficult. She plucked and pulled until her fingers screamed with pain, but finally the knot gave and Katrina's rope fell free.

The youngest girl flexed her fingers and cried, "Yeow! It feels like I've got a hundred needles stuck in me."

Necessity made her ignore the pain as blood rushed back into her hands. With ankles still bound, and at Emma's direction, she hopped to the front of the wagon, bent over Big Jack's motionless body, and removed the gleaming Bowie knife from its sheath.

"Now, be careful," Emma said as Kat started slicing at the rope around her ankles. "Don't cut yourself."

"I won't."

She didn't. Ten minutes later, the three girls stood a short distance away from the wagon, their wrists and ankles sore, their mouths thirsty, and their stomachs growling. But at least their bladders felt better.

Maribeth set down the shotgun she'd confiscated from Big Jack and raised her arms above her head for a good long stretch. "What do you think, Em? Should we roll Big Jack out of the wagon and drive it back to town?"

Emma pointed the Colt revolver she'd taken from the captor's holster toward the circling buzzards. "I'd say yes if we had any clue what direction to go. The horse wandered for who knows how many hours without someone at the reins."

"Are we lost?" Katrina asked around the thumb stuck in her mouth.

"Well . . ." Emma said. "Once the clouds covered up the stars I lost all track of the direction we traveled."

"Then we're as lost as an outhouse in fog," Maribeth observed, studying the countryside as she turned in a slow circle. "If we go the wrong way, we could be lost on the prairie for days. Even weeks!" She looked at Emma. "What do you think, Emma? What do we do next? Have you come up with a plan?"

"I have a plan," Katrina said, perking up. She pointed toward the bottle peeking out of the top of Maribeth's dress pocket. "We can dose him up with love potion. If he is in love with us, he'll do whatever we want. We'll make him take us home. What do you think, Em?"

Emma nibbled at her lower lip and considered her youngest sister's suggestion. Slowly she shook her head. "I don't know, Kat. It's a good idea, but I'm a bit concerned at the idea of Big Jack Bailey being in love with us. What if he wanted to marry us?"

"Yuck," Kat said, shuddering. "Never mind. I don't like that plan after all. Do you have another one in mind?"

Emma nodded slowly. "It's not much of one, I'm afraid, and a lot depends on Big Jack's mood once he wakes up. But it's the best I can do at the moment."

Once she explained, her sisters pitched in and followed her directions. The hardest part proved to be rolling Big Jack from the wagon seat down into the back of the buckboard. "Talk about dead weight," Maribeth muttered.

Emma took the reins and ordered the grazing horse forward toward the tree line Maribeth had pointed out along the western horizon. Soon enough, they found a stream. Once the girls and the horse had drunk their fill of the sweet, refreshing water, Emma retrieved the wool blanket from the back of the buckboard and dipped it in the stream.

The wet blanket did the trick. Moments later Big Jack Bailey came awake spouting a rousing stream of curses.

Emma and Mari knelt on the buckboard's seat facing the back of the wagon, their guns aimed at the rancher. Katrina knelt beside them, gripping the handle of the knife.

Bailey groaned and tried to sit up. He couldn't. "Son of a bitch! I'm all tied up!"

"Yep." Maribeth pointed the Colt at his chest. "You're tied up, and you're gonna stay that way until you direct us back to town. Our knots are real good, too. Better than yours. Papa taught us. You'll be wasting your time if you try to work them loose."

"You!" He gasped. "The three of you! The McBride Menaces." Lying on his stomach, the rancher moaned pitiably against the bed of the wagon. "Oh, no. Not you. I thought last night was all a dream, a nightmare."

"It was a nightmare," Maribeth snapped. "Our nightmare. You kidnapped us, Mr. Big Jack, and you got us lost. That was not a smart thing to do. Now you have to tell us how to get home."

"Kidnapped? Oh Lord, the curse!" The big man actually blubbered. "Listen to me, girls. I didn't mean to. It was all an accident. I never intended to have anything to do with your family again."

At his reaction, Emma relaxed a little bit. "Then why did you do it?"

"I don't know! I don't remember." Bailey lifted his head, and his wild eyes met her gaze. "Wait a minute. Yes, I do. I remember now. I looked at the moon through the bushes. That's what did it I drank a little too much down at the Snake Pit and I was walking it oft when I slipped and fell. There it was—the moon shining through the holly. That's what brought on the bad luck."

"Bad luck?" Maribeth frowned in confusion.

"Getting tangled up with the likes of the McBride Menaces,"

he moaned. "I no sooner climbed to my feet than the three of you appeared."

Emma's mouth dropped open as she eyed Big Jack incredulously. He was well known for being the most superstitious person in a superstitious town, but moon shining through holly bringing bad luck? How ridiculous!

Big Jack levered himself over onto his back and shut his eyes against the sun. "I know your mama is out of town, but curses don't need proximity to work. She can't find out what's happened. We can't let her find out."

Maribeth nudged Emma's sleeve. "That would probably be best for us, too. Think of what she'd do to us. Think of what *Papa* would do to us. Uncle Tye is one thing, but Papa? Our hind ends wouldn't be worth sitting on for years."

Slowly Emma nodded, whispering in reply, "Actually, I'm afraid that this time we might have crossed the line, even with Uncle Tye. He's bound to be worried sick about us by now, and if he learns about the spelling bee plan and the love potion, well . . . he is Papa's twin brother, after all."

"We're doomed," Maribeth declared.

"Oh, I hurt," Bailey groaned. "My body. My head. I have a herd of cattle running through it How long was I out?"

"It's going on mid-morning now."

He muttered something beneath his breath. "Someone will have missed you?"

"Yes."

"Damn."

Emma thought the word summed up the situation quite well.

"Wait a minute." Puzzlement stole through his voice as he cocked open one eye and said, "My bad luck aside, what were the three of you doing down in Hell's Half Acre that time of night? That's no place for young children. Why, I'd have walloped my girls if they'd pulled a stunt like that. What were you up to?"

"We were visiting Madam LaRue," Katrina explained before

Emma managed to clamp her hand over her younger sister's mouth to shut her up.

"The witch. I should have guessed. What mischief are y'all up to now? I reckon without your stepmother around to practice her voodoo, you need a substitute."

"Don't you talk bad about my mama," Katrina warned, lifting the knife in an unspoken threat.

Jack Bailey scowled at the youngest McBride, then addressed Emma. "Look, I've admitted this was all a mistake, so you can lower the weapons and untie me. We need to work together. We all need to get y'all back to town in such a way that the adults in your family don't find out what happened. We need a plan, a story. Let's start thinking of one, all right?"

Emma scowled at him. "Why should we trust you?"

"Because if we don't work this right, you'll be in as much trouble as I am. Think about it. What would your folks do if they knew I'd found you haunting Hell's Half Acre after midnight?"

The three sisters met each other's gazes, communicating wordlessly. After a moment Maribeth lowered the Colt and massaged her aching arm with her free hand. "You won't fight letting us go?"

"Of course not. I don't want to cause you any harm. You're little girls. Little *McBride* girls. I want you to go home." He had the nerve to look offended as he added, "What kind of man do you think I am?"

"You're a bad man," Katrina said, dropping the knife onto the wagon seat and folding her arms in a huff. "You hurt our Uncle Tye and our mama."

Big Jack closed his eyes at that. For a long moment the only sound to be heard was Kat's indignant sniff and the horse's nicker. Then the rancher spoke in a troubled tone. "It was wrong of me. I know that. But then I was caught up in grief for my son. I'm through the worst of that now. Losing my boy, and the troubles my daughters had, well, it changed me. I've reformed."

Maribeth gave a snort of disbelief. "If you reformed, then how come you stole us?"

"It wasn't my fault. I told you that. It was bad luck."

"I don't think it was bad luck," Katrina stated. "Bad luck is good for us. The Bad Luck Wedding Dress brought us a new mother, so now it's the Good Luck Wedding Dress. I can't figure out anything good about being here with you. You tied us up and got us lost. I'm hungry. You are a bad, mean man, Mr. Big Jack."

"All right, I'm bad and I'm mean," he said, impatience heavy in his voice. "But we're not lost. We can't be lost." He struggled to sit up and finally managed to get his head above the wagon's side slats.

The girls watched silently as he slowly panned his head around. "Oh, Lord," he muttered.

"What is it?" Emma asked, fearing she already knew the answer.

He sighed loud enough to scare a mockingbird from a nearby tree. "Looks like we might just have plenty of time to come up with a story to tell your uncle. You were right. We *are* lost."

At the end of the longest night of his life, Tye watched daylight dawn in a muted pallet of pink, purple, and mauve. He paced like a panther along the southern bank of the Trinity River, waiting for the morning to grow light enough to search the muddy slope for signs he prayed he wouldn't find. His eyes were gritty; his body weary. He had not slept in almost twenty-four hours.

He didn't much expect to discover evidence of the Blessings here along the river. The amount of time they'd remained missing combined with the clues he and Claire had found in their room led him to believe they'd hopped the train for New Orleans. But until responses to his telegrams arrived, he didn't know what else to do other than search for them in Fort Worth. So that's what he did.

His mind drifted back to the previous day, recalling the many efforts he and the townspeople had made, wondering if they had overlooked any possibility and unable to imagine what it might be. The citizens of Fort Worth had come out in force to look for the McBride children. Officially, the sheriff led the search, but as the hours passed it became obvious that the indomitable Donovan family directed the townspeople's efforts.

The Confederacy could have used a few generals like John Donovan. Some majors like Claire's brothers wouldn't have hurt, either. Still, despite a thorough exploration of every nook and cranny in town, no one discovered even a hint as to the girls' whereabouts.

For a little while Tye had pinned his hopes on young Casey Tate since the boy had partnered the girls in their pranks a time or two in the past. Tye had questioned the boy, and once he'd convinced him of the seriousness of the matter, Casey had rattled off a stream of schemes and pranks that had Tye shaking his head in wonder at the scope of his nieces' imaginations. He'd tracked down teachers and playmates and merchants. He'd even spoken with a fortune-teller down in Hell's Half Acre. All he'd learned there was that Madam LaRue had sold Spike to Casey Tate.

Tye lifted his face toward the brightening sky and sent yet another prayer heavenward. Then, as the sun climbed above the treetops, he began to follow the Trinity's shoreline, his gaze sharp, his footsteps heavy, weighted by the burden of his brother's misplaced trust.

If the Blessings had come to harm on his watch, Tye would want to die.

A flash of red near the water caught his gaze and shook his composure. He scrambled down the bank and with trembling fingers lifted a twisted length of cloth from the cool water. Droplets of water scattered like rain as he shook the cotton open.

Relief swept over him. A cowboy's bandanna. Most likely lost while driving cattle across the river.

He'd never seen the girls wearing bandannas.

For the first time in hours a smile lifted the edges of his mouth. At the same moment, he heard the sound of Claire Donovan's voice calling his name. He scrambled back up the bank and spied her driving his way in a coal-box buggy. She looked happy. Emotion clutched his chest as he called out hopefully, "They've been found?"

He saw it in her eyes before she shook her head. "No, I'm sorry, Tye. Not yet."

He kicked a rock and sent it flying toward the river. It entered the water with a plop that sounded like his heart felt.

"Brian told me I'd find you out here," Claire said, pulling up beside him. "He took the next shift at the telegraph office when the operator went back to my house to sleep." She held up a basket and added, "I brought you coffee and fresh muffins."

"Thanks. I'll take the coffee." He'd leave the muffin alone, however. He knew if he tried to force down one of the Blessings' favorite breakfast foods he'd choke on it.

Tye secured the horse and buggy for her while Claire carried the basket to a large flat rock beside the river. Setting it down, she flipped back the lid and removed an earthenware jug. She pulled the cork and the aroma of strong coffee rose along with the steam and teased Tye's senses. After filling a mug with the brew, she offered it to him. "Did you get any sleep at all?"

He accepted the coffee with a shrug and lied, "Sure."

She studied him, then wrinkled her nose with disbelief. "I saw Brian at the telegraph office. He said to tell you replies are beginning to come in from every train stop between here and the Louisiana border."

"Good," he replied, nodding as he sipped from the mug. "I don't suppose we've received any word from New Orleans?"

"Actually . . ." With an apologetic look, Claire reached into her basket and brought out a sheet of paper. "Under the circumstances I won't apologize for reading it. It's the longest telegram I've ever seen. Mrs. West hasn't heard from the girls, and I'm afraid the tone of her message is . . . well. . . it's not very nice. I don't know if you really want to read this."

Tye scanned the page, his scowl deepening with every word. It wasn't difficult to see where Constance had gotten her character. *Bitch* was too nice a term for Beatrice West.

If my granddaughters arrive on my doorstep, I won't allow them to leave.

"I won't allow them to stay," Tye muttered, crumpling the telegram in his fist. No way in hell would he let Beatrice West's influence corrupt his Blessings. Look what she'd done to her own daughter.

He reared back and threw the paper into the Trinity, the left-handed toss sailing the ball farther than he would have guessed. Hot coffee sloshed over the rim of the cup with the movement, scalding his skin. He hardly noticed the outer pain, because inside he hurt so fiercely.

As much as he hated the idea of his nieces being within spitting distance of that old crone and her cold mansion, he prayed they'd turn up there. "It's a helluva deal."

"Wouldn't you like a sweet roll, Tye?" Claire asked. "They're Patrick's, and he's the best roll maker in the family."

Tye took one even though he didn't want it. During this nightmare, Claire had displayed such concern and caring. In fact her whole family had acted that way. Shocked the hell out of him. Maybe there was something in those folks worth her love after all. Taking a small bite of the sweet, he swallowed and said, "Thanks, Claire."

"You're welcome. I hope you enjoy it."

"I didn't mean breakfast. Well, I did . . . but I meant more, too. You and your family have been a big help. The search through town took half as much time as it otherwise would have if your father hadn't been there directing the sheriff."

Claire's mouth twisted in a rueful smile. "No one is better than my da when it comes to organizing and directing people. Besides, everyone wanted to help the Menaces and Lord McBride."

For once he didn't argue with either term. Instead, he took a long sip of coffee, studying her over the top of the mug. She looked a bit bedraggled herself. Noticing it, Tye realized he'd been so caught up in his own troubles, he'd all but forgotten about hers. Clearing his throat, he asked, "So how is it going with your father? You showing your sand?"

"I'm trying," she said simply. This time she was the one who kicked a stone toward the river. She stared at it as it rolled down the slope, but once it splashed into the water, she looked up at him. Sorrow and the slightest hint of shame glimmered in her eyes. "I can't say I'm making much headway. I'll know better if he's learning anything once the girls are found and life settles back to normal."

"From your mouth to God's ears."

"Oh, Tye." She reached for him, then paused. Their gazes met and held as the memory of their last embrace rose like a specter between them. He needed her comforting touch. God, how he needed her. But he couldn't ask.

He didn't have to ask. Smiling tenderly, Claire wrapped her arms around him and hugged him tight.

His own arms stole around her, and he buried his head in her hair, inhaling her sweet scent of faith and hope and drawing on her strength.

She was strong, probably the strongest woman he knew. He hoped she'd come to see it, too.

With her in his arms, he was able to confess, "I'm so afraid for them."

"I know."

They stood as they were for some time, holding each other, until the thunder of approaching horses broke through Tye's consciousness and he looked up. Patrick Donovan galloped toward them. The wide grin wreathing his face faded as he saw his sister in Tye's arms. He reined his mount to a halt a few short steps away and snapped, "McBride, get your paws off our Claire."

Instead of letting her go, Tye held her tighter. A lump the size of one of Claire's Magical raisin muffins rose in his throat as one possible reason for Donovan's presence occurred to him. He managed to squeak out only one word. "Claire?"

She glanced from him to her brother. Slowly a smile broke across her countenance like sunshine from behind a thundercloud. "Patrick, they're home?"

"Aye. They drove into town a few minutes ago. Now, let go of my sister and climb in the buggy, McBride. Your Blessings are home safe and sound."

CHAPTER 11

CARRY PEAS HOME FROM THE PEA-PATCH IN A SPLIT BASKET TO AVOID HAD LUCK.

TYE DROVE the buggy like a Roman chariot back into town, deaf to all of Claire's cautions from her seat beside him. His gut was a ball of anxious nerves as he raced down Throckmorton Street toward the crowd gathered in front of Fortune's Design. At his approach, the congregation parted, and he caught his first sight of the trio sporting pigtails and worried smiles. Tye breathed for what seemed like the first time since the previous morning. The pressure suddenly present at the back of his eyes felt suspiciously like tears.

The Blessings, home safe and sound. Thank God.

I'm gonna kill them.

"Uncle Tye!" they cried in a chorus as he yanked the buggy to a stop, vaulted to the ground, knelt, and swept all three of his nieces into his arms. They smelled dirty and dusty and so damned good. For a long moment he held them, his eyes closed, his heart full.

"Oh, Uncle Tye," Katrina said, her voice muffled against his shirt. "I'm so glad to be home."

He couldn't speak. He opened his eyes, and his gaze met

Claire's. Tears spilled from her eyes as she sent him the purest, sweetest smile. His heart overflowed.

A hundred questions fired in his mind, but for now he remained content to absorb the reality of the moment. Gradually, however, he grew aware of the world beyond these three shining faces and Claire's weepy one.

What looked like half of Fort Worth swarmed around them. He spied the sheen of wetness on nearly every third person's face. He overheard snippets of the other two-thirds' conversations, enough to piece together a pair of troublesome facts. First, the girls apparently had driven Big Jack Bailey's buckboard into town, and second, the wealthy rancher himself rode into Fort Worth with them, propped upright in the back of the wagon with his leg wrapped in bandages.

Big Jack Bailey. Tye's blood ran cold.

Behind him he heard Patrick Donovan ask, "Who is Big Jack Bailey?"

Wilhemina Peters's distinctive voice replied, "Big Jack owns the Lucky Lady ranch southeast of town, and he's the richest man in this part of Texas. Meanest, too. Or at least, he used to be the meanest, but ever since he tangled with Lord McBride and Jenny and Mr. Trace, he seems to have sweetened up a bit."

"What happened?"

Tye tuned out the other murmurings of the crowd, zeroing in on Wilhemina. "Bailey claims that Jenny dabbles in voodoo," she was saying. "She threatened to curse his grandbaby if he ever went near her family again. Nobody in town believes it, of course, other than Big Jack. But he does believe, and that's what has everyone in such a state here this morning. We can't imagine what the Menaces are doing with him. He shot Lord McBride, you know. In the shoulder. Almost killed him and almost caused dear Jenny to lose her baby."

Wilhemina paused a moment, then added, "Your sister is

friends with the McBrides. Miss Donovan? Where do you think the Menaces have been? Why do you guess they were driving his wagon?"

"I don't know."

Neither did Tye, but he reckoned it was time to find out. Slowly he unwrapped himself from the Blessings and climbed to his feet. He stepped forward, toward the wagon, and shot Big Jack Bailey a lethal look.

"Now don't be jumping to conclusions," the rancher said, tilting his broad-brimmed, brown felt hat back off his forehead. "Nothing bad happened to these girls. Unless you count being heroines and saving a man's life as a bad thing."

Tye loomed over Bailey. "Explain."

Big Jack struggled to sit up straighter. "Your nieces saved my life, McBride. A rattler got me. I'd fallen in a gully just off the trail to the Lucky Lady. They came and they saved me."

Tye twisted his head to look at his nieces. "At the Lucky Lady? What in the world were you doing out at the Lucky Lady ranch?"

Katrina stepped forward and clasped her hand dramatically against her chest. "It was my dream that started it all."

"No it wasn't." Maribeth shoved her aside. "It was Spike who started it all, Uncle Tye. Kat wouldn't have had the dream if not for Spike."

Emma braced her hands on her hips. "You're both wrong. I'm the one—"

"Enough." Tye threw Claire a "help me" look.

She said, "Emma, why don't you begin the tale for your uncle?"

The oldest girl nodded, sucked in a big breath, then recited in a rush. "We were talking about lizards when we went to sleep night before last. Lizards led us to horny toads and we decided to have our own horny-toad hunt like you and Miss Claire did, Uncle Tye. So we asked Spike questions about what direction we should go to find good hunting this year, and we whittled it down to an area out near the Lucky Lady. Then Kat had her dream about Big Jack."

"It was *sooooooo* scary." The young girl's eyes rounded like saucers, and she clasped her hands and shivered. "The lizard turned into a horny toad, and that turned into a snake. I saw it bite Mr. Big Jack. He screamed like a banshee."

The crowd buzzed with reaction to that. Bailey protested. "I didn't scream. I may have hollered a bit, but I didn't scream."

Kat's chin came up and her nose wrinkled. "In my dream you did. Loud. Anyway, I woke up and I felt this . . . this . . . this need to go look for Mr. Big Jack."

Maribeth nodded. "It was strange, Uncle Tye. It was like she was in a trance. Nothing was going to stop her from going, so Em and I thought we'd best go with her. And you know what? She led us right to him."

"I did." Katrina nodded sharply.

Emma cleared her throat. "Mr. Bailey was drifting in and out of consciousness, but he managed to tell us how to save him."

Bailey nodded. "It was a struggle, but I managed it."

Tye scratched skeptically at his day-old beard and glanced at Claire, looking to see how she was taking the story. She wore her disbelief like a shawl. So, she wasn't buying it any more than he. Good. He'd been afraid his lack of sleep might be interfering with his ability to think. In a soft, southern drawl, he asked, "And just what did my nieces do to treat your snakebite, Bailey?"

"The usual. They read three verses of Matthew, Chapter One, and called my name after every sentence they read."

"I even read one sentence," Kat added. "Some of the words were very hard, but Emma helped me." She smiled at her older sibling. "She's a good sister sometimes."

"Of course, we had to go fetch a Bible first, Uncle Tye," Maribeth said, continuing the wild explanation. "Since we were closer to the Lucky Lady big house, we went there to find one rather than come back to town. It was our bad luck all the men were out rounding up cattle or we could have had help."

"And sent word back to town," Emma added. "You see, Uncle Tye, by the time he recovered enough for us to leave him, it was too late to start back to town. It would have been too dangerous to travel in pitch-dark. We had to wait for moonrise. So that's why we were a little late getting home. We had to save Mr. Big Jack Bailey."

The three girls looked at one another, nodded, then smiled angelically at their uncle.

Tye didn't believe this hogwash for a minute, although he did have to give them credit for a good delivery. They must have practiced it for hours.

Bailey spoke up. "I sure am grateful they showed up when they did. I was halfway to heaven. Could all but see Saint Peter smiling down at me, and fact of the matter is, I'm not ready to meet up with the old guy yet."

Someone from the crowd called out. "Ain't much of a chance of that, Big Jack. Saint Peter ain't the one who'll be giving you the howdy on the other side."

The rancher showed his teeth and growled. "You hush your mouth, Brent Archer. I'm dancing to a new tune these days. Why, I even gave these sweet little girls a reward for saving my life."

"Well, I swan," Wilhemina murmured. "Big Jack's known for pinching pennies almost as much as for his superstitions. I must mention this tidbit in my newspaper column." She pulled a pad of paper and a pencil from her bag and called in a loud voice, "How much of a reward?"

"Thirty dollars."

Thirty dollars. At that, Tye jerked his head around to meet Claire's gaze. He watched her mouth the words, *Oh, those girls. They are Menaces.*

This time, Tye had to agree.

～

CLAIRE HAD WATCHED the children tell their unbelievable story and wondered if they had half a clue of the grief they'd put their poor uncle through. Someone needed to take those children in hand. As Tye knelt once again and took his nieces back into his arms, she had serious doubts that he'd be the one to do it.

"They need their parents," she murmured to herself with a sigh. Those girls desperately needed someone who wasn't afraid to discipline them. Someone like John or Peggy Donovan, who knew just how to keep a mischievous daughter out of trouble.

Even when that daughter was all grown up.

Claire closed her eyes. Now that the Menaces were home, she would be forced to rejoin the battle with her da. At that realization, irritability threatened to overtake the euphoria she'd felt since learning the girls had returned safely. When Tye climbed up into Big Jack's buckboard and addressed the gathering, she was grateful to return her attention to the McBrides.

"I want to thank everyone for their help in looking for my nieces," he said. "I know if my brother and his wife were here, they'd thank you too. Fort Worth truly looks after its own. Now, I don't know about y'all, but I'm dog tired and played out. I think I'll take my Blessings home and put my feet up for a time."

Slowly the crowd dispersed, many of the folk pausing long enough to give the girls a hug or pat on the head. "He was right," Claire said to her brother, observing the scene. "I know the townspeople love to complain about the girls' mischief-making, but they certainly gave their all when they thought the Blessings were in danger."

Tye sauntered up beside them and extended his hand toward Patrick. "I appreciate your family's help more than I can say. Please pass along my thanks to all the Donovans."

Patrick accepted Tye's handshake and his gratitude, then

turned to his sister. "I'm going back to the bakery. Claire, are you coming?"

Tye touched her sleeve and spoke in a low tone. "Would you mind hanging around for a bit? There is more to this story than the girls are letting on. Something tells me I can use the benefit of a female mind while I get to the bottom of this."

She agreed without hesitation. Patrick had to whisper in her ear about it for a moment because he wasn't comfortable with the amount of time she was spending with the McBrides. After promising to make the visit a short one, she secured his word on seeing to her horse and buggy.

Tye muttered something about overprotective brothers when he slipped his hands around her waist and swung her up onto the buckboard's seat. Claire didn't even think of arguing with that. Next he told the girls to hop into the back for the short trip to Willow Hill. Bailey protested, claiming his snakebite required a doctor's attention, but Tye discounted his claims by pointing out that the rancher had already proclaimed himself saved. Another half-hour or so shouldn't adversely affect his health.

They made a brief stop at the telegraph office to send word of the girls' safety to Beatrice West and the other out-of-towners Tye had contacted, then continued on to Willow Hill. Except for the clatter of wagon wheels, the drive took place mostly in silence. Exhaustion was setting in.

When the wagon rolled to a stop in the front drive, Tye ordered his nieces and Big Jack Bailey into Trace's office. "Miss Donovan and I will join you directly."

"Could we eat breakfast first, Uncle Tye?" Maribeth asked. "We sure are hungry."

He handed her the basket Claire had brought to the river. "Grab a muffin and wait for me inside."

The sweet perfume of roses drifted from the garden as Claire stood beside the wagon, waiting for Tye to speak. He shuffled his feet, rubbed at his eyes, then sighed heavily. Finally she lost her patience. "Tye? What are we waiting for?"

He scratched his day-old beard and gazed toward the room where his nieces were waiting. "You caught the bit about thirty dollars?"

"Yes."

"This wasn't any snakebite rescue. They cooked something up with Bailey."

"Yes, I think you're right."

He scowled and began to pace back and forth across the front porch steps. "I don't care what he or they or anyone else says, that man is dangerous. I have a hole in my shoulder that says so. The Blessings went too far this time." He halted abruptly and shot Claire a look. "I'm going to have to punish them."

"I think that's a wise decision."

"But I don't want to punish them."

"Yes, I know."

"I don't know how."

She rolled her eyes. For such a strong, masculine man, he acted like such a little boy at times. "Sure you do, Tye. You think of what your brother would do under the circumstances, then you do the same thing."

"Yeah. I guess. But I know Emma will do that wounded-doe imitation with her eyes. Katrina will suck her thumb, and Mari will look everywhere but at me. I hate it when they do that." He again gave a heavy sigh. "Guess we'd better go in. I don't like leaving them alone with Bailey."

They heard a buzz of conversation as they approached the office. It stopped as soon as Tye turned the doorknob. Inside, Big Jack Bailey sat in Trace's big leather chair, smoking a cigar and sipping whiskey. Claire thought he intended to be intimidating. He hadn't quite pulled it off.

Tye dismissed Bailey with a look and turned to the girls. "I'd like to hear the rest of your story now."

"What rest of the story, Uncle Tye?" Maribeth asked.

Tye scratched behind his ear. "I think there is a piece or two of this puzzle missing."

Maribeth looked at Emma. "Can you think of anything we left out?"

Emma shook her head. "Not me. What about you, Kat?"

Wide-eyed, Katrina stuck her thumb in her mouth and shook her head.

Tye met Claire's gaze, silently saying *I told you so*.

Claire had already figured out that where the Menaces were concerned, Tye McBride was a pushover—as undoubtedly the girls had, also—so she wasn't completely surprised by his next move.

"I want you three to skedaddle up to take your baths and think about it awhile," he told them. "We'll discuss it some more after breakfast." He waved his hand toward the door and said, "Go on."

Claire rolled her eyes as they darted for freedom. Tye scowled at her, then turned his attention toward Big Jack Bailey, all amusement wiped from his expression. Trepidation shuddered across the rancher's face as Tye placed a hand on each arm of the chair and leaned forward, lowering his face to within inches of Bailey's. "Just so you know, Jack, I'll get to the bottom of this story, and when I do, if I find that you harmed so much as a hair on their beautiful, innocent little heads, I'll have yours on a platter."

He drew a knife from his boot and with a quick jerk of his wrist, sliced away the bandage around Bailey's calf. "Claire, double-check me here, would you? Does that wound look like a rattler's bite to you?"

Claire had never seen a rattlesnake bite before, but she questioned the absence of swelling in this case. "Those two little holes could have been made with a knife."

Tye nodded and tossed the bandage in Bailey's face, then turned away. "Go on, I'm tired of looking at you."

Bailey huffed a protest that Tye ignored. Once the rancher finally made a show at limping out of the office while he muttered about ungrateful young pups, the McBride Menaces' uncle slumped into his brother's desk chair and started to laugh. "Have you ever heard such corral dust in your life?"

Claire couldn't decide whether to laugh with him or screech at him. "You're not going to let them get away with it, are you, McBride?"

"I think they're due a few points for creativity." She fired a glare at him and he added, "No, I won't let them get away with it. First I need to find out what really happened. Any guesses, Miss Donovan?"

Claire thought about it a moment, then shrugged. "Except for the fact they obviously needed thirty dollars badly enough to go through the entire spelling bee mischief, I haven't a clue. Do you?"

"I have my suspicions. It wouldn't surprise me if this doesn't have something to do with their matchmaking plans for me and Loretta Davis. The Blessings do get serious when it comes to matchmaking." He slumped back in his chair. "I'll find out the truth and dole out a punishment. Later, though. I know I should get it over with, and I intended to. I did. But I'm too tired, Claire. I don't have the sand for it right now. All my energy was used up being happy they got home safely."

Claire sank into a chair. Tenderness stole over her as she watched Tye McBride lean his head back against the high-backed chair and close his eyes. He was a good man, a loyal man. A loving uncle. "You're just a chicken, McBride."

He cocked open one eye. "Excuse me?"

"It's true." She folded her hands primly in her lap and observed, "You're too chicken to discipline those girls even though you know they need it, and they need it now. That's why you wanted me to tag along. You knew I'd make certain you finished the job."

"I did?" His brows furrowed into a scowl.

"Yes. I agree you can take some time to ferret out the truth. They obviously worked a long time on their story, and you're more liable to catch them off guard at a later time. But the punishment can't wait. Even if it's only a small part, you need to do something this morning."

"Ah, Claire."

"Don't 'ah Claire' me. There's no need. You did the right thing by bringing me with you to Willow Hill, Tye, because I've thought of the perfect penalty."

"You have?"

"Yes." Watching the dread drip across his face, Claire could hold back her smile no longer. Standing, she reached for Tye's hand and pulled him to his feet. "Come along, McBride. I'll fill you in on the way upstairs."

Twenty minutes later Tye stood in front of his freshly bathed nieces and cheerfully swung the punishment stick. "All right, girls. Whatever else transpired, you broke the rules by leaving the house at night, correct?"

They nodded.

"Well, I can't ignore it. It's a serious infraction. I've given the situation careful consideration, and I have arrived at a decision on how you will be disciplined."

Kat yanked her thumb from her mouth. "Don't spank us, Uncle Tye."

"Please don't make us work for Sister Gonzaga," Maribeth pleaded.

Emma clasped her hands in front of her chest. "We haven't eaten in a long time. If you could give us one good meal before we're put on bread and water?"

Claire swallowed a snort when Tye folded his arms and spoke in a strong, definitive voice. "There will be no spanking or slaving for the nuns or bread-and-water meals, children."

"Then what are you going to do?"

"I'm sorry, girls, but I have no other choice. As your punishment, I'm going to tell your father exactly what happened. Every single detail."

The children gasped as one. "Oh, Em," Kat said. "You said he wouldn't do anything bad. This is terrible!"

Emma clapped her hands over Kat's mouth and repeated in a horrified tone, "You are going to tell Papa?"

Tye nodded solemnly, and Maribeth slowly shook her head. "Call the undertaker, sisters. We're dead."

FOUR DAYS later the citizens of Fort Worth gathered for an afternoon picnic to celebrate the dedication of Fort Worth's new fire station. Braving the inevitable stream of women-come-a-courting, Tye attended with the girls. Since the Blessings' return, the world looked as pretty as a rainbow after a drought-ending storm, and he was happy to be out enjoying it.

The girls were having a high time, too, between the sack races and the taffy pull. Through it all, Tye didn't let them out of his sight for a minute.

At the moment the task wasn't difficult because they'd all stopped to eat. While Maribeth and Emma bickered over the last dill pickle, Tye noticed Katrina staring past him, a contemplative look on her face. Twisting his head, he realized his niece was watching Claire, who carried a pitcher of water from blanket to blanket, refilling glasses as needed. After the baker stopped by the McBride's spot, exchanged pleasantries, and moved on, Kat looked at Tye and asked, "Why does Miss Claire look sad? Is it because her papa took down the pretty window curtains at her bakery?"

"I don't think she's sad," Emma observed, holding her pickle up out of Ralph's reach. "I think she's angry."

Angry? Tye paused in the midst of taking a bite of fried

chicken, his eyes narrowing as they focused on Claire. She didn't look angry to him. More like depressed. The fight with her family must be wearing on her. Then, because he wondered if Emma saw something he didn't, he asked, "Why do you say that?"

Emma shrugged and tossed Ralph a piece of meat, then scratched him behind the ears when he climbed up on her lap and whined for more. "She reminds me of Mother."

Tye almost swallowed a bone. *Mother*, she had said. Not Mama. Jenny was Mama to the girls. Emma was referring to her birth mother, to Constance. *Dear Lord.*

He jerked his head around and fired a look at Claire, who smiled as she refilled Sister Gonzaga's glass. He searched for signs of wickedness or evil. All he saw was sweetness.

He called forth a picture of Constance from his memory and compared her and Claire. Other than extraordinary beauty, the two women had little in common. What did Emma see? "How does Miss Donovan remind you of your mother, sweetheart?" he asked.

The girl glanced over at Claire. "Her smiles don't reach her eyes for one thing. But mainly it's not on the outside. More inside. She's too quiet. She hardly talked to us earlier. Mother was always quiet like that when she was the most angry. I remember she was angry a lot."

Damn Constance. For perhaps the thousandth time, Tye wondered what extent of wickedness the woman had served up to those sweet wee ones.

Tye wouldn't put anything past Trace's first wife. Lies, manipulations, and betrayal had been Constance's stock and trade. Her plot to destroy her own family for the sake of coin and Tye's stupid foreign title proved she lacked the normal maternal instincts to protect and defend her young. The way she'd lied to pit brother against brother, to drive a wedge of hatred and betrayal between them, showed how truly evil she could be.

Now, looking at his brother's daughters, Tye speculated about what other secrets may have died with Constance on that awful, bloody afternoon so long ago. What other ways had she abused her children? What other horrible memories might Emma, the eldest, have tucked away; recollections waiting to rear their ugly heads when she grew older?

The complete lack of emotion on Emma's face when she spoke of Constance McBride made Tye shudder. It wasn't natural and it filled him with regrets.

Katrina interrupted Tye's black thoughts when she licked a ring of custard from her mouth and said, "I think we should do something to cheer up Miss Claire. After all, we'd be dead from the gas lamp if not for her, and her muffins make my tummy happy."

"I think you're right, Kat," Maribeth said, feeding the last of her potato salad to Ralph. "And I know just the thing. Let's invite her to go to the swimming hole with us. You're still taking us swimming on Saturday, aren't you, Uncle? You promised, remember?"

Tye had a mental flash of Claire dressed in wet, clinging, minimal clothes. He cleared his throat. "Uh, I remember. But maybe it would be better if y'all came up with another way to cheer up Miss Donovan. She might not even know how to swim."

Kat shrugged. "I'm sure she does. She grew up on the Gulf, after all."

To Tye's relief, Emma shot her sisters a meaningful look and said, "Uncle Tye is right, sisters. Let's help Miss Donovan later. After all, she has that beautiful Mr. Sundine to cheer her up. First I think we should visit with Miss Loretta. Remember how Maribeth promised her she'd share the secret of her spelling success? Look, sisters, there she is. Why don't we go say hello?" She jerked her head toward a sprawling oak tree off away from the main body of the picnic, where Loretta Davis stood speaking to her blacksmith beau. Neither one of them appeared too happy.

"But Emma," Katrina protested. "Think how Miss Donovan

helped Uncle Tye look for us. Don't you think she should be the one we—"

Tye saw Maribeth reach over and pinch her younger sister. He didn't bother to correct her; he was too busy worrying why the Blessings' ringleader had brought up Loretta's name.

He had thought the girls had given up on their matchmaking attempts. Had these recent days been the proverbial lull before the storm? He wasn't at all ready to jump back into the tempest again. "I don't think now is the time to approach Miss Davis about anything," he told his nieces. "It looks like she and Gus are having a private conversation."

"Not anymore." Maribeth reattached the ring on Ralph's collar to the leash tied around a nearby pecan tree. She shook her finger at the dog and said, "Stay." Then she jerked her thumb over her shoulder. "Miss Loretta is bawling like a lost calf, and I think she needs something to cheer her up."

Tye grimaced when he looked back and saw the black-smith stomping off toward town. Mari was right Loretta was crying her eyes out. *Well, hell.* He glanced around for signs of her mother or another woman who might offer Loretta a comforting shoulder, but from what he could tell, nobody else noticed the drama taking place beneath the large oak. *Leave it to the Blessings*, he thought with a sigh. "It's really none of our business, girls, and your apology can wait After all, we—"

"Sure it's our business, Uncle Tye." Emma shot her sisters a purposeful look that put all Tye's suspicions on alert. She reached over and patted his knee. "It's part of the penance Sister Gonzaga gave us when she stopped us on our way to the bakery yesterday."

"Penance? What do you mean, penance? You're not Catholic."

Maribeth nodded. "She said in our case that didn't matter, that any penance we did would help us in the long run."

Try as he might Tye couldn't make a connection between the Blessings, penance, and the woman currently watering the wildflowers beneath an oak tree. "But what does all that have to do with Miss Davis?"

Emma answered. "We're supposed to spread kindness and caring wherever we see a need for it."

"That's right," Maribeth concurred. "And if we ignore a need when we see it that counts against us." Standing, she held out a hand toward Tye as the other girls scrambled to their feet. "Come on, Uncle. Let me help you up. You don't want our souls to get another black mark, do you?"

Well, what could he say to that? Against his better judgment he followed the girls on their mission of mercy, his attention so focused on what might happen that he only vaguely noticed that Emma remained at their picnic spot long enough to pour iced tea into a pair of glasses.

Katrina haled Loretta Davis first. The young woman spun around, quickly wiping her eyes, and when her gaze flew up to meet Tye's, an embarrassed flush stained her cheeks. Thank goodness the girls filled the moment with their chatter.

"Hi, Miss Loretta," Maribeth said. "We're to help you with your spelling and officially apologize for the tricks we played on you while we were trying to get you to fall in love with our Uncle Tye."

Clasping her hands to her chest and sighing dramatically, Katrina said, "We were mean and we're sorry."

"That's right Please accept our apology, Miss Loretta. Here, have a drink of tea," Emma added, shoving one of the glasses she carried into the young woman's hand. "It will help you feel better."

Loretta tried to talk, but the girls wouldn't let her. Instead, they kept encouraging her to drink. When she finally did as directed, Emma turned to Tye with a huge smile on her face. Smoothly she handed him the second glass. "Here, Uncle. Share a drink with Miss Loretta. It's rude of us to ask her to drink alone. It's sweet tea. Your favorite."

Then it was as if a petticoat dust-devil swept across the meadow. In a whirl of motion and chatter, the McBride Menaces departed, leaving Tye and Loretta standing alone. *Well, hell*, he thought, and took a gulp of tea.

The taste of it surprised him, distracted him from the moment. "This isn't the way tea normally tastes."

"It's good," Loretta said, her teary gaze sliding past Tye to focus on something behind him. "I was thirsty."

No wonder, considering all those tears she cried out. A body needed hydration. Tye scowled down at his glass. "Reminds me of something . . . I can't quite put my finger on it"

Tye paused, searching for a polite way to end the small talk and get the hell out of there. Deliverance came in the form of a tall, blond-headed man who sauntered up with concern written all over his expression. "Loretta, my dear, you talked to Gus? You told him? It is done?"

"Hello, Lars. Yes, the deed is done. He said he'd leave town rather than stay and watch me make such a big mistake. He said he'd leave tonight."

Nodding, Lars said grimly, "We'd best prepare for the consequences."

"That sounds ominous," Tye began. "What did the blacksmith —" He broke off suddenly as something bumped against his legs then streaked on by. *Ralph*. Leash trailing along behind him like an extra tail, the mutt dashed straight toward the Trinity. The three Blessings raced after him.

"Ralph, you bad dog!" shouted Katrina.

"Come back here, boy," called Maribeth.

"No, Ralph, not the river!" hollered Emma.

"Can he swim?" Katrina screamed. "Oh, no. He might drown. Get him before he gets in the water, sisters, or we'll have to go in after him, and the snakes might get us all!"

"Damn." Tye shoved his glass of tea at the Viking god and took off after his nieces. He overtook them at the crest of the riverbank, yelled at them to halt, then plowed down the slope toward the river. Just as the puppy prepared to spring into the water, Tye made a flying lunge for the leash. Even as his face plowed into the mud, his hand grasped the leather and he held on tight. He came up spitting dirt and dirty words. He yanked his handkerchief from his back pocket, wiped off his face, and muttered, "You've had some dumb ideas before, McBride, but giving the Blessings a dog has to take the cake."

He climbed the bank to the sounds of the girls' cheers. His muddied pride recovered quickly at the sight of three shining faces gazing worshipfully up at him.

"Oh, Uncle Tye, you are the most wonderfulest uncle."

"Ralph might not be able to swim. You probably just saved his life."

"Oh, Uncle Tye. You're our hero."

He wiped some mud off his tongue and grinned. Those girls sure knew how to make a man feel good. So good, in fact, that when he dropped to his knees and they flew into his arms for a muddy hug, he didn't even mind the fact that Loretta Davis and that Viking son-of-a-bitch friend of Claire's stood watching the production, chuckling as they sipped their tea.

That was the last time Lars Sundine crossed Tye's mind until two days later when he sat at his breakfast table reading the newspaper and enjoying his steak and eggs and peace and quiet. As he started Wilhemina Peters's "Talk About Town" column, he heard the door behind him swing open and assumed Emma had returned from the garden with her hands full of flowers. The Viking god's name jumped out at him from the page, and he started to chuckle. "Well, what do you know about that. Now I understand why ol' Gus Willard left Fort Worth. Seems there has been an elopement in town, Emma. Loretta Davis has run off with Lars Sundine."

He heard a gasp, then Claire Donovan said, "My Lars married Loretta Davis?"

Before he could twist around in shock at why Claire was standing in his brother's kitchen, Maribeth spoke up from the doorway. "Married? Miss Loretta married? To Mr. Sundine? Oh, no. It's all our fault."

Then she started to scream.

CHAPTER 12

IT'S BAD LUCK TO STRIKE A MATCH ON A COOKING POT.

TWENTY MINUTES later Claire held a still-wailing Katrina in her arms in Willow Hill's front parlor. To her right on the sofa sat Maribeth, tears pouring silently down her face and occasionally accompanied by hiccups. On her left, Emma cried softly, but with such strength of emotion it all but broke Claire's heart to watch her.

Tye stood frozen in front of them like a statue carved from a glacier.

His voice was raspy as he repeated the words Emma had just confessed. "You accidentally dosed Miss Davis and Mr. Sundine with a love potion?"

"Yes," Maribeth sobbed. "It was supposed to be for you. We doctored up the tea we gave you and Miss Loretta at the picnic, except you only took a sip before Ralph got loose, and then you gave your glass to Mr. Sundine and he drank the rest. That's why they ran off and got married."

The wailing swelled in volume, and Claire attempted to offer comfort. "Oh, girls, it's not your fault. Now that I think about it I should have seen this coming. Lars and Loretta have been making eyes at each other at The Confectionary for weeks. She came into my shop every day at lunchtime, and they carried on their flirtation in front of half the town. Believe me, their elopement had nothing to do with any love potion."

Tye cleared his throat. "This love potion. Is it Miss Donovan's Magic?"

Emma shook her head, her lips dipped in a frown of confusion. "It wasn't Magic. It was *magic*. Madam LaRue's magic. We bought it from her."

"Madam LaRue." Tye dragged a hand through his hair. "I talked to her after you disappeared. She never said a word." He heaved a heavy sigh and said, "Tell us the rest of it."

Katrina lifted her face from Claire's bosom, and the three girls looked at one another. "Go ahead and tell him, Emma," the middle sister directed. "Get it over with so he can kill us fast instead of dragging it out."

Tye shot Claire an apprehensive look as Emma nibbled at her lower lip. Claire reached over and patted her knee. "Go ahead, honey. Your uncle needs to know the truth."

What followed was a tale that left Claire shuddering in fear at the thought of the dangers the girls had faced. Hell's Half Acre past midnight. A black-arts priestess. A drunken Big Jack Bailey. Lost on the vast prairie west of town. "Oh, my."

At one point during the story Tye had leaned against the wall for support. When Emma relayed the part where they pulled the gun on Big Jack, his knees appeared to give out, and he slid slowly to the floor, his head hanging between his knees.

Emma wrapped up the tale, sniffling as she said, "And now it's all ruined. Miss Loretta can't marry you, so you won't stay here and live in Fort Worth like we want you to."

Tye lifted his head. His face looked ravaged. "What are you talking about, Em?"

"We want you to stay, Uncle. Papa does, too. We heard him tell Mama right before they left on their honeymoon. Papa said he wished you would settle in Fort Worth for good instead of going back to South Carolina when they get home. He said he worried you'd never be truly happy as long as you lived where you fought the War and where you had lots of bad memories. Then Mama said marriage would be the best way to keep you here, and Papa told her he thought that of all the available women in town, Loretta Davis would make you the happiest."

Tye rubbed his temples. "So, what you are saying is that the purpose of all this matchmaking nonsense was to keep me living in Fort Worth?"

The three youngsters nodded, and Maribeth said, "We want you to be happy, Uncle Tye. We love you."

Tye let out a groan. "Oh, girls, I love you, too. I just wish you'd have said something. I decided weeks ago to make my home here in Texas."

"You did?" Maribeth asked, her voice trembling with hope and wonder.

"Yeah, I did." As the three girls' tears started drying, he continued, "I like it here. I realized I want time to get to know your father again, and I want to be around to watch you three grow up."

Katrina wiped her nose on her sleeve and asked, "But what about your sisters and your grandmother. Won't you miss them?"

"Of course I'll miss them, but with rail travel becoming more convenient every year, regular visits will be easy to arrange."

"So you are gonna stay? You promise? Even without having Miss Loretta as your wife?"

"Even without the fair Loretta. I bought some land, girls. I'm going to build a ranch."

After a moment of frozen joy, the girls erupted into cheers that all but deafened Claire. They rushed from her arms into their uncle's, climbing on him, covering him with kisses, babbling about pets and houses and their parents.

Claire watched with tears in her eyes. Such love, she thought. Such concern and caring. Such . . . family. How did her own family compare? The Donovans loved her, she knew. They cared for her and were concerned for her. But when was the last time they said it? Had they ever once told her they wanted her to be happy?

Every morning Claire went down to the bakery. Every morning her father tried to send her home. She'd refuse and they'd bicker about that and a thousand other items for the rest of the workday. Then every evening, because she had put down her foot and refused to leave the cottage, Da had her mother come by and offer yet another reason why Claire should move into the rental house with the rest of the Donovans.

It was hard to keep fighting, to keep demanding her due. That's one reason why she'd stopped by Willow Hill this morning. She needed a good dose of Tye McBride's encouragement.

Eventually the hugs and kisses amongst the McBride clan slowed, and Tye looked up and met her gaze. "I guess I'm remiss for not asking what brought you to Willow Hill today, Claire. Is there something I can do for you?"

As Claire opened her mouth to answer, Katrina piped up. "I invited her to go swimming with us today, Uncle Tye. Remember we talked about it?"

Claire didn't find his wince reassuring, or for that matter, flattering. She didn't need to fight this man, too.

Rising from the sofa, she said, "Actually, I had stopped by to tell Katrina I wouldn't be able to go after all. I have some family business to take care of. I'd best be leaving now, in fact."

He need not look so relieved, she thought, hiding her pique behind a polite smile. She gathered up her purse, grateful she'd left the bulging picnic basket out in her buggy rather than toting the heavy thing up to the house, and turned to go.

"Hold on," Tye said, setting the girls away from him and pushing to his feet. "Before you get out of here, I have something I'd like to discuss with you. Do you have a few more minutes to spare?"

"Well, maybe a few."

"Good. Let me get the girls settled and then we can talk. Out on the porch, perhaps? It's a fine morning."

Claire nodded her agreement, and as Tye accompanied the children upstairs, she walked out onto the veranda. It was a gorgeous spring day; warm, but not hot, the air perfumed with the fragrance of roses and alive with the music of songbirds. Strolling around the corner, she took a seat in a rocking chair that looked out onto the rose garden, and tried to relax. What a morning, and it wasn't even eight o'clock yet.

She should never have agreed to go swimming with the McBrides anyway. Even though he said he didn't want her at the bakery to begin with, her father gave her grief when she mentioned she wanted time off. But the girls had caught her with the question during a weak moment, and she'd said yes without giving it any thought. It had been forward of her to agree to spend the morning with the McBrides, out away from town . . . Thinking she and Tye might find themselves alone together again. . . . Hoping he might wrap her in his arms again and pull her close . . . and kiss her . . . use his tongue like he had . . .

The door slammed open with a bang, jerking her from her reverie. Tye stormed out of the house. "Where did you go, Claire Donovan? I want to talk to you."

She gawked at the fury in his voice. What in the world had happened?

"Claire! You damn well better still be here."

She froze. *Damn well better?* He was cussing at her?

It started as a spark but quickly swelled into a glorious, raging temper. She was tired of being told what to do and not to do. Sick and tired of it. She shoved out of her chair and marched back around the corner of the house, hollering right back at him. "What is your problem, McBride?"

That shut him up. For just a moment he stood stock-still. She'd have smiled about it had she not been so angry herself.

Fire burning in his eyes, he slowly reached into his shirt

pocket and pulled out a bottle. Even as he took an aggressive step toward her, a liquid sense of strength poured into Claire like hot iron into a mold.

His tone was low and rough. "What's my problem? You're my problem, lady. You and that damned aphrodisiac you cooked up."

Aphrodisiac? "Not that again."

His eyes narrowed to slits. Anger radiated from him in waves. After a long moment, he sucked in a deep breath in a visible effort to gather his control. "When I went upstairs I asked my nieces about the love potion. This danger they lived through? It's your fault."

She blinked. "Excuse me? Did you say my fault?"

Nodding, he yanked the cork from the bottle in his hands, then shoved it beneath Claire's nose. "Smell it. Tell us what it is."

The familiar aroma rolled past her senses like a song. "It's Magic."

"That's what my nose told me."

"Where did you get it?"

"The Blessings."

"Where did they get it? I didn't give it to them. And what does Magic have to do with anything?" After a second's pause, her eyes went wide and she added, "Don't tell me they intended to bake for you again."

She flinched when the bottle came whizzing past her ear and crashed against the wall. The scent of Magic filled the air along with Tye McBride's curses. "It's the love potion, damnit. My nieces didn't steal it. They bought it for twenty goddamned dollars from Madam LaRue."

"Madam LaRue?" Clare made the connection then. The love potion they bought that night in Hell's Half Acre was a bottle of her Magic. "They paid twenty dollars for a bottle of my Magic?"

"Yep. They spent the other ten on incidentals." His eyes snapped as he advanced and she retreated. "What sort of profit did the witch make, Claire? How much did you charge her for it?"

She felt the edge of the rocker against the backs of her legs and she sank down into it in shock. Her Magic? Sold as a love potion? "I didn't sell it. I've never met Madam LaRue."

"You're lying."

The accusation rankled. She lifted her chin and glared up at him. "No, I'm not. Don't you dare say I am."

He shoved at the chair with both hands then backed away, speaking in a low, angry tone. "Madam LaRue sold my nieces this bottle of your Magic. Even if you are telling the truth, and you didn't supply her with the stuff, you are still responsible for its existence. Just like you'd be responsible if any lasting harm had come to my nieces as a result of this mess. And it could have happened that way so easily."

He braced both hands on his hips and ground out through clenched teeth, "Hell's Half Acre. In the middle of the goddamned night." Claire gasped a breath as he plowed on. "Are you familiar with the types of amusements that take place in that hellhole after midnight? They could have been murdered or drugged or raped. It happens every night in that end of town. And some men—some monsters—they like little girls. Think about that, Claire."

"Dear Lord."

"Makes a person's fingernails sweat just to think about it, doesn't it? Reckon we should be grateful Big Jack kidnapped them. Of course, none of it would have happened if not for your witches' brew."

Claire shook her head, nonverbally denying his accusation while she tried to figure just who this Madam LaRue was and how she got her hands on a bottle of Magic. Her family couldn't have done it. The Donovans had only just arrived in town the night of the spelling bee.

One possible answer occurred to Claire. The Galveston store had been burglarized a couple of years ago. The Donovan Baking Company lost almost thirty bottles of Magic. Could at least one of them somehow have made its way to Hell's Half Acre?

Possibly. It was common knowledge that stolen goods were offered for sale all over the Acre. People like Big Jack Bailey didn't quibble with acquiring ill-gotten gains. She glanced at Tye and asked, "Now that you know the truth are you going to have Bailey arrested?"

"Arrest Big Jack?" Tye's mouth twisted into an ugly imitation of a smile. "I could. But then I'd have to have you arrested, too, wouldn't I?"

"Me?" Claire pushed to her feet once more. "Look, McBride, I told you I didn't do anything. I didn't sell any Magic to anyone. I do have an idea, though, about how that bottle might have ended up at this Madam LaRue's."

He dismissed the notion with a wave of his hand. "It doesn't really matter how she got it, does it? You are the one who cooked up that poison to begin with, so the responsibility comes back to you. You are the root of all this trouble."

His scorn rocked Claire, but before she could defend herself, he pressed on, ticking each point off on his fingers. "We have the Blessings' near-miss with serious danger. We have Loretta Davis throwing away her life on a pretty-boy bun-maker. No telling what other misery you've caused that we don't know about yet. I don't doubt you've ruined at least one or two marriages since you came to town."

Claire's mouth bobbed open and shut like a fish out of water. She couldn't believe what he was saying. "Let me get this straight, McBride. Are you saying I'm responsible for your nieces' misbehavior? That I'm responsible for Loretta having run off with my friend?"

"Yes, I am. He drank the doctored tea and boom—" Tye snapped his fingers "—they run off and tie the knot."

Claire blew a frustrated breath. This was the biggest bunch of foolishness she'd ever heard. "Where did you get this stupid idea that Magic is an aphrodisiac anyway?"

"Don't try to deny it." He folded his arms and glared at her. "Hell, one whiff of that stuff is more potent than hundred-dollar French perfume."

Claire threw out her hands, scaring away the mockingbird that had just landed on the porch rail. "That's just ridiculous, Tye. Magic is an extract, like vanilla. It's a food additive, that's all. Adding it to their tea did not make Lars run off with Loretta. That's pure silliness."

"The hell it is. Maybe it doesn't affect everyone that way, but it damn sure does some of us. I know. Believe me, I know. And I'm telling you, good ol' baker Lars got his buns warmed when he got a good dose of Magic."

Claire wanted to scream. "If Lars's buns were the least bit warm it was because Loretta Davis had been eyeing them for weeks. It had nothing to do with Magic."

"It has everything to do with Magic. You said it yourself: They carried on at The Confectionary—the scene of the crime."

"He worked there."

"That's obviously not all he did there, now is it?"

Now she wanted to hurt him. She wanted to punch him in the stomach like she used to do to her brothers when they all were young. "You are so hardheaded, Tye McBride."

"Yeah? Well my head's not the only thing that gets hard when your damned Magic is involved. Admit it, Claire. It's an aphrodisiac. And you and your family are using it against the citizens of this good town. You should be in jail."

"And you should be in a hospital for mental patients. *Aphrodisiac,*" she said scornfully, whirling away from him. "I thought you were an intelligent man, but obviously I was wrong. No wonder those Menaces have you wrapped around their little fingers. If you believe this, you'll believe anything. I swear I'm beginning to think your brother made a huge mistake when he left you to care for his children."

She regretted her words as soon as they left her mouth. All the fire seemed to drain from Tye's body, replaced by an icy chill she recognized as infinitely more dangerous. Long seconds passed silently before he spoke again. "Don't you think I know that? Only days ago the Blessings dodged a bullet on my watch."

Fear of what might have been carved furrows in his brow, and icicles dripped from his tongue as he swore. "If your Magic had hurt them, I'd have made you pay."

Claire started to shiver, but she knew she was innocent, so she didn't back down. "Why are you doing this, Tye? You can't truly believe . . ."

His mouth twisted into an ugly smile. "What I can't believe is that I thought you were different. I was wrong. Emma called it. She saw it. You're just like her, like Constance." He laughed then, and the sound was chilling. "Constance. Medusa. A Borgia bride. Eve from the Garden and Claire Donovan. I swear, you women are all alike."

"Tye, listen to me."

But he was beyond listening. Though he looked straight at her, he seemed to be lost in the past. He stepped forward, backing her up against the veranda's railing. "Lying and luring to get what you want. It doesn't matter if you destroy those who get in your way. It doesn't matter if you tear families apart and turn brother against brother. As long as you get what you want. As long as you make your unholy dollar. It doesn't matter if it's twenty dollars or a damned fortune. God, I hate you all."

What was going on here? Claire wondered. She made little sense of his irrational speech, but the venom in his voice rocked her. More was happening here than a misguided opinion about the power of Magic. She'd never seen Tye like this. She'd never imagined he had this . . . nastiness inside him.

Claire shivered at the raw, ugly emotion painting the face of the man she'd so admired. She took a step sideways, intending to scoot by him. "There is obviously no reasoning with you at the moment. I'm going home now. We can discuss this further once you've calmed down."

"Oh, you're not going home, Miss Donovan," he drawled, reaching out and grabbing her arm as she attempted to walk past him. "Not until I've finished saying my piece."

She waited, biting her tongue to keep from railing back at him and dragging this meanness out further. Instead, very quietly and with great control, she said, "All right. What do you want to say?"

He opened his mouth to speak, then he paused, faltering, a look of confusion darting across his face. He dropped her arm as though it had burned him. "Hell. I don't know. I don't know what I want" Looking over her shoulder, he grimaced. "That's a lie. I do know what I want, and that's the problem. It's you. I want you. Even after all this."

He raked his hand through his hair. "Go on, get out of here. Go home and stay away from me and mine, Claire. You are the problem. You and your damned Magic. You are both dangerous as hell."

ANGER FUELED Claire's footsteps all the way from Willow Hill to the bakery. Outside the building she paused and stared above her at the sign that read DONOVAN'S CONFECTIONARY. Then she started to laugh. Softly, hollowly. The repainted sign symbolized so much. None of it was particularly good.

Inside the shop, she found her mother at the corner table sharing a cup of tea with her father as was their habit during the midmorning lull. So it had been for as long as Claire could remember. Her mother would drop whatever business she'd been doing at home and rush to have tea with John Donovan, always at his convenience. This morning, the midmorning lull suited Claire's purposes just fine.

As she approached the table, John Donovan scowled. "What mischief are you up to now, Daughter? Didn't you throw a fuss about not coming to work today? What are you doing in my bakery?"

It was, she thought, a singularly poor choice of words. Her temper fizzed like vinegar and soda. "Your bakery, Da? Is it really? Did you start this bakery from nothing? Did your hard work make it the viable business it is today? Or was it my efforts that built this shop?"

Her father leaned back in his chair, his chin dropping in shock. "She's doing it again, Peg," he said, his voice perplexed. "What's gotten into the girl?"

Her mother asked, "What is the matter, Claire?"

"What is the matter? I'll tell you what's the matter. I'm tired. I'm tired of fighting all the time. Tired of losing. My bakery, my friends, my freedom. The curtains I sewed for this shop. Lars eloped with Loretta Davis, did you know that? I didn't even know she was the one for him. I've hardly talked with him since the Donovans came to town."

"Lars eloped?" John said, his eyes rounding with surprise. "I don't believe it. Why, he hasn't—"

"See?" Claire interrupted, glaring at her mother while pointing toward her father. "He's doing it again. I'm in the process of telling you my deepest feelings, and he glosses right over them and zeroes in on the man in my conversation."

Tears stung her eyes and she furiously blinked them away. "Why don't I matter as much as your sons, Da? Why do you value them so much more than me? I have hopes and wishes and dreams just like Patrick and Brian. Why do theirs count and mine not?"

"Catherine Claire." His mouth hung open and he shook his head. "How can you say these things?"

"It's easy. It's been this way all my life. I've just never understood it. Why should the boys be allowed to marry the women they love, but I must marry according to your decree? Why shouldn't I get the same choices and opportunities as they? I'm as talented, as intelligent. I know I'm better at figures than both of them put together."

"But you're a girl," John Donovan declared. "Girls aren't equal to boys. That's not the way the world works."

"I'm not talking about the world, Da. I'm talking about our family. Whether I like it or not, men run the world and that's not about to change anytime soon. I can live with that. But I can't live with my place in this family. You should love me as much as you love your sons."

"I do, pumpkin. You know I do." John Donovan looked helplessly at his wife.

"Apparently not, John." Peggy Donovan patted her lips with her napkin, then set it on the table. Rising from her chair, she stood beside her daughter. "Claire is right. You do treat her like a second-class citizen."

"I don't treat her any differently than I treat you."

Peggy turned to Claire. "I never knew you, Daughter, and it shames me. I should have realized what lay at the source of your rebellion. You are so like your father." She reached out and tucked a stray curl behind Claire's ear. "Do you know that? I see so much more of him in you, than of myself."

"Mama, I—"

Peggy lay her finger against Claire's lips. "My turn. You are right. We have never listened to you. You were the little girl your father and I wanted so desperately. Our princess. We wanted to cosset you and protect you and provide for you. I never realized that your fairy tale might be different from mine."

"Peggy," John broke in.

"Hush," she told him, never looking away from her daughter. "For once, my daughter has my attention at the moment."

215

Her mother was actually standing up for her. Suddenly it was too much for Claire, and the tears she'd fought back since leaving Willow Hill spilled from her eyes and trickled down her cheeks.

"Oh." Peggy clicked her tongue and wiped her daughter's tears with her husband's napkins. "Come along, water pot. We need to talk, and I know just the way we should go about it." She extended her hand, palm out, toward her husband. "Give me money, John. Your daughter and I are going shopping."

THE RECEPTION HONORING newlyweds Loretta and Lars Sundine was Maybelle Davis's attempt to socially save face. Her housekeeper admitted to Peggy Donovan—who told Claire—that privately, Maybelle despaired at the thought of having a baker-accountant for a son-in-law rather than the titled gentleman she'd longed for. In other words, Tye McBride. Publicly, the doctor's wife told a different story. When Maybelle Davis hired Claire to provide sweets for the party, she acted tickled to death with the husband her dear, darling Loretta had chosen.

Maybelle's attitude didn't make a bit of difference to Claire. She was too busy being thrilled with having been hired for the job. Maybelle had wanted her to make the cake. Not her father or any of her brothers. Her. She'd said she trusted the quality of Claire's products after having purchased various items over the course of many weeks. She didn't have that extended experience with the baked goods the male Donovans produced. She also acted surprised that Claire even asked, when she denied any input from Lars in making the decision.

The work came at an opportune time for Claire—on the heels of her confrontation with her father. It subtly proved her point.

Overall, Claire was pleased with the progress she was making with her family. Her mother had listened to her—truly listened—for the first time in forever, and Da no longer protested her presence at the bakery every morning. True, lasting change came in little steps, she knew, and she was encouraged with the strides made so far.

Now if only she knew how to step where the McBride family was concerned. She had not spoken with Tye since the scene at Willow Hill two weeks earlier. Every time she recalled his charges, her anger erupted all over again. Throwing all her energies into reception delicacies had proved to be a welcome distraction, and as she carried the last plate of cookies to the serving table in the Davises' backyard, she smiled with satisfaction at a job well done.

The setting was everything a bride could hope for. The sun was shining and a light, airy breeze carried just a hint of chill. Splashes of yellow ribbon decorated the yawning branches of the giant pecan trees that shaded a space of open lawn a perfect size for dancing. Purple irises swimming in clear glass bowls served as centerpieces for linen-draped tables placed in friendly groupings around the yard. Near the house magnolia blossoms perfumed the air, while closer to the makeshift dance floor a string trio tuned their instruments in preparation for the party.

And, on a round table at the foot of the back steps, Claire applied the finishing touches to the pièce de résistance of her career, her first bride's cake. Her first Magical Wedding Cake.

She wondered what Tye would think when he saw it.

"Not that I want to see him," she muttered, touching up a swirl of Magical vanilla icing. She was determined to put the man completely out of her mind.

She wondered if he'd be here today.

"Come on, Claire," she softly scolded herself. "Concentrate on business. You want this cake to be perfect."

And it was. Finished with the last of her touch-ups, she stepped away and allowed herself a moment of admiration. It was beautiful. Her best work ever. Perhaps the love she felt for the groom had somehow made itself known during the creation of this cake. Whatever the reason, Claire knew—and the family would certainly recognize—that with this effort she had proven her talents equal to those of her brothers.

It was a delicious feeling.

At that moment Lars Sundine appeared with his blushing bride on the back steps. He took one long look at the cake, then dipped into a bow. Loretta clapped her hands and squealed with delight. "Everything looks so beautiful and perfect. Why, this is going to be the most successful party this town has ever seen."

For the first two hours of the festivities, Claire was inclined to agree. Wilhemina's bright and airy laughter set the mood, and guests ate and danced and drank with gay abandon. For a time she kept an anxious eye on the arrivals, wondering if Tye might show up, take a look at the wedding cake, and start yammering about aphrodisiacs.

Of course, it might be a good thing if he did. Look what the Magical Wedding Cake legend had done for the Donovan family business. Imagine what kind of a stir an Aphrodisiac Wedding Cake would cause.

Despite herself, she grinned and murmured, "It would be something to see."

"What would be something to see?" asked the groom from behind her.

Claire turned with a smile. "Me on the dance floor. I love this tune."

"Great minds think alike." Lars extended his elbow to escort her toward the swirling crowd. "That's exactly what I was thinking, Claire."

They danced two waltzes. It took that long for Lars to successfully tease her out of her pique over not being informed of the nuptials before the fact. "She's a lovely young woman, Lars, and I'm very, very happy for the both of you. And now that you're happy, I finally feel free to tell you, I never liked that Millicent Ayers."

He grinned, and his gentle, loving gaze found his wife, laughing as she twirled in the arms of Patrick Donovan. "It was the luckiest day of my life when she dumped me."

After Lars, Claire danced with a number of customers, then rested for a time, conversing with the ladies. Relaxed and enjoying herself, she grinned at Lars, who had stopped in the middle of a dance to lay a lusty kiss on his blushing bride.

Then Claire's pleasure ground to a halt with the arrival of her family—and the snake in a suit coat that slithered in with them.

"Look here, Claire," said her da, his face wreathed in smiles. He gave the man beside him a hearty pat on the back. "Look who rode in on the morning train."

She looked, all right. Looked and about lost the oysters she'd swallowed a moment ago. Must be the slime they have in common, she thought irreverently.

"He's brought us good tidings," John continued. "He's managed to buy up our debts, and we'll be able to get the company back. Isn't this glorious news!"

Claire's stomach went sour as Reid Jamieson took her hand. He lifted it to his mouth for a kiss as his gaze delved into hers, sending messages she couldn't quite interpret. When she felt his lips touch her skin, it was all she could do not to jerk her hand away and wipe it on her skirt.

"Hello, love," he said, his voice a husky drawl. "Fancy meeting you at a wedding reception."

TYE PLUCKED a pickle from a tray on the serving table and plopped it in his mouth, ruefully observing the trouble Katrina was having choosing between the potato salad and baked beans. "Take a little of both, honey. You're holding up the line."

"That's right." Maribeth nudged her sister with an elbow.

"You'd better get some and hurry up or you'll miss out on the sweet potato pie."

With that as a lure, Katrina skipped both the beans and the potato salad, leaving room on her plate for extra sweet potatoes. Tye knew she should eat more than one piece of roast beef and a stomach full of dessert that posed as a vegetable, but he simply didn't have the heart to force the issue. This was the happiest he'd seen Katrina and her sisters in days, and he didn't want to do or say anything that might dampen their spirits.

They'd come down with a severe case of missing their mama and papa.

Tye didn't know what brought it on, but it sure had hit them hard. Kat came down with it first, waking up one night sobbing for Papa. After that the malady spread through the family like the chicken pox. Shoot, even he felt a twinge or two wishing Trace would come on home. Not that he didn't enjoy his time with the Blessings, but truth be told, they had just about worn him out. Learning the truth about the girls' business with the Magic and his subsequent call on Madam LaRue in the Acre still had him waking up with night sweats going on two weeks after the fact.

The witch had put a hex on him. He'd gone down to the Acre and given her the sharp side of his tongue for the better part of an hour. By the time he'd finished with her, she'd not only sworn never to give, sell, or otherwise distribute her wares to any person under the age of sixteen, she'd also found religion and sworn to lose twenty pounds to boot. But as he was leaving, she'd experienced a moment of bravery and done the deed. She'd predicted he'd tangle with a woman who would bring him to his knees. Each night ever since, he'd tussled with Claire Donovan in his dreams.

How was it, he wondered, that despite his never having taken her on that swimming trip, he dreamed of how she looked in dripping, detailed color damn near every time he closed his eyes? It was enough to make a man swear off sleep.

He felt bad about the way he'd talked to her. He sort of hoped he'd see her here today so he could apologize. Not that he didn't mean most of what he'd said, but he could have said it nicer. And besides, once he said he was sorry, maybe he'd start getting some sleep at night.

The Blessings carried their laden plates to a table with their school friends while the string trio segued into a popular waltz. After helping the girls get settled, Tye dodged a gaggle of approaching women who had that "Lord McBride" look about them by sliding into the lone empty chair beside Lars Sundine. "Pretend to talk to me."

"Is it lord season again?" the groom asked, looking decidedly unhappy for a man at his own wedding party.

"*Still,* and the hunting's gotten worse than ever." Tye gave his head a woeful shake. "Maybelle told me the Blessings had convinced most of the women in town that I was in love with your Loretta. Now they think I'm free again."

Lars smirked. "And brokenhearted, too. They'll be wanting the chance to heal you, all right."

"With cream pies, it seems. I hate cream pies."

For the next few minutes Tye questioned the Swede about his job at the bank and whether he'd continue working at the bakery now that he was a married man. His sudden interest in Lars's life was mainly an effort to avoid accidentally catching a woman's eye. When he finally thought it was safe to look away from the groom and glance around, he got his first good look at the centerpiece of the dessert table—the wedding cake.

Somehow he knew it was Claire's work.

Well, hell. The girls can't have any cake. No matter what Claire said, he knew how Magic affected him, and he damn sure wasn't going to let the Blessings have any. They'd be sore as blisters at him, but he couldn't let that stop him. "Magic strikes again."

Then the little voice of truth inside him whispered, *Be honest, McBride. It's not the Magic that gets to you, it's the woman herself.*

"Did you say something?" Lars asked.

Tye shrugged, then gestured toward the table. "I'm surprised y'all haven't already cut the wedding cake. We arrived late because the horny toads escaped their box and Maribeth wouldn't leave home until we found them."

Lars scowled and sipped his champagne. "So you didn't hear the news?"

"What news?"

"The rumors about Claire's cake," he replied. "I could strangle John Donovan for bringing Reid here today of all days. The perfect day for him to spill his story. I can't decide if John knew what he was doing or not. I'd like to doubt it, but . . ." he lifted his shoulders in a shrug.

"What the hell are you talking about, Sundine?"

Lars Sundine sighed and tossed back the rest of his champagne. "You didn't hear the talk? All that nonsense about what a close call dear Loretta had today? How it was pure good luck she decided to wait until later than normal to cut the cake? Maybelle has sent word to the hotels and restaurants in town to deliver any cakes they might have on hand. My mother-in-law is beside herself with embarrassment, and my wife and I have had the first fight to break our wedded bliss."

Tye couldn't follow this conversation on a bet. "Embarrassment about what? I'm following only about half of what you're saying. What are you talking about?"

"You haven't heard about the—" he cleared his throat and sneered "—Bad Luck Wedding Cake?"

"The Bad Luck Wedding Cake?" Tye repeated.

Lars thumped his empty champagne glass, tipping it over. "That's what folks here in town are calling it. They're saying Claire shouldn't have risked Loretta's and my happiness. I swear I want to box the ears of each and every one of these superstitious fools."

Tye narrowed his eyes. "Does this have something to do with this fiancé person?"

"How did you guess." Lars made a fist with his right hand and stared at it. "He needs more than his ears boxed, I'm telling you. I'm just about drunk enough to do it, too." After a slight pause he added, "Loretta threatened to sleep at her mother's house tonight. She didn't like me defending Claire."

"I'll take over that job, I promise. You can keep your bride happy." Tye reached over and set Sundine's glass upright, then motioned for one of the waiters to come refill it. "But first you have to tell me the story. And start at the beginning so I can follow it this time."

Sundine nodded sadly. "It's that damned Reid Jamieson. I can't believe he fooled us all. Everyone but Claire, that is. He's the one who told Wilhemina Peters, and telling Wilhemina is telling everybody."

"What did the son of . . . what did Jamieson say!"

"He told Wilhemina about the Bad Luck Wedding Cake. Actually, of course, it's a Donovan's Magical Wedding Cake. Do you know the story, McBride? The cakes have become quite famous in recent years, not only because they taste so delicious, but because of the legend."

"I've heard some talk about it, but I don't remember exactly what."

Lars brushed a butterfly off his sleeve and continued, "One of Claire's ancestors wrote in a journal that the marriages of those couples who served a Magical Cake at their weddings appeared to be blessed with an extra measure of happiness and prosperity. Well, Reid shows up here at my reception saying Claire broke the enchantment when she left him standing at the altar. Now everyone thinks the Magical Cakes are bewitched, that they are bad luck for brides and grooms and even for the Donovan family. They say the Donovans lost their business because of the Magical Wedding Cakes, not because of ill-considered business loans."

"And—" Tye spat the name "—Reid Jamieson spread this story around?"

"Yes. Around Fort Worth, anyway. The news has already spread up and down the coast. And the people of Fort Worth bought into the idea."

Tye nodded. "They would. They're the ones who embraced the idea of a Bad Luck Wedding Dress, after all."

Lars lifted his glass to eye level and stared over the top. "So what happened to the Bad Luck Wedding Dress?"

"Jenny turned it into the Good Luck dress," Tye replied. He rubbed his hand slowly across his jaw. "That's what Claire will need to do. She'll need to somehow reverse the appearance of bad luck."

"And Reid thinks he knows just the way to do it, curse him." Lars flicked his wrist and drained his glass. "I'm hoping Claire will come up with something better. She might. She's pretty smart and she sure as hell doesn't want to do what Reid wants her to do."

"And what's that?" Tye asked, almost afraid to hear the answer.

"Ruin Claire's life, to my way of thinking." Lars propped both elbows on the table then rested his chin in his hands. "He said he's come to give her a second chance.

Tye's throat went suddenly tight. "A second chance?"

Lars nodded. "Reid said he and Claire are rescheduling their wedding."

CHAPTER 13

BAD LUCK RIDES A BLACK HORSE.

Standing in the kitchen at Donovan's Confectionary, Claire would have covered her ears with her hands had they not been sticky with bread dough. The clan was at it again.

She stared vacantly at the dust motes that danced in the sunshine beaming through the alley window and shuddered. In the front of the store her parents and brother planned out her future in loud, argumentative tones. Thank heavens Patrick had taken Reid over to the Cosmopolitan hotel to get a room. Claire couldn't bear the thought of trying to hash all this out in front of her former fiancé.

"Not a single customer since the ladies took to whispering about Claire's Bad Luck Wedding Cake," Peg Donovan said, clicking her tongue. "This isn't good."

"No it's not," Brian declared. "She should be glad Reid is still willing to wed her."

Her father observed, "The question on the table is, Will she marry him? We thought he was a good match for her a few months back, and I tend to think he's an even better match for her today. He's handsome, prominent, and he can hold his whiskey."

There was a moment of silence while the Donovan family agreed on the importance of the last characteristic.

"I don't know, John," Peggy said. "Have you looked at your daughter lately? That headstrong set to her face hasn't gone away. We need to listen to what she has to say about this."

Brian piped up. "Well, she can just be a stubborn old jenny. She can bray all the way to the altar if she wants, but she has to marry Reid."

"Brian Michael," her mother scolded. "Don't call your sister a mule."

Claire kneaded her bread dough with added vigor. They thought she'd been stubborn of late? "Just wait," she murmured softly. "Just you wait."

"You know, Claire doesn't have to do anything," Peggy continued, the lone voice of reason in the group. "This is her life that we're talking about. I wonder if we shouldn't let her live it the way she wants."

"It's all our lives," her father snapped back. "Let me remind you that when Claire bolted on Reid, it destroyed the Magical Wedding Cake's reputation and that destroyed our business. By buying up our debts and offering Claire an opportunity to restore the cake's image, he is giving this entire family another chance. If Reid is family, then the Donovan Baking Company will be back where it belongs, in the family."

With that, Claire's hands stilled and an uneasy sensation fluttered in her stomach.

"But Da," Brian protested.

"No 'buts' about it, Son. You want to marry your Cynthia, don't you? Patrick wants to tie the knot with his Eloise. What's been standing in your way? A way to support them, that's what. It doesn't have to be that way any longer. We won't have to rebuild our company almost from scratch with this little store here. You heard Reid. He needs us. Revenues have fallen way off in the bakeries."

Claire's gaze shifted to the bottles of Magic lining the shelves.

In the outer room Brian said, "That's because they've run out of Magic. Magic is what made Donovan Baking Company products so special."

"You are exactly right," John agreed. "And we—the Donovan family—are the only ones who know the recipe to make Magic. That's why Reid will return us to the helm at Donovan Baking Company. It'll be just like before."

Claire's movements were slow as she rolled her dough into a big ball and put it in a bowl to rise. She covered the bowl with a clean tea towel as Brian said glumly, "No it won't, Da. This time we'll be working for Reid instead of ourselves."

"We'll be working for family," John insisted. "Reid will be one of us."

"Only if Claire marries him," Peggy pointed out. "I'm not certain she should. He didn't have to repeat the talk about the bad luck cake, you know."

"A slip of the tongue," John defended. "And of course she'll marry him. She'll do it for the family."

Plunging her hands into a basin of wash water, Claire grimaced at her father's words.

Brian said, "She didn't do it for the family before."

"That's because she didn't know what her actions would cost us. Your sister is a Donovan and Donovans stick together. She won't let us down."

She won't let us down. The words echoed in her mind as she wiped her clean hands dry with a towel, then with heavy steps walked into the outer room. No one even noticed. They continued to debate the question as if she wasn't there. Claire smiled at the irony of it. This was the Donovan family in action. It had been this way all her life. Nothing had changed.

But she had changed. She had that backbone now, for one thing. She had learned to take a stand for what she wanted. She'd had a taste of freedom and she darn well liked it. The thought of giving up made her queasy.

But the thought of refusing her family in their time of need made her shudder in shame.

The Donovan Confectionary's greeting bell rang and Claire had never heard a more welcome sound. She twisted her head to identify her customer, but instead of calling out a salutation, she bit back a groan. Just what she needed.

Tye McBride.

But the Menaces' uncle did the strangest thing. He sauntered up to the counter and ordered every cinnamon roll in the case. Claire's mouth dropped open in shock.

"For the nuns across the street," he muttered, tossing money on the counter. He then accepted the boxed rolls from her mother and left without another word.

Once Claire got over the strangeness of the event, she breathed a sigh of relief. Thankfully, his visit had interrupted a conversation she was not prepared to have—not yet, anyway.

Following Tye's departure, and obviously believing the marriage question settled, John Donovan turned his attention to the Donovan Baking Company. Soon he sent Brian off with instructions to check on this supplier, then that piece of equipment.

By the time Tye returned to the bakery some twenty minutes after purchasing the cinnamon rolls, only Claire and her parents remained at the shop. This time he bought lemon tarts for the Baptist preacher's family and a pecan pie for the Methodist minister.

On his third appearance, he ordered cookies for the residents of Miss Rachel's Social Emporium, then casually inquired after her parents.

"They had an appointment elsewhere."

"You're alone?"

Claire hesitated only a moment before nodding.

"Good. Then cancel the cookie order and fry me up a steak and eggs, would you?" He pulled a chair away from a table and straddled it "I didn't get a chance to eat at Loretta's party, and I'm hungry enough to eat an armadillo on the half shell."

Claire dropped the box of ginger snaps on the counter hard enough to break them. "Why are you really here, McBride? It's not because you are hungry, I know."

He frowned defensively. "I am too hungry."

"Then why didn't you go to Delmonico's or another restaurant?" Her tone grew louder with every word, and she was only warming up. She'd been spoiling for a fight for hours now. "Why did you come to a bakery and order steak and eggs when I have never served them to you, despite your having ordered them every single morning when you lived upstairs?"

"Excuse me, Miss Donovan," he drawled and gestured toward the empty room. "Under the circumstances, don't you think this interrogation is a bit out of place? I would think you'd be grateful for every customer you get."

Then suddenly, to her distress, tears stung at the backs of her eyes. Blinking them away, she ignored his protest and asked again, "Why are you here, Tye? Are you happy my reputation is in the process of being ruined? Did you come to gloat?"

He muttered a curse, shoved to his feet, and headed for the door. Halfway there, he stopped. "I didn't come to gloat." Slowly he faced her, his eyes snapping with angry confusion. "I don't know why I came, all right? I just wanted . . . I needed . . . I don't know. I thought I'd better check on you."

Beneath a flush of embarrassment, Claire felt a little surge of pleasure. He'd worried about her. Even after that scene between them about the Magic, he'd cared enough to check on her. It was a soothing balm to the wound her family had given this day.

She brushed some imaginary dust off her sleeve and said, "If you want to take a seat, I'll see to your order."

For a minute, she didn't think he'd stay. Then slowly, he lifted

EMILY MARCH

his arm and took off his hat, and at once her heart felt lighter. She saw him settled at a table with coffee and a newspaper, then slipped out the back door and cut across the alley to the butcher's, where she purchased the thickest steak he had cut. A short time later, she set the sizzling meat and steaming eggs in front of Tye and waited for him to comment about the food. Instead, he folded his paper, set it aside, and picked up his silverware. "Join me," he said, pointing to an empty chair with his fork.

"I should probably mix up a cookie dough."

"Why?" He gestured toward the display case. "Looks like you have plenty to me already. You're not exactly swamped with work here today."

She sank into the seat. "That's because my customers are all at Maybelle Davis's eating my pies and tarts for free."

He rolled his tongue around his cheek. "They're not eating your cake, though, are they?"

That observation drove her back onto her feet. For something to do, she refilled his glass of water. Like a good hostess she asked, "How is your steak?"

"Delicious."

It all got the better of her, then, and she set the pitcher down hard on the table. "Delicious? I'll show you delicious. Delicious is that wedding cake in Maybelle's backyard." She slumped into a seat beside him.

He forked a slice of steak into his mouth and studied her thoughtfully as he chewed. He swallowed, sipped his water, and said, "You want to talk about it?"

"No. Yes." Swiping her finger across the ring of moisture his glass left on the table, she said, "You heard what happened?"

"The girls and I went to the reception, but we were late and you had already left when we arrived. I saw the cake, Claire. It was pretty."

A sad smile fluttered at her lips. "It was the first wedding cake I'd ever baked and it wasn't just pretty. It was beautiful. Perfect."

230

"I'm sorry I didn't get to taste it." The man sounded like he meant it. Sometimes life truly took a strange twist.

Claire looked up at the ceiling. "What are you doing here, McBride? Why are you being nice? I thought you hated me now. I imagined you'd be out there castigating me along with the rest of Fort Worth."

He set down his fork. "I wanted to talk to you."

"About the Bad Luck Wedding Cake?"

He looked away, focusing on the street outside. His profile drew her gaze. All angles and pride, with a raw masculine air. His Adam's apple bobbed as he spoke. "I said some pretty ugly things to you the other day. I'm sorry."

Her mouth twisted. "You mean 'I'm sorry I was wrong'?"

"I mean I'm sorry I said them." He drew a deep breath and exhaled loudly. Abruptly he pinned her with his stare. "Lars told me your fiancé showed up at his party."

She leaned back in her chair. "He just thinks he's my fiancé. But then, my family thinks so, too, so maybe I'm the one who is wrong." She chuckled without amusement. "Yes, Reid arrived just in time to spread the word about Donovan's Not-So-Magical Wedding Cakes. I swear if he walked through that door right now I'd let fly with a pie."

"Cream or fruit?"

"Something sticky."

Tye dragged a napkin across his mouth, then pushed back away from the table. "This town is exceptionally superstitious, Claire. My sister-in-law learned that the hard way. She made it work for her, though, and I don't see why you couldn't do it, too."

"McBride, if you agree with my family and tell me I have to marry Reid Jamieson, I'm going to find a special pie for your pretty face."

His mouth slashed a grin. "You think I'm pretty?"

She pointedly eyed the display case.

231

He reached over and squeezed her hand. "I'm not gonna tell you to marry anyone. That's not what I meant."

"Then explain yourself."

Abruptly he stood, gathered up his plate and utensils, and carried them back to the kitchen, speaking to her over his shoulder as he went "You don't love him, Claire. You wouldn't have kissed me like you did if you loved him."

Recalling the passion that had sizzled through her body with his kiss, Claire closed her eyes and rubbed her forehead with her thumb and forefinger. What did love have to do with anything? This wasn't a question of love, not romantic love anyway. Familial love was what had her backed up against a hot oven.

She thought of Patrick and Brian and the women they wished to marry. She recalled how her mother hummed while concocting new recipes in her kitchen. She pictured Da poring over the business's books, cackling with glee when he discovered a transposed number. All of them—always working, giving their best toward the betterment of the family. Just because they and Claire had different goals didn't detract from their efforts.

Claire stood and followed Tye into the kitchen. "There are different kinds of love, McBride."

He slid his empty plate into the dishwater. "True enough. But only one kind is worth marrying for."

She folded her arms. "And who made you the expert? Last time I looked, you didn't have a wife."

"Exactly." He propped a hip on her worktable and sat casually swinging his foot. "I haven't found that marrying kind of love. Maybe I never will."

"Then how can you presume to offer me advice on the subject?"

An emotion—something deep and dark and painful—flashed in his eyes. Then he said flatly, "Believe me, Claire, tying the knot with anything less than that kind of love is asking for trouble. I know. I've seen it firsthand."

"You've alluded to this before. What's your story, Tye?"

For a long moment he studied her, saying nothing. "I let myself get caught up in some ugliness between a man and his wife. I was dead wrong to do it, and I'm not making excuses. I just believe the trouble never would have happened if they'd truly loved each other."

"What trouble? What did you do?"

"Does it matter?"

As his gaze shifted away from her, instinct told her that yes, it did. Ugliness, he'd said. "Did you love her?"

Without answering, he pivoted and returned to the other room. Claire followed and found him standing in front of the window, his hands shoved into his back pockets, staring out at the street. "Tye?"

"It shames me, Claire. Maybe someday I'll get past it, but for now . . ." His shoulders shuddered as he blew out a breath. "That's all beside the point. I only mentioned it because I don't want to see you land in trouble like mine."

He turned and met her gaze, his emerald eyes flickering with an emotion that caused Claire's heartbeat to accelerate. "I care about you. I care what happens to you. I don't want to see you make this mistake."

He cared, even after the mess with the Menaces and the Magic. A ribbon of warmth spiraled through her. He'd told her before that he wanted her, but he'd never said he cared. Not until now. Claire took an inadvertent step toward him, then abruptly stopped as the events of the day came roaring back and Reid's image rose like a specter in her mind.

Slowly, sadly, she said, "I don't think I have a choice. My family needs me to marry Reid."

"Your family needs you to ruin your life?"

Claire repeated some of the arguments her father had used, ending by saying, "Donovan Baking Company is their livelihood. I took it away from them, and now I can give it back."

He waved away her justifications. "That is a stupid reason to marry a man you don't love."

"Is it?" she replied defensively, arguing with herself as much as with him. "You wouldn't marry for your family's sake? Put yourself in my place. What if your brother was in trouble? What if the Blessings were in trouble? Wouldn't you do anything in your power to help them?"

"Of course I'd do what I had to do to help them. But marrying? Look for another solution, sugar." He walked toward her, stopping an arm's length away. He reached out and slowly trailed a finger down her cheek. "Nobody understands family obligations more than me, Claire. Just make sure that when you think of what is best for family, you include yourself among the number, all right?"

"My da thinks Reid is perfect for me."

"Perfect for you, or perfect for him?"

"Tye, don't. They do love me. I know they do."

He brushed his finger across her lower lip. "They may love you, but they don't know you, do they? Tell me this, Claire Donovan. Are your loved ones going to be happy when this Jamieson character starts stepping out on you or hitting you or doing some other wickedness because you aren't giving him what he needs? Because you can't give him what he needs, because you don't love him. Are the Donovans going to be happy about that?"

Claire closed her eyes. "That's a stretch, McBride. You can't know that any of those things will happen."

"Honey, I've seen it happen. I've seen it happen and my family is still paying for it."

"But—"

"Listen to me. You think you are talking about marrying for love—your love for your family. But that's not it." His hand fell to his side as he took a step backward. "What you are really talking about in this case is marrying for money."

"Money!"

"Yeah, money. You can hide it behind talk of family loyalty and love, but when you strip it down to the nut this marriage is about cash."

"You're wrong." Claire felt the unwelcome sting of tears in her eyes. "It's not that at all."

He smiled crookedly. "Cash, cold and hard, Claire. Just like your bed is going to be if you marry this Jamieson fella." With that, he turned to go.

Claire refused to leave it at that, following him out into the front of the shop. "Blast you, Tye McBride. I thought you of all people would understand. Watching you with those girls, I thought you'd do anything under the sun for them. Apparently I'm wrong. You don't understand one thing about family loyalty."

"Family loyalty?" His laugh was bitter as he grabbed his hat off the rack near the door. "I've heard that one before. That was her excuse, too. Right before my brother killed her, she told me she'd done it for family—for the children."

Before his brother killed her? My God, was he talking about Trace? Claire tried to recall whether he'd ever mentioned another brother, but couldn't. She shook her head in confusion. 'Trace killed a woman?" Tye nodded and she asked, "Who was she? What did she do to create all this . . . rancor in you?"

He met her gaze then. His eyes were granite-hard and empty. They frightened Claire. "I've mentioned her before. Constance. Constance McBride. The Blessings' mother."

Their mother. Oh, my. A chill of sorrow swept through Claire. "Trace killed his wife? How terrible. It must have been a horrible accident."

"Yeah, it was definitely an accident."

His tone—a dry, obnoxious amusement—should have warned her, but it didn't. He caught her completely by surprise when he added, "He was aiming to kill me."

"You!" She gasped, shock widening her eyes. "Why? What happened?"

Tye's smile was ugly. "Money and greed, Claire. Guaranteed marriage killers. Take my advice and think long and hard before you agree to marry a man you don't love. I'd hate to see it kill you, too."

The door shut softly behind him.

～

TYE SAT at Willow Hill's kitchen table trying to work up the energy to read the paper or sip his morning coffee. His eyes were gritty, his movements sluggish. He had slept poorly. Between memories of Constance and worries about Claire, he'd been haunted by nightmares each time he slipped into sleep.

He stared unseeing into his cup of black coffee and wondered why the two women had gotten tangled up in his head. Claire wasn't anything like Constance. He could admit that now. So why did his mind keep trying to connect them?

Or was it his heart doing the dirty work?

He groaned and closed his eyes. Was that it? He had told himself he had gone to the bakery yesterday to caution Claire against making a foolish decision. Had he lied to himself? Was that truly the reason, or was it something else? Something more? He'd told her he cared, but did his feelings go deeper than that? Did he want her for himself?

"Of course I want her," he muttered, reaching for his coffee cup. He got hot every time he even thought about her.

But do you want her?

Tye's hand shook, rattling the cup in its saucer. Want her? As in *love* her? Had he gone and fallen in love with Claire Donovan?

Tye couldn't answer that. He wouldn't answer that. Look what happened the last time he'd loved a woman. Hell, he cared about Claire too damn much to love her. She deserved a better man than him. And if she married a man she didn't love, well, she deserved whatever she got. At least he'd warned her.

He shoved the newspaper away and it fluttered to the floor. "Let her marry Jamieson. It's no skin off my teeth."

"You have skin on your teeth, Uncle Tye?"

He glanced up to see Katrina standing in the doorway in her nightgown. She carried a stuffed bear and rubbed her eyes sleepily.

"Better than fur, don't you think?"

She giggled, then crossed the room to crawl into his lap. "I'm hungry, Uncle Tye."

"You're always hungry." He gave her the usual good-morning hug and kiss, then lifted her into the seat beside him. "What would you like for breakfast?"

"Hen seed and a raisin muffin and a . . . what's a viscount, Uncle Tye?"

Tye was too busy trying to translate his niece's Tex-anese for an egg to pay attention to the entire sentence. "What, honey?"

She pointed toward the newspaper lying on the floor between them. "In the big black letters. It says TYE MCBRIDE, VISCOUNT OF WEXFORD. See? It's right below the line that says WOMAN BAKES BAD LUCK WEDDING CAKE."

Tye scooped the paper up off the floor, scanned the front page, and winced. Poor Claire. That Wilhemina Peters had done a job on her. She'd be lucky to sell a glass of water to a thirsty man once Fort Worth got a load of this.

He paid less attention to the article about his ancestry.

Apparently, Wilhemina had kept her promise to research his title. She explained to everyone that calling him Lord McBride was incorrect, that the proper address was Lord Wexford. Then she wiped out her effort at observing the social graces by naming in the next paragraph a respectable sum of money the title was thought to be worth. Tye sighed at the invasion of privacy, but he knew it could have been worse. She could have discovered the extent of the fortune his first offspring was due to inherit. News like that would have vultures like Constance circling him for the next twenty years.

Firmly he dismissed all thought of trouble from his mind and concentrated on scrambling eggs for Kat. With the youngest girl settled at the breakfast table, he woke the older girls and hounded them all into getting ready for church on time for a change.

An hour later he hitched the horses to the buggy and drove it from the carriage house around to the front of the house. His nieces brought Ralph outside with them. "We're not taking the dog this week so you might as well let him off that rope."

Three pairs of pleading eyes stared up at him, and Tye crumbled. Just like always. "Girls, how does your daddy stand living in a house with four women?"

But his nieces didn't answer because their attention shifted toward the rider coming fast up the hill toward the house. "Mr. McBride!" the man called breathlessly as he reined his mount to a halt near the buggy. "I need to see you."

Tye recognized the man as the clerk from the telegraph office who'd been a big help when the Blessings went missing. A cold chill washed through him. Trouble just rode up to Willow Hill's front steps. He'd bet a week's worth of Blessings' hugs on it. "Mr. Jones, is it?"

"Yes, sir. Uh, I mean, Lord McBride. I mean . . . oh, what is the right way?"

"Tye." He swung out of the buggy and gestured for Jones to follow him.

"Better hurry, Uncle Tye, or we'll be late again."

"Just a minute, Katrina. Y'all stay in the buggy. I'll be right back." He led the man around the side of the house out of sight of the Blessings, then turned and said, "What is it? You got news for me?"

"Yes." Timothy Jones reached into his jacket and pulled out a folded sheet of paper. "This telegram just came. I got here as soon as I could. I'm sorry, sir. You have my condolences."

Condolences, hell. Tye's stomach took a fall to his feet. He cleared his throat and eyed the paper as if it were a rattlesnake poised to strike. *Condolences. Who?* His grandmother? Mirabelle was getting on in years, true, but she'd been so strong when he left South Carolina. *God, I don't want...*

His hand trembled ever so slightly as he reached out and took the paper from Jones. For a moment he paused, soaking in the sunshine and smelling the sweet perfume from Jenny McBride's rose garden. *Condolences*. "Hell."

He unfolded the telegram and scanned the contents. Something sharp sliced across his chest, pain so strong it caused his shoulders to hunch. His heart seemed to stop.

Lost at sea. No survivors. Ship's manifest lists ...

"No," he groaned softly. "God, no."

Mr. and Mrs. Trace McBride.

CHAPTER 14

TO BREAK A RUN OF BAD LUCK, BURN CEDAR CHIPS IN YOUR STOVE FOR FIVE DAYS RUNNING.

TYE HELD on to his control until the messenger left, then he staggered and fell to his knees. A band of pain encircled his chest, squeezing the air from his lungs. Trace and Jenny lost at sea. His brother dead. "Oh, God."

The news soaked into his soul and he waited for the sensation of being ripped in two. His twin. The other half of his whole. Dead.

Dead.

Tye shuddered. He had lost family members before. He remembered as if it were yesterday the moment he learned of the accident that had claimed his parents' lives. He knew how a protective fog descended at such news, muting the agony, and he waited for that blessed numbness to come.

But this time it didn't happen. The fog didn't come; but neither did the renting, slashing hurt.

Trace is dead. He silently rolled the words around in his head, testing them. *My twin brother is dead.*

He didn't believe it.

Tye's heart pounded. Slowly he climbed to his feet, breathing hard and heavy. He dragged a hand across his mouth, swallowed the lump in his throat, and closed his eyes. *Could it be? Dear Lord, was it possible?*

He knew how to find out.

The bond—the link. If Trace lived, if Tye searched for him, he could find him.

Gathering the talent he'd possessed his entire life, he retreated inside himself, journeying to that innermost part of him where he'd always connected with his other half, with his twin, even during the seven interminable years of their estrangement. *Trace. Are you there?*

The answer came swiftly and with absolute certainty. It warmed the chill inside him soothed his troubled heart, sent him soaring. "He's alive."

The day looked suddenly brighter, the sky bluer, the leaves on the trees leading down Willow Hill greener. His brother *was* alive. In trouble, perhaps. In a bind of some sort. But somewhere out there in this big, wide world, Trace McBride's heart continued to beat.

Tye heaved a shaky sigh of relief, and immediately his thoughts turned toward the girls. Gossip spread fast as a brushfire on a windy day in Fort Worth, and the news from the telegraph office was certain to reach the church ahead of the McBrides. He would need to deal with this now. He grimaced and muttered a curse.

All in all, he'd rather have his toenails pulled off.

He trudged back to the buggy. "I've changed my mind about church, girls. Think we'll skip it this week. Here, let me help you down. Maribeth, hand Ralph over to me.

The Blessings shared wide-eyed glances, then allowed him to swing them onto the ground. Emma said, "I don't understand. We never skip church."

"Would you please hush before he changes his mind?" Maribeth tossed her sister a glare before beaming at her uncle and passing over the dog.

Tye wouldn't change his mind. He couldn't take them anywhere in town before he explained the situation to them. Briefly he considered loading them up and taking them off on a holiday somewhere. If this trio were any less curious, he might try it. But they were curious, and they'd pester him to death about any spur-of-the-moment journey. They'd weasel his reasons out of him eventually. They'd all be better off if he dealt with the matter now.

Just how you gonna do that, McBride? he asked himself. What words would he use? How would they react? Would they believe him? Would he be able to give them the comfort and assurances they would need?

Heaven help him. "I'm in the mood to push some girls on backyard tree swings. Anyone want to help me?"

"I do," cried Maribeth and Katrina simultaneously. Emma's eyes narrowed as she shot him a curious look, but she nodded.

"Good."

Chattering with excitement, Mari and Kat dashed around the side of the house, making a beeline toward the swings. Emma followed more slowly beside Tye, who tossed a stick for Ralph to fetch. As the dog bounded off after the prize, Emma slipped her hand into her uncle's. She gazed up at him with wide, solemn eyes and asked, "Is something the matter, Uncle Tye?"

His Adam's apple seemed to double in size. "Aw, honey," he said gruffly. "It's gonna be all right. I promise you that."

That and the wink he gave her appeared to satisfy her. She walked with him up toward the old, spreading oak and the swings that hung from three of its branches.

Tye decided to wait awhile to tell the Blessings about the telegram. Thoughts of Trace weighed heavily on his mind as he pushed the girls on their respective swings. Soon he found himself relating stories about his childhood, of some of the pranks and troubles he and their father had gotten into.

And what about this time, Trace? What sort of trouble are you in now? Were you on that ship when it went down? Have you washed up on some deserted Caribbean beach?

The desire to set off in search of his brother was a fire in his blood, but it was tempered by the knowledge of the responsibility he faced right here. *I promised I'd keep them safe for you, brother, and I'll do it Just get yourself and your bride back to town as fast as possible.*

The children had been playing for almost an hour when Tye decided he'd put off the moment long enough. No telling when someone from town would show up at Willow Hill to express their condolences. It was important he get the deed done before that happened. Among other things, the girls needed a chance to believe him before the townsfolk told them they shouldn't.

The people of Fort Worth would probably label him crazy. Although, considering their superstitious nature, maybe not. He wondered how Claire would react. He'd like to think she'd believe him, but he couldn't worry about it. It didn't really matter what Claire Donovan or anyone else in Fort Worth thought. Right now the Blessings were all that counted.

He glanced across the yard to where the girls lay in a three-pointed star on their backs in the grass. Heads touching, legs outstretched, they gazed up at the clouds naming pictures while Ralph made a game out of jumping over their legs. Taking a seat in one of the rope swings, Tye called for the children to gather round. "I need to talk to y'all about something."

"It's a dragon, I tell you," Maribeth insisted as she and Katrina settled at his feet a few minutes later. Emma hung back, standing beside the tree, her grin fading as she studied her uncle's countenance.

Katrina sat cross-legged with Ralph nested down into her lap. She scratched the dog behind the ears, then looked up at Tye with an impish grin. "What is it, Uncle Tye? What do you want to talk about?"

His heart broke a bit as he gazed into their shining, innocent faces. He rubbed his thumbs along the rough hemp as he searched for the right way to say it. "I have something important to say, and I want y'all to listen to me very carefully, all right?"

The girls' expressions reflected curiosity and a hint of concern. "We'll listen," Maribeth said.

Tye worked up a smile. "The three of you are sisters, and it's a close bond. I've seen times when you look at one another and say a whole lot without speaking a word."

Their gazes met and silently asked what in the world Uncle Tye was talking about.

"Let me ask you a question," he said, searching for just the right words to get his point across. "Have you ever been somewhere doing something and you get a certain feeling that one of your sisters is in trouble?"

Maribeth's brows arched in surprise. Katrina nodded her head briskly and clutched the dog a little tighter. Emma's eyes took on a frightened look and, seeing it, Tye grimaced. He needed to tread carefully here. "It can work the other way, too. Did you ever hear the story about the time I fell down the well?"

They shook their heads.

Remembering, Tye could almost smell the earthy, wormy stink of the well. "It wasn't long after your father's and my tenth birthday. I'd snuck out of the house for some reason—I don't remember why. It was dark and I'd forgotten about the new well being dug out behind the carriage house. Fell straight to the bottom."

"Wow." Maribeth shuddered. "That must have been scary."

He nodded. "Very scary. I lost my voice early on shouting for help. They looked for me for two days before they found me. Afterward one of my sisters told me they never once worried I was in serious danger because Trace told them he could feel that I was all right."

Katrina nodded decisively. "That's cause you are twins and y'all have an extra-special connection. Papa told us about that before he left on his trip."

"He did?"

All three girls nodded, and Maribeth added, "During his lecture for us to mind you. He told us he'd know it if we misbehaved."

"He even said Fairy's Promise," Kat added.

"Fairy's Promise? What's that?"

The youngest McBride's eyes grew solemn. "It's what we say when we really, really, really mean it."

"Oh, I see. I'll have to remember that." Returning to his point, Tye said, "Your papa was exactly right about our connection. You see, girls, the bond Trace and I share is special. I always know he's with me. I even knew it all those years when we were apart. And I can feel him now. I know as sure as I'm sitting here that your papa is all right."

Emma took a step forward, her hands clasped at her waist. She started trembling. "Why wouldn't he be all right, Uncle Tye?"

Damn but he hated to see worry like that on a child's face. He sucked in a deep breath, then dragged a hand wearily along his jaw. "The man who came to the house this morning works at the telegraph office. He brought news, girls. Bad news. Now, some folks will say it's wrong of me to do this, but I don't think so. Not feeling like I do. I want you to know that I don't believe it's true." He thumped his chest with his fist. "The knowledge is in here. Trace is still here."

A moment of silence dragged out until Maribeth asked, "What are you saying, Uncle Tye?"

He grimaced at the quaver in her voice. They were bright children. They would put it together quickly. He decided not to prolong the moment any longer. "Your mother and father were listed as passengers on a ship that sank off the Florida coast. The authorities claim your parents didn't make it. I'm saying I don't believe it's true."

"Didn't make it?" Emma asked, her voice a reedy squeak. "Didn't make it like dead?"

The younger girls gasped. "Dead!"

"But it's not true, girls," he insisted, his throat tight. "My twin's heart tells me so. I don't believe it."

Like a trio of falling dominoes, the girls reacted to the news. First, Katrina pushed Ralph out of her lap and stuck her thumb in her mouth. She scrunched up her face for a few seconds of thought, then shrugged. "I don't believe it either. Papa promised he'd be home for my birthday in July. A Fairy's Promise. Papa never breaks a promise." She got up and skipped toward the other side of the yard where Ralph now stood yapping at a stray tabby cat stepping haughtily along a fence rail.

Next, Maribeth, her complexion pale as a new moon, picked at the grass blades clinging to her skirt. She didn't meet his eyes as she spoke in a low, hesitant voice. "Uncle Tye, this feeling you have? What is it like? Is it warm or cold or what?"

He saw she blinked furiously and his heart cracked. "Warm, honey. Very warm. Like a glowing coal in my heart."

"But how do you know it's Papa? And what about Mama? Do you feel her, too?"

Tye reached out, grabbed Maribeth's hands, and pulled her up into his embrace. The tremors racing down her limbs tortured him. *Dear God, help me. Give me the words to make them believe.* "Because it's familiar, Mari. I know it like I know my own name. It's been part of me and your papa from the moment our hearts started beating. It's still there, still glowing. That's how I know your papa is all right."

"Mama?"

This time his heart split right in two. *Jenny.* He couldn't know about her, not like he could Tye. Unless . . .

"Uncle Tye, what about Mama!"

He hugged her tight "Aw, honey, about your mama, well . . . I'll be truthful with you. I admit I can't be totally certain, but this is what I think. Your papa loves Jenny with all his heart, and he'd be devastated if something bad happened to her and the baby she carries, right?"

Mari nodded against his shoulder.

"Well, I'm pretty sure that if he were hurting that much, I'd know it. And I haven't felt a thing, not even a twinge. I really think he's fine and your mama's fine and that baby she's growing is fine, too. Do you believe me, Maribeth?"

Again, she nodded. "I think so, but it wouldn't hurt to run it past Spike, would it? Just to double-check?"

"If you want sweetheart," Tye told her. "I'd like to ask the questions this time, though, if you don't mind." He'd make damn certain to word them so that no matter how the fish flopped, Mari would have the answers she needed—that her mother and father were alive.

Maribeth pulled away and smiled tremulously up at him. Tye looked past the tears clinging to her lashes and spied the hope shining in her eyes. Reassured, he leaned down, kissed the tip of her nose, and asked her to go check on her younger sister.

Then he turned his attention to Emma. He saw no sign of hope on her face. The child looked sad enough to cry a waterfall and scared like she was strangling on her own heart. *She doesn't believe me.*

"Emma?"

The tears started then, plump pearls of misery rolling down her face. Tye rocked from the swing onto his feet. He knelt before her and thumbed the wetness off her cheek. Gently he said, "Darlin', what's this? Don't tell me you listen to what a perch's tail tells you but not your uncle. You have to believe me, Em."

"I can't."

"Ah, baby, you must. Listen to me. In my heart, I know your pa is alive."

Her body trembled. Her voice quavered. "It might be Papa's ghost in your heart. You don't know, Uncle Tye." Her fists clenched into tight little balls and her voice sobbed out in anguish. "Don't lie to me. I'm not a little baby. I'm not stupid."

"Em, I'm not lying."

"But you can't know!" She lifted her little fists and pounded his chest, every blow a bruise to his aching heart. "Papa's never been dead before! Maybe you'll always feel him, no matter what. Maybe it's true and he's dead and Mama's dead and we'll never see them again!"

Helpless, Tye watched Maribeth approaching with Katrina in tow. He saw them hear their sister's fear. Kat's thumb went farther into her mouth, her eyes as round as a Comanche moon.

Maribeth stopped in her tracks, and her pigtails started swinging as she shook her head, slowly at first, then faster and faster. "You hush, Emma McBride," she said, taking a threatening step forward. "They're not dead. They're not!" She was a half-pint warrior, fierce and furious as she shouted. "And you don't say that ever, ever again!"

Emma—the leader, their strength—trembled like a willow in a gale. "But Mari, their ship sank!"

"No!" Maribeth launched herself at her sister, shoving her to the ground.

Tye grabbed Mari around the waist, ignoring her flailing fists and kicking legs, and pulled her back against him. He murmured soothing words into her ear like he would a skittish horse, his gaze darting between Kat and Emma, who lay sobbing into the green grass of spring.

Never in his life had he felt so helpless, so impotent. So overwhelmed. What should he say? What should he do?

Brother, I could use a little help here.

Help arrived, bearing chocolate and the soft, cradling comfort of feminine arms. Without so much as a word, she shoved the cake into his hands and dropped to her knees on the ground beside Emma, gathered her close, then held out her arms to the others.

This time she wove her spell with compassionate words and maternal gestures, and Tye gave thanks for Claire Donovan's magic.

She lifted her head and their gazes met and held. Her eyes glimmered with empathetic tears. A surprisingly strong need for her understanding and belief swelled inside Tye, but as he searched for words of explanation, Emma broached the subject for him. Lifting a tear-stained face, she said, "Uncle Tye says it's not true. He says he'd know in his heart if our papa was . . . was . . . gone. What do you think, Miss Donovan?"

Beneath the focus of her troubled gaze, Tye lifted his chin defensively and tried to explain. "He's my twin. We share this . . . connection. My heart tells me he's all right."

She addressed Emma, but kept her gaze on him. "Well, sweetheart, I do know this. Much of this world God gave us is beyond our understanding, and if your uncle believes he has a special connection with his brother, well, I'm not one to naysay."

It wasn't the most resounding show of faith he'd ever received, but it seemed to console Emma. She calmed down and dried her tears. Then all the girls indulged in large slices of Claire's chocolate cake. Tye never once considered denying them the Magic.

Condolence calls began with a vengeance, and by two o'clock, bereavement foodstuffs filled the McBride family larders even fuller than those first days of the impress-Lord-McBride movement. By three P.M. Tye's patience had run out. He climbed halfway up the central staircase, fumbled in his pockets, and pulled out Katrina's hairbrush. For a moment, he frowned down at the object—he couldn't remember how it got there—but then he banged the handle against the banister, calling for the softly murmuring crowd's attention.

"I want to thank you all for your consideration in stopping by here this afternoon, but the fact of the matter is, you can cart your casseroles right on back home. Your hearts are in the right place, but my family doesn't need the condolences. My brother and his bride did not perish in the shipwreck."

He went on to give them a brief explanation of the tie between twins, and once he was finished, the visitors scattered like buckshot.

The evening edition of the *Daily Democrat* ran the story, quoting Tye's assertion that Trace and Jenny McBride survived the sinking of their ship. A sidebar to the account gave the results of a survey of the townspeople conducted by the newspaper shortly before press time. According to the report, the people of Fort Worth were evenly divided on the question of Tye McBride's sanity or lack thereof.

By midnight, almost a dozen healthy-sized bets concerning his mental state had been placed in venues ranging from a Hell's Half Acre saloon to the Episcopalian Ladies' Sunday Night Sewing Circle. At one A.M. Monday morning Tye laid down a hundred dollar bet on himself at the Green Parrot Saloon. Two A.M. found him feeling run down, run over, and wrung out.

Two-fifteen found him rapping on the cool glass pane of Claire's bedroom window.

CLAIRE GAVE HER HEAD A SHAKE, trying to dispel the fog of a fitful sleep. Had she dreamed it? She glanced again toward her window. No, this dark shadowed figure peering through her gingham curtains was no figment of her imagination. *Of her fantasies, perhaps.*

Rising on her knees, she pushed aside the curtains.

"Tye?"

With the nights having grown warmer, it was her habit to sleep with her windows cracked open. He slipped his fingers into the narrow opening and tugged the window fully open. "Hi, sugar."

"What are you doing here? Where are the girls? You didn't leave them home alone?"

"I telegraphed Mrs. Wilson. Figured that leg oughta be good and healed after all this time. She agreed that the girls needed her more than her daughter did at the moment, so she came over from Dallas on the evening train. She'll stay at the house for a while rather than sleeping at her place. I don't have to hurry home."

"How are you, Tye?"

"Do you mean, am I crazy for thinking they're still alive?" He laughed then, but it wasn't an amused laugh. It was an anguished noise that cut her to the core.

"Oh, Tye. Why have you come? Do you need my help?"

"What I need is a little of your magic. Meet me on the porch swing?"

She knew this probably wasn't the best of ideas, but she couldn't tell him no. She didn't want to tell him no. Lifting her robe from the foot of the bed, she slipped it on and padded barefoot across the polished wood floor. She turned the lock on the front door, quietly pushed it open, and slipped outside.

Moonlight bathed the yard, but the porch where the swing hung was cast in deep, dark shadows. Although she couldn't see him, she knew he was there. His sadness hung like a ghost across the darkness.

"C'mere, sugar."

The porch swing gave a squeak. Claire's eyes slowly adjusted to the lack of light, and she made out the profile of his body settled at the far end of the swing. She intended to take a seat at the opposite end, but as she went to sit, he reached for her and dragged her down next to him, tucking her beneath the shelter of his arm. She didn't have the heart to resist, so she lay her head against his chest and relaxed.

They sat gently swinging, not speaking, for a good quarter-hour. With the passing of each minute, Claire felt his tension ease, and the knowledge pleased her. She was helping him and that made her feel good. When Tye finally spoke, his choice of topic surprised her.

"So what's the latest with you and Jamieson? Have you booked the church?"

Claire groaned. There went her good feelings. "Not yet. I've been thinking about what you said, Tye, but I don't know what's right. I don't know what to do." After a moment's pause, she added, "I love my family, very much. But they are so blind where Reid is concerned."

She could have said more, but she didn't want to. She didn't want to think about her difficulties at all. Of course, that's probably how Tye felt, too, and as far as troubles were concerned, an unwanted marriage paled in comparison to the death of loved ones.

Claire relaxed against him, offering her comfort without words, accepting his in return. Long moments passed with only the chirp of the crickets and the creak of the swing breaking the silence. She startled when he asked, "Do you think I'm crazy?"

"Crazy?" It took her a second to make the connection. "Do you mean because you believe Trace is alive?"

He drew a deep breath, then exhaled it slowly, saying on a sigh, "Yeah."

Claire reached up and grabbed his hand, lacing her fingers with his. "What I told Emma was the truth. I believe that a lot of our world is beyond our understanding. I can accept that you and your twin share a connection that is something . . . more. So, no, I don't think you're crazy." After a moment's consideration she added truthfully, "What I do think is that you have a difficult road ahead of you where your nieces are concerned; at least, until the day Trace and Jenny return to Fort Worth."

His hand squeezed hers hard. "And there is no telling when that'll happen."

She didn't know how to answer that, so she remained silent,

holding his hand, listening to the soothing, steady creaks of the swing. Tye spoke next in a voice so low Claire had to strain to make out his words.

"I've catered to them, spoiled them rotten."

"You've loved them."

"Yeah, but I've let them get by with too much. It was easy being an indulgent uncle. I haven't worried about discipline and the likes because I've known Trace would be home soon to straighten out my mistakes. But now . . . well . . . it could drag on. What if I can't do it right? What if I ruin the girls?"

"Oh, Tye." She shifted, turning toward him. She touched his cheek. His insecurity was understandable under the circumstances, but difficult to watch. Tye McBride wasn't an insecure kind of man. "You won't ruin them. Now that you know it must be done, you'll figure out how to deal with the more . . . challenging aspects of their behavior, I feel certain of it."

"I want to do right by them."

"Then you will."

She felt him smile. "I wish I could be as confident about it as you seem to be."

"Give it some time, Tye. That's all you need."

"No, you're wrong." The pain in his voice sliced to her heart, and she wanted to weep. "I don't need time. I need my brother. I need you. That's why I came here tonight, sugar. I need a little taste of your magic."

His lips brushed hers once, then twice. Longing gripped her, and she whispered his name. He responded with a long, deep, life-affirming kiss that Claire surrendered to completely. Tye McBride literally stole her breath.

He eventually released her mouth and nibbled his way along the curve of her jaw to her neck. Lost in the sensual haze he created, she barely heard him murmur. "I've figured out the secret ingredient."

Her head was still spinning. His comment made no sense. "What?"

"Your aphrodisiac." He nipped at her ear. "It's you. You dip your finger in the brew."

He made her shiver and tingle all the way to her womb. She felt so very alive. "I do not," she replied in a husky voice. "I'll have you know I keep a very clean kitchen."

"The kitchen isn't the room I had in mind, sugar." He again brought his mouth to hers, and the passion in his kiss left no doubt as to which room he referred.

Claire knew she shouldn't be kissing Tye McBride on her front porch. Her brothers had been known to pay calls in the middle of the night in the past. Just two days earlier, in fact, Patrick had mentioned strolling past her house to check on her while on his way to the bakery for the earliest morning shift. If she had any smarts at all she'd tear herself from Tye's arms and retreat to the safety of her house. Instead, she burrowed in a little deeper.

Then, all of a sudden, he was gone, standing away from her beside the porch railing. The swing rocked crookedly as a result of his abrupt departure. "Tye?"

"Are you going to marry him?"

The question was a bucket of January well water. She slumped back in her seat, her emotions swaying like the swing. She hated him for asking, for bringing up Reid and spoiling a truly magical moment. "The situation was different when I refused him last time. They had the bakeries. They had their reputations. Now they have nothing."

"They have each other," he snapped. "They have you. That makes them damned lucky."

Oh, Tye. Suffering so at his brother's disappearance. Claire shrugged. "That's true. But I love them, Tye, warts and all. With this one act, I could make their lives so much easier. I could make them happy again. How can I not marry Reid?"

"Fool. You don't love him. I warned you, Claire."

A band of misery tightened around her chest, allowing the bitter truth to break free. "Maybe I'm safer not loving the man I marry. My mother loves my father, and I've seen what it has done to her. She's John Donovan's wife instead of Peggy. She's lost herself in him. I don't want to lose myself."

He snorted. "So you're going to tie yourself to a man for life? Excuse me, but I can't quite get the pieces to fit."

"It's family, Tye. I'd think under the circumstances you should be a bit more understanding about the lengths one will go to for family's sake."

"Yeah, well . . . oh, forget it." His footsteps shuffled away and when he descended the porch steps without another word, Claire thought their tête-à-tête was done. She was wrong.

Halfway down the front walk, she heard the rattle of gravel as he turned and came back. He climbed the steps, stopped, and asked, "Do you believe in ghosts?"

Now she was totally confused. "What?"

"Emma asked if what I feel could be Trace's ghost. She thinks since he's never been dead before, I couldn't know if the sense of life I feel is him or his ghost."

Her ire melted as her heart wept for him. But sensing his need, she forced a scathing note into her tone. "Quit doubting yourself, McBride. Especially when it concerns something the children say or do. It's not attractive and besides, if you do it in front of anyone but me, Trace is liable to hear about it when he gets home. Imagine how that will make you feel. You don't want him to think you had any doubts about your abilities to care for the Menaces, do you?"

Her strategy worked. "They are the Blessings, and I can care for them just fine," he insisted. "See that you don't forget that."

He left then, and even the crickets grew quiet. Claire rose from the swing, reentered the house, and crawled back into bed. What a day. What a night.

But as she drifted off to sleep, she did so with a bittersweet smile upon her face. The man who had marched away from the cottage walked with confidence rather than doubt. *All in a night's work, Donovan. Now if only you could do the same trick for yourself.*

She had told him she'd probably marry Reid after all.

Against her pillow, her smile melted into a frown.

TYE GOT through the next two weeks on what felt like determination alone. Katrina's thumb took up permanent residence in her mouth. Maribeth carried that damned fortune-teller fish around with her all the time, asking questions about Trace and Jenny. And Emma, poor sweet Emma, was grieving. She wasn't sleeping, wasn't eating, and she threw a conniption fit if she went looking for a family member and couldn't find them right away. Tye didn't know what to do with the child. He tried to keep her busy, but she was even giving him trouble about getting up and going to school.

He figured an extra dose of security might do the girls some good, so he brought them with him to the meeting with his attorney to sign over the Oak Grove plantation to his sisters. His plan backfired. As he scratched his John Henry across the contract, and while her sisters cheered because their Uncle Tye owned only one home and it was in Texas, Emma's eyes sparkled with tears.

When they left the attorney's office, Tye gave Maribeth a nickel and sent her and Katrina ahead to the candy counter in the mercantile. He wanted a few moments with Emma by herself. "What is it, honey?"

She shrugged and drew a circle in the dirt with the tip of her shoe. It took a little more coaxing, but he finally got her to explain her weepy eyes. "It's 'cause of the plantation."

Exasperation gripped him. "I thought you wanted me to settle in Texas. I thought this would make you happy."

"I do. It does," she insisted, a tear overflowing and spilling down her cheek. "But you didn't do it before. I can't help but worry why you are doing it now. Is it 'cause you think you're wrong about Papa? Have you changed your mind? Do you think he's dead?"

Tye knelt right there in the middle of the dusty—and, thankfully, lightly traveled—side street. He drew Emma into his arms for a hug. "No, baby, that's not it at all. I've been meaning to do this ever since I bought my ranch land. I just never got around to it. It has nothing to do with your father."

He told the child the truth, more or less.

The deeper he got into this cattle ranching, the less certain he felt about making it his primary business. Investing in the land didn't bother him; he had enough Southerner in him to believe it never hurt to own a substantial amount of land. And he had to do something; he wasn't the type to sit around spending an inheritance he didn't care about having. Nor did he care to do nothing more than baby-sit the Blessings. That wouldn't set a good example for the girls.

Cattle ranching on a temporary basis had been one thing. Doing it long-term was something else entirely. He liked beef much better on the plate than on the hoof. And with every day that passed without word from his brother, Tye feared that long-term was exactly what they faced. Once life settled down a bit, he thought he might spend a little time investigating the infant industry of oil exploration. The idea of hunting oil appealed to him. A throwback, he guessed, to the days of his childhood when he and his twin had spent day after day searching the Carolina coastline for signs of lost pirate treasure.

Emma reclaimed his attention by tugging on his sleeve. "We'd better hurry, Uncle Tye. Kat and Mari are inside the store and I can't see them."

She gave his heart another little crack with that, and he reassured her he could see her sisters' heads bobbing in the storefront window.

All in all, it proved to be a fine afternoon. The girls took half an hour picking out their sweets at the mercantile while Tye placed orders for supplies he'd need out at the new place. On the way home he asked the Blessings to start thinking of a name for the ranch. Their suggestions, both silly and serious, had them all laughing as Tye drove the buggy up Willow Hill.

Tye's smile died when he spied the visitors seated in the white wicker furniture on the front porch. *What the hell was this?*

He recognized the woman right off. He wouldn't have known the man if he hadn't seen him with her. It had been a long time since the trial. They had aged poorly. Grief would do that to a person. Concern was a caterpillar crawling up his spine.

"Who are those people, Uncle Tye?" Maribeth asked before taking another bite of her licorice rope.

Tye didn't want to announce it out here in the open, in front of the trees and frogs and roses. He didn't want to tell them at all. He figured their lives would have been much better off never having known these particular people even existed. God knows his would have been.

He ignored Maribeth's question, instead saying, "Girls, I need you to hop out of the buggy, run around back, and up to your rooms. This is important, Blessings. I need your Fairy's Promise you'll do this."

"What is it, Uncle?" Emma said anxiously, ignoring her sister. "Is it about our parents? Do these people know something about Papa and Mama? I can't leave, Uncle Tye. I have to know the truth."

Damn. Tye set his jaw. This time Emma broke his heart right in two. *Dammit to hell and back.* He took the time to meet her gaze. "I know these folks from back home. They don't know anything about your parents. You have my word, Em. I have some personal business to discuss with them, and it's nothing you and your sisters need to overhear. Now, I need to talk with them. Alone, Emma. Mind me on this, all right?"

Slowly she nodded.

"Fairy's Promise?" Tye insisted. Once she agreed, the others nodded also. Tye pulled the buggy to a stop and the girls hopped out. In a flash they disappeared around the side of the house.

In front of the house Tye jumped down from the buggy and secured the horses. His pulse pounded like a locomotive's piston as he turned around slowly and politely tipped his hat. "Afternoon, George. Beatrice."

As usual, the dragon lady spoke first. "Well, if it's not the man who murdered my daughter."

Tye forced a crooked grin. "Now, ma'am, I didn't actually shoot her. And besides, the judge ruled it accidental death, not murder."

The man took off his hat and twirled it on one finger. The woman's eyes shot fire. "That was no trial, that was a travesty of justice. Thank heavens your brother finally got what he had coming, even if it is years too late. Trace McBride deserved to die."

Tye held on to his temper with great effort. "Shut up, Beatrice," he warned. "It's plain to see where Constance got her meanness. Now, what are you doing at my brother's house?"

"Your brother's house?" she laughed. The sound made Tye's skin crawl. "Not anymore. A dead man doesn't own property."

"He's not dead."

"Yes, he is. I read it in your own newspaper and confirmed the contents of the telegram you received. Your brother is dead and I'm here—" she glanced at the silent man beside here "—we're here, to take our grandchildren home to New Orleans." Time froze in its tracks. "The hell you say," Tye spat. Her eyes took on a predator's gleam. "You are an acknowledged drunkard, Tye McBride. It is public record that you molested your own brother's wife."

A cold chill washed over him. "That's a lie."

Beatrice West's eyes gleamed with wicked satisfaction. "And, to make it even more tidy, you are a bachelor. No court in the country will give you custody of my three minor granddaughters."

"Their father gave me custody."

She shrugged. "Their father is dead. Their mother is dead, too, and it might as well have been by your hand. Call them, McBride. I want to meet my granddaughters. We'll be leaving for New Orleans on the morning train."

His rage came on fast and furious and so strong that, had he been wearing a gun, he'd have pulled it and fired. "*Over my dead body.*"

George West spoke up for the first time. "Yes, well, that can be arranged."

CHAPTER 15

BAD LUCK CAN LAST A LIFETIME IF A MAN TAKES NO STEPS TO CHANGE IT.

DINNER AT DELMONICO'S was a dismal affair for Claire. She kept wondering how Tye and the girls were making out. She kept wishing she were somewhere other than Fort Worth's premier restaurant.

The entire Donovan family was in attendance, along with soon-to-be-in-law Reid Jamieson. Right now Claire doubted it could be any different.

She'd lived with the knowledge half the night and all day long, ever since Tye forced the issue. What choice did she have? When she'd left Reid at the altar she hadn't dreamed it would cost the Donovans the family business, but in a roundabout way it had. Whenever she wasn't feeling self-righteous, guilt ate at her like an acid. Now, for reasons she couldn't quite fathom, Reid had offered her—and her family—another chance.

Of course, he'd also taken away their one alternative. Reid and his big mouth had all but ruined the bakery's business.

The only surprise of the evening so far was that her father had actually called him on that. Reid apologized, claiming he'd never intended to do any harm, but that seeing a Magical Wedding Cab brought the pain of his own aborted wedding to mind and subsequently loosened his tongue.

Claire didn't believe it for a minute. She wasn't certain how her family took it, either.

She stabbed her fork at her serving of beefsteak, picked up her knife, and cut a small piece of meat. The Bad Luck Wedding Cake. What foolishness. It was as if Reid had set out deliberately to force Claire's hand.

As she brought her food to her mouth, she glanced across the table toward Reid. A few moments ago he had announced his intention to open a Donovan Bakery in Dallas. This started a storm of discussion because neither of her brothers wanted to live in Dallas, and they didn't like the idea of a business bearing the family name if none of the family worked there. Claire agreed and attempted to offer her opinion. For once, her father and brothers actually halted their argument and listened to her. Reid didn't. He resumed speaking with her father as if she had not spoken.

Worry shined in Peggy Donovan's eyes as she met Claire's gaze across the table. She glanced from her daughter to Reid then back to Claire again. Could it be that her mother might actually have realized Reid Jamieson wasn't the paragon everyone believed?

Wonderful. Now that it appeared to be too late, someone in her family finally opened their eyes.

Her food tasted sour. Claire swallowed, then set down her fork. She was through eating. She had no appetite for anything at this table.

Why does he want to marry me? She asked herself the question for at least the hundredth time. Men usually had reasons for wanting to marry a woman, love or money being the two that first popped to mind.

Obviously money wasn't the reason. Reid had five times more money than Claire or her family. He also didn't need to marry her gain control of the Donovan Baking Company. He did that wh he bought up her father's loans.

So that left love, and Claire seriously doubted the man was in love with her. How could he be after she'd left him practically at the altar, embarrassing him in front of all of Galveston society? Besides, he certainly didn't act like a man in love. He spent most of his time with her family. He didn't seek her out when she was alone. He hadn't tried to kiss her since his arrival in Fort Worth.

No, he wasn't motivated by love. Heck, it wasn't even lust. Now that Claire had some experience with true sexual sparks, she realized nothing of the kind had ever existed between her and her former fiancé. After all, what kind of man didn't even try to sneak a kiss from the woman he'd traveled hundreds of miles to marry? Claire had received more kisses from Tye McBride than from Reid Jamieson.

Now that, Claire thought with an impish smile of remembrance, *was lust*.

She sipped at her glass of water, observing her erstwhile fiancé over its rim. So if Reid didn't need her money or her love or her lust, what did he need? What *did* he want? Why did he want to marry her so badly?

The question apparently didn't bother her family. She was the only one who had expressed the slightest interest in the idea. She'd hinted at the question before in conversation with Reid, but he'd always sidestepped an answer. Now that it looked as if this wedding might actually take place, she thought she deserved an answer.

I'll ask him right out, she decided. Revenge, pride, whatever the reason, she'd demand he come right out and say it.

She stewed on the notion throughout the rest of the meal and while her brothers escorted her home. Unable to relax, unable to put aside the idea, she threw caution to the wind and returned to the hotel where she knocked on Reid Jamieson's hotel room door. Her mouth went a little dry as she listened to his footsteps approach.

The door swung open. "Why, Claire," he said, his thin brows arching in surprise. "What in the world are you doing here?"

"Funny, that's the same question I'm here to ask you." She stepped into his room without invitation and gave a curious glance around. Green velvet draperies, gilded rosewood furniture, a silk counterpane filled with down—this had to be the most expensive room the Cosmopolitan had to offer. No, Reid wasn't after her little cache of cash.

Reid started to reach for the jacket lying at the foot of his bed, then stopped abruptly. His eyes suddenly narrowed, and she could all but see his speculative thoughts. He walked out into the hallway, glanced to the right and to the left, then stepped back into the room and closed the door. "What can I help you with, my love?" he purred.

My love, hah. If she was his love, Davy Crockett didn't die at the Alamo.

Claire drew a deep breath and prepared to lay all her cards on the table. "Reid, why do you want to marry me?"

"What kind of question is that?" he replied, attempting a shocked and hurt demeanor.

He didn't fool her for a second. "You don't love me. You don't lust after me, and I have no material goods or social connections you might covet. I don't understand. Please, Reid, tell me what you want, and maybe we can figure out a way for us both to be happy."

"Claire, Claire, Claire. You are misreading the situation entirely."

He made her think of a snake. A charming snake. At her skeptical look, he laughed and reached for her right hand, giving it a reassuring pat. "Of course I love you. You are everything I want in a wife: beautiful, witty, loyal to your family. Brian told me just this afternoon that loyalty has always been one of your most admirable qualities."

"If you need loyalty, you should get a dog."

He took her hand in his and lifted it to his lips for a kiss. "You'll make me the perfect wife."

"No, I won't." Claire yanked back her hand, wanting to wipe it on her skirt. "I won't make you happy, Reid. I don't love you."

Straight white teeth flashed. "Love will grow. And even if it doesn't, you'll be an asset to me. Look at what you did with Donovan's Confectionary all on your own."

Claire scowled and muttered, "And look at what you did to the business with a few dropped rumors."

Reid began pacing the room, warming up to his subject. "You surprised me, Claire. I never expected you to create such a success all on your own. Your idea of adding tables and chairs in the bakeries was inspired. Once we're married and I have the recipe for Magic, I hope to open new shops to complement the ones I already own. We'll make certain to occupy only those buildings large enough to accommodate table service. Why, I may even put you in charge of the details, Claire. How do you like that?"

"I'm positively beside myself with good cheer," she drawled in a desert-dry tone. "I know you would listen to my ideas, just like you listened to my opinions tonight at dinner."

Pausing in his pacing, he chastised her with a look.

She folded her arms and retaliated with a sweeping, scathing glare. "You don't want my opinions, you don't want my love, you don't want my lust, you don't need my money, so what is it, Reid? Tell me what you want."

"Don't be so certain of *my* lust, my love," he said, his stare drifting down to her bosom. "You are quite attractive when riled."

Her hand itched to slap him. "Why, Reid? What do you want? You are wealthy. You have a family and a business. The Jamieson Bank is extremely successful."

"The Jamieson Bank is my father's, not mine. The Donovan Baking Company is—" he thumbed his chest "—mine. My father has no say in how I run it. It's a small start, true, but it's a stepping stone to bigger and better things. I intend to build an empire, my own business empire, and you are going to help me do it."

Light dawned. A father-son competition. That's what this was all about. Heaven knows with her brothers she'd seen her share of that, but in her home the contests usually revolved around games of one sort or another, never business. "You want to build an empire of bakeries? Bakeries? Wouldn't shipping or railroads be more appropriate for that kind of thing?"

His dark eyes gleamed with a fanatical light she'd never seen in him before. "Bakeries are a start. My start. I don't have a railroad or sailing ships. I'll do it with Magic." With that, he yanked her into his arms and despite her struggling protest, kissed her with more passion than he'd ever shown her before.

Good heavens, the man is a lunatic. Claire wrenched herself away and swiped the back of her hand across her mouth. She stood staring at him, her chest heaving, as her thoughts whirled like a springtime twister.

Slowly everything fell into place. *I'll do it with Magic*, he had said. That was it. That's why he wanted so badly to marry her. *For the Magic*. She should have seen it. They all should have seen it. She'd bet her favorite mixing spoon he tried to buy the recipe for Magic from her father. She asked him about it.

"Of course," he replied, his stare fastened on her mouth. "The stubborn old cuss refused to sell."

Claire nodded. Of course he'd refused. Each person who was given the recipe swore an oath to keep it in the family. John Donovan might be a blind, stubborn man, but he would never break his word.

Reid took a step toward her, his dark eyes burning with lust.

I don't believe this, Claire thought, backing away. The man lusts over a recipe. Maybe Tye had the right of it all along.

He lunged for her but she darted away, scrambling toward the door. "Claire," he protested when she wrenched it open. "We're not done here. Don't you dare—"

She slammed the door in his face. Fleeing down the stairs she exited the hotel and turned toward home. Well, her mission had been a success. She had certainly learned the answers she'd sought. Reid Jamieson lusted after Magic and dreams of commerce. "He can go kiss his account books," she muttered.

She had to think about this. For her sake, for the family's sake, she must find a way out. Reid Jamieson would not get his hands on her Magic.

DAWN CREPT across the sky like a thief, stealing away the pleasures of the night down in Hell's Half Acre, leaving behind a fresh new morning. Tye glanced above him as he climbed the courthouse steps, shaking his head and sneering at the three-storied, boxy design. "Ugly as sin," he grumbled as he entered the building and tugged off his hat. The town fathers should have hired Trace as the architect. He'd have done a damn sight better. Of course to be fair, at the time the courthouse had been built, Fort Worth knew Trace McBride only as the owner of the End of the Line Saloon—not a talented, accomplished architect.

Tye dismissed thoughts of the past and focused on the present as he made his way up to the top floor of the courthouse where W. G. Rawlins, Attorney at Law, had his office. He wanted all his wits about him when he talked to the lawyer. This was one battle he intended to win; one war he simply refused to lose.

No way in hell would he allow the Wests to take the Blessings away from him.

He didn't have an appointment with the lawyer, but he'd sent word around to Rawlins's house the night before that he needed to see him first off this morning. Tye didn't expect the man to be here this early, but he had run out of patience for waiting around at Willow Hill. Waiting here at least made him feel like he was doing something.

He rounded the landing expecting to see an empty hallway leading down to Rawlins's office. Tye didn't find an empty hallway,

"God bless, Claire. What are you doing here?"

She sat on the floor beside the door to Rawlins' office, her feet tucked in beside her. She wore a modest gray dress and hairpins poked from her disheveled braid. She looked weary as a kitten walking in new mud.

"You're out awfully early this morning," she said with a wan smile.

"I could say the same about you, but this is the middle of the day for you, isn't it?" He sat down beside her, stretching out and crossing his legs at the ankles.

"Ordinarily, yes. But nothing is normal today."

"Oh." Tye placed his hat on the floor beside him. "So you're not here to deliver muffins?"

"Not today. I need to speak with Mr. Rawlins."

"You do?" In a familiar movement neither of them questioned, Tye slipped his arm around Claire and pulled her close. "How come?"

"Oh, it's Reid and the bakeries and the Magic and the marriage. My family has been up all night long trying to figure a way around it."

"Around what?"

Her smile was apologetic. "It's a long story and I'm not up to going through it right now. I'm so tired of it all. I'm just so very tired."

Tye could understand that. He'd been up all night himself, worrying to death over this situation with the girls. Finally, about an hour earlier, he'd gone and rousted the Blessings from their beds and stashed them in the Rankin Building apartment, hiding them from the Wests while he worked on the problem. Weariness had its claws in him, too.

He hugged Claire a little closer, and she rested her head against his chest. Little by little, he felt her relax. He smiled to himself when she drifted into sleep.

Resting his head against the wall, Tye closed his own eyes and enjoyed the moment; a respite of peace during an ongoing storm. *It's like the eye of a hurricane*, he thought as her scent wafted over him: sunshine and soap and Claire's own magic. With her in his arms, for the first time since the Wests had darkened Willow Hill's front porch, Tye relaxed. Just a little.

They slept until the sound of a door slamming downstairs woke them half an hour later.

"What Wilhemina Peters wouldn't give to see this," Claire muttered as she eased away from Tye. "Get up, McBride, before you cause a scandal."

"I am a scandal," he muttered, standing and stretching. He helped her to her feet, and as she blinked sleepily, he smoothed a thumb over the shadow beneath one of her eyes, wishing he could kiss it away. Instead, he bent and retrieved his hat. "I figured Rawlins would be here by now."

"Me, too. I wonder what is keeping him?"

Tye paced up and down the hall for a moment, then, just for something to do, tried the doorknob. To his surprise, the door was not locked. "Let's wait inside. It'll be more comfortable."

The attorney's office had no anteroom, just a broad mahogany desk, two black leather visitors' chairs, a small matching sofa, and a console table against one wall. Claire took a seat in one of the chairs. Tye strolled over to the window, pushed aside the draperies, and stared outside.

His stomach was tied in knots, and he was anxious for Rawlins to arrive. He needed answers and he needed them fast. "Wonder where that son of a gun is," he muttered.

She must have heard the impatience in his voice. "Has something happened with the girls, Tye?" Claire asked.

He laughed without amusement. "You could say that. Remember those letters we found in Emma's room?"

"The ones from her grandmother?"

"Please," Tye replied, grimacing. "Don't call the woman that. Especially not now that she's arrived in Fort Worth." At Claire's look of surprise, he nodded. "Yep, the dragon lady and her demon husband showed up at the house yesterday. She says she's going to take the girls from me."

"What? You're kidding."

"I wish I were." In short, succinct sentences, Tye told her of the Wests' arrival, finishing with, "I'll do anything I have to do in order to keep those girls with me. They're my Blessings, and I'll keep them until my brother returns home to fetch 'em. I figured it'd be good to have a lawyer tell me how to go about it legally."

Claire opened her mouth, then abruptly closed it.

"What? What were you going to say?"

"Nothing."

"Tell me, woman."

She shrugged as if to say *You asked for it*. "Well, keep in mind that I have not been schooled in the law, but at first glance, I'd say you need to quit claiming you know Trace is alive because you have a 'feeling.'"

"Damnit, it's true." Tye raked his fingers through his hair. "They're not dead, I tell you. My brother will come back for his children, and I damn well intend to see they're here when he does."

"Fine." Claire leaned forward, entreating him. "Believe it in your heart, but quit saying it with your mouth. People will forgive you a temporary bout of craziness under the circumstances as long as you keep it short. And you don't want the Wests to charge you with insanity if the matter goes to court."

Tye thought about that for a moment. "You have a point, Claire, but what will the girls think if I . . ." He shook his head. "No, I can explain it to them. They'll understand I'll do anything to protect them. Even lie about this. Maybe . . ." he mused, rubbing his hand along his jaw. "Maybe I should speak to the newspaper and confess I was beside myself with grief when I made that announcement. What do you think?"

"I think that would be an excellent idea. Tell Wilhemina Peters. She'll stir up plenty of sympathy for you."

In the midst of rubbing the back of his neck, Tye grinned. "Shoot, you should move around to the other side of the desk, sugar. You're doing as good a job as Will Rawlins would have done."

A masculine voice rumbled from the doorway. "I don't doubt that for a moment." Rawlins hung his hat on the rack and stepped farther into the room. "You might ought to hire her, McBride. You'll need somebody good to defend you on the breaking and entering charge I'm fixing to file."

Tye raised his hands, palms out. "The door was open, Lawyer. Have at me if you want. I'll put my faith in Miss Donovan anytime."

Rawlins smiled at her. "I can see why."

As the lawyer assumed his rightful place behind the desk, he motioned for Tye to take a seat in the second visitors' chair. "So, what can I do for you?"

His mind already engaged by his own problems, Tye didn't think to ask Claire if she wanted to go first. He relayed the story about the Wests' arrival, including the details he and Claire had just discussed. "Like I told Miss Donovan earlier, I want an attorney's advice on what to do next."

Rawlins leaned back in his chair and linked his fingers behind his head, elbows outstretched. "So, aside from the question of sanity, do the Wests have any other information they could possibly use against you?"

Tye hesitated. He should have guessed he'd have to tell it. Maybe in the back of his mind he had figured it out. But knowing it and actually doing it were two different things. Especially with Claire here to listen.

Feeling the weight of her stare, he glanced over at her. Did he have the sand to do this; to let her know the depth of his shame? If he asked her to leave, she'd go. But the soft, gentle encouragement he saw in her expression compelled him to begin. "The War of the Rebellion. Did you join the fight, Rawlins?"

The attorney nodded. "Hood's Texas Brigade. Wounded in the Battle of the Wilderness."

"I was there. From the Wilderness to the siege at Petersburg. They say it was the bloodiest six weeks of the war. When it was over, well, I had . . . memories."

Their gazes met in a moment of shared acknowledgment. He could have stopped there, Tye knew. Rawlins had seen it. He didn't need the words.

But Claire did.

Tye drew a deep, fortifying breath. He looked at Claire, held her stare, and told of blood and screams and tears. As best he could, he put the horror into words, mentioning severed legs, but stopping short of decapitated heads. "Some managed to live with it better than others," he finished, shame licking at his conscience. "I started drinking to forget. I didn't stop for years, not until Trace helped me to stop. The Wests know this. They could use it against me."

Rawlins removed a sheet of paper from his desk drawer, inked his pen, and scratched a note. "Any trouble since then?"

Trouble. Tye's stomach took a yawning dive off a cliff and he closed his eyes. He'd had trouble since then, all right. The silence dragged out, seconds taking hours to pass. His heart drummed like a smithy's hammer, pounding faster and faster. *Trouble.*

He could still ask her to leave. He was crazy to be thinking of telling her everything. Only a fool would tell her like this. Only a fool would want her to know the truth.

She took hold of his hand.

I'm a fool.

Tye realized he wanted her to know it all. He wanted her to know the very worst about him, but he couldn't say why. Self-protection maybe? Telling her would certainly kill any tender feelings she harbored for him. Once she knew him for what he really was, maybe he could rid himself of the foolish notion that hit him upon occasion—the idea that with Claire Donovan, he could have the kind of home and family he'd always wanted, the kind of life that Trace had with Jenny.

The kind of life Tye didn't deserve.

He opened his eyes and spoke to Claire, answering Will Rawlins' question. "I fell into serious trouble another time. Seeing as how the Wests are Constance's parents, they know about that, too."

Claire asked the question with her eyes. Rawlins voiced it: "What happened?"

Tye opened his mouth to reply, but the words stuck on his tongue. He shoved to his feet and paced to the console table against the wall, where a water pitcher sat. He filled a glass half full, drained it, and slammed it back onto the table. Pivoting, he looked Claire in the eyes and said, "I bedded my brother's wife."

Her sharp intake of breath was the stake in his heart he had expected. Rawlins's only reaction was to ask, "What were the circumstances? Was this an ongoing affair?"

The old shame shuddered over him. "God no, once was more than enough."

"Tell me how it happened."

"Does it matter?"

The attorney shrugged. "Depends on how badly you want to keep those kids. Give me something to work with, McBride. Give me details."

The Blessings. Grimacing, Tye forced his focus back to the Blessings, where it must remain. *Details, hell. All right.* He'd tell them the excuses he'd tried to make to himself, excuses that weren't worth the spit it took to speak them aloud.

"My brother's first wife learned of this *title* silliness and the substantial inheritance that would go to my eldest child. So, she set out to have it. This was eight, going on nine, years ago. I was already a little in love with her, so it didn't take much more than showing me some bruises and tears to convince me my brother was beating her."

"She had bruises?" Claire asked.

Tye nodded. He couldn't look at her. "Constance wanted the money badly enough to have her cohort beat her. When she claimed Trace was responsible for it, I believed her. It was just about the stupidest bit of thinking I'd ever done. Shows what liquor does to a person." Tye resumed his seat while the lawyer penned a few notes.

Bold thing that she was, Claire took over the questioning. "So you were still drinking at the time?"

"No." He gazed at her, then, needing her to read the truth in his eyes. "I hadn't had a drink in over two years. My lemonade was spiked."

"What villainy," she muttered.

Clearing his throat, he continued the sorry tale. "Anyway, Constance cried and I comforted and threw away the last little bit of honor I had left. After that I left the country and pretty much stayed drunk for an entire year."

"Where did you go?"

"Europe. I'd probably still be there but Constance summoned me home with word she had borne me a child. That bit of news eventually led to a confrontation between me, Constance, and Trace that left her dead."

The attorney stopped writing and looked up from his page wearing a troubled frown. He asked, "You killed her?"

"I was certainly part of it, but Trace actually pulled the trigger."

"Thank God for that," Rawlins muttered. "And the child?"

"Katrina. Trace took all three girls and ran. That's how he came to live in Fort Worth. I finally tracked him down last year."

"This is good," Will Rawlins said. "With the youngest being your blood daughter, we'll stand a better chance—"

"She's not," Tye said, his mouth tightening in a thin line against the wave of tangled emotions rolling through him. "For years I believed she was, but that was a lie, too. She is Trace's. They are all Trace's."

"Oh, Tye," Claire whispered.

He braced himself, waiting to hear her disgust or contempt. He couldn't look at her.

"That must have been so hard for you."

He blew out the breath he'd been unaware of holding, and his gaze met hers. Never had he dreamed he'd see support shining in her brilliant blue eyes. But he did. Support and something more; something he dared not name. *Son of a bitch.*

Tye sat a little straighter when he turned back to the attorney. "The children are Trace's, and he entrusted their care to me during his absence. I won't allow the Wests to take them, and I need you to tell me what my legal options are. I'd like to try it that way first."

"First?"

"I will not betray my brother again."

After that the office fell silent but for the click of Rawlins's pen as he tapped it against the desktop in thought. Finally he asked, "So what is Miss Donovan's place in all of this?"

"What do you mean?" Claire inquired.

"What are you asking?" Tye demanded simultaneously.

Rawlins drew a large number one on his paper. "Why did you bring her with you this morning?" He added a number two. "Are the two of you involved?" Number three, he underlined twice. "Will she be a factor in a custody fight?"

Tye floundered like Spike outside his fish bowl in the face of the lawyer's questions. *Involved?* He didn't think that was quite the word. But then, he didn't really know just what that word might be.

Claire's skirts rustled as she rose and approached the two men. "Tye didn't bring me, Mr. Rawlins. I was already waiting for you when he arrived. I have a legal problem of my own to discuss."

"I see."

Tye sure as hell didn't see. "What happened? Are you all right? Nobody hurt you, did they?"

She waved a hand and took a seat beside Tye. "My question involves business assets. It can wait. Please, Mr. Rawlins, tell us what Tye needs to do to make certain those West persons can't hurt the girls."

Tye's chest grew tight "So you do support me, Claire? Still?"

Her dainty nose wrinkled in scorn. "Of course I support you. Why wouldn't I?"

He waved a hand. "Weren't you listening a few minutes ago?"

"Yes, I was listening." From her tone he'd have thought she were talking to a three-year-old.

"You heard what I did?"

She raised her eyes to the ceiling and gave a long-suffering sigh. "Tye McBride, I swear you are as stubborn as a chocolate stain. You want to know what I think? I think what you did with your brother's wife was wrong, but human. I think that it's a shame that woman's manipulations cost her her life. Finally, I think since Trace's obviously forgiven you, it's time you forgive yourself. Now, Mr. Rawlins, can we continue? What does Tye need to do?"

The lawyer stretched back in his chair. "Well, I can think of one move, right off. His legal position isn't helped by the fact he is a bachelor caring for three young females. My best advice, McBride, is to find yourself a wife."

THE BAD LUCK WEDDING CAKE

"A wife?" Tye's throat constricted. *A wife. Marriage and all that entailed. Intimacy and commitment. Trust.* "No, I can't."

The attorney shrugged. "If you'd rather run with them, that's your choice. You did ask for my opinion, though, so I have to tell you that under the circumstances, I don't think you'll win a fight with the grandparents."

A wife. Marriage. It would never happen. "Why would marrying help my case?"

"For one thing, the grandparents will claim they can accord the children both a father figure and a mother figure."

Possibilities bombarded Tye. "Mrs. Wilson has returned to Fort Worth. I can ask her to give up her house and live at Willow Hill permanently. She loves the Blessings. She's a good mother figure. She's already raised a passel of kids."

"But she isn't blood kin."

"Neither would be any woman I married."

"True, but she'll be family. Family is what counts in a case like this. What you want to do is show the court that the grandparents won't be giving the girls anything more than what you're already providing. Circumstances being similar, age would work in your favor, too."

"And if I prove that, it will be enough?"

"Not necessarily." The lawyer leaned back in his chair. "It depends on how far they're willing to take the fight. Considering most of what you've told me here this morning concerns their late daughter, they might not want to bring it up in public. But if they do . . ." he shrugged. "The facts don't paint you in a very flattering light, McBride. But what about the grandparents? Do you know anything we could use against them?"

Tye lifted his hands to his face and rubbed his eyes. "The Wests are wealthy and successful. As far as I know they are well respected in New Orleans. But Constance was raised in their household. I'm not one for blaming all a child's troubles on her parents, but neither can you discount it altogether. I wouldn't doubt we could sling a little mud right along with them if need be. I'd need some time to check into it."

"I don't think time is a luxury you're gonna have. A case like this will be heard quickly. Folks don't like to see children with their lives left hanging unsettled. You're better off hedging your bets with a wife."

"A wife," Tye groaned, burying his head in his hands.

The word conjured up images of Constance McBride at her most devious—and her most desirable. "That cursed woman is still wreaking havoc from the grave."

Claire's arm appeared within his vision. She held something in her hand; a small bottle.

Tye looked up. "What's this?"

"It's my habit to carry a small bottle of Magic with me. I thought you might appreciate a little flavor as you eat your words."

"Eat my words?"

"You gave me grief about marrying for family's sake. Looks like you are facing the very same situation."

Tye considered the bottle. His life looked like it could use a little magic at the moment. He tossed the brew back like a shot of raw whiskey, then said, "No, I won't marry. I'll find another way."

"That's what *I* thought," she observed. "In fact, that is why I came here today." She glanced at Rawlins. "My father used the Donovan Baking Company as collateral for a number of loans. When the bank unexpectedly called the notes, my father was unable to meet the demand. Another party stepped in and covered the debts, gaining control of the company. The question I put to you, Mr. Rawlins, is this: The man who bought the Donovan Baking Company purchased the buildings, inventory, and the other supplies, correct? He didn't purchase the people. He doesn't own their baking talents or the knowledge they have acquired after years in the business. Am I right?"

"Correct."

"So then, am I also correct in concluding that while the purchaser has a right to the products we had on our shelves, he does not have a right to the recipes for the items the company produced?"

Rawlins laced his fingers behind his head, elbows extended, and lifted his gaze toward the ceiling in thought "I'm not certain about that, Miss Donovan. I'd have to research the question. If the recipes were maintained in a journal or collection of sorts, then it's likely those recipes would be counted as assets."

"Yes, but what if a particular recipe has never been recorded? What if it exists only in a person's head? How could it be an asset of the company if the person who memorized the recipe is not?"

The attorney thought a moment and said, "Well, *hmm*. Miss Donovan, your question deals with an area of the law in which I am no expert. However, I think it is safe to say a case could be made either way, so again, I'll need to do some research."

"But it's possible the purchaser has no rights to the recipe?"

"Very possible, I'd say."

Claire sat back in her chair wearing an extremely satisfied smile. Had he not been so mired in his own dark imaginings, Tye would have wondered just why Rawlins's answers had pleased her so. As it was, he could hardly think at all.

Wife. The word circled round in his head like a buzzard over dead meat. *Wife. Wife. Wife.*

How long he sat that way he didn't know, but when he looked up, Claire stood beside him, tugging on his sleeve. "Come with me, Tye. I want to talk with you about something."

He didn't have the heart to continue the discussion with the lawyer at the moment, so he saw no reason to protest. He requested that billing be sent to Willow Hill and made an appointment for the following day to further consider the problem facing him. Then he trailed Claire from the office, out of the building and into the sunshine.

Halfway down the courthouse steps, the fog began to lift from his head. He reached out and touched her shoulder. "Claire, what's this all about?"

Something flashed across her eyes. Hesitation? Uncertainty? It disappeared before he identified the emotion. While she made a show of retying her bonnet strings, her tongue ringed her lips, betraying her nervousness.

"Claire?"

Her shoulders went back and her chin came up. She looked him directly in the eyes and said, "I want to speak of it in private. Tye, I know a way to solve both our problems."

CHAPTER 16

STIR THE SOUP POT COUNTERCLOCKWISE TO BRING GOOD LUCK.

"So what's your idea?" Tye impatiently demanded as Claire led him toward the Trinity River and the path that ran along its bank.

Claire tossed a glance back over her shoulder. "When we get to the riverbank, all right? What I have to say is best said in private." *And with plenty of room to move around. Getting through this might well require some pacing.*

Ordinarily the path along the riverbank was deserted this time of day, making it a good place for her to outline her idea without interruption. Plus, they could walk side by side and she wouldn't be forced to look at him. She wouldn't need to see his reaction when she put it into words.

Nervousness clawed at her belly. She couldn't believe she was fixing to do this. She'd gotten downright bold over the past few months. At the edge of the river, she stopped and stared at the water.

Maybe I should just jump in.

Muddy from recent rains, the Trinity flowed slowly from west to east. Claire's mouth twisted in a rueful smile as she spied a driftwood log spinning in a circle in the middle of the river. "In some ways I feel like a hunk of flotsam myself. My family is the

Trinity, and I'm an uprooted log being swept wherever the river wants to take me."

"Tell me that's not what you dragged me out here to tell me." Following the path of her gaze, Tye added, "Besides, you're not a log, Claire. Not big enough. A branch, maybe."

"What kind of branch?"

"What kind of branch?" he repeated. "What kind of question is that? Come on, Claire, spill your story. I'm feeling pretty-danged-desperately in need of a good idea."

But because she was intrigued by the notion, and because she was putting off the moment of truth for as long as possible, Claire asked again, "What kind of branch?"

"I swear, woman, you're as stubborn as Maribeth. You want to *know* what type of tree you are? All right, then. You're a peca—"

His eyes narrowed and cut to hers, and she could tell he'd changed his mind about what he was going to say. "Cedar. You're a cedar," he declared in a low, husky rumble. "Your bark is soft, but underneath, the wood is strong and so very beautiful. And cedar burns hot and fragrant. The aroma reminds me a little of your Magic, in fact."

A tremor skittered up her spine. Her gaze dropped to his lips as her mouth went dry.

"Then there's the other thing about cedar," Tye continued, stepping closer even as she attempted to move away. Her skirts brushed his legs. "When I think of cedar, I think of pests."

"What!" Claire jerked away.

"Pests," he repeated. "Like you. Enough of this nonsense, Claire. What's your solution?"

Miffed, she shifted her gaze toward the far bank. "That's a contradiction McBride. Cedar is a pest repellant."

"Well you're a pest and I'm feeling repellant at the moment, so it fits. Talk to me, Claire. Lay it out, here. Tell me how to solve my problem."

"All right, I will. Marry me."

He froze. "Excuse me?"

"I said, marry me. That's how we'll solve both of our problems."

For a long moment he stood frozen in shock. Then he belted out an unamused laugh. "Marry you. Hell, Claire, you never struck me as stupid before."

"You're lucky I never struck you, period," Claire muttered. "This is a perfect solution. I'd provide you the wife you need for the girls' sake, and you can help me out of this situation with Reid."

He shoved his hands in his pockets and stalked down the path. He snapped over his shoulder, "No."

Heavens, this was hard on a woman's pride. But whether it sat well or not, too much was at stake to let feelings stand in the way. Picking up her skirts, she ran after him. "Get the stubborn out of your ears and listen to me, McBride. You heard what Rawlins said. In order to protect those children you must marry someone."

His strides grew longer, faster, as his feet carried him away from her. "I don't know anything of the sort. You are a forward woman, Claire Donovan. Asking a man to marry you. You must truly be desperate."

She put on a burst of speed and ran around him, stopping in front of him. She jabbed him in the chest with the palm of her hand, saying, "Stop. You're right I am desperate. But so are you, Tye McBride. That's why you'll listen to me about this."

Halting, he stood glaring down at her, his eyes flashing with fury. Not at her, Claire knew in her bones, but fury at the situation. He yanked off his hat and stabbed his fingers through his hair.

Claire said, "You heard Mr. Rawlins."

"That doesn't mean I agree with him."

"They say he's the best lawyer in town, maybe even the state. With your nieces at stake, how can you dare to disregard his advice?"

Tye lifted his face toward the sky and spouted a string of ear-singeing curses. Then, shooting her a furious look, he marched on down the path, fleeing both her and the truth she was forcing upon him.

Claire followed him for half a dozen steps, then changed her mind. She'd give him some time to get used to the idea. She'd give him some space. When he was ready to listen, he'd come back to her. Tye would give his life for those Menaces, and though he might fight it, he'd give his hand in marriage, too.

Noting a flat rock a few yards away, Claire made her way to it and took a seat. Idly she picked strands of buffalo grass and milkweed and tossed them into the water, her gaze following the path of a yellow butterfly as it rose and dipped its way across the Trinity.

Almost ten minutes later Tye plopped down beside her. He yanked off his hat and swiped his brow with his sleeve. "I know what I'd get from the arrangement. Tell me how it would work for you."

Claire eyed the perspiration clinging to strands of his dark hair, then glanced toward the puffy white clouds currently shading the sun. The morning breeze blowing in from the northeast carried an unseasonable degree of chill. Tye wasn't sweating because of the heat. *It must be the thought of marrying me.* How flattering.

Claire plunged ahead. "Last night I found out why Reid is so anxious to marry me. It's why I wanted to speak with Mr. Rawlins."

"It has something to do with the bakeries?"

"Yes." To keep her hands busy, Claire picked three long stems of grass and started to braid them together. "You know that my father took out loans to expand the business so each of his sons could have his own bakery, and when the notes were called he lost everything to the bank."

"Yes." Tye fiddled with the brim on his hat.

"Reid stepped in and bought the company—lock, stock, and lemon jelly cake. Now he's offered to give day-to-day management of the bakeries back to my family if I'll agree to marry him."

"So how would marrying me help you?"

The tension and impatience in his voice made her grimace, but Claire believed it important that he have a clear understanding of her motives for proposing this marriage. "I'm getting to that."

She finished the braid, then ripped another three stems of long grass from the ground. "Reid didn't stop with the offer. He made certain I'd need to accept him by coming to Fort Worth and repeating the stories being told in Galveston about our Not-So-Magical Wedding Cake. It ruined the business here and left me without any options. Or so I thought."

"That's what I am? An option?"

Claire ignored the interruption. "Last night Reid told me the Donovan Bakeries will be the cornerstone of a business empire he intends to build. Now, for that to happen, the shops must continue to operate at the level of success they'd achieved with my family at the helm. I believe that success is the direct result of two factors: my family's work ethic and Magic."

Tye's gaze had drifted away toward the southwest side of town. Claire followed its path and spied Willow Hill. For a moment she felt a flush of shame at the idea of using his troubles to alleviate her own. Yet the fact remained she'd be helping him, too. She had to remember that. She was proposing this solution for her family *and* for his family. Not for herself. She wasn't doing this because she *wanted* to marry him.

Was she?

She cleared her throat and continued her story. "With the right incentive, Reid could probably hire hardworking employees for the bakeries. Nothing, though, will make up for the lack of Magic in the products those people produce. And without Magic, he'll be hard-pressed to achieve the success he craves to impress his father. Obviously Reid realizes it."

"Why do you say that?" Tye asked, his attention returned to Claire.

"Because he's been so sneaky. Da won't sell the recipe. And if Mr. Rawlins is right, and taking the question to court couldn't guarantee a win, then Reid would have burned his bridges with the family so he'd never get the Magic."

"So he figures to marry for the recipe? What makes him so certain you'd give it to him?"

"Da married into the recipe himself, and he's never made a secret of the fact he intends to carry on the tradition with his own children. Once we married, Reid would have complete access to Magic."

Tye cut his eyes toward her and snorted. After muttering something she couldn't quite make out beneath his breath, he added in a louder tone, "You must have thrown a fly into his buttermilk when you left him at the altar."

"I imagine so. And I'm fixing to do it one better right now. If only you cooperate, that is."

The moment seemed to drag on forever as he sat without speaking.

Finally, anxious to interrupt the silence, Claire tossed away her grass braid, dusted off her hands, and said, "So you see, Reid wants my recipe, and the only surefire way to get it is to marry a Donovan. I'm his choice."

Tye's lips twisted. "Bet Brian's relieved."

No one could put as much sarcasm in a drawl as Tye McBride, she thought.

"Your father should sell him the recipe."

Claire shook her head. "That's what he said last night when I told them the news. We all feel so stupid for not figuring this out before now. Da is ready to sell the recipe, even though he swore an oath he wouldn't when he was given the secret himself."

"Well, I'm glad to hear your father has finally come to his senses. Let him sell the Magic and y'all can go about your business. You won't have to marry Reid and you certainly don't need to marry me."

"Da can't sell the recipe, Tye. Breaking his oath would break his heart, but that's only part of it. Magic is what makes our products special. If anyone could make it, then every bakery in town would be exactly the same."

"If anyone could make it, no man in this country would be safe."

Claire swallowed a groan. She was sick and tired of Tye and his talk of aphrodisiacs, and because of her frustration she skipped directly to the meat of the matter. "All the pieces fell together in Mr. Rawlins' office. I help you and you help me and my family has their livelihood and you have the Men—Blessings. It's actually quite tidy."

"Tidy?" Tye shook his head and winced. "Sugar, believe you me, marriage is anything but tidy. You still haven't explained how marrying somebody other than Jamieson can help you."

"You'll listen?"

He shrugged. "Might as well. No skin off my nose just to listen."

Claire smoothed her skirts and soothed her temper. "It came to me in the middle of the night—not marrying you, mind you, but the idea of the factory."

"What factory?"

"A Magic factory."

Tye winced and rubbed his eyes. "Now you sound like Katrina."

"It's a matter of thinking beyond the parameters of the moment," Claire explained, ignoring his comment "My family doesn't need bakeries to support themselves, because they have Magic. And Reid Jamieson wants it. It would be foolish of them to sell the recipe, but why not sell the product? They could bottle it and sell it to Reid. They could sell it across the country. It's not difficult at all for me to imagine bottles of Magic next to bottles of vanilla extract in kitchens all across America."

"The population of our country would boom," Tye observed in a mocking tone.

"Would you be serious?"

"I'm always serious when I'm talking about weddings. Of course, I've yet to hear what Magic factories have to do with them."

"Oh. Well." Claire inhaled a fortifying breath and said, "It's money. Da doesn't have any, not enough to build a factory. You told me once that you had plenty. I thought maybe you could—"

He shoved to his feet. "Money? This is all about money? You want to marry me for my money!" Disgust laced his voice as he added, "Hell, honey, I never took you for a prostitute, but then I've been wrong about women before. Way wrong." Shoving his hands in his pockets, he turned and left her sitting beside the river, her thoughts as murky as the water drifting by.

A lump of emotion weighed Claire down like an anvil as she slowly stood. Tye McBride could be as mean as a cornered cottonmouth when he wanted. She started after him, and slowly, with every step she took, the hurt drained away. Anger took its place, and her pace increased.

She didn't move fast enough to catch him before he hitched a ride on the trolley down Main Street. By the time she retrieved her buggy from the square by the courthouse and drove to where she guessed he might be headed, Tye had made it halfway to the apartment above her bakery.

She drove the buggy right up beside him and picked up the conversation as if it had not been interrupted. "I'm not prostituting anything, Tye McBride. I'm not proposing a real marriage with love and babies and death-do-us-part vows. I'm talking about a simple business proposition; a marriage of convenience to last only as long as you need. As soon as your brother returns for his family, we can have the marriage annulled. And I'm not asking you to give us the money. It would be a loan. A business loan that the Donovans would repay with interest. That's what I'm asking for my part of the deal."

He drew to a halt and looked up at her. "A marriage of convenience. As in platonic marriage? Between you and me?" The smile that spread across his face held no hint of amusement. "You do live in a fantasy world, don't ya, hon."

She ignored his sarcasm. "It's a good deal for you, McBride. You get a temporary wife who will not betray you or manipulate you or cause you and those you love any grief at all. You get me, McBride. To use as long as you need, then discard with impunity when you're done. Think about it. What other woman in town is going to make you such a deal? You could not find a more perfect weapon to use against Constance West's mother if you tried."

At the mention of the dead woman's name, Tye shut his eyes. The temper appeared to ebb from his body, leaving behind an air of guilt that drained away Claire's temper. She fixed the reins and climbed down from the buggy. Standing beside him, she softly said, "It's a good plan, Tye. I could help you with your Blessings. If it takes Trace and Jenny some time to find their way home, the girls will need a woman in their lives. I promise I would do my best by them. I could love them so easily, if only you'd allow it."

His rigid stance and pained expression spoke volumes, and Claire felt the sting of his rejection. He must have seen it, because he grimaced and muttered a curse, then attempted to explain. "It's not you, Claire, it's me. Constance broke something in us—in Trace and me. Jenny came along and helped my brother glue himself back together, but I'm still all in pieces. I swore I'd never tie myself to a woman. Not until I'd learned to . . . trust."

She couldn't keep the bitterness from her tone as she asked, "Is it all women you don't trust, Tye, or only me?"

"No, it's not you. It's not even women in general. It's myself I don't trust. I've tried to tell you this before. Even if I dared to roll the dice and take a chance at having what I'd like, having the family my brother has, how could I possibly rid myself of the doubt? Think how that would wear on a man, and on a woman. It wouldn't be fair to anybody."

"So what are you saying, Tye? You won't follow your attorney's advice in this? You'll take that risk?"

"I can always run."

Claire had never seen a man look so fierce and yet so frightened at the same time. She slowly shook her head. "You're thinking with your heart rather than your head. If you're right and Trace is alive, how will he find you if you run?"

"I'll think of something."

"Why should you need to? I've already thought of something."

He closed his eyes, tilted his head, and rubbed the back of his neck. "Ah, sugar, I was wrong before spouting off like I did. I know you mean well. But believe me, a marriage between us wouldn't solve our problems. I know for a fact it would create more, in at least one area. No, marriage is not the answer."

Claire wanted to know what area he meant, but before she could ask, a movement in front of the Rankin Building caught her attention. The McBride Menaces filed out the front door and stood in front of the Donovan Confectionary front window. They wore matching, frilly, lilac dresses and worried expressions, and stood with hands folded primly beside a strikingly beautiful older woman. She had to be the grandmother.

This woman had tracked down the girls despite their being hidden in the apartment? And she'd talked them into those dresses? Even Maribeth? It looked as though Tye had better find his answer fast.

She decided to make it easier on him. "You made me a promise when the gas leaked and I saved your and your nieces' lives. You said if ever I needed anything, I had only to ask. Well I'm calling in the marker now, McBride. I expect you to marry me."

"Blackmail? You bow to blackmail now, Claire?"

"I'll do anything for my family." She grabbed his arm and made him turn toward the house. "Look at that and remember your promise and tell me you won't do anything for your family, too."

Tye's eyes narrowed and his jaw hardened. In a cold, flat voice, he said, "When do you want to do it?"

Claire slipped her arm through his and said solemnly, "As soon as I can bake a cake."

FROM THAT MOMENT ON, time passed in a rush for the bride and groom. While she baked the wedding cake, he dealt with the problem of physically removing his nieces from their grandmother's clutches. He thanked God he was poker buddies with Fort Worth's marshal before all was said and done. Beatrice had been determined to get the girls on an outbound train. Tye had brought the marshal into the matter, and Beatrice had been forced to settle for a court date two days later, for a custody hearing.

Later that day the Donovan family met with the McBride family at Willow Hill to cuss and discuss the upcoming nuptials. Tye provided liquor for the Donovan men and Mrs. Wilson's fresh lemonade for the women. It proved to be a long afternoon.

"I'll not marry me daughter to the likes of you," John Donovan said, pouring his third four-finger glass of Trace McBride's finest bourbon.

"I'll take good care of her, John," Tye replied, taking a hit of lemonade. "Better than that slug Reid Jamieson ever would."

"Aye." He propped his head in his hands. "I cannot believe I allowed myself to be so taken in by that . . . that . . . Magic thief."

Two glasses later, Claire's Da had changed his tune and was singing the praises of Claire's new fiancé. "A fine idea. A partnership with my new son and my old sons. Imagine that." He made

L's with each thumb and forefinger, as if framing a sign. "The Donovan Magic Factory. I love it."

"Don't fall in love too fast," Tye warned, motioning for Claire to come stand by his side. "It's the McBride-Donovan Company, and my bride will be the majority stockholder." He glanced at Claire, and couldn't help but grin as he added, "Claire will be your boss."

"No!" the three Donovan men cried.

"Yes," Tye asserted. "It's my money buying you out of this predicament."

"But it's our Magic," Brian protested.

Tye chuckled and reached for Claire's hand. "But it's Claire's Magic, too, isn't it? Now, she and I haven't discussed it yet, but I'm hoping she'll decide to leave the factory concerns to y'all so that she can concentrate on running The Confectionary."

"Donovan's Confectionary," Patrick corrected.

"No, The Confectionary. Y'all were wrong to take it away from her. Now I'm making sure she gets it back. If that's what she wants. Claire gets to decide."

He'd shocked her speechless with that, and his chuckle broadened to out-and-out laughter.

"Well, I'll be," Patrick drawled. He folded his arms and started to laugh. "He's got us, Da. Slick as snot."

"Slick as snot," Katrina McBride repeated, her nose wrinkled up tight. "Eeeyeew."

Tye acted surprised to find the McBride Blessings hiding behind the sofa. He'd known they were there, of course, but he'd found himself reluctant to face them. He knew he should have broached the subject of his marriage to Claire with them before her family arrived, and he'd tried. But he never managed to get the words out of his mouth. He didn't know how he'd handle it if they pitched a fit.

Now, however, the moment of truth had arrived. Nervous, Tye sat in a chair and asked the girls to gather around him. "So," he said, "what do you think of my plan to marry Miss Donovan? Any objections?"

Emma folded her arms. "Well, if we did have any we couldn't very well tell you here and now, could we? Not in front of her family. That would be rude."

Maribeth said, "That's right, Uncle Tye. You should have come to us ahead of time and asked our permission."

Tye arched a brow and tried to look stern. "Oh, really?"

Katrina patted his leg, saying, "It's all right, Uncle Tye. I've liked Miss Donovan for a long time, even before Mr. Sundine stole Miss Loretta away from you. Now Mari and Emma think she's a good wife for you, too, and Spike told us it's fine for you to marry her."

"Spike has given me his blessing?" Claire asked. "Well, if I'd known that, I wouldn't have worried so much about getting my family's approval."

John Donovan scowled. "Oh, really? And just who is this Spike?"

Claire and the three McBride Menaces turned to her father and said in unison, "He's Spike the fortuneteller fish."

After a moment's pause John said, "Oh." Then he poured himself another bourbon.

Tye poured the girls lemonade and told them to have at the tray of canapés Mrs. Wilson had prepared.

Brian spoke up next, toasting the bride and groom and their plan, confessing he was tired of being a baker anyway, and that he liked the idea of being a prince of industry—even if his kid sister was the queen.

Patrick, on the other hand, needed a little more persuasion to agree to the marriage. He clung to the solution he had proposed the night before when Claire told them why Reid wanted to marry her. Patrick dreamed of solving the problem by taking Reid Donovan out behind the nearest woodshed and beating the tar out of him. After hearing Tye's reasons for wanting the wedding, he offered to haul the Wests out to the woodshed, too.

Calmer heads prevailed, and Tye and the three Donovan men drew up a contract on the spot forming a new company, settling on the name The Magical Partnership of McBride and Donovan after consultation with the three McBride girls who in turn brought Spike the fortune-teller fish in to assist with the final selection.

Peggy McBride's actions were the ones that surprised Tye the most. She took to mothering the girls like cinnamon to sugar, and when Claire commented on her obvious delight, Peggy mentioned how much she'd always enjoyed having a little girl around. Claire looked stunned at that one.

The festive atmosphere continued until approximately four P.M., at which time the front doorbell chimed, announcing the visitor Tye had summoned.

He asked Peggy and Mrs. Wilson to take the girls upstairs and keep them there. On their way from the room, he overheard Claire's mother ask for Mrs. Wilson's canapé recipe.

Then a voice filled the foyer like a plague: "Lord Wexford, I believe? Reid Jamieson, here. I received a note you had business with me?"

"Jamieson." The name tasted sour in his mouth. "Come in, please. I believe you know my bride-to-be, the future Lady Wexford, Miss Claire Donovan?"

Jamieson's complexion flushed like a peppermint, going red, then white, then red again. "What is the meaning of this?"

What happened next was ugly, but satisfying. Before all was said and done, Reid, representing the Donovan Baking Company, had signed a one thousand dollar purchase order for the first batch of Magic produced by the McBride-Donovan Magic Company. Claire signed the contract on the manufacturer's behalf.

Reid's objectionable response to that led Tye to lure him outside for a taste of that woodshed-justice Patrick favored.

The Donovan men and Tye then hauled Reid down to the train station just in time to pour him into an outbound car. Upon their return to Willow Hill they broke out the Irish—root beer for Tye—and set about bonding in a manly sort of way.

The party didn't break up until the wee hours of the morning.

HER WEDDING DAY dawned all too soon.

At half past seven, Claire sat at her kitchen table drinking her first cup of coffee of the day when the knock sounded on her front door. Expecting that her mother had come to help her dress for the ceremony, she called out, "Come in, Mama."

Her screen door squeaked open and footsteps approached. Tye's husky voice rumbled, "I'm not Mother."

She looked up to see white silk taffeta overflowing his arms. Claire stared at him in surprise. "I didn't expect to see you until the ceremony."

"Bad luck to see the bride, I know. But I've got something here to take care of that. Come see." He jerked his head for her to follow, then made his way through the small cottage until he found her bedroom. Entering, he moved to her unmade bed and spread his burden across it. While he fussed with the fabric, she scurried toward the bed, kicking her corset beneath it as she silently berated herself for the previous night's laziness.

Now, because in her exhaustion the night before she'd left her clothes where they fell and collapsed into bed, Tye knew she wore lavender lace adorning her corset. Heat stained her cheeks.

"No sense being bashful, sugar. Not under the circumstances."

She opened her mouth to comment on the role of her under-wear in their marriage of convenience, but before she managed to speak, she got her first good glimpse of what he'd brought to show her. "A wedding gown? Why are you bringing me a wedding gown?"

"You mean, other than the fact you are marrying me today and are in need of something to wear?"

"I have a pretty blue organza. It would do just fine."

"I'm sure it would, but this will do better. This is not a wedding gown. It's a wedding dress. *The* wedding dress."

She blinked. "The Bad Luck Wedding Dress?"

He clicked his tongue. "No, Claire. You're a bit behind the times. The dress had a change of luck. It's now the Good Luck Wedding Dress. The Blessings suggested you wear it today."

"They did?" It was on the tip of her tongue to mention that maybe the dress's luck hadn't turned, after all. Wasn't the last bride who wore it presently lost at sea? Claire was superstitious enough to think twice. "That's nice of them, really, but I'd prefer to wear my own. Besides, it probably wouldn't fit."

"It'll fit. You and Jenny are two peas in a pod, figure-wise. Come on, sugar." He stroked her cheek with his finger. "Wear it for me?"

When he used that voice, that touch, she knew she'd do darn near anything for the man. Speechless, she nodded her acceptance.

The moment dragged on, their gazes locked, asking questions without words. Finally he turned away as if to leave, and Claire reached out a hand to stop him. "Why does it matter to you, Tye? Do you believe in lucky talismans?"

He dragged a hand across his jaw and nodded. "I do. I believe in Good Luck Wedding Dresses and Magical Wedding Cakes."

Claire glanced from him, to the dress, then back to him again. "But I don't understand. Your attitude . . . well . . . it's changed."

Tye dipped down and snagged her corset from beneath the bed. He dangled it before her, watching her as he said, "I've had time to get used to the idea, and I've realized we might as well make the best of the situation. For your sake I had hoped for a better man for you, but now that's no longer the question. You and I are getting married today, and I'm honest enough to recognize it won't be any marriage of convenience. Not the way our blood runs hot when we're alone."

Claire's heart hammered. "Are you saying . . .?"

"We'll have a wedding night tonight. Whether we like it or not, we'll be having ourselves a real marriage. That's why I want you to wear Jenny's dress. That's why I want us both to have some of that Magical Wedding Cake."

He pulled her to him and pressed a swift, hard kiss to her lips. "I reckon you and I can use all the good luck we can get."

CHAPTER 17

GOOD LUCK COMES TO THOSE PATIENT ENOUGH TO WAIT FOR IT.

SHORTLY AFTER TYE LEFT, a second knock sounded on Claire's door. This time she didn't bother to say "Come in." She couldn't. She was crying too hard.

Her mother entered the room anyway. "Claire? Why, Claire Donovan. What in heavens has you so worked up?"

Claire lifted her tearstained face toward her mother and said, "Oh, Mama, I'm so very afraid."

Concern dimmed Peggy Donovan's expression. Depositing the rose bouquet she carried on a nearby table, she approached the bed. She gave the wedding gown a curious look, then shifted it aside making room for her to sit beside her daughter. Taking Claire into her arms, she said, "What happened? Why are you afraid?"

"Oh, Mama. I don't know how to explain."

"Don't you want this marriage, after all? Have you had second thoughts? Last night you seemed happy to be marrying Mr. McBride. Did I read that wrong?"

"I was happy. I am happy. That's the problem."

Peggy Donovan reached into the pocket of her skirt and withdrew a handkerchief. She wiped the fresh flurry of tears from her daughter's face. "Maybe you should explain."

Claire was such a mass of confusion she didn't know how to articulate it. The words bubbling up inside her made little sense, but she assumed her mother knew her well enough to put it all together. And maybe then she could explain it to Claire.

"He brought me a dress, Mama. Everything is for the children, of course, and I used it for what I wanted, but now it breaks my heart. I all but blackmailed him, and he brought me a wedding gown and wants to have a wedding night. I know if that happens I'm doomed. It will be the end of me. The end I won't be able to stop it."

"Stop what, child? Does this have something to do with the partnership he formed with your father?"

Claire shook her head.

Peg Donovan's face grew grim. "Has Tye McBride given you reason to believe he'll be a bully in the bedroom? If so, we'll call a halt to this wedding immediately. I won't have my baby hurt."

"He won't be able to help it. It's not his fault. It's mine. I'm the one who . . . oh. Oh, my. Oh, dear Lord no." Her entire body froze as realization swept through her like a January wind. "It's already too late."

"Too late for what, Claire?"

"Me. It's too late for me." She gazed at her mother, noting the worry and concern that dimmed the older woman's eyes. In a thready tone, she gave voice to the words that shook her to her soul. "I love him, Mama."

Gentle amusement colored Peg Donovan's slow-dawning smile. She smoothed the hair away from her daughter's face and teased, "You love the man you are about to marry? What misery."

"It's a catastrophe."

"Just the thing for Catastrophic Claire."

"Mo-ther. You don't understand."

"Then explain it to me, dear."

"Oh, Mama." Claire dropped her chin to her chest. "I can't."

Her mother placed a finger beneath her chin and forced it back up. "Try."

Claire shut her eyes for a moment, gathering her thoughts. How could she put this confusion into words? Maybe it would help to compare her feelings for Tye to her mother's life with her father. Claire took a deep breath, then asked, "You love Da, don't you?"

"Yes, very much."

"That love you feel for him has changed who you are. I don't want to change like that, Mama. I'm still trying to figure out me, who I am. I don't want to be Mrs. Tye McBride. I mean, I want to be his wife, but I don't want to be his . . . his . . ."

"His what?"

Twenty-odd years' worth of unexpressed objections and observations baled out from her mouth like accusations. "You love Da, so you iron his underwear and cook his favorite foods. You read the books he wants you to read and make friends with those he wants you to befriend."

"Now, Claire."

But she pressed on. "You let him pick out the new stove for the kitchen at home—your kitchen. You let him pick out the names of your children. You became a baker when you wanted to be a teacher."

Peggy frowned. "This is a fine way to be speaking to your mother, young lady."

Claire saw the hurt in her mother's eyes and she winced. "I'm not trying to be mean, Mama. I just don't understand. Because you love Da, you gave up who you are. How could you do that, Mama? How could you let him do that to you?"

"Oh, Claire," her mother said with a sigh. "Is that what you think?"

"What I think is that loving someone shouldn't make a woman toss away her own dreams and desires. It shouldn't steal her freedom. That's not right. It's not. But it's reality. It's the way of this world, and it's why I didn't want to fall in love. I don't want to lose who I am, and who I am becoming, to Tye McBride."

"My dear child. And to think I've always considered you my bright one. How can you be so blind?"

Claire didn't know her mother considered her bright. She certainly had never said so. At the moment, fresh on the heels of self-revelation, Claire didn't feel exceptionally intelligent. But neither was she stupid.

"I'm not blind, Mama. My eyes are very much open. I've seen the lengths to which we go for the sake of love. You've been cooking on that stove you hate for three years now." Tears over-flowed once more. "And now I love Tye. Oh, Mama, I love him so much. What lengths will I go to for him? Who will I become? Will I end up just like you?"

"Perhaps," Peggy replied, a razor's edge to her tone. "If you are very, very lucky."

Her words brought Claire up short. She was horrified and ashamed at the things she had said.

"Do us both a favor and listen to me, please?"

Drying her tears, she met her mother's gaze, offering a silent apology. Never before had she been so . . . impolite with her mother, but today of all days she felt she had to be completely honest. She had no energy for anything else. Softly she said, "I'll listen."

"I never realized you labored under these misconceptions. If you had mentioned them earlier, perhaps we could have avoided much of this. So you think I threw away my wants and wishes for John, hmm?"

"Mama . . . I . . . well, yes. Yes, I do."

Her mother sighed. "I cannot believe I have raised a daughter who thinks falling in love means the end of a woman's dreams and the loss of her sense of self."

"But that's what I have seen at home," Claire defended.

"Is it? Or is it what you only thought you saw?" Before Claire could comment on that, her mother said something that left her all but speechless. "Of all my children—and despite your gender—you, Claire, are most like your father."

"What?"

"Yes. You are brave and courageous and independent and loyal. You're willing to do absolutely anything for those you love. But sometimes, Claire, you are truly dense."

Claire reared back, but her mother pressed on. "For example, it is true I give up the idea of being a schoolteacher when I married your father. And haven't I suffered for it?"

She said it such a way that Claire knew she meant exactly the opposite.

"Instead of teaching dozens," Peggy continued, "I've been forced to concentrate my educational efforts on a handful. God blessed me with two boys and a girl. Now, what kind of job did I do? Not too shabby, I would think. Texas has a pair of strong, young, learned men to help lead it into the next century. And the girl, well, up until today I'd thought I'd done a masterful job teaching her. Apparently I missed a few important lessons."

"Mama, I—"

Peggy ignored Claire's interruption. "Apparently I forgot to teach her about compromise. No marriage can exist without it."

"Compromise?" Claire scoffed. "You don't compromise with Da."

"You don't think so? Then you, my dear, haven't been paying attention. You should have noticed the give and take on financial matters concerning brands of stoves and expensive family holidays to resorts like Lake Bliss."

Oh. Claire winced as her mother drove that point home.

Peggy wasn't through yet. "Of course, you were at a disadvantage because I relegated many such discussions to the privacy of your father's and my bedroom. I am a firm believer that it isn't right and proper for parents to argue in front of their children, and I always made it a point to save my stiffest backbone and hardest head for behind closed doors."

Claire was in shock. "I never realized that happened. I always thought Da's word was law."

"Your Da's word is loud, not necessarily law," Peggy replied dryly.

Claire thought back to all the times she'd assumed her mother had given in to her father's wishes. Had they fought behind-doors battles every time? "You make it sound so . . . difficult."

"Oh, no. Don't think that. Love is nothing to dread or fear. It is the sun and the moon and stars and the sky all wrapped up in a wondrous gift."

Watching the blissful smile on her mother's expression, Claire saw that for Peggy, it surely was true. But couldn't her mother understand that her needs might be different? "Mama, I don't want the moon and the stars. They were fine for you, but I need something different. These last few months on my own have been wonderful. I want the freedom to be myself—whoever and whatever I want to be."

"Oh, Claire," her mother said, shaking her head. "What do you think true freedom is?"

"Independence."

"That's where you're wrong. True freedom is not independence, not really. It's *choice*."

"Choice?"

"Yes. True freedom is the ability and opportunity to choose how you live your life. It's what loving your father gave to me. The choice."

"I don't understand."

Peggy drew a deep breath, then sighed. "All my life I had wanted no more than to be a wife and mother. The teaching was a substitute for what I truly craved— a family of my own. Loving your father didn't curtail my freedom; it gave me my freedom."

Claire thought about that a moment "So you are saying you chose to give up teaching?"

"And I chose to allow him the honor of naming our children. Those things you mentioned —all of them— were choices I made. Your father never forced anything upon me that I didn't choose to allow."

"Even the stove?"

Humor lit her mother's eyes. "Perhaps the stove wasn't my choice, but it was my compromise." She reached for her daughter's hand and gave it a squeeze. "Your father and I have a partnership, a good, strong, healthy partnership that is rooted in mutual respect and, most important, in love. Can you see that honey?"

It took effort for Claire to speak past a lump the size of a raisin muffin lodged in her throat. "I guess so. But Mama, Tye and I don't have that."

Peggy smiled. "It takes time, child. A marriage is a partnership that takes time and effort to develop. It doesn't happen overnight, not like this partnership between your father and your husband-to-be. Give yourselves some time. Listen to your Mama. Don't be afraid of love."

Then, all business, she stood and reached for the wedding gown. Holding it up, she clicked her tongue. "A beautiful design. Simple but elegant. You'll be the most beautiful bride Texas has ever seen. And here I was, afraid that the cake might outshine you."

Claire glanced toward her mother with anxious eyes. "You saw the cake?"

"Don't ask me to admit it to your father, but you, darling daughter, have baked the prettiest Donovan Magical Wedding Cake I've ever seen. That magnolia blossom you used for the top is truly spectacular."

Pleasure melted like meringue through Claire. She had worked so hard on that cake. It held a special place in her heart.

While she bathed and dressed, she reflected on the conversation with her mother. Maybe love wasn't automatically a sentence to a life of servitude and drudgery like she had feared. Maybe with the right man, marriage would mean freedom of choice for her like it had for Mama.

The question remained whether Tye McBride was the "right man." She didn't dare forget that while she might be marrying with love in her heart, Tye certainly was not. For him, lust was as close as it got.

But could lust be nurtured into something deeper?

Claire viewed her reflection in the bedroom mirror and said softly, "Perhaps."

If she acted bravely and showed him at least through her actions, if not her words, how much she cared, then perhaps this marriage could succeed. If she made him happy—truly and deeply happy—then perhaps this marriage could grow into a partnership like her parents', one filled with strength and joy and laughter. And love.

Hope sparked a flame in her heart. She'd do it. She'd do her best to make him happy, and maybe given enough time and effort, lust would grow into love. "It could happen," Claire murmured, slipping her feet into her shoes. She stood and took one last glance in the mirror.

A bride looked back. Rosy cheeks and glittering eyes. Hopeful. Almost even confident. She'd make Tye forget about that Constance woman and the trouble she had caused. She'd redefine his entire perception of what he now considered a four-letter-word: wife. "I'll make him happy, I will."

She walked into the parlor where her father had joined her mother, waiting to escort them to the hastily reserved church. It wasn't until she climbed into the waiting buggy and smoothed her skirt around her that she realized what she had said. *I'll make him happy*.

Dear Lord, she'd become her mother, after all.

But this time, for the first time ever, that didn't seem such a bad thing.

EMMA and her sisters lay on their bellies in their favorite Sunday dresses, peering through the choir loft railings at St. Paul's Methodist Evangelical Church. At one end Maribeth kept hold of Ralph, who chafed at the unaccustomed leash. Spike the fortune-teller fish acted the opposite bookend. In honor of the occasion, yellow roses adorned both Ralph's collar and Spike's bowl. The added touch had been Emma's idea, and even Uncle Tye had appeared pleased at the results.

He certainly didn't look too happy at the moment.

Five minutes earlier, Miss Claire's siblings and the friend she loved, that pretty Mr. Sundine, had shown up at the church with scowls on their faces and threats in their voices, asking for a few moments alone with their future brother-in-law. Tye sent Emma and her sisters outside. They chose to hide in the choir loft instead. Now they watched and listened in wide-eyed amazement as the Donovans took their uncle Tye to task.

"What the hell is this all about?" Tye demanded, his hands braced upon his hips as he scowled at the men surrounding him. "Last night y'all were all for this wedding. What happened since then? Did you rob the bank overnight to get the money for your factory or something? You figure you don't need my cash anymore?"

Patrick Donovan snarled. "We did a bit of thinking, McBride."

"Now, why does that surprise me?"

Lars Sundine narrowed his eyes. "I don't like his attitude."

"Yeah, me neither," agreed Patrick.

Brian brushed his knuckles on his sleeve. "I say we hit him a time or twelve. Just in case."

Above the tableau, Maribeth armed herself and her sisters

with a stack of hymnals to bombard the Donovan brothers if needed.

"Just in case of what?" Uncle Tye looked seriously close to losing his temper.

Patrick answered. "Just in case there is more to this hurried wedding than you and our sister let on last night."

"More? More what?"

Brian took over the conversation after that. "Have you touched our sister, McBride? Is that the reason for this haste? Is her belly fixin' to pop?"

Tye frowned and shook his head. "Her belly? What are you fellows talking about?"

As one, the men shouted, "Have you gotten our Claire in a family way?"

The echoed resounded through the church. In the choir loft the McBride Menaces shared a scandalized look. Emma knew about making babies. Mama had explained about it not long before she and Papa left on their trip, when she sat Emma down and talked to her about monthly courses. At the time Emma had been too appalled at the idea of bleeding that she'd hardly paid attention to the rest of it. The one thing she had remembered when she, being a good sister, related the tale to her younger siblings was that the husband put his boy part inside the wife to give her a baby.

So the Donovan brothers and Mr. Sundine thought Uncle Tye had done that to Miss Donovan even though they weren't married yet? How rude.

Apparently, Uncle Tye thought so, too, because he hauled off and punched the closest Donovan brother, Brian. As blood gushed from the bride's brother's nose, the other Donovans' fists started flying and Mr. Sundine launched into the fray. Uncle Tye defended himself, of course, and the event became a free-for-all. Especially once Maribeth launched the first hymnal. The grunts and groans and whacks and cracks rose to the rafters like a song.

It all ended abruptly with a scream, a crash, and a splash.

"Spike!" Katrina squealed as the glass bowl went sailing over the railing, knocked from its inadvisable perch by an errant elbow.

Emma grabbed at her youngest sister and pulled her away from the rail, fearful she'd follow the fish. Maribeth's howl of horror joined Kat's as she darted for the stairs, the other girls right behind her, Ralph nipping at their heels.

Just as the sisters reached the ground floor, the front doors of the church opened. Claire and her parents walked inside. John Donovan let out a bellow and rushed forward.

Seeing that Spike flopped on the floor tile directly in his path, Emma made a diving leap in front of him and attempted to scoop up the fish. To her dismay, Spike spurted from her outstretched hands and sailed beyond reach.

Claire's father tripped over Emma and stumbled toward his sons as Katrina rushed for the group yelling, "Spike! Spike! Don't step on Spike!"

Brian and Patrick caught their father just before he fell. Mr. Sundine's elbow also caught Mr. Donovan, only in the nose. More blood began to flow.

As Maribeth snagged Spike and deposited him in the holy water font at the back of the church, Ralph took a dislike to Patrick, his teeth closing down hard on the man's pant's leg at the ankle. In the midst of it all, Emma climbed back onto her feet, watching her uncle as he first caught sight of Miss Claire.

The grin on his face abruptly died. He looked as if an invisible fist had given him one more punch. *Stunned*, Emma thought. *He looked stunned*.

He wiped a smear of Donovan blood from his cheek with the back of his hand, his eyes never leaving his intended. Claire, in turn, offered a tentative, shy smile. Neither one paid the gathering any attention as Tye walked up the aisle toward his bride. "You are positively beautiful, Claire," he told her.

"It's a gorgeous dress. Thank you for allowing me to wear it."

"Not the dress. You. You're beautiful."

Her smile widened, then amusement filled her eyes as she responded. "You look pretty good yourself, McBride. The blood-stain on your shirt almost looks like a rose boutonniere."

"Does it?" He glanced down. "I never have been one much for flowers."

"I take it my brothers decided a little family initiation was called for?"

"Something like that."

They stood frozen in place, grinning at each other, until slowly, one by one, the others joined Emma in watching the pair.

Brian Donovan finally spoke up. "Good Lord, he looks like he's about to gobble her up. Where's the preacher? We'd best get the show on the road quick-like."

The minister called the bride and groom to the altar, and the families took their places in the pews. Five minutes into the nuptial ceremony, Ralph started barking and straining at his leash. Just as Emma spied the source of his excitement—a mouse crawling along the back of a pew halfway down the aisle—the church's back door opened to reveal Wilhemina Peters.

When the reporter dipped her hand in the holy water and squealed, the minister paused in the midst of his scripture read-ing. He didn't resume until Mrs. Peters took a seat and Kat managed to muzzle Ralph with her hand.

The balance of the ceremony took place without incident. When it was done and Uncle Tye drew their brand-new Aunt Claire into his arms for a long and thorough kiss, Emma heard Mrs. Peters speak from behind her.

"Well, I can't say I'm surprised. Rodents, dogs, fish, and a kiss that doesn't quit. Just a typical McBride family wedding."

TYE POURED himself a lemonade and gazed longingly at the whiskey decanter. He hadn't wanted a drink this badly in years. He was alone in the parlor of Rankin Building apartment with his brand new wife, who was currently taking a bath.

Preparing herself for her bridegroom and the marriage bed.

The waiting was hell. He'd fought arousal off and on all day, a condition that developed into a lesson in pure masculine misery the moment he and his bride had left the small reception the bride's family had hosted at the Cosmopolitan Hotel.

Claire's mother and Mrs. Wilson had waged a full-blown battle concerning who would watch the girls while Tye and Claire honeymooned. A compromise was reached when Peggy and John chose to stay at Willow Hill temporarily until Tye and his bride returned. Tye liked the idea of the Blessings having extra protection until he managed to run the Wests out of town, so he readily agreed to the plan. He even went so far as to suggest that Brian and Patrick close The Confectionary for a few days and spend the time at Willow Hill, too.

None of the Donovan men had seemed too happy at the plan. Mainly because they knew that, while they watched over the McBride Blessings, Tye McBride would be watching over their Claire. So to speak. The last words out of Patrick's mouth when Tye and Claire left the reception had been a warning. "You take care of my little sister. You treat her gently. When you make love to her, remember she has two blood brothers and Lars who will make you pay if you don't treat her well."

Remembering, Tye gripped his glass with such force he halfway expected it to break. *Make love*, no. What a disaster that would be. He and Claire had a nice healthy dose of lust going, but that was all. It would never be more, never could be more.

Deep within himself, a little voice dared to whisper, *Why not, McBride? You could love Claire if you'd let yourself.*

He slammed the glass down hard on the parlor table and stalked out into the entry hall, staring up the stairs. She'd looked so lovely in that wedding dress. The gown fit her perfectly, the elegant display of her curves attracting the gaze of every man within eyesight. Throughout the ceremony and the small, hastily thrown together reception afterward, his gaze had returned to her time and again. Elegant. Graceful. Radiant. Her smile had been sweeter than the cinnamon sticky buns she baked up Saturday mornings at The Confectionary. The fragrance of Magic had clung to her and branded his senses.

Surely she'd finished her bath by now.

He muttered a curse and took the first step up the staircase. Lust flowed like molten glass in his veins. Tye blamed his condition on an extended length of celibacy. That, and, of course, Claire's own magic.

He knocked upon his bedroom door. "Claire? It's me."

"Come in."

The door swung open and Tye lost his breath.

She stood beside the bed dressed in a peignoir of diaphanous emerald silk. Her feet were bare, her golden hair loose and flowing in thick waves to her waist. She was every man's fantasy. She was Tye's fantasy.

She was his wife.

His wife. Yearning as strong as his lust swept through him and time seemed to freeze. Wife, family, home. Happiness. All right here, his for the taking. His stomach took a dip and his eyes closed.

Forced by circumstance, he had grasped the idea of a "convenient" marriage like a lifeline. No promises, no permanence; a solution to both of their problems with the added bonus of sex with Claire. He never once guessed the vows would matter.

They did. The vows mattered a lot. This marriage wasn't just a solution-and-sex. It was more.

It could never be more. Claire deserved a better man than him.

Tye swallowed hard. And what of her? Had the vows caught her by surprise, too? Did the vows give rise to unexpected dreams? Would she hope for something from him he would not, could not, give her?

If so, even if it killed him, they needed it settled before anything went any further.

Within himself he searched blindly for a seed of self-control, some last, decent impulse to cling to. "I want you, Claire McBride. God, I want you. More than I have words to express it. But I have to be fair."

He dragged his gaze away, unable to say this while looking at the picture she made. He stared blindly toward the wardrobe. "I don't know what you're thinking, but just in case . . . well. . . I have to say something. This marriage of ours can never be more than what we agreed to yesterday. Don't expect more from me. If you take me to your bed, I can promise you pleasure—"

His stare darted to her and he couldn't help but lick his lips. "Toe-curling, knee-melting, out-of-your-mind passion—"

This time she dragged her gaze away. Tye saw her shudder.

"But I won't give you a lifetime," he continued, forcing the words past his mouth. "This marriage won't last past my brother's return. So it's your call, sugar. Do I go or stay?"

Half a minute passed, the longest year of his life.

"Well, I probably shouldn't admit this," she finally said, giving her shoulders a shrug. Her robe slipped to the floor. "But right now, I'm only concerned that this marriage last for the next hour."

All the air left Tye's body. Her gown plunged to a deep V between her full, creamy breasts and ended high on her thighs, revealing shapely legs that seemed to stretch on forever. Legs that stepped right up next to him. On the verge of passing out, Tye sucked in a deep, lung-filling, Magic-scented breath.

"One hour, Tye." She slipped her arms around his waist. "Or am I wrong about how much time these matters take?"

The false bravado he saw in her eyes almost gave him pause. She was scared, vulnerable, but so very brave. Typical Claire.

But Tye was only human. A mere mortal. "An hour? Hell, sugar. With you, nothing less than all night will do."

Then he kissed her and she melted, hot, spiced Magic in his arms.

Magical Claire. Damn, he was hungry for her. Running his tongue along the soft, sleek surface of her lips, he coaxed her to open, then dipped inside, brushing, stroking, lapping up her sweetness and tasting the zest of her desire.

She sighed her pleasure, and he answered with a low-throated rumble.

Releasing her mouth, he nibbled and nipped and licked his way down her neck. The warm caress of her breath brushed his skin as she sighed her delight.

Tye groaned and swept her off her feet. He carried her to the bed and lay her down like a cherished prize. He drank in the vision before him, his heart pounding like a smithy's hammer. He wanted this woman like hell on fire. He wanted her naked and against him. Around him. Now.

Slow down, McBride. His needs would have to wait. This was her first time. She should have fireworks and rainbows and joy. That much he could do. He'd promised her. Lying down beside her, he gave himself over to the delicious task of bringing pleasure to this remarkable woman.

He kissed her again, his mouth skimming over hers. She opened and he delved inside, their tongues touching and teasing and tasting. "I'll make it good for you, Claire," he swore. He trailed his tongue up the satin skin of her neck until shivers racked her body. "I swear I'll make it good."

"It's already delicious," she murmured.

"Well, it's fixin' to get even better." He tugged the gown off her shoulders until it pooled around her waist, pressing kisses against every inch of skin revealed. "Magnificent," he murmured, drinking in the sight of her full, rosy-tipped breasts.

Masculine instinct drove him. He had to taste her. Now. Slowly he lowered his head and lapped at her nipples, circling first one, then the other, with his tongue, until they drew up into hard, taut peaks.

"Oh, Tye," she whispered.

Holding the silken weight of one breast in his hand, he stroked and kneaded as he suckled the other. Her flavor seeped into him, a starburst to his senses. Her gasp went straight to his loins.

Moaning softly, she arched against him, the motion wanton yet innocent, reminding him of the significance of the moment. No matter what the future held for them, she would always remember this moment, remember him. He was her first.

The notion humbled him, but dwelling upon it became impossible when her fingers skimmed impatiently up and down his back, her nails scraping the linen shirt separating them. Tye paused long enough to shrug it off, then they touched, bare flesh against bare flesh, eager mouths mating.

She trembled and whimpered, each sound a ripple lapping away at his control. His hands stroked her, explored her, searching out those particular places that pleased her most. His mouth worked her and teased her and whispered words that made her blush.

With Claire's untutored help, he shed the last of his clothes. When he stripped her gown completely away, she neither protested nor attempted to hide, though her smile betrayed a maidenly shyness. Tye cupped her cheek in the palm of his hand, smiled into her eyes, and reassured her with the tenderest of kisses. Then, kneeling back, he drank in the sight of her beauty. "I knew you'd be exquisite. You take my breath away."

He pressed a courtly kiss to the back of her hand, then he turned it, exposing the tender flesh of her wrist where her blood pulsed. He laid his tongue against it and tasted the pounding, erotic rhythm. His own pulse kept time with hers, beating fierce and hot and aching. *Slow, slow, slow,* he told himself, battling his own needs while he nibbled his way up her arm.

"Hurry, Tye," she pleaded while his hand drew lazy circles over the flat of her stomach, slipping lower and lower toward his ultimate goal.

Questing fingers found the folds of her flesh slick and wet and hot. At his touch, she stiffened and gave a little cry, a melding of pleasure and pain. "Tye?"

"Give in to it, sugar," he urged, finding and thumbing the tiny ball of nerves in gentle, steady strokes. "Let it happen, Claire. It's good, so very good."

Her entire body pulsed and shuddered, and Tye's breathing quickened right along with hers. Her ache became his. The tension swirled and spiraled ever upward, tugging them along together. "Please," she whimpered.

It was almost his undoing.

Her first time. Slow. Take it slow. He slipped a finger inside her, and her virgin body gripped him tight.

Tye groaned, his hand working her flesh as she twisted in a sensual, sexual frenzy. "Please," she sobbed, the husky plea nearly his undoing. 'Tye . . . oh . . . hurry, please."

She surged against him, her movements sheer instinct. His own hips flexed against her, pressing, seeking to quench the heat searing his loins. Desire drove him, hammered at him, weakening his restraint. "Do it, Claire. Let go and do it for me."

She arched against him, little noises winging from her throat, as her hands clawed at his back.

Then, finally, she stiffened, her entire body growing taut. "Tye!" she cried as her honey poured into his hand and she gave him the gift of her release.

"God, Claire." No longer able to ignore his body's demands, he eased her legs apart and knelt between them. Leaning forward, he probed her moist opening with the tip of his shaft. He summoned every ounce of will not to thrust hungrily inside her. "I don't want to hurt you, sugar," he rasped. "I don't . . ."

As she gazed up at him, her eyes glowed with an unnamed emotion. She reached for him, arching her hips, taking him deeper, until together, they broke her innocence.

Tye sank into her with a groan. "Claire? Are you all right?"

"*Mmm* . . ." she purred and rolled her hips. "You fill me."

Pleasure bathed him at her words. His body throbbed with the need for release, but he battled for some semblance of control. She was so hot, so tight, and she felt like . . . home.

It was then, in a lightning flash of clarity, that he admitted how close he was to falling in love with his wife.

In that brief moment in time, the sky lit with dreams: wife, home, family. Children of his own.

Then the dark clouds of desire came billowing back. His own climax rushed toward him, a raging storm of sensation that threatened to destroy him. *No, God. I can't*. He met the tempest head on, braved it, battled it, and, with a wrenching shout, won.

He yanked free of her body, his life force jetting harmlessly across her stomach.

When his breath returned a million years later, he rolled off her and lay on the bed beside her. Without speaking or meeting her gaze, he cleaned her with his shirt. He sensed her watching him, but he refused to acknowledge it.

Claire wasn't so shy. When he'd turned off the lamps and returned to bed, lying with his arm flung across his eyes and trying desperately not to reach for her again, she asked, "Tye? Why did you . . . ?"

Because I saw a little angel with my green eyes and your blond hair, that's why.

"It's a method of preventing conception," he replied.

"Oh."

Unreasonable anger flared inside him and he snapped,

"Damned right, *Oh*. I told you this marriage won't last. It would be beyond cruel for us to bring a child into this world under the circumstances."

"Oh."

Beneath the cover of his arm, he sneered and silently repeated, *Oh. Is that all she can say?*

A few minutes later, he wished that were true. He flinched when she laid her hand on his belly and asked, "Is that the only method for preventing pregnancy?"

Bold little thing. What kind of deflowered virgin was she anyway? He'd be damned before he'd discuss such things with her. "Didn't your mother teach you anything?"

"Not really, no."

Haunted by the vision he had glimpsed, Tye's words turned raw and cruel. "It doesn't matter. I'll take care of it. I won't be trapped into staying with you."

Beside him in the dark, his wife went stiff as a fence post

"Oh, hell," Tye muttered, then followed the curse with a litany of words bad enough to turn the air blue three times over. Shame and frustration beat his spirit to a pulp. With every word, Claire grew colder and stiffer so that when he finally wound down, she could have passed for an ice wagon delivery.

Tye didn't blame her for her reaction one bit.

He found her cheek in the dark and gently slid his thumb across her silken skin. "I'm sorry, darlin'. I know better. You are not a scheming woman, and I never should have said that."

"No, you shouldn't have."

He took her hand and pressed an apologetic kiss to the back of it. "What you made me feel . . . well, it scared me and I reacted poorly. I have all this . . . stuff going on in my head and it makes me crazy sometimes. You got caught in the backwash, and that wasn't fair. I'm sorry, sugar. Forgive me?"

After a long moment, she said, "I don't know. Kiss me again and I'll think about it."

The petulance in her voice cued him to her teasing. He grinned in the darkness, pleased she'd heard his apology and accepted it. His wife wasn't a pouter, a grudge holder, and Tye was glad of it. He didn't like pouty women. He liked Claire Donovan McBride very much.

He set about showing her how much.

Claire showed him a thing or two right back. The woman proved herself to be a fast learner.

This time when he loved her, Claire didn't hold back. She explored him with bold hands and mouth and tongue. When she held him, stroked him, and spoke in a throaty, curious voice about the contrast between soft, velvet skin and the steel-like hardness beneath it, he damn near erupted in her hand.

Better that he had.

Because this time when she accepted him into her body, she knew what she was doing. This time, Tye had absolutely no desire to get loose. This time, when Tye McBride climaxed, he remained buried to the hilt in his wife's soft, slick, infinitely welcoming body.

When dawn finally broke the following morning, he'd repeated his carelessness three more times.

And he'd loved every damn minute of it.

CHAPTER 18

SET A WHITE LACE DOILY BENEATH THE BEDROOM LANTERN FOR GOOD LUCK.

CLAIRE WOKE STIFLING hot and clinging to the edge of the bed. Groggily she shoved away the covers piled on top of her. She blinked twice, frowning as the opposite wall came into view. Blue floral wallpaper? Her bedroom was yellow.

An elbow nudged both her kidney and her memory, and the events of the previous day and night came crashing back. A cat-and-cream smile spread slowly across her face, and she would have added a feline arch and stretch if she could have moved without falling to the floor. Tye McBride hogged the bed.

After a bit of thought, she decided against launching an assault of nudges and shoves to regain her rightful share of the mattress. He'd certainly wake up then, and she found she wanted a few moments' solitude to reflect on her feelings in the wake of the night's events.

Sliding from beneath the covers, she lifted her robe from the floor and slipped it on, the modesty that deserted her the night before having returned with the light of morning. Thus fortified, she sneaked a look at her husband.

No wonder she'd been hot. He'd kicked all the covers off of himself and onto her.

He sprawled across the bed on his stomach, naked and tanned and Greek-god beautiful. Claire sucked in a breath as a ribbon of desire fluttered through her, then her lips tilted in wry self-amusement. Such a short trip from virgin to vixen, apparently. And how did she feel about that? Ashamed? Embarrassed? Upset?

Smug. She felt gloriously, deliciously smug.

A smile played about her mouth as she acted the voyeur and allowed her gaze to drift over her husband's muscular flanks. Along with being smug, she felt so wonderfully wicked. How strange that with the simple recitation of a few words, acts once labeled sinful transformed into a blessed event.

As many times as Tye had invoked the Lord's name last night, she figured their marriage bed should be considered extra-blessed.

Outside on the windowsill a mockingbird stretched out his neck and greeted the day in song. Inside, Tye grumbled some unintelligible words and tugged a pillow over his head.

He was an exceedingly complex man. So fierce and loyal. Funny and witty and sweet. And loving. She'd never known such an openly loving man before. Tye proclaimed his love for family and friends back home in South Carolina each time he mentioned them. The vehemence with which he expressed his absolute faith in his brother's continued existence said it eloquently, also.

But the most telling example of the depths of Tye McBride's love were the three little girls he called his Blessings. His every word, act, and deed reflected his love for those children.

Now if only he could learn to love himself, to defeat his inner demons and forgive himself for the mistakes he had made. Claire had figured out that along with being loyal and loving, Tye McBride was wounded. The damage done by the trouble with that wicked Constance had yet to heal.

"I can help you," she whispered softly so as not to disturb his sleep. With her love, she could help this man who gave so much of himself in order to help others. She could show him the way out of his self-doubt and back to believing in himself again. Her love could help him heal. Then maybe he could love her in return and they could forget the notion of having a temporary marriage.

It was a heady thought, one that gave her new insight into the ideas her mother had tried to convey about loving and liberation. Claire's love for Tye empowered her in a manner she had never felt before. The feeling had carried over into their lovemaking last night, she realized, pushing along the evolution from virgin to vamp. From bride to lover.

Tye mumbled something beneath the pillow then tossed it away and rolled restlessly over onto his back. Claire's gaze trailed slowly over him and she grinned. From bride to lover. Her da liked to say that the love of a good woman cured many a man's ills. Perhaps in this case, her father's dictum required a little editing. In Tye's case, he had the love of a woman who was, for the most part, good, but who had just enough bad thrown in the batter to make it interesting.

The flesh between her husband's legs began to lengthen and lift, and Claire jerked her stare upward to his face. Sure enough, he had awakened.

Jade eyes watched her, glowing and gleaming. "Good morning," he said, his rough, raspy tone sending a shiver down her spine.

"Yes, it is."

"Is it?"

"Very good."

He smiled; a slow, satisfied, totally male smirk. Obviously Claire wasn't the only one feeling smug this morning.

With no apparent concern for his nakedness, he rolled onto his side and propped his elbow on the bed, his hand supporting his head. Cognizant of his gaze upon her, Claire continued to brush her hair. "It's a waterfall of sunshine," he observed, reaching out to pull a curl.

"It's a pain in the neck to brush when I go to bed without braiding it first."

"If you leave it loose for me when you come to bed, I'll brush it in the morning for you. I've always enjoyed sleeping surrounded by sunshine."

Claire wrinkled her nose. "I don't care to hear about your past amours, Husband."

He laughed and sat up, appropriating the brush. "I'm talking the great outdoors, sugar." He stroked the bristles through her hair. "And afternoon naps."

"Oh."

"There you go again."

"What do you mean?" She almost purred beneath his attentions.

"*Oh*-ing me."

"Owing you? What do I owe you?"

He paused and a moment later she felt his lips nibbling at her neck. "A good-morning kiss," he murmured softly in her ear. He guided her back down onto the mattress and accepted the tribute she joyfully afforded him, a boon that evolved into more than just a kiss.

Later, they lay side by side, spent and so exhausted that Claire thought she might never have the energy to leave her bed again. Tye, however, obviously didn't similarly suffer. After a short moment of recovery, he rolled from the bed and reached for his pants. "This is ridiculous," he grumbled. "I'm an idiot. I should have suspected this might happen. I should have been prepared."

"Prepared for what?"

In the process of tugging on his shirt, he tossed her a frustrated glare. "Prepared for the fact I have the self-control of a gnat." He grabbed his boots off the floor and shoved first one foot and then the other into them and headed for the door.

Claire sat up, the sheet clutched to her chest. "Tye, where are you going?"

"The druggist."

"The druggist? Why? Are you ill?"

326

"Oh, I'm ill, all right." At the door, he paused. Retracing his steps, he walked to the bedside table and hunkered down in front of it, scanning the row of books lined up along its lower shelf. Not finding what he sought, he crossed to the matching table on the opposite side of the bed. He touched the spine of each book as he searched the titles, finally grunting in approval as he pulled one volume from the collection. He tossed it to Claire.

"Read this while I'm gone. It gives a good explanation."

When he quit the room, Claire lifted the book and read the title printed on its cover. "*The Fruits of Philosophy*, by Dr. Charles Knowlton."

Philosophy? She didn't understand.

"I think it's Chapter Three," came Tye's shout from downstairs. "And while I'm out, I'll probably run by Willow Hill and check on the Blessings."

She heard the front door slam as she opened the book to the title page. It carried a most interesting subtitle: Or, *The Private Companion of Young Married People*. Quickly she turned to Chapter Three, the heading for which read "Contraceptive Advice."

The third paragraph ended with the sentence, "Condoms may be purchased from many druggists."

Claire's stomach took a dive and she shut the book with a snap. Well, she shouldn't be surprised. Why should one night change his mind about such a dearly held tenent? She'd been a fool to have hoped for more once he'd changed the way he made love to her after that first time. So Tye didn't want to have children with her. She shouldn't feel hurt by it. She was in no hurry to start a family. He didn't love her yet, and a child truly should be conceived in love. Besides, with her family gone, she'd need to concentrate her efforts on getting The Confectionary back on track, not growing babies.

No matter how appealing the idea sounded.

She gave the book a long, speculative look, then slowly reached for it. The notion of growing babies might be premature this morning, but the practice of making them—or not making them, as the case might be—was quite appealing, itself.

"Besides," she said to herself as she opened the book to intriguing Chapter Two, "We got married only yesterday. There is no rush. Once he loves me, I can bring up the issue of children again."

She read the first two pages of the chapter, then added, "Yes, now that I think about it, I am very glad we have plenty of time."

TYE EXITED the druggist's shop and headed up Main on his way to Willow Hill. While passing the mercantile, a set of items in the window caught his eye. He stopped. Polished blue stones the color of his wife's eyes adorned each piece of the silver dresser set. The comb, brush, and mirror seemed to have Claire Donovan McBride's name written all over them. Without further thought, he entered the shop and made the purchase.

He didn't feel foolish until he'd covered half the distance to Willow Hill. Not because he'd bought her a gift—it was appropriate for a man to buy his wife a bridal gift. Claire would love it and he'd love watching her use it. What bothered him was how glad he was to have a weight in his hand to counteract the weight in his pocket.

His own embarrassment while making his purchase had caught him by surprise. Because he'd always exercised the withdrawal method while engaging romantic pursuits, he had never bought this particular essential before. Hell's bells, he'd felt like a green boy. Of course, the damned druggist hadn't helped matters at all. Having read about the day's nuptials in the morning paper, the fellow had laughed and made a comment having to do with locking barn doors after the horses have escaped. Tye prayed the fellow wasn't a gossip. He sure as hell didn't want to see this particular purchase written up in Wilhemina Peters's "Talk About Town" column.

Tye instinctively checked his jacket pocket as he approached the house. The package remained neatly tucked away. It wouldn't do for curious Kat to see it and ask him what was in the paper-wrapped parcel. Or, God forbid, Claire's father.

Maybe that's why he'd gone bashful at the druggist.

Something about carrying condoms around while in the company of the Blessings and the Donovans left him feeling more than a tad uncomfortable.

He heard Emma's giggling as he climbed the steps of Willow Hill and he smiled at the most welcome sound. Opening the door he called out a loud hello and then the Blessings were in his arms, laughing and squealing and telling him how much they missed him. "Since yesterday?" he questioned. "It was all of a day, girls. You didn't have time to miss me, not with all this company around the house."

Katrina tore open his heart with a solemn observation. "Ever since Papa and Mama got lost, I miss you anytime I'm not with you."

Tye dropped to his knees, laid aside his gift, and took her in his arms, wrapping her in a fierce hug. "Ah, Kat, it'll be all right. I promise."

Maribeth asked, "Do you still feel Papa in your heart, Uncle Tye?"

He started to answer by rote but instead, out of respect for these children, he stopped and considered it. "Yeah," he replied a moment later. "Yes I do, sweetheart. Your papa is there deep in my heart just like he's always been." Unable to miss the skeptical plea in Emma's eyes, Tye held her gaze and repeated, "He's alive and doing his darnedest to get home."

The four of them shared a poignant, hopeful moment before Peggy Donovan made her presence known by asking, "Is Claire with you?"

"Uh, no. She's . . . uh . . ." He darned sure didn't want to say home in bed. "She's getting ready for our meeting with the judge later on."

"What time is that?"

"Two o'clock."

"Do you want us to bring the children to the courthouse?"

Tye considered the question before answering, "After their shenanigans at the wedding, I think it's best they stay here. Besides, I don't want them around the Wests any more than necessary. If the judge wants to see them, I'll come get them myself." From the corners of his eyes, Tye saw the Donovan men descending on him like guard dogs. He gave his nieces one last hug, then beat a hasty retreat—before the condoms burned a hole through his pocket and dropped at his wife's father's feet.

Tye wasn't surprised to find her down in The Confectionary's kitchen. She wore a pristine white apron over blue gingham and she smiled brightly as she greeted him. Tye was struck by both her beauty and the cloud of Magic he detected in the air. He cleared his throat. "Whatcha baking?"

A blush painted her cheeks as she met her husband's gaze. "Banana muffins."

Tye was struck by the need to do some painting of his own, using his mouth as a brush and her body for the canvas. Desire warred with dismay in his heart. He'd worn himself out last night, and here he was randy as a stud horse again this morning.

He watched her, unable to look away while she bent over and peered into the oven. "I debated whether to make muffins or cinnamon buns, but the muffins were quicker and I thought you might be hungry when you came home. It won't take me but a few minutes to fry up steak and eggs."

Buns and hunger and Claire McBride's magic. Tye yanked his gaze away from her rear and focused on the window. He'd best get control of himself before he laid her out like a pie crust on the kitchen table. He cleared his throat. "I brought you a present."

Her blush deepened. "I read Chapter Three."

Tye slapped a hand against the small package in his jacket pocket. Damned if he didn't feel his own cheeks heating. "Not those." He ducked into the outer section of the shop and retrieved the dresser set. "This," he said, shoving the package at her.

Her exclamation of pleasure only made his condition worse. When he found himself seriously eyeing the table, he decided he'd best retreat and regroup. "I'll go wash up for breakfast."

Her attention focused on the gift, Claire paid him scant attention as he hurried upstairs. In the bedroom, he stored his package, then turned to flee the site of his total loss of control. But something stopped him, drawing him slowly, inexorably, toward the bed.

Bloodstained sheets. The physical proof of Claire's loss of innocence. Of the fact that he'd rejected the notion of a marriage of convenience and made her his wife, in truth.

Tye stared at the bed for a long time.

Emotion slowly built a lump in his throat. Marriage vows and all they symbolized. Had he been wrong yesterday? Did they have a chance? Could he give her forever?

He felt better about himself today than he had in a helluva long time. Claire knew all about him, every one of his shameful secrets. And yet, she'd given him so much. And he knew, if only he found courage enough to reach for it, she'd give him everything.

"Maybe in time," he said softly. Maybe in time, Claire could work enough magic to make it happen. Maybe they could work together to bring that rainbow of joy a little closer. Maybe, just maybe, she could help him find the backbone to reach for the prize. "If anyone can, it's Claire."

Tye left the bedroom saying to himself, *Maybe all we need to make it happen is a little time.*

～

SHORTLY BEFORE TWO, Tye and Claire climbed the front steps of the Tarrant County Courthouse.

"Are you ready for this?" Tye asked, his gaze both intense and nervous.

The pounding in Claire's heart had little to do with physical exertion. She drew a deep, steadying breath and nodded. "Yes."

"You'll say the stuff that needs to be said? The stuff about love?"

The stuff about love.

Claire bit her tongue to stop it from betraying her. She wanted so badly to tell him the lies he'd requested she tell weren't lies at all. She wanted to be honest, but in her bones she sensed he wasn't ready for her to tell the truth.

So rather than tell him, she'd show him. Now and tonight and for as long as he would let her.

She took his hand and gripped it tight. Meeting his gaze, holding it, she made him silent promises as she said, "I'll say what needs saying. You can trust me, Tye."

"Trust," he repeated. "It's a nice thought. I'm afraid it's been a heck of a long time since I used the words 'trust' and 'woman' in the same sentence."

"I'm not Constance West, Tye."

"I know that." He squeezed her hand in return. "In fact, you make me think of Jenny."

"Oh?" Claire liked the thought of that. "In what way?"

Tye shrugged. "She's good for my brother."

With that interesting bit of news, he reached out and opened the door to Judge Remington's courtroom. A clerk met them and escorted them back to the judge's chambers.

George and Beatrice West sat in two of four chairs lined up in front of Remington's desk. "He is five minutes late," the woman accused. "Take note of that. And why did he bring that woman with him? This is a private affair, is it not, Judge?"

Tye ignored her as he gallantly took Claire's elbow and escorted her to one of the empty chairs opposite the judge, then took a place behind her, laying his hands on her shoulders. "Judge Remington, before we get started, have you had the opportunity to meet my bride, the best baker in Texas?"

Beatrice West gasped.

The judge smiled. "I saw the morning paper. Congratulations." Patting his stomach, he added, "I've had the pleasure of sampling your German chocolate cake, Miss Donov—I mean, Mrs. McBride."

"Mrs. McBride?" Beatrice West blazed an angry glare toward Tye. "What skullduggery are you up to this time?"

"Didn't catch a look at the morning paper, did you Bea?" Tye drawled lazily as he took the last vacant seat.

Obviously threatened by the judge's goodwill toward the McBrides, Beatrice launched into her attack. Without allowing any break in conversation, she took almost ten full minutes to outline her arguments why Tye wasn't fit to raise her granddaughters. Accusations shot like venom from her mouth, some true, some false, all of them ugly.

Three times Claire swelled up with a protest. Three times her husband warned against it by squeezing her hand. They'd known to expect this. The plan called for letting Mrs. West empty out her guns. With Claire on his side, Tye had told her, he didn't anticipate any fatal volleys.

Finally she wound down, shot him a vicious look, folded her hands in her lap, and sat back in her chair. George West apparently thought she'd covered it all because he never said a word.

Judge Remington looked at Tye. "McBride? Care to respond?"

Tye dragged a posturing hand down along the line of his jaw. Upon occasion in the past, Claire had observed high stakes poker games. Never before had she seen a bet being laid on the table as large as the one her husband now placed.

Here's hoping the Good Luck Wedding Dress did its thing.

"Yes, Judge," Tye said. "I do. First, let me say I'll be happy to answer any and all questions you might have concerning the charges Mrs. West laid against me. I'll go into as much depth as you wish. But as far as I can tell, it all boils down to a few relevant facts."

He ticked them off on his fingers. "Number one, my brother entrusted his daughters into my care. He did so with full and prior knowledge of the personal failures Mrs. West mentioned. Knowing all that, he trusted me to keep his girls safe and happy. If I'm good enough in Trace's eyes, then I should be good enough to do the job from the court's point of view."

Claire glanced at the judge, trying to gage his reaction, but Remington had a darn good poker face himself.

"Number two," Tye continued. "In Claire, I have provided my nieces with an exemplary mother figure. She has promised to love them like her own, and I have no doubt that she will. Number three, Emma, Maribeth, and Katrina love me. They want to live with me and my wife at Willow Hill. They do not wish to be ripped from their home and taken to the sinful city of New Orleans."

"Wait a minute," George West roused himself enough to interrupt.

"And last, but certainly not least," Tye said, plunging ahead as though West had never spoken, "are the feelings I harbor for my nieces. I love them, Judge Remington. With my heart, my soul, every breath I take. Love. It's a word, you'll note, that Mrs. West never spoke."

The understated accusation rippled through the room like a water wake. Claire knew Tye had more lined up to say, but that last bit had been extra-effective. Utilizing another good poker strategy, he fell silent, quitting while he was ahead.

Judge Remington steepled his fingers and brought his hands to his mouth in contemplation. Perhaps sensing a pending defeat, Beatrice leaned forward and snapped, "You can't believe a word he says. Those McBride boys were always good liars. I don't doubt this marriage is a lie, too. A tactic to bolster his attempt to hold my dear granddaughters hostage. Don't allow it to work, Judge. Don't fall prey to his false charm like my poor, departed Constance, the woman he so wickedly seduced."

Remington's brows arched. "It's a fair question, McBride. Why the sudden marriage?"

Claire cleared her throat and spoke up. "My former beau, Mr. Reid Jamieson, refused to accept the fact that I had severed our relationship. Since we already planned to wed, Tye and I decided to advance the date of the ceremony in the hope of finally proving to the man that he and I had no future together."

Tye patted her shoulder in support. It was a nice bit of side-stepping, technically the truth. He was impressed.

"I see," said the judge. "And where is this Mr. Jamieson now? Could he possibly be a threat to you and thereby the children?"

"Not at all," Tye declared. "He has left town and I am certain he will never come back."

The judge pinned Tye with a look that said he guessed there was more to this story than stated, then turned and addressed Claire. "So this is a true marriage? It's not something McBride here cooked up in order to complicate the Wests' plans?"

Claire clasped her husband's hand as it lay upon her lap. In a voice strong and sweet and sincere, she said, "Sir, I love my husband. Exchanging wedding vows with him was a dream come true for me. I will be a good wife to him, Judge Remington. And I will love Emma, Maribeth, and Katrina like my own. You have my word on it."

Tye shot her a warm, approving look, then leaned over to kiss her cheek. While there, he whispered in her ear. "I'd like to drag you from that chair and plant a kiss right on your lips. You are as convincing as a spade flush."

"Enough of that," Remington scolded mildly. "You're making me jealous." Then he addressed Tye. "Now, what about this nonsense I hear about you thinking your brother didn't die?"

Tye nodded. "You said you read this morning's paper. I discussed this same question with Mrs. Peters yesterday, and she wrote it up today. Did you see her column?" He reached into his jacket pocket, pulled out a copy of the article and handed it to the judge. "She made a good summary."

Handling the matter in this way had been Claire's idea. The less lies they actually told the judge, the better, to her way of thinking.

Remington read the column and a few moments later, following a few more questions and a handful of legal cautions, he said, "Now, this meeting here today doesn't dot all the legal *I*'s and cross all the legal *T*'s, but if the question of the McBride girls' guardianship comes before my court, I'm telling you now that unless I'm presented with a compelling new argument, I'll decide in favor of Tye and his bride."

Tye burst into a smile as big as Texas as Beatrice lurched to her feet and exploded in argument. Claire tuned her out, her attention caught by the warmth of Tye's celebratory gaze. She decided that under the circumstances, a kiss wouldn't be out of order. Actually, the judge probably expected it.

More than willing to do her wifely duty, she pulled his head over to hers and captured his lips with her own. She vaguely heard Beatrice say something about filing suit in New Orleans as Remington escorted the Blessings' grandparents from the room, but she let that worry fly right on by. He pulled her over into his lap and she was lost in her husband's kiss, afloat in the riot of sensations he brought to life within her.

When they finally paused to draw a breath, he said, "I swear, you must use Magic for mouth rinse, too."

"Oh, Tye, you did it. You won."

"*We* won. That last bit you said . . . that did the trick. You said it like you really meant it."

She pulled away from him then, and stood. If her smile had dimmed just a little, he appeared not to notice.

"Thank you, Wife," he said softly, sincerely.

"You're welcome, Husband." She tucked her arm through his and led him toward the door. "Let's go home and tell the children, shall we?"

OUTSIDE THE COURTHOUSE, while Claire paused to accept felicitations on their marriage by a few of her customers, Tye turned his thoughts inward. His eyes half-closed, he searched his heart for his brother's presence. Finding him, linking in his mind, he sent a silent message. *Don't worry. They are safe. I've seen to it and I'll keep on seeing to it. Until you get home, Brother. Until you get home. I won't betray you this time.*

AFTER THEIR ONE-NIGHT honeymoon Claire and her husband returned to Willow Hill, the Donovans departed, and Mrs. Wilson went back to working days at Trace's home and spending nights at her own. The McBrides' patchwork family settled into a pleasant routine. After getting the girls off to school Claire and Tye would both go down to The Confectionary where she would help with the baking while he held meetings in the upstairs apartment with her father and brothers and suppliers and builders as they planned the construction of their Magic Factory.

After the wedding, business at The Confectionary rebounded, and soon all of Fort Worth was talking about how the Donovan's Magical Wedding Cake legend had once again come true. Obviously Claire's wedding to Reid Jamieson had never been meant to happen. True love won out in the end. When "Talk About Town" quoted Emma as saying that the McBride-Donovan partnership had turned a Magical Cake into a Good Luck Wedding Cake, the bakery's success was assured.

The Wests' continued presence in town did paste a pall over the days. Beatrice was a dog with a bone, and every day brought another threat or attempted legal maneuver. Tye fended each one of them off, but everyone in the family looked forward to the day Beatrice gave up and went home. The Blessings added that hope to their nightly prayers.

On the afternoon of Mrs. Wilson's day off, early in the second week of married life, Claire slid the last tray of molasses cookies into the oven at Willow Hill and sighed. "Finally," she said gratefully, rubbing the small of her back. "If I'd known you girls would take to baking with so much zeal, I'd have had this lesson down at the bakery. My oven holds double the amount of this one. We'd have finished much sooner."

"Nah," Maribeth said, cookie crumbs clinging to her lips as she munched happily on the fruits of her labor. "We would have wanted to make even more stuff. This has been fun."

"That's right." Katrina gleamed a molasses smile. "And eating is the funnest part."

Emma held out a plate with a sampling of their baked goodies artfully arranged. "Can we take this to Uncle Tye now? I think his meeting is over. I saw Mr. Hayes leave Papa's office when I went upstairs to change my clothes."

The unfortunate recipient of a buttermilk spill, Emma had returned to the kitchen a few moments earlier. Claire listened to the news of the visitor's departure with interest. Hayes was the third architect Tye had interviewed to draw plans for the ranch house he intended to build. From the brevity of the meeting, Claire guessed he'd soon be talking to architect number four.

Claire wondered when her husband would realize he'd never find a professional as talented as his brother. In his mind, anyway.

Not that she cared. She was happy living at Willow Hill. She was happy, period. Each day of their marriage brought them closer, each night strengthened the bond slowly growing between them. This morning when Tye collapsed on their bed following a particularly physical bout of lovemaking, he'd smiled at her so sweetly, so lovingly, that all thought had flown from her mind and left her stuttering for words. Claire had begun to hope that in time, he might actually let down his guard and come to love her.

"Auntie? Can we take him the cookies?" Emma said, her tone suggesting she'd repeated her question a number of times.

Claire wiped her hands on her apron. "Of course. Let's go find your uncle, shall we?"

They had to look a few minutes, but finally located him on the second-floor front veranda, busy replacing the porch rail spool Ralph had chosen for a chew toy. They all sat, drinking milk and eating cookies while Tye shared the details of his meeting with Claire. "Getting the house built is going to take longer than I'd figured."

"Don't worry about it, Tye," Claire replied. "I think—"

"Look at this," Emma interrupted, standing at the railing and pointing toward the bottom of the hill.

Katrina's eyes went round. "Look at all the people!"

"Are we having a party?" Maribeth asked. "It's a good thing we baked those cookies."

Claire glanced at the drive, then toward her husband. He appeared as perplexed as she. "I count five wagons and there must be thirty horses. Are we having a party, Tye?"

"Not that I know of," he replied, frowning.

The five of them lined the veranda, peering out at the gathering crowd. Katrina said, "I don't think anything bad has happened, do you? Look, most everyone is smiling."

"Uh, oh," Maribeth groaned. "There's Mrs. Peters. She'll turn us in to the truancy deputy, you just wait and see."

"Could it be a shivaree, Tye? A couple weeks late and the wrong time of day for it, I know, but what else . . . ?" She allowed her voice to trail away when she heard Emma's soft gasp and saw Tye's grip clamp like a vise around the rail.

"Good Lord," he murmured.

Tears spilled from Emma's eyes and began to roll down her cheeks. "Uncle Tye?" she begged in a little voice.

"What!" Maribeth demanded. "What is it?"

"The second wagon," Tye replied in a raspy voice. "Son of a . . ." He stopped and cleared his throat. "Girls, quick. Look at the second wagon!"

CHAPTER 19

IF A LADYBUG LANDS ON YOUR RIGHT ARM, YOU WILL HAVE GOOD LUCK.

THE two younger girls strained forward, then Katrina let out a long, high-pitched squeal. Maribeth didn't take time to make noise; she whirled and dashed into the house. Claire squinted toward the crowd, trying to identify the source of the excitement while Emma repeated, "Uncle Tye? Please, is it true?"

His hand shook, Claire saw, as he oh-so-slowly lifted it in a wave. "Yeah darlin', I do believe you can believe this."

When a figure—a man—stood in the bed of the second wagon rolling up the hill and returned Tye's wave, Emma moaned and melted, sinking to her knees, tears streaming down her face.

"Emma!" Claire moved toward her, but Tye reached the child first. He looked haggard, yet joyous, as he scooped young Emma into his arms and exited the veranda without a word to his wife.

Taken aback, she turned once again to the commotion brewing in the front yard just in time to see the man jump down from the wagon and hit the ground running.

At the same time, Katrina and Maribeth burst down the front steps.

The man's arms reached, opened wide, and even before his hat flew off revealing an extremely familiar face, Claire realized who it was. He dropped to his knees, arms outstretched, as Tye stepped into view and set Emma down so she could run with her sisters.

Tears stung Claire's eyes at the sound of the most beautiful music in the world—the McBride Menace's joyous voices lifted in the cry of a single word: "*Papa!*"

Trace McBride had come home.

And judging by the size of the stomach on the woman who approached the blubbering father-daughter foursome, he'd brought his Jenny home with him.

Claire observed the reunion through blurry eyes. She smiled as Tye wrapped his sister-in-law in a hug. Her breath caught on a sob when the identical brothers shook hands, hesitated, then pulled each other into an embrace.

"Thank you, God," she prayed, wiping her eyes and smiling and trying to ignore the worry pricking at her brain. The McBride family celebrated below while she stood apart. Alone. Very much afraid she had just run out of time.

HALF AN HOUR after his brother's arrival, Tye leaned against the doorjamb in the parlor, his arms folded, a sappy grin on his face as he watched the Blessings demonstrate Spike the fortune-teller fish's amazing capabilities.

Jenny lay stretched out on the sofa, her feet propped up by three pillows—one from each daughter—while Trace sat on the floor in front of her, all but covered up in ecstatic little girls. And a dog. And, when Spike did a double-left flop, one out-of-water fish.

The laughter in the room was sweet enough to steal the tart from one of Claire's rhubarb pies. Tye remained silent, however. He doubted he could force so much as a sigh past the boulder-sized lump in his throat.

Emma, especially, stayed plastered against her papa. It was she who finally turned the tide of the conversation away from the girls' activities of late with the questions Tye himself had been burning to ask. "Where were you, Papa? Why didn't you come home? They told us you drowned and that was a very horrible thing. Uncle Tye told us you were all right, that he felt your connection, but still it was . . . hard."

"Ah, Emma." Trace's voice was rough with emotion. "It breaks my heart you had to go through that. Your mama and I didn't know the ship sank. We didn't know you'd be so worried."

"We were scared to death," Katrina exclaimed in an accusing tone.

Tye pushed away from the doorjamb and strolled into the room. "What did happen, Trace?"

His brother's lips twisted in a grim smile. "Jenny got stubborn and apparently saved our lives, that's what."

The woman in question smiled a madonna's smile. "Remind me to remind you of it when the shipment arrives."

Shipment? Tye quirked a brow at his brother.

Trace nodded. "The day we were due to leave she meets a native woman and falls head over heels for the lady's dress."

"Now there's a picture," Jenny said ruefully, frowning at her baby-filled belly.

Grinning, Trace lifted his hand to pat her stomach. "Anyway, my Jenny balks at boarding the ship. She wants to travel inland to the woman's village and purchase Caribbean cloth for Fortune's Design. She refuses to listen to reason, so I write a letter for you explaining our change in plans and give it to the ship's captain. He promised to telegraph, too, in case the letter took too long getting home. With that supposedly settled, Jenny and I rattle away in a rickety wagon bound for an island village whose name I never did learn to pronounce."

Tye grimly added, "And the ship sailed off to sink."

A moment of silence filled the room as the occupants considered the vagaries of fate. Then, with eyes rounded in wonder,

Maribeth broke the silence by saying, "Maybe you should make another wedding dress out of the cloth you bought, Mama. Talk about good luck."

"What I think I'll do is say extra prayers for those poor people who lost their lives." Glancing at Tye, she added, "Maybelle Davis told us the news about the ship's loss. It came as quite a shock."

After that, they spent some time discussing the rest of their trip and catching up on all the happenings back home. Tye chafed to explain about the Wests, but didn't want to drag all that baggage out in front of the Blessings. Of course, from the looks of things, it might be a year or more before they let their beloved parents out of their sights.

Occasionally Tye thought about Claire, wondering why she'd made herself scarce. Once or twice he started to go look for her, but he couldn't quite make himself leave his brother. *Hell, I'm just as bad as the girls.*

Having heard the news of her employers' safe return, Mrs. Wilson blew through the front door in a whirlwind of happiness. As Jenny repeated their story to her, Trace wandered over to where his brother stood. "Something tells me we'll be telling this tale till we're sick to death of it."

"Why don't you give an interview to Wilhemina and let her print it up in the newspaper?" Tye suggested. "That would ward off a few of the questions, anyway."

"Good idea. I might just do that." He paused, his gaze drifting back to where his wife sat surrounded by his children. A pained grimace etched his face. "It must have been hell for them."

"Emma took it the worst. She didn't completely believe me when I told her you were all right."

His brother shot him an intense look. "You felt. . . ?"

Tye shrugged. "For me, the connection never disappeared. Faded, maybe, during the bad years. But since I've come to Fort Worth it's grown as strong as when we were boys. I knew you were safe. I knew you'd come home when you could."

Trace blew out a sigh. "Thank you, Tye. For everything, but especially for making my 'death' easier on the girls."

Emma approached as her father spoke. "I always believed you, Uncle Tye. It's just that sometimes I got so very scared I didn't think straight." To her father, she said, "Uncle Tye took care of us real, real good, Papa. Why, he even saved us when our wicked grandmother tried to steal us away to New Orleans."

"What?" Trace's gaze snapped toward Tye. "What wicked grandmother? Surely not . . ."

Had Tye his druthers, he'd have eased into that story a little differently. "Afraid so. Once news of your demise got around, George and Beatrice paid us a little visit."

"How the hell did they find us? Except for the letters we exchange through my attorney about the Louisiana property, I've had no contact with them since Constance died. How did they find me?"

Tye winced. "I'm afraid that's my fault."

"What happened?"

"Papa," Emma cried, pouting her lip. "Don't get upset. Please, don't get upset."

Chastened, Trace gave his daughter a hug even while his eyes demanded an explanation from his twin.

Tye twisted his mouth and scratched behind his ear. "It's a long story."

"You're not gonna tell him about the spelling bee plan, not already," Maribeth protested. "He just got home. I think we should at least get one day before the punishment starts."

"Spelling bee plan? Punishment?" Trace eyed his daughters sternly. "What in heaven's name have you Menaces done now?"

"Blessings," Tye corrected automatically. "They're your Blessings. And Maribeth, don't worry about punishment. I can't explain about your grandparents without talking about the spelling bee, but I'll make sure your father understands that as far as punishment goes, I've taken care of it. You three have been through enough."

Trace's sternness melted into amusement. "You're going to protect my daughters from their own father?"

Shrugging, Tye replied, "I don't think that will be necessary."

"But you'd do it." With a laugh, Trace clapped him on the back. "If I read you right this story is better told without an audience. How about you and I adjourn to my office? I feel the need for a cigar coming on, and my wife turns green in the face at the scent of smoke these days."

A keen sense of anticipation hummed through Tye's veins as he followed his brother toward his office. Crossing the foyer, he hesitated and glanced up the stairs. Briefly he considered asking Trace to wait while he located Claire. She was part of the Blessings' shenanigans and she could help relay the story.

Besides, a part of him wanted her with him during this momentous conversation. She knew the truth about him, and he'd like to have her at his side witnessing the moment when he finally earned his redemption.

But, he realized, if he asked her to join him, then he'd have to explain about the wedding right off. He'd have to tell the story backward. It was probably simpler to keep the telling of this tale between brothers for the time being.

So minutes later, settled into deep leather chairs, cigars in one hand, whiskey for Trace and plain water for himself in the other, Tye started the story with his nieces' misbegotten efforts to make a match between their uncle and Loretta Davis. Trace just about busted a gut laughing during some of it. He buried his head in his hands during other sections. Twice Tye thought he saw tears in his brother's eyes.

The difficult part came when he spoke of the Wests' arrival. "When the girls were missing and I found Beatrice's letters to you in Emma's room, I felt I had no choice but to contact them. But I never dreamed they'd show up later in Fort Worth trying to take the Blessings away. Such a possibility never once occurred to me."

"I wouldn't have thought of it either," Trace agreed. "So what happened? How did you, to use Emma's words, 'save them from their wicked grandmother'?"

Tye pursed his lips and studied his fingernails. "Well, little brother, I got married."

Trace dropped his cigar in his lap. "You *what?*"

"I got married. It neutralized the most serious arguments the Wests had against my continued guardianship of your daughters."

"Married. Are you saying you got married just to save my children?"

Tye shrugged, wanting to downplay that aspect. "Partially, yes. Of course, my bride got something out of it, too. She had her own set of troubles that marrying me solved."

"Good Lord, Tye, I think I left you with my daughters too long. Sounds like some of their mischief-making rubbed off on you. Who? Who is she and what did she get?"

"You know Claire. Claire Donovan, your tenant?"

In the process of brushing ashes from his lap, Trace froze. "You married Claire Donovan?"

"Yes. Sort of."

A slow grin blossomed across Trace's face. "You 'sort of' married Claire Donovan?"

Uncomfortable with his brother's reaction, Tye stumbled a bit through the explanation. "It's not a real marriage, but . . . well . . . an arrangement. It was convenient for both of us."

"I imagine you did find marriage to that beauty . . ." he stressed the word ". . . *convenient.* Most men would."

"Now, Trace, it's not like that."

"You mean you're not bedding her?"

"Well, uh . . ."

"Yes?" he asked, smirking.

Tye stubbed out his cigar. "Hells bells, Brother, that's none of your damned business." Trace's chuckles soon turned to guffaws that pricked Tye's temper. "Why don't you stick that Havana back in your mouth before my fist takes a notion to fill the spot, all right?"

Emerald eyes twinkling, Trace said, "Sometimes I amaze myself. I predicted this, you know. I told Jenny that Claire was dangerous to your bachelorhood. Damn, but I like being right."

The smug expression on his face drove Tye over the edge. "Well I wouldn't trumpet too loudly if I were you. That's what started all this trouble to begin with. The Blessings heard you say I should marry Loretta Davis, so they set about making it happen."

"You said you married Claire, not Loretta."

"That's right. But your daughters wanted me to marry Loretta, and it was that misguided matchmaking that led to the foolishness that caused me to wire the Wests, which brought them to town and me to the damned altar."

All seriousness, Trace asked, "You didn't want to marry Claire?"

Tye wasn't certain how to answer that question, and his uncertainty pricked his temper. "No, I sure as hell didn't. The woman's not normal, and she has me tied up in knots. What I wanted, Brother dear, was to defeat Beatrice West. I wanted to protect your children. I wanted—God help me—to do something for you that was so important, of such value, that it balanced the scales and made up for what I did to hurt you."

"Constance," Trace spat, laying it out between them like a filthy rug.

"Yeah, Constance."

Trace rattled out a vicious stream of cuss words long enough and vile enough to turn the red light district of Fort Worth blue. "If you're not dumb as a box of rocks. You don't think saving Jenny's life last winter was of value to me? Hell, Tye, you busted the scale on that one. And besides, did I not accept your apology?

Did I not come right out and say I forgave you for that mess with Constance?"

Tye lurched to his feet and pounded his fists on the desk. "But I can't forgive myself, Trace. I can't forgive myself."

Trace waited a full twenty seconds before he said, "You block-head. So you let Constance fool you. You let her lead you along by the pecker. That was years ago. It no longer matters. Constance is dead, and we need to leave her that way."

"I know. It's just . . ."

"Listen to me, Tye. I'm happier now than I've ever been before. Jenny has given me that gift. Last winter you saved her life and the life of the child she carries, and got yourself shot up in the process. This spring you saved my daughters from a fate almost as deadly, and got yourself tied up in matrimony in that process. Don't you think that's enough? Don't you think you've atoned? I sure as hell do. You've more than made up for the hurt you caused."

Absolution and atonement. It's what he'd wanted for so very long. "You *are* happy now, aren't you, Trace?"

"With my girls and my Jenny and a new baby on the way? Damned right I'm happy. I'm ecstatic. And it's due in a big part to you. Can't you see that?"

Yes, he could. And it terrified him. He had his absolution, he'd made his amends.

But the guilt and shame that had weighed him down for years still clung to his back like a stone coat.

Trace continued, "I'm happy, Tye, and I believe that if you'll let yourself, you can be happy too. Claire Donovan could do for you what Jenny has done for me. If you'll let her, that is. If you'll let go of the guilt."

Tye didn't acknowledge him because he barely heard him speak. Trace's absolution. His own atonement. It wasn't enough. Goddammit, it wasn't enough.

Cold to the depths of his soul, Tye shuddered. For him, redemption obviously wasn't in the cards.

CLAIRE WAS A GOOD COOK; adventurous with spices and methods of preparation, and always willing to learn from the various people who passed through her life. As a result her personal collection of favorite recipes spanned a dozen different cuisines, from French sauces to Italian sausage, Indian curried rice to Mexican refried beans, and many others in between.

While she'd grown up baking for business, when it came to cooking she tended to plan her menus according to mood. Weather affected her choices, as did her emotions. She made thick, spicy Louisiana gumbo on rainy days. She fried chicken when she was in pain. High moods and happiness meant soufflés and meat sauces; confusion, corn tortillas and vegetable sauces.

Tonight, as she voluntarily prepared the welcome-home celebration dinner for Jenny and Trace McBride, she dredged chicken pieces in flour and waited for her grease to heat. It was a fried-chicken kind of night.

Unwilling to intrude upon the family reunion, she had retreated to her room until Tye came to get her, hours after Trace's return from the not-quite dead. He'd acted strange, happy for his brother's safe homecoming, but detached and distant in a way different from ever before.

For their part, both Jenny and Trace accepted her warmly, welcoming her to the family and thanking her profusely for the help she'd given Tye in caring for the girls. When Claire suggested moving out of Willow Hill and leaving the family to their reunion, Trace wouldn't hear of it. "You are family," he told her. "You and my brother move one bag out of my guest room and I'll just send my Jenny to fetch you back. Believe me, y'all don't want to mess with Jenny, especially not these days."

Uncomfortable in the face of their graciousness while her husband acted with such reserve, Claire had seized upon the idea of fixing dinner, which allowed her the opportunity for escape. Or so she'd thought.

Five minutes earlier Jenny McBride had waddled into the kitchen begging for a before-dinner snack. She now sat at the kitchen table, her feet propped on a pillow on a second chair, eating an apple and half a roast beef sandwich even as she eyed the chicken Claire added to the heated grease in the skillet.

"Mmm . . . I love that smell," Jenny rattled on. "I can't wait. I haven't had fried chicken since long before we left home. For the first half of this pregnancy, greasy food made me sick. In fact, most food made me sick." She paused to take a bite from her apple, then sighed. "I'm afraid I've more than made up for it since. I fear I'll never get my figure back, that I'll never fit back into my clothes."

"I wouldn't worry if I were you. I don't doubt caring for four children will whittle your waist away in no time."

"I do hope you're right."

Claire waited a moment before saying, "Speaking of clothes, I should confess I made free with one of your creations. Tye and the girls . . . well, never mind, that doesn't matter." She paused, took a deep breath, and said, "I'm afraid I wore your wedding gown when I married your husband's brother."

"You did?"

To Claire's surprise, delight painted Jenny McBride's face.

"That's wonderful. Now your marriage will be blessed with good luck just like mine." She paused in the midst of biting into her sandwich to sweep Claire with a critical, dressmaker's measuring gaze. "The dress must have fit you to a tee. I bet Tye's eyes all but popped out when he saw you. Where did you marry?"

"St. Paul's."

"Oh, that's a beautiful church. If only you had waited a few more days, Trace and I could have been there. I hate it that we missed it."

If they'd waited a few days, Tye wouldn't have needed to marry her, Claire thought. Her family would still be in financial trouble, and she'd be preparing to marry Reid Jamieson. "Life is all about timing, I guess," she finally replied. Good timing and poor timing.

"Do you love him?"

The personal question caught her off guard. "Love him?" she repeated, turning the sizzling chicken. "I uh . . . well. . . it's complicated."

"Actually, it's not." Jenny McBride licked her fingers. "It's a very simple, yes-or-no answer." She waited, watching Claire expectantly, until Claire surrendered.

"Yes, I love him. I love him very much. But it's—"

"Obvious the two of you belong together," Jenny interrupted. "This is truly the best news. We'll all be so thrilled to have Tye here in Texas. You are going to stay here, correct? He won't move you back to Charleston?"

"I don't know what Tye plans to do." She feared his plans had little to do with her beyond ending this marriage. *Oh, why couldn't we have had more time.*

Claire could tell by the look on her sister-in-law's face that she had plenty more questions to ask. Thankfully Maribeth and Katrina arrived with an offer to set the table and do any other dinner chores Claire might have. "I'll do Emma's share," Maribeth said. "I don't mind. She's having a hard time letting Papa out of her sight." Lowering her voice confidentially, she added to her mother, "I think she's been scared that Uncle Tye was wrong about you and Papa being alive."

Katrina stood in front of the growing platter of fried chicken and sniffed deeply. "Yummy, yummy. That smells almost as good as your raisin muffins, Auntie."

Jenny agreed. "Between the chicken and whatever it is you have baking in the oven, Claire, my stomach is growling out loud."

"The baby is growling?" Katrina asked, her voice sounding intrigued.

"No, silly," her sister replied. "Babies can't growl in their mommy's tummy. All they can do is grow."

Katrina pursed her lips and nodded. "'That's something I've wondered about. How does it get started, Mama? What makes a baby start growing in the first place? Emma didn't tell me that."

Jenny sent Claire a panicked look, and for the first time all afternoon, Claire laughed. "Don't look at me, she's your daughter."

While Jenny stumbled around trying to provide an answer appropriate for a seven-year-old, Katrina pondered her mother's big belly, then switched an appraising glance toward Claire. "How about you, Auntie Claire? Do you have a baby in your tummy, too?"

Her gaze scuttled over Jenny McBride's belly and yearning gripped her. *A baby. Tye's child.*

Katrina said, "I want a cousin. I hope you do have Uncle Tye's baby in your tummy."

Tye, demonstrating his infinite ability for poor timing once again, walked into the kitchen just as Katrina made the last observation. His gaze flew to Claire's, and the emotion lurking in the fathomless green of his eyes struck her like a fist.

Dread.

And that, Claire thought, dusting the longing from her heart like flour from her hands, *was that*.

Hours later, when they retired to their room for the night they lay side by side in the darkness without touching. Claire was tense, certain that at any moment he would speak, bringing up the subject of ending their marriage. Instead, he remained silent. Even when he finally reached for her, pulling her into his embrace, he did it without so much as a word.

She sensed the war in him immediately.

This was no patient seduction, but a desperate claiming. His hands tore down her back, over her thighs and hips and buttocks. They swept up to her breasts, where he caught her taut nipple between thumb and forefinger, tugging it. Twisting. Sending pleasure spearing through her. His mouth plundered, teeth nipping and lips sucking. Demanding.

And Claire leapt recklessly into the chaos he created.

She matched him, frenzied movement for frenzied movement. Her hands stroking, pressing, possessing. Her tongue impatiently thrusting, spearing into his ear, licking down his neck, lapping at his small round nipples. They battled across the bed, every moan he uttered her victory, every cry he wrested from her a glorious surrender.

She rolled and writhed, losing herself in the wondrous war they fought. Desire consumed her doubts and passion devoured her pain.

At least for now, for tonight.

Spiraling rapidly to the heights, she gasped as his relentless fingers worked Tye's own brand of magic, urging her higher, forcing her ever upward toward the climax. She hung there forever, sweetly suffering, while exquisite sensations teased her to the point of pain. Then she shouted and shattered, dying and flying in a shuddering free fall of pleasure. Calling out his name.

As she lay panting, gasping for breath, he claimed his prize. His growl of satisfaction as he filled her echoed in her womb, and when he drove himself hard and deep into her, she answered with a blissful moan. Eyes closed, he bent his head and savaged her mouth while his body took hers, plunging again and again. Mindlessly, she matched his pace and lost herself to the rhythm of movement as old as time.

Low groans escaped him with every thrust of his hips, driven by throbbing, elemental need. Then his muscles coiled, went taut. He thrust once more. Twice. He threw back his head and shuddered his release.

Grasping, Tye collapsed on top of her, his muscles quivering, sweat dampening his flesh. As Claire basked in the languorous afterglow, stretching sensuously against him, she thought she heard him whisper her name. She thought she heard the echo of love.

But she feared it was only a dream.

HELL WAS A COLD PLACE, Tye decided as dawn broke over the eastern horizon. A fellow always expected heat, but in truth it was a frigid, icy emptiness.

Seated in a wicker rocker on the veranda outside his bedroom, his bare feet crossed at the ankles, he held up the whiskey bottle and studied the rich, amber color of the liquid inside. Like a ghost from his past it called to him, promising warmth. Promising forgetfulness.

Tye had been to hell before; battle and its carnage playing gatekeeper for the devil. He hadn't minded the actual fight so much; it was the stumbling over bloody pieces and parts of neighbors and friends afterward that had sucked the man right out of him, leaving behind the fear, the weakness, the grief.

He'd warmed up with whiskey then—or tried to, anyway. The bottle hadn't rescued him from hell, just took him to a different level—one just as cold. Trace had been the one to rescue him the first time. Yanked him out of the cold amber ocean, dried him out, and bullied him into wanting to live again, until Constance McBride led him back to the devil a few years later.

Katrina, or more specifically, the lie that he'd fathered a child, had made him claw his way out of his whiskey-walled perdition. Then Trace disappeared with the baby, the daughter Tye had thought was his, and anger had kept him warm for years.

Finding out it was all a lie had been tough, but it had also been a relief. Fool that he was, he'd thought he could start over. He'd thought the slate had been wiped clean, that redemption waited just around the corner.

But the goddamned cold simply wouldn't go away.

He held the bottle by the neck and turned it in a circle, until its contents swirled in a little whirlpool of manmade misery. He could dive in so easily, drown himself. Fill the hollowness, the emptiness inside him with liquid death.

But however appealing, whiskey was a coward's way to hell. If this was his existence, he should at least attempt to accept it like a man. Claire deserved that much.

Claire deserved so much more, which was why he was getting an up-close, personal look at Hades all over again.

For a brief shining moment he had thought it might happen. Claire his wife. A home. Someday maybe even a family.

With that thought, Tye brought the neck of the bottle up to his nose and inhaled the malty scent.

He'd been working on his redemption, thinking he could earn back the right to be happy.

"Bullshit." He licked the mouth of the bottle and the taste of whiskey stung his tongue. He'd finally learned the truth. Trace was wrong. He hadn't done enough. Yes, he'd rescued Jenny. Yes, he'd protected the children. But that hadn't done it. Nothing would ever be enough. Nothing absolved him of the deed. No atonement was powerful enough.

He had betrayed his twin brother by bedding his wife and making possible the lie Trace ran from for seven years, the lie that Tye was Katrina's true father. Actions beyond redemption.

Tye's grip tightened like a vise around the bottle. He rose to his feet, reared back, and flung the whiskey as hard and as far as he could. It crashed against an oak tree. Shattered.

Shattered. Like his heart.

Waves of pain rolled through him as he finally admitted the truth. He loved Claire. He loved her with every fiber of his being.

He loved her too much to condemn her to an icy cold pretense of a life with him.

His knees turned to water and he grasped the veranda's railing, breathing hard. After a moment he chuckled, the ugly sound grating against his ears. *God, McBride. Aren't you wallowing in a slop of self-pity. Guess it's too much to ask a pig like yourself to act like a man.*

"Shut up," he said to himself. He could still act like a man. For Claire's sake, he would.

He walked back into his bedroom, where his wife lay peacefully sleeping, a heart-wrenching, contented smile on her angel's face. Reaching down, he lifted a silken lock of her fiery hair and allowed it to slide through his fingers like tears.

God damn him, he had failed to protect her last night. Again. Caught up in the moment, in his own anguish and pain, he had acted the irresponsible fool and left the goddamned condoms in the goddamned drawer.

Bracing himself, he laid his hand on her shoulder and shook her. "Wake up, Claire. We need to talk."

CHAPTER 20

BURY A TEAR-SOAKED HANDKERCHIEF BENEATH A COTTONWOOD TREE DURING A FULL MOON TO HAVE GOOD LUCK.

CLAIRE WOKE, took one look at her husband, and felt as if the temperature in the room had dropped thirty degrees.

This Tye was a cold, forbidding stranger. His eyes were flat and empty, his jaw hard. He made her want to shrink back into the mattress.

"We need to talk," he said, his gaze flicking imperviously over her nudity.

A chill shuddered down Claire's spine. She sat up, gathering the sheet and her composure to her breast. "All right. What is it you wish to talk about?"

Had she not been watching closely, she wouldn't have seen him flinch at the sound of her voice. So, he wasn't as unaffected by her as he let on.

"Our situation. Obviously, with Trace and Jenny's return, it has changed."

"All right," Claire said cautiously, trying not to get angry. In her opinion, a woman—especially a wife—deserved more . . . softness from a man on the morning following a night like the one they'd just shared.

He wouldn't meet her gaze, looking past her, instead. "If we'd known Trace would come home so soon we could have managed all this a little differently. Not that I regret helping your family. The factory will be a good investment. But we could have avoided this other . . . uh . . . trouble."

"Trouble?"

"Marriage."

"Oh." Claire's heart pounded. "Our being married is trouble."

"Yeah."

She reached for her robe lying at the foot of the bed, no longer trying to hold back her anger. The man certainly hadn't had a problem with being married to her last night.

Knowing well the value of silence in an argument— her mother was a master of the technique—Claire said nothing more as she slipped into her robe and calmly knotted the sash. Then she sat on the edge of her bed and looked up at her husband, waiting. Showing no sign of the temper and hurt building within her.

He dragged his fingers through his hair. "You're a nice girl, Claire," he began.

A nice girl? Her fingernails dug into her skin as she clenched a hidden fist. That one got her good.

"You're beautiful, funny, and talented. You'll make a man a good wife someday. But that man . . . well . . . it can't be me. I told you that going into it. We need to get this marriage annulled."

An invisible weight on her chest forced her to take shallow breaths, and her anger suddenly went cold. "Annulled."

He still wouldn't look at her. He walked over to the vanity, where he lifted the silver hairbrush and started flipping it around and around in one hand. "Yeah. It's been such a short time. An annulment shouldn't be a problem."

An annulment. A rejection. He didn't want her. The chill spread like a cancer through her body.

"An annulment." As she repeated the word yet again, she felt a sudden surge of anger. Hot anger that battled the iciness of her pain. "But we consummated our marriage."

He shrugged. "You and I are the only ones who know it I won't tell if you won't tell."

She wrenched to her feet. "You're asking me to *lie?*"

"I thought it would be easier that way." He set down the hairbrush and picked up the comb. He ran his thumb along its teeth as he casually added, "We could get a divorce, instead. Divorces are easy to get in Texas, and it doesn't matter to me one way or the other. I just thought you'd prefer an annulment."

She was breathing hard. An annulment rather than divorce. How considerate of him. Wasn't it his good luck she had no weapon at hand at the moment.

He continued in an offhand manner. "We'll need to do it in a way that won't play in to the townspeople's superstitions and hurt your business at The Confectionary. I'm sure if we put our minds to it we can figure a way to prevent another Bad Luck Wedding Cake disaster."

"I'm sure you're right," she agreed, her voice rapier-sharp.

He darted a quick glance her way at that, but his gaze remained unreadable. "I'll come up with something. I just need to think on it a bit. But other than that I don't see any problems. Do you?"

Problems? Oh, maybe one or two. Little things, like the fact that she loved him. And the fact that she might even now be carrying his child.

Faced with his outright rejection, that alone, she could not ignore. Fury bubbled like chili on the stove as she asked, "And if I'm increasing?"

The comb slipped from Tye's grasp.

He started pacing the room, muttering in a low, angry tone. "I can't believe I did this to myself," he muttered. "Knew better. Went to all that trouble to buy the damned sheaths then didn't have the patience to stop and put one on. Got the self-restraint of a randy rabbit."

"Oh, be quiet." Claire reached the end of her patience. She was dying inside and he was being such a . . . man. "And don't curse at me."

"I'm not cursing. I cussed and that's different and I was doing it to myself, not you, anyway."

"You you you." She threw out her arms, anger and anguish adding fuel to her temper. "What *you* are, Tye McBride, is the most selfish man I have ever seen."

That brought him up short. They stared at each other, his face going red, her chest heaving. "Selfish?" he repeated, bracing his hands on his hips. "Me? Honey, I'll own up to a whole buckboard full of bad traits, but I'll be damned if selfishness is one of them."

"Well it's one of those 's' words then," she shot back, blinking away furious tears. "Scheming, or scurrilous. Spineless, perhaps? No, I know. It's stupid. You are stupid, Tye McBride. Your head is full of stump water instead of sense."

She had captured his total attention now. Exaggerating his drawl, he said, "Not that I can argue with you, sweetpea, but I admit to being curious as to how you reached that particular conclusion."

Her heart pounded. Her mouth was dry. Grief rolled over her in waves. How could he do this to her, to himself? It was so needless, so wasteful, so . . . stupid. "Lord, I hate stupid people. You want to know? Fine, I'll tell you. It's because you could have had so much and you are throwing it away. You're throwing *me* away. And that, McBride, is completely, totally, absolutely, *stupid* because . . . because . . ."

"Why, Claire?" His gaze burned into hers. "Why?"

Too angry to control herself, she shouted it on a sob: "Because I love you!"

He took it like a lance, closing his eyes, flinching as if in pain.

He took two heavy breaths, exhaling them audibly, sounding like he'd just run a mile long race.

"Then God help you, Claire."

Suddenly weak, she sank down upon the bed.

Tye's chin came up, his jaw hardened. He met her gaze with flat, emotionless eyes. "We'll wait on the annulment until you know whether or not you are carrying my child. At that point we can decide how best to proceed. In the meantime, I'll move into another bedroom."

It would have been kinder, Claire thought, for him to use a real sword to slash her heart into shreds rather than the weapon of words.

He turned to go, but the thought of him leaving before everything was said drove her past reason. She stopped him at the door by speaking a single word, proudly stated, that demanded so much: "Why?"

As if against his will, he made a half turn. His voice ragged, he said, "I'm not the right man for you. My sins are too big . . . I'm not . . . I'm too . . ." He mouthed a curse. "You've offered me a gift I can't in good conscience accept, Claire. No matter how much I . . ." his voice trailed off.

Something—the light in his eyes, the pain in his voice, the tension of his body—something gave her hope. "How much you what?"

He opened his mouth. She held her breath.

Then he shifted his gaze away from her and in that instant she knew the words he would speak were not the words he originally intended.

"How much I enjoy you in bed."

The door slammed behind him, leaving her with the impression of a man running for his life. Claire would have been insulted had the realization of the truth not burst upon her like a cloud of smelly, half-cooked Magic vapor. She wrinkled her nose. "Why, that fraud. That big, tall, strong fool."

A slow smile tilted the corners of her mouth. Her husband didn't want to throw her love away. He was too scared to keep it. His excuse of sins too big to be forgiven was just that, an excuse.

Tye McBride was afraid to be happy.

She thumped her lips with her index finger as she thought. Tye McBride was afraid to be happy. It made perfect sense. Stupid, but she understood why he might feel that way. That old "Constance" wound again.

So Claire McBride needed something to conquer his fear. Some strong medicine. Something sweet and soothing and strengthening. Something tasty. Something spicy. Something irresistible.

The perfect treatment came to mind.

She felt better, rejuvenated. He thought to push her away, but she refused to accept it. She wanted this man, and she'd fight for him. Walking to the wardrobe to select a dress, she spied her reflection in a mirror and said, "That's a good thing about being a baker. Always have a recipe or two up my sleeve."

After washing and dressing, she headed straight for the kitchen. She crossed to the cupboard, removed a bottle from the shelf, then dabbed a little Magic behind her ears.

Then, a woman on a mission, Claire went off to find her husband.

"THAT WOMAN IS DRIVING ME CRAZY," Tye said to his twin a little over a week later as he burst into Trace's office and dropped into a chair.

"Tell me about it," Trace replied, tossing down his pen and glancing up from his latest architectural drawing. "I guess I shouldn't have teased her so. But in my defense, she had just referred to herself as a whale, so why did my comparison to a circus elephant send her into such a torrent of tears?"

"I'm talking about my wife, not your wife, Trace," Tye said with disgust. He drummed his fingers along the padded arm of the leather upholstered chair. "You know what she's doing? Among other things I'm too polite to mention, the woman is sending me gifts. Courting gifts. Embroidered handkerchiefs. A new pocket knife. This morning I found a bouquet of posies on my damned pillow when I woke up."

"What's wrong with that?" Trace leaned back in his chair and linked his fingers behind his head, elbows outstretched. "Gifts are nice. I could use a new pocket knife myself. Shoot, I wouldn't even mind flowers from Jenny. They'd be a helluva lot better than the buckets of tears I'm getting these days."

Trace snagged the Blessings' candy box off their father's desk and opened it. "Well it was pur-dee stupid of you to make a crack about an elephant to a pregnant woman. You should have known better."

"Yeah, well," he grumbled. "She's not the only one who is anxious about this baby."

"True, but she's the one who has been toting your kid around all this time. She has good reason to be acting a bit touchy. My wife doesn't." He chose a peppermint stick and returned the box to the desk.

"Oh, really?" Trace drawled, going for a piece of candy for himself. "Her husband moves out of her bed before she's been married a month and she has nothing to get upset about? I don't think so, Brother." After a moment's pause, he added, "What the hell is the matter with you?"

Tye stopped mid-lick on his candy. "Just let it go, Trace."

"No, I don't think I will." Trace popped a lemon drop into his mouth. "This is my house. You're miserable. Claire is miserable. It makes me miserable to look at you." The look on his face turned sour and frustration sounded in his voice. "Dammit, Tye, y'all hardly speak, but the looks you give each other on the sly are hot enough to peel the paint from the walls. Why are you doing this to yourself? Why are you doing it to me?" He crunched his candy, swallowed, and said, "I haven't had sex in a month."

"Sounds like a personal problem to me."

"Well, it is my problem, but you aren't making it any easier." Trace took a second piece of candy and slapped the box closed. "Since I married Jenny, I'd gotten accustomed to frequent relations. Pregnancy is hard on a man, you know, and all this . . . this . . . tension in the house keeps a man's mind on something he ought not to be thinking about when he's got a good month or two left to sweat."

Tye pointed his peppermint stick toward his brother. "I thought the baby was due any time now."

"I'm not talking about the baby. I'm talking about sex and why neither one of us is getting any. At least I have a damned good excuse. What the hell is yours?"

At that point, Tye didn't know whether to deck him or drink with him. Observing the wild look in his brother's eyes and understanding his frustration—after all, he was suffering himself —he took a good lick of his candy and said, "Trace, do you remember Lieutenant Jenkins? Red-headed and covered with freckles."

Trace nodded. "He got killed at Chickamauga, didn't he?"

"Nope. Bought it at the Wilderness. Anyway, he had a saying I think fits this situation. Jenkins used to say that a man has two emotions: horny and hungry. Now, neither one of us can do much about the first at the moment, but it's nigh on to noon and the Green Parrot Saloon serves a beefsteak special on Wednesdays. Besides, your daughters got into my root beer last night, and I need to restock my supply. What do ya say, want to buy me dinner?"

"No, but you can buy mine."

Forty minutes and two rounds of root beer later, the McBride brothers sat at a table in the Green Parrot finishing up their meal. Their bickering over who should pay the charges ended when Big

Jack Bailey and a pair of Lucky Lady ranch wranglers walked through the door, giving Trace his first opportunity since returning to town for a personal "discussion" with Bailey concerning his part in the love-potion mishap.

Because the rancher had been good to the girls once he sobered up, Trace had decided not to kill him. But because Bailey had kidnapped them to begin with, he had some trouble coming to him. Besides, Trace and his brother both needed a good fight.

It proved to be a most welcome distraction. The McBride brothers dusted the floor with Bailey and his minions.

"Damn, I feel better," Trace said when the fisticuffs were finished. He wiped the blood dripping from a cut on his chin onto his shirtsleeve, flexed his bruised and scraped hands, and grinned. "Nothing like a little fight when a fella can't . . . you know."

Tye finished checking the status of his teeth with his tongue, then stuck a finger through a knife slit in his shirt and checked the skin beneath for blood. "You should have handled your visit with the Wests this way instead of making those calm, cold demands."

"Nah. As much as I'd like to knock Beatrice's teeth down her throat, I couldn't hit a woman. I did get to tell them both what I thought of them, though, and sending them packing was pleasurable enough."

"You know, I like trains," Tye observed, dusting off his filthy pants. "They come in awfully handy for getting rid of enemies." He gazed around the saloon and added, "We're gonna owe the proprietor some money for the chairs we busted."

His brother waved a hand. "Doesn't matter. It was worth it. Bailey should be glad I gave him nothing more than a broken nose after he messed with my Menaces. Hell, he's lucky I don't let Jenny loose on him. As mean as she's feeling these days, she'd at least have broken a rib or two."

Accepting the raw steak one of the dancers brought him for his rapidly swelling eye, Trace plopped it against his face and added, "I must say, that lie you told him about Claire and her Magic hex was inspired. On top of the threat of Jenny's voodoo curse, he'll be checking the color of his—" Trace broke off abruptly midsentence. "Emmaline Suzanne McBride! What in tarnation are you doing in Hell's Half Acre?"

Tye jerked his head around toward the saloon's swinging front doors just as Maribeth and Katrina burst into the building on the heels of their older sister. "You have to come, Papa," Emma pleaded.

"Hurry, Papa!" Maribeth shouted. "You must hurry."

Katrina hopped up and down. "Come on, Papa. Come on!"

Trace shoved to his feet, the beefsteak hanging forgotten in his hand. "What's the matter, girls? What's wrong?"

The three children hollered together. "It's the baby!"

Trace's Adam's apple bobbed. "The baby?" he squeaked.

"Mama's having the baby."

"You've gotta come quick!"

Tye and the girls tore out of the Green Parrot, then skidded to a halt as they realized they'd left Trace behind. Dashing back in, Tye found his brother glued to his spot, silently mouthing the words "having the baby" over and over again. Tye muttered a curse, then yanked his brother's arm. "Put some git in your gitalong, Brother, or you'll miss this whole show."

"She's having the baby."

Tye snorted, tugged the steak from Trace's hand, and slapped him with it. That managed to get the father-to-be moving, and soon they raced neck-and-neck on a sprint through the Acre, Emma, Maribeth, and Katrina following at their heels.

CLAIRE REMOVED the cool cloth from Jenny's forehead and stepped away as Trace burst into the room. "Where's the doctor? Honey, are you all right? Did you have it yet?"

In the waning moments of a contraction, Jenny cut her eyes toward her husband and snarled. "Get him out of here!"

Even as she wondered about the bruises painting her brother-in-law's face, Claire couldn't help but smile at his shocked expression. He'd had no warning, of course. He had not been here to hear his wife call him a selection of mean-spirited names for getting her in this condition. But, as Trace would soon see, Jenny did that only during her contractions. In between times she called for him, desperately wanting him to be with her and hold her hand.

The labor had come on quickly, and Jenny had demanded that the girls summon the doctor before their father. The physician had arrived a short time ago and confirmed what Claire and Jenny had both suspected. This was shaping up to be an extremely fast delivery for a first-time mother.

Over the course of the next half hour, Claire sponged Jenny's brow as Trace hurried into and out of the room on his laboring wife's strident demands. With every entrance and exit, signs of his frustration grew until finally, when the pains were hitting Jenny about a minute apart and she was yelling some particularly unflattering things about him, he exploded with frustration. "Dammit, my love, I've worn out the damned door hinges, and I'm staying put. Now, let's get this over with. I'm tired."

Lying prone in her bed, Jenny actually took a swing at him.

Their son was born five minutes later.

While a bathed and dressed William Wesley McBride was introduced to his adoring sisters and relieved uncle, Claire slipped from the room and made her way downstairs to the parlor. Seeing that precious little bundle another minute longer was more than a woman rejected by her man could stand. She'd done her feminine duty by helping Jenny during the labor, but now was family time. She didn't belong.

She was beginning to think she would never belong.

For more than a week now, she'd worked her wiles on her

husband. For more than a week, he'd resisted. She'd tried everything from seduction to sedition. He ignored everything.

Yesterday had been the worst. She'd had the bright idea to tell him she loved him every time their paths crossed. By noon he had been going out of his way to avoid her. By suppertime, he'd taken to hiding in his room. With the door locked.

"Scaredy-cat," she'd called from the hallway. He hadn't bothered to deny it. He hadn't bothered with anything at all.

Now, standing at the parlor window and gazing outside, she watched a pair of squirrels scamper along the front lawn. From upstairs came the sweet music of an infant cry, quickly hushed, then the delighted laughter of the three McBride girls. The sound pierced Claire's heart like an arrow.

The new parents' display of love, joy, and devotion made it impossible for Claire to ignore the likelihood that she had been living a fool's dream. Tye cared about her. Of that much, she was certain. But as Trace and Jenny exemplified, caring and loving were two very different things. If the fear she sensed in Tye was stronger than his feelings for her, perhaps she fought an unwinnable war.

Maybe the time had come to let the dream go.

"Claire?" Tye's voice washed over her like a warm tide in winter.

Bracing herself, she turned. "Yes?"

He drew a deep breath. "I just wanted to thank you for helping Jenny. She said having a woman with her—having you with her—was a comfort."

"I was happy to be of help. It was a magical moment to be part of."

"Yeah, I imagine it was." He walked toward her. "Have you ever witnessed a birth before?"

"Just kittens. Never a baby." Praying her voice wouldn't break, she added, "Isn't he beautiful?"

Skepticism twisted his mouth, and worry dimmed his eyes.

Lowering his voice, he asked, "Do you think babies all have that . . . sort of . . . monkey look to them?"

Claire found the expression on his face so comical that she spoke without thinking. "He's a beautiful little boy and don't you dare say a word otherwise. Just wait until you have a newborn child. Then you'll see—"

He cut her off in a cold hard tone that matched the look in his eyes. "Are you telling me something, Claire?"

Fissures of pain crept across the surface of her heart. "No, I wasn't."

"Thank God."

His fervor hurt, driving home to her how little progress she had made in the past week. Numbness spread slowly throughout her. "Are you afraid of me, Tye? Is that it? Do I threaten you in a way I don't understand?"

He clenched a fist. "Claire, don't. Not now."

Even as he spoke, she shook her head. "Yes, now. I think now is the perfect time. We have just witnessed an event that is the very essence of what love and family is all about. I can't think of a more appropriate moment to discuss it."

"There is nothing to discuss," he snapped, whirling away from her, storming across the room to stand gazing out the window. "We've said it all. Just let it go."

She almost did. Upstairs, the baby started crying and Claire almost fled the room, the house, her husband, so much did the blessed sound bring heartache to her soul. But to her own surprise, she stayed. The love she felt for this man gave her the strength to demand her due, to force the issue one more time.

"You didn't explain why you're so dead set on ending this marriage. I deserve to know that, Tye. I deserve to hear the words."

"Damnit, Claire, don't you see?" His head dropped back, his face lifted toward the ceiling. His words sounded pulled from his soul. "You don't deserve anything I have to give you. You deserve so goddamn much more."

"And what's that, Tye?" She marched over to him, gripped his sleeve and tugged. "You answer me, Tye McBride. You tell me the truth. What do I deserve, love? Is that it? Love?" Voice cracking, she demanded, "Why won't you love me?"

A shudder wracked him. He met her gaze. Emotions swirled in the deep green current. Agony. Anguish. Hopelessness.

"Oh, Tye." Even she heard the pity in her tone.

He jerked as if she'd struck him. "Fine," he said, yanking away from her, his eyes shooting fire. "You want to know the truth? I'll tell you the truth. I won't love you because I can't love you. I don't have it in me to love you. That's asking more from me than I have to give."

Inside, Claire began to crumble. She wanted to shout, *Liar, Liar*. Every act this man did shouted of his ability to love. His Blessings. His brother. Why couldn't he see it?

As fast as it had occurred, his fury died. "You need to get on with your life, Claire. You have so much to offer a man. You're sweet and generous and smart and so damned beautiful. You deserve the very best life has to offer. And believe me, sugar, that ain't me."

He was wrong, so wrong. Claire's body trembled and she wrapped her arms around herself.

Tye muttered a curse and again his head dropped back. He gazed at the ceiling for a long moment before he calmly met her gaze. "If I could love any woman—make a family with any woman —that woman would be you, Claire. But I can't love you. I'm cold inside. I'm dead inside. I just can't love you. You must believe me. I want you to be free to find someone who can give you what you want and need. What you deserve."

Claire never knew pain could feel this way. Hollow and cold. So empty. Expanding. Bigger and bigger until it threatened to consume her.

Tye cleared his throat "That's why I pray my lack of discipline and restraint doesn't bear fruit. I'm not the right man to give you babies. Hopefully that won't be an issue and we can call this marriage quits. Soon. It's better for us both that way."

His words pierced like bullets, shattering her heart. Nothing she'd done had mattered. She'd failed at flirtation, at temptation, at seduction. No demonstration of wifely skills captured his notice, and thus, his heart.

He wanted to call the marriage quits. He wanted to run in spite of all she had to offer, and she had offered him her best. Maybe she had been wrong, and he wasn't afraid to be happy. Maybe he told the truth.

Claire nearly doubled over from the pain. Tye didn't love her. Never once had he said the words, not even when she barraged him with declarations of her own love. He had stated just the opposite, in fact. *I can't love you.* She'd heard the words. Perhaps the time had come to accept them. Perhaps the time had come to let go.

No matter how much it hurt.

Then, like a bugle call, again came the sound of little Billy's cry. For Claire it was the signal for surrender.

"This morning." It came out as a dry, cracked whisper. She hadn't wanted to share this news, tempted to give herself—give them—a little more time. Now she recognized the fallacy of her thinking. Tye refused to love her.

She didn't want him unless he did. He was right about that. She did deserve her husband's love.

Gearing her throat, she tried again. "This morning. I learned . . . it didn't. . . we didn't. She exhaled a fierce, heavy breath. "I do not carry your child. There is no baby. I'll move out of Willow Hill immediately."

"No baby?" Tye repeated in a strangled voice.

"No baby."

He closed his eyes. Half a minute passed before he said, "It's over then."

Tears clogged her throat, so she nodded rather than spoke. *Over.*

He sucked in a shuddering breath. "I'll take care of the legalities. Might even be able to get it wrapped up this afternoon. And I don't want you worrying about leaving Willow Hill. I know Trace won't mind you staying here as long as you need, and I won't be here to get in your way. With the baby safely here and everything settled with Trace, I'll be returning to Charleston just as soon as I can make the arrangements."

"What about the ranch?" she managed to ask.

He shrugged. "Maybe I'll deed it over to the Blessings. Never was all that het up about ranching anyway."

After that, there seemed little left to say. They stood awkwardly for a moment, then Claire said, "I think I'll go up and check on the girls. They might need a little attention right about now."

"Good idea."

Claire picked up her skirts and all but dashed from the room, bumping into Trace as she went about it. "Excuse me," she said, glancing up at him, fighting back her tears.

He was staring past her into the parlor, his scowl filled with disgust and focused on his brother. "You have no need for excuses, honey," Trace gently replied. "Not like somebody else I know."

CHAPTER 21

KISS YOUR TRUE LOVE EVERY MORNING TO WARD OFF BAD LUCK FOR THE DAY.

THE LEGAL PAPERS lay like a carcass on Tye's bed. All they lacked was Claire's signature to make them official.

It had taken three days to iron out the details of the dissolution of his marriage. Not the legal details, those had been easy. The difficult part was arranging matters so that he could leave town—leave Claire—without triggering the townspeople's superstitions and ruining The Confectionary's business all over again.

In order to preserve the legends of the Magical Wedding Cake and the Good Luck Wedding Dress, Tye had requested another interview with the doyenne of Fort Worth gossip, Wilhemina Peters. With a clever mixture of truth and fiction, he'd explained away the marriage by calling it a marriage in name only that Claire kindly and generously consented to in order to save the Blessings from a fate worse than death—going to live with their maternal grandparents. He'd heaped honest praise upon Claire's name and cast wicked aspersions upon the Wests. He explained how the legend of the Donovan Magical Wedding Cake remained intact because Reid Jamieson had acted out of greed rather than love when he proposed marriage to Claire, and that an argument could be made that the cake had, in fact, protected her, leaving her free to someday meet her true love, her destiny. He'd enlisted the aid of Jenny and Trace, and by the time Wilhemina left Willow Hill, she was ready to declare Claire Donovan McBride the compassion queen of Texas and most eligible woman in the state.

Tye figured men would soon be lining up in front of The Confectionary with masculine versions of cream pies and chocolate cakes.

He could now leave town with a clear conscience. Too bad he couldn't do it without leaving what functioned as his heart behind.

He set his valise upon the bed next to the annulment papers and started packing. He didn't intend to take much with him. Experience had taught him physical reminders made the memories more difficult to handle. Somehow, though, the case filled up quickly with mementos like drawings and snips of pigtail ribbons and even a program from the night the Fort Worth Literary Society had hosted a spelling bee.

Tye shut the case and was buckling the strap as his brother marched into the room. "Are you sure you want to leave this way, Tye?"

Actually, he didn't want to leave at all. "I have to go."

"Do you know my daughters are downstairs bawling their eyes out? I never have taken kindly to anyone who makes my little Menaces cry."

"Blessings. I told you, Trace, you shouldn't call them Menaces. It might affect them as they grow up, make them think poorly of themselves."

Sarcasm dripped from Trace's reply. "Well we can't have a member of this family thinking poorly about himself, now can we?"

"Let it go, Trace," Tye said quietly.

"You've already let go, Brother." Trace walked to the window and gazed outside. "You are making a huge mistake."

"Look, you don't know the particulars."

"I know enough. I eavesdropped on your parlor conversation with your wife the day Billy was born. I think it's likely I found it more enlightening than poor Claire." Turning, he folded his arms and faced his brother. "Do you know you always intimidated me, Tye?"

"What?"

"It's true. From the time we were boys. I used to tell myself I felt that way because you were older than me."

"By all of a handful of minutes," Tye drawled.

"In my heart I knew it wasn't true. You intimidated me because you were my mirror image, but I wasn't nearly as brave as you."

"Brave?" Tye scoffed. "I hardly think so."

"You were always the risk taker. You climbed higher in the trees, swam out farther in the ocean." Lips twitching in a smile, he added, "The first to bed a woman."

"I think that should be considered a tie. Mrs. Watson and her twin fantasy. I wonder what ever happened to her? Didn't she go North before the War?"

Trace ignored the bait. "Somewhere along the way, you stopped taking risks. It didn't happen during the War. You were the most foolhardy soldier in our regiment. I saw your back on every charge we made. Never had time to be scared for myself during battle because I was so busy being scared for you. I still to this day have nightmares about the time you went after that live grenade."

"Get to the point, Trace. I have a train to catch."

Again his brother ignored him. "I think it started after the War, when the memories started getting to you."

"You mean when the bottle started getting to me," Tye said, yanking at the strap on his brown leather satchel.

"They beat you down, didn't they? The memories. I heard your nightmares."

"You lived them, too."

"Yeah, but they didn't haunt me the way they did you. You always felt things deeper than I did, Tye. I think it was part of that risk-taking edge of yours. You always lived just a little bit bigger than me. Half a step . . . more. I drank to forget, too. But I didn't have quite as much to forget, so I didn't drink as much as you. That's when you started to change. I saw timidity in your character for the very first time."

"Oh, yeah? I was timid as a mouse when I was breaking up barrooms in drunken brawls, wasn't I?"

"You didn't sleep for days on end. It wore you down. The War and its aftermath wore you down." He exhaled in a deep sigh and added, "Then Constance finished you off."

"Hell, Trace." Tye feared his voice would crack. "Don't talk about her. Please."

"Those risks you took on the battlefield had nothing on the risks you took with her. You took the biggest risk of your life, you believed her lies about me despite your better sense, because you couldn't bear to see a woman hurt. Not a woman you loved."

"I didn't—"

"Yes, you did. I knew you did. I saw it long before that night she did her best to steal your soul. So when you thought I was beating her, you took a risk and laid your heart out there for her to stomp on."

"What I took, Brother dear," Tye sneered, "was your wife."

Trace smiled sadly. "What you did that night was give part of yourself away, that last little part that made you more than me."

Tye blew a dismissing breath. "This conversation makes me think you've lost a chunk of your brain."

"I had thought when you came here to Fort Worth, when you saved my Jenny from that damned Big Jack Bailey, that you had begun to reclaim that part you had lost. When I learned of everything you had done for my children, I thought you'd finally cauterized the wound. But then I listened to that rot you told

Claire down in the parlor the day before yesterday. You haven't reclaimed squat, Tye. You still won't take a risk."

He folded his arms and challenged. "You are still afraid. Not of love. I know you love me and my family. I know you love your wife. But you're being a selfish son of a bitch. You, Tye McBride, are afraid to let us love you."

Tye made a grab for the handle of his case. "Why didn't you tell me that during your runaway years you took time to study psychology?"

"It's plain as the nose on my face because I've been there myself. My love for Jenny required a leap of faith, and thank God when the time came, I wasn't afraid to make the jump. But you apparently are. The risk-taker twin won't take the same vault as his brother. That's a damn shame."

"I'm leaving now," Tye said, a band of misery squeezing his chest. He had to get out of here, but his feet wouldn't move.

Trace continued to talk. "But the worst part about it is the suffering your fear has brought to bear upon a very fine woman. I saw her, Tye. She was tortured, completely devastated by your rejection."

Tye choked back a silent scream, his brother's words whipping flesh already raw and bleeding. He grabbed the legal papers with one hand and hoisted his satchel with the other, then headed out the door. "I can't miss the damned train."

His brother followed him, his words echoing along the hallway and down the stairs. "You think you're doing her a good turn, don't you? You think there is someone else out there for her to love, someone who has never made a mistake. You are wrong Tye. She doesn't want perfect. She loves you."

At the front door, Tye paused. "She'll get over it."

"Maybe. But will you? I know you still feel bad about betraying me by bedding Constance. What you are doing to Claire is ten times worse than the hurt you caused me and you know it. You wear your guilt poorly now, Tye. Claire is a damn fine woman whose only mistake was to love you. Think of how heavy that mantle of guilt is gonna feel in years to come."

Trace's words replayed in his head like a nightmare all the way to the train depot. Tye tried his best to shut them out. He already felt bad enough. He didn't need Trace making it worse.

At the station he bought a ticket then wandered out onto the platform to await the boarding call. A crowd milled, laughing and talking and hugging good-byes. Smoke puffed from the locomotive's smokestack, as black as Tye's thoughts.

A home, a family. Claire. His dream. Giving it up was damn near killing him.

Then don't do it. The notion whispered through his mind like the devil's own temptation.

"I have to," he muttered to himself. It was the right thing to do, the best thing for Claire.

Is it? Or could Trace be right?

A tiny kernel of hope penetrated Tye's heart as his mind cracked open just enough to give his brother's argument a moment of consideration.

You're a selfish son of a bitch. She doesn't want perfect. She loves you. You are afraid to let us love you.

Tye scrunched his eyes closed against the blaring glare of the sun. His chest grew tight and he struggled to draw a breath. Hell, he was confused. *You are afraid.* Was that what this was? Not guilt or distrust, but fear? Was he giving up on Claire and on the life she offered out of cowardice? Was he too damned yellow to risk being happy?

The engine's whistle blew, yanking him from his reverie. The conductor framed his mouth with his hands and yelled, "All aboard!"

The ticket burned a hole in Tye's pocket. Leaving burned a hole in his heart.

Tye shuffled slowly toward the train.

EMMA BLEW into the depot ahead of Maribeth, who dragged Ralph on a leash, and Katrina, who carried Spike, both water and fish splashing back and forth in the bowl. They ran straight through the building and back outside to the platform. They stopped short.

The tracks were empty.

"We're too late," Emma cried, steepling her hands over her mouth. "The train is already gone. Oh, sisters, we're too late."

For a long minute, the three girls stood frozen, staring in horrified shock at the empty track. As if on cue, tears started falling from each girl's eyes.

"I can't believe he up and left without telling us goodbye," Maribeth said with a sniff.

"He left. He really left. I'm so angry at Uncle Tye." Katrina shifted Spike's bowl to free one hand, then shoved her thumb in her mouth with a flourish.

Emma slowly shook her head. "I'm worried to death about him."

Ralph started to whimper, and Maribeth reached down to pet him. "Em, you don't think Uncle Tye thought we didn't need him anymore because Papa and Mama are home, do you?"

"Uncle Th-ye'th not that th-upid," Katrina sobbed around her thumb. "He knowth we love him."

Emma nodded, wiping her tears with her sleeve. "And he knows we need him desperately. A papa is one thing, but an uncle is something else entirely."

"That's right," Mari agreed, her silent tears spilling in wet circles on her blouse. "We simply can't do without him. If Uncle Tye isn't here, who's going to give us candy when we shouldn't have it? Who will buy us toys at the mercantile for no reason. And most important of all, who will help us hide our mischief from Papa?"

"We've got to go after him, sisters." Emma insisted, angrily wiping at her eyes.

"But how?" Katrina wailed. "What do we do?"

Maribeth tugged a wad of paper from her pocket and blew her nose. "Does anybody know where he went?"

"Nowhere."

The masculine voice sounded from directly behind them. The girls whirled around. Leaning against the depot wall, his suitcase on the ground beside him, stood Uncle Tye.

The two younger sisters gasped. Emma doubled up her fist and punched him in the stomach.

His eyes bulged and his chin dropped. "Emmaline Suzanne! I can't believe you hit me."

"Well I can't believe you were running away!"

"It didn't happen. I couldn't make myself get on the train."

"Well it's a good thing," she scolded. "Otherwise we'd have had to chase you down and drag you back by the pigtails just like our papa does us."

Their uncle grinned and tugged at the ends of his hair. "Pigtails, huh? Guess I do need a trim."

With him standing safe and sound in front of her face, Emma started to calm down. It took an effort. She kicked at a small stone beside her foot and said, "This was mean of you, Uncle Tye. Really, really mean. Do you know how worried we were?"

"Yeah," Maribeth piped up. "You didn't even tell us good-bye. Is this any way to treat family?"

"You even broke Ralph's heart," Katrina accused.

Tye glanced down at the dog. "I did? How can you tell?"

" 'Cause he's crying!" Maribeth yelled, showing him her fiercest scowl. "Just like Emmie's crying and Kat's crying and I'm crying. Mama's crying, too, and baby Billy, although all he ever does is cry."

"And pee and poop," Kat added.

"It wouldn't surprise me if Papa cried, either," Mari continued, putting her fists on her hips and glaring up at him. "And what about poor Auntie Claire? You think we've been crying buckets? You should see her. We've been watching her from the peephole. Why, she can hardly bake for all her crying. You've been very bad, Uncle Tye. You shouldn't have made her cry. That's not how you treat someone you love."

Tye looked away. He stood without moving, staring out at the train tracks for what seemed like a very long time. Emma and Maribeth shared a worried glance. He had a funny, strangled sort of look on his face.

"You're right, girls," he said finally. "I have acted badly. This isn't how you treat people you love."

The three sisters sniffed and nodded sharply.

"I have one question, though," he said, pulling his train ticket from his jacket pocket and tearing it into little pieces.

"What makes you so certain I'm in love with your Auntie Claire?"

The sisters looked at one another and rolled their eyes. Emma said, "That's easy, Uncle Tye."

"Simple," Katrina added.

"A piece of Magical Wedding Cake," Maribeth said with a grin.

"Oh." Tye tossed the torn ticket into the air. "You mean you figured it out because Claire and I had a Good Luck Wedding Cake?"

"No, silly." Maribeth snorted.

" 'A piece of cake' is just an expression that means something was easy. I just added the 'magical' and 'wedding' parts because it sounded right."

"I see." He picked up his case. "So if it wasn't the cake, how did you figure it out?"

Emma tucked her arm in his and stepped toward the street. "Like we said, it was simple. We asked Spike."

CLAIRE WOKE up wrinkling her nose. The horrible odor hit her like a fist. What in the world was that awful smell?

It took her a few minutes to get her bearings. Only the fourth morning since moving into the apartment above The Confectionary, she sometimes woke up forgetting where she was. The nightmares that haunted her sleep didn't help the situation any. Invariably she dreamed of being in Tye McBride's arms and she woke either crushed or angry or happy. Happy was the worst because reality was always right there waiting to dash her down.

Today, though, she woke up to something different. To a stink.

At first she suspected she was still asleep, still dreaming, and that the stench was the scent of her dreams going up in smoke. Wilhemina Peters had dropped by the day before with the news that she'd just come from the Texas & Pacific depot where Tye was preparing to depart on the afternoon train. Claire had smiled and continued her task of mixing molasses cookies. It wasn't until she'd put them in the oven to bake that she realized she'd left out the Magic.

No surprise in that. Seemed like the Magic had been left out of a lot of things lately.

Claire's head cleared and she frowned. She wasn't asleep and the smell wasn't her dreams; it was real, very real, and coming from downstairs. She glanced at the clock. Three A.M., still thirty minutes before her da arrived to help with the baking.

Thinking about Da, her tears welled up again. He'd been so sweet to her through this. Her whole family had been sweet. And supportive. Of course, it hadn't been easy to convince the Donovan men to refrain from going after Tye and beating him to a pulp. But she'd managed to convince them this way was the best. They had listened to her. Her family had actually listened to her. She could take comfort in that change.

Claire threw off the sheets and climbed out of bed. Grabbing her robe, she tugged it on even as she started downstairs, pausing only long enough to gather up her keys.

Exiting into the Rankin Building vestibule, she halted abruptly. A light shined in the bakery's kitchen. Had Da or one of the boys come in early? She doubted it. They were always on time, but they never, ever came in early.

Claire chewed on her lower lip and considered what to do. She left no valuables in the shop. Could someone be stealing the Magic? Maybe Reid Jamieson decided not to wait for Da to get the factory up and running. Or maybe it was simply some poor soul looking for something to eat. That might explain the smell. Perhaps this person had attempted to cook.

She had to investigate.

Quietly she tried the doorknob. Unlocked. She slipped silently into the shop and made her way to the counter where she stored a bread knife. It wasn't much of a weapon but with any luck at all, she wouldn't need one.

Any luck at all. From out of hurtful memories came the sound of Tye's voice as he spoke of his hope she would not prove fertile during their time together. She shook her head. She didn't need tears or a distraction at the moment. A skunk of one kind or another was loose in her kitchen and needed to be dealt with.

She tiptoed toward the doorway that led into her kitchen. Raising the knife, she drew a deep breath and peeked around the corner.

Her gasp was loud enough to wake the nuns in the convent across the street.

Tye McBride stood in front of the stove. He wore one of her aprons and stirred a steaming, stinking soup pot with one of her long-handled wooden spoons. Twisting his head toward her, he flashed a smile. "Morning, sugar. Did I wake you?"

Shocked speechless, she nodded. Her heartbeat sped up to double-time and her knees began to knock.

"Sorry about that," he said flippantly. "I had this new recipe I wanted to attempt, and I just couldn't wait. I'm hoping you'll try it out on me."

EMILY MARCH

What in the world was he talking about? Try it out on him?

She had to swallow three times before she could force the question past her lips. Tye paused and took a swig from the bottle of root beer he had sitting on the counter beside the stove. Then he grinned at her, but it was a nervous grin. Somehow, seeing that made her feel better.

"It's a recipe I've been working on for years now, but I only discovered the perfect last ingredient yesterday. I believe I finally have it right this time. I'll warn you up front that depending on the person, it can be a very bitter concoction to swallow. But once I got it down, well, it seems to have worked for me. I'm hoping—praying—that you'll give it a fair shot. What about it, Claire? Will you taste it for me, Claire? Will you give it a try?"

"What is it?"

He dipped the spoon into the soup pot and drew it out filled with a molasses-dark liquid. He blew a stream of breath across the spoon's bowl, cooling the contents. Then, his eyes glittering with a fierce emotion she couldn't quite name, he held it out to her. "You make Magic. I took a shot at Forgiveness."

"Forgiveness?"

He nodded. "You see, I'd tried to whip this up before, but I left out the secret ingredient."

"And that is . . . ?"

"Guts."

She drew back. "Guts?"

"Courage. I found out that, for me, it takes a full pound of courage in the recipe to cook up a good batch of Forgiveness strong enough to work on me. I gave myself a good dose, sugar, and I'm pretty sure it worked this time. I feel good now. Good about a lot of things. I'm done looking backward and I'm ready to go ahead. I've got the courage in me to trust in the future."

Her mouth was dry and her voice squeaked. "You do?"

"I do."

She watched his Adam's apple bob as he swallowed hard. Then

386

he held out the spoon. "What do you say, Claire? Is your tongue in the mood for a little Forgiveness? If you like it, we can bottle up the rest. I imagine you'll go through a lot of it, married to me."

Married to me. When his words finally filtered through her mind, her heart started to sing. She licked her dry lips, and said, "Hmm . . . it's something to think about. What other ingredients did you put in your recipe?"

"A gallon of love. A cup of hope. Two tablespoons of spice and a pinch of good fortune—Spike clued me into that last one."

"Hmm . . ."

"Please, Claire. Take a taste and forgive me? Might as well warn you, I'm not leaving until you do. If you want to bake your muffins, you'll just cook around me."

"I'd rather cook with you," she said, smiling. "I've developed quite a taste for your particular heat."

Leaning forward, she sipped from the spoon. A shudder racked her body. "*Bleh.* That's as bitter as gyp water."

He tossed down the spoon and grabbed her hand, pulling her toward him. "You're the baker, sweetness. I had to come to you to get the sugar." He bent his head and took her mouth in a kiss so tender, so loving, that her heart overflowed.

She was crying when he finally lifted his head. Somberly he stared into her eyes. "I was a coward, Claire. I was afraid to risk loving again. You and Trace and the Blessings finally got it through my thick skull. You made me happy, Claire, and it scared the stuffing out of me. It had been so long. It hurt so much when I lost it. I didn't want to risk going through that again."

A pair of fat tears spilled from her eyes to roll down her cheeks. He thumbed them away, saying, "Fear is one of the most powerful motivators on earth, and where I was concerned, for a little while it had love beat all to hell. It makes me shudder to think of how close I came to letting the fear conquer me. Too damned close, because I hurt you. I'm more sorry about that than words can say."

"Oh, Tye."

"The Blessings gave me hell for it. They said that's not how you treat the ones you love, and they were right. I always wanted you, sugar. From the first time I met you. Somewhere along the way, I fell in love. But I was too afraid to admit it. I thought my heart was dead but it wasn't; it was frozen in fear. But loving you melted that ice, Claire. Loving you has made me feel alive again."

He loves me. Claire closed her eyes and swayed beneath the weight of her emotions; relief and joy and sorrow for his pain, a thousand different feelings so intense they overwhelmed her. *He loves me.*

"Say it," she demanded.

"I love you, Claire Donovan McBride."

Love for him filled her heart and her soul to overflowing. Her voice broke as she reached out and touched his cheek. "You are a good man, Tye McBride. A very good man. I wouldn't love you if you weren't."

His smile was bittersweet. "I figured that one out, too. You have a pure heart, Claire McBride, and I know I can believe in your love. I'm sorry I was too chicken to realize it before."

She smiled through her tears and sniffed. "You were wrong."

Sighing, he brushed the tip of her nose with his finger. "I reckon I'll hear that a time or two during the next fifty years or so." Then he grew serious, pleading with his eyes and words and tone. "Will you ride the rainbow with me, Mrs. McBride? Will you stay my wife and have babies with me, make a home and family with me? Share my dream?"

Overcome, she couldn't at first answer. That easily, he was handing her all her fantasies, her most fervent wishes.

Love melted through her like hot caramel, leaving her feeling delicious enough to tease. Drawing away, she put her hand to her breast and said, "I don't know, Mr. McBride. You're not saying all this just to get my Magic recipe, are you?"

He scoffed and yanked her back into his arms and nuzzled her neck. "Honey, you are all the aphrodisiac I need. Keep your danged old recipe. Now tell me yes."

She smiled from the heart. "If I get to keep my recipe and remain the proprietress of The Confectionary . . ." She paused and questioned him with a look. Tye nodded rapidly and she continued, "Then yes, Tye. I'll be proud to be your wife, and thrilled to be the mother of your children."

"Good." He kissed her. "Wonderful." He kissed her again. "I'm thrilled." He kissed her one more time, and said, "Now that everything is settled, I have only one thing to say to you, Mrs. McBride."

"And what is that, Mr. McBride?" She batted her eyes flirtatiously. "You love me? You need me? You passionately desire me?"

"Well, that's not exactly how I intended to say it, but yeah. All those things."

She licked her lips and smiled a siren's smile. "So, how did you plan to say it?"

He shrugged, and glanced away from her. "Well, I was gonna say . . ." He shot her a leering grin. "Woman. Get your muffins in the oven and your buns in my bed."

She hit him with a raspberry tart.

EPILOGUE

THE BEST KIND OF GOOD LUCK IS TO BE LUCKY IN LOVE.

CLAIRE ADDED a cup of honey to the brew cooking on the stove in The Confectionary's kitchen. It was the first time she'd visited the bakery since selling it to Lars a month earlier, and while she was happy to pitch in for a few days while he stayed home to help Loretta with the new baby, she'd rather be home at the Magic Lady Ranch. She enjoyed baking and socializing with the customers, but as she had realized shortly after moving to the ranch, she loved working with Tye. She was awfully glad she'd convinced him to forgo the cattle in favor of raising horses.

"You were right, Mama," she said softly, stirring her brew. Freedom was choice, and her choice to sell The Confectionary had given her a sense of independence as pleasing as the choice to build the business to begin with.

She and Tye had moved into the house Trace had designed for them four months ago, right before the first cold spell of winter, and already the place felt like a home. Having family around was a big part of that, she knew.

Tye and Trace's grandmother and sisters and their families had traveled from Charleston to spend part of the winter in Texas, and they split their time between Willow Hill and the ranch. The

McBride family reunion had been an event the entire city continued to talk about, considering the Blessings had chosen to mark the occasion by setting off fireworks a little too close to a storage shed containing a keg of gunpowder. The family tradition of good luck held, in that no one was injured in the mishap, despite Maybelle Davis's claims.

Hers had been one extremely ugly hat, anyway, Jenny and Claire had agreed.

Claire dipped a spoon into her brew for a taste. The honey had helped but it wasn't quite there yet.

Hearing the swing of the back door, she turned with a smile. Tye strolled into the kitchen rubbing his hands in an effort to warm them. "Hello, beautiful," he said, bending down to give her a kiss on the cheek. He removed a letter from his jacket pocket and handed it to her. "Letter from Peggy," he said before glancing into the soup pot. "Whatcha cookin'? Smells like ambrosia to me."

"Just a new recipe I'm working on," she said absently. The letter from her mother distracted Claire. The decision to build the Magic factory along the Texas coast rather than in Fort Worth had been tough for her to accept. Though she had recognized the business sense of it, she had mourned the Donovan clan's removal to Galveston. She missed her family desperately.

Peggy Donovan's weekly missives were a balm to that particular sadness. Her mother always entertained, and today's letter was no different. Scanning the page, Claire gasped a laugh, then said, "Listen to this, Tye. Mama says that when Mr. Barnum's circus came to Galveston, Reid Jamieson had a very loud and very public fight with his father, then he ran off with an acrobat."

Tye snapped his fingers. "Dadgum, that reminds me. That trapeze I ordered for the bedroom came in last week. Remind me to get by the mercantile and pick it up before we head home."

Claire didn't bother to comment on his questionable humor. She had already read past the next three paragraphs containing news of her family. "Brian and Cynthia are back from their honeymoon. Patrick and Eloise have decided to spend the winter in Bavaria. He's apparently enamored of strudel."

"More likely he's found a new market for Magic," Tye observed. "The man is truly a born salesman."

"*Hmm* . . ." she replied, finishing her letter. "Oh, dear. My parents met Jenny's mother's ship when it docked in Galveston. Monique is resting at their house for a few days before making the final leg of her trip home. Mama says Monique brought an organ grinder's monkey to give to the girls."

Tye laughed loud and hard at that one. "I want to be at Willow Hill the day she delivers that particular gift. Trace is gonna love it."

"A monkey might finally get you off his trouble list for bringing Ralph into the family. Every time I see him he goes out of his way to say what a menace that dog is."

"So what? He calls his own children Menaces. I can't believe I haven't broke him of that habit yet." Tye licked the spoon he'd just dunked in the soup pot. "Honey, what is this stuff? It's pure heaven. Tastes almost as good as you do."

Claire glanced down into the soup pot. Retrieving a clean spoon, she gave the mixture a thorough stirring, then leaned over and sniffed. "It smells good, too, doesn't it? It reminds me of you."

Tye put his hands around her thickened waist and tugged her back a step. "Don't get so close there, sugar. Don't want to burn the baby."

She thunked his hand with the spoon. "My belly's not that big yet."

"Give it another month."

"You say a word about elephants and you're a dead man, McBride."

He swiped her spoon and dipped it into the pot, drinking down another spoonful. "*Mmm* . . . *mmm*. I do believe I could drink this stuff by the gallon. What is it?"

"I've been playing with the recipe for Magic. I thought it might be time to add a new recipe to the family cookbook."

"This is an extract? Like Magic?"

"Yes. It has Magic for a base, but I added a few of my own ingredients. I've been playing with it for a few months, and I've about decided it just can't get any more perfect."

"It sure does taste perfect." He stopped and sniffed the air. "Seems like you took all the stink out, too."

She smiled sweetly and stood on her tiptoes to kiss his cheek. Tye took advantage of the opportunity to ply her with a deliriously breath-stealing kiss. "Could you turn the fire down low and keep it simmering for a while, sugar? I've a mind to put one of those trapezes in the apartment upstairs, and I could use your help figuring out exactly where to hang it."

"Always glad to assist, sir," she replied primly, then spoiled the effect by answering his wiggled brows with a wicked wink.

Tye crooked his head toward the soup pot. "Seriously, though, it won't hurt your brew to simmer for a bit? I know this kind of creation takes work, and I don't want to ruin it for you. I can wait to take you upstairs. Five minutes or so, anyway."

Claire laughed and caught his hand. "Husband dear, you can't ruin this recipe, not when you are its inspiration."

"Inspiration? I like the sound of that." Arching a curious brow, he asked, "What are you calling this stuff again?"

"It's Magic plus a whole lot more. I've decided to call it Love."

"Love." Tye pursed his lips and thought about it a moment. Then he nodded derisively. "Makes perfect sense to me."

Wrapping his arms around his wife, he added, "After all, the only potion more powerful than Magic is Love."

AFTERWORD

Dear Readers,

I find it appropriate to be writing this letter on Valentine's Day. I've just put the finishing touches on *The Bad Luck Wedding Cake*, and the heart-shaped cake I bake every year for my family is now ready to go into the oven.

This cake is not a Magical Cake by any stretch of the imagination. In fact, it's heavier than the Snow Cake Claire dumped in the trash can behind The Confectionary. It is a version of my Colorado-born mother's high-altitude recipe that doesn't quite have all the adaptations required for Texas baking. But even though it's heavy as a doorstop, I love it. My kids love it. Having this heavy, heart-shape white cake with chocolate icing every Valentine's Day is a family tradition. As you might have guessed from my books, we are big on family and tradition here at my house.

Most writers put a lot of themselves into their work and I am no exception. *The Bad Luck Wedding Cake* is sprinkled with pieces of my life. This story is set in my hometown of Fort Worth, and much of my research was done on family outings to the historical sites in town. I guess that's why my oldest, Steven, keeps trying to convince me to set a book in Hawaii. My son John brought home the fortune-telling fish, and my daughter Caitlin is the original Katie-cat. That thumb-sucking is the reason for the orthodontist appointment we have next week. The part of Tye that makes him fall head-over-heels for his nieces is drawn straight from my husband. He is an awesome father, but little girls wrap him around their thumbs without even trying.

But the best research I do for my love stories is done each day here at home. This is where, every day, I learn something new about my family and about love.

Thanks for sharing your reading hours with me and my fictional families. I hope my story made you smile a lot, laugh out loud a time or two, and maybe even cry just a little. Here's to family and romance and, most of all, to love. I hope you are as blessed in yours as I am in mine.

Happy reading!

Emily March

ALSO BY EMILY MARCH

The Bad Luck Wedding Historical Romance Series

THE BAD LUCK WEDDING DRESS

THE BAD LUCK WEDDING CAKE

Bad Luck Abroad Trilogy

SIMMER ALL NIGHT

SIZZLE ALL DAY

THE BAD LUCK WEDDING NIGHT

Bad Luck Brides Quartet

HER BODYGUARD

HER SCOUNDREL

HER OUTLAW

THE LONER

Stand Alone Historical Romances

THE TEXAN'S BRIDE

CAPTURE THE NIGHT

THE SCOUNDREL'S BRIDE

THE WEDDING RANSOM

THE COWBOY'S RUNAWAY BRIDE

The Brazos Bend Contemporary Romance Series

MY BIG OLD TEXAS HEARTACHE

THE LAST BACHELOR IN TEXAS

The Callahan Brothers Trilogy

LUKE—The Callahan Brothers
MATT—The Callahan Brothers
MARK—The Callahan Brothers
A CALLAHAN CAROL

The Eternity Springs Contemporary Romance Series

In order:

ANGEL'S REST
HUMMINGBIRD LAKE
HEARTACHE FALLS
MISTLETOE MINE *(novella)*
LOVER'S LEAP
NIGHTINGALE WAY
REFLECTION POINT
MIRACLE ROAD
DREAMWEAVER TRAIL
TEARDROP LANE
HEARTSONG COTTAGE
REUNION PASS
CHRISTMAS IN ETERNITY SPRINGS
A STARDANCE SUMMER
THE FIRST KISS OF SPRING
THE CHRISTMAS WISHING TREE

The McBrides of Texas trilogy
JACKSON
TUCKER
BOONE

ABOUT THE AUTHOR

Emily March is the *New York Times, Publishers Weekly*, and *USA Today* bestselling author of over thirty novels, including the critically acclaimed Eternity Springs series. Publishers Weekly calls March a "master of delightful banter," and her heartwarming, emotionally charged stories have been named to Best of the Year lists by *Publishers Weekly, Library Journal,* and Romance Writers of America. A graduate of Texas A&M University, Emily is an avid fan of Aggie sports and her recipe for jalapeño relish has made her a tailgating legend.

Please register for Emily's newsletter at www.emilymarch.com to receive information about new releases and special offers, including

Printed in the USA
CPSIA information can be obtained
at www.ICGtesting.com
LVHW042134130923
758153LV00031B/336

9 781942 0026